Blind
Spot

DOUBLEDAY

new york   london   toronto   sydney   auckland

Blind
Spot

A NOVEL

Terri Persons

This book is dedicated to my wonderful, supportive sister,

Bernadette, who said I could use her name as long as

her character wasn't a whore or an ax murderer.

Love you, Bern.

Acknowledgments

I owe everything to my husband, David, and our sons, Patrick and Ryan, who keep me energized with their unwavering love and loyalty.

My brother, Joseph, and his wife, Rita, continue to bolster my efforts with their encouragement and faith.

I am immensely grateful to my agent, Esther Newberg, and to my editor, Phyllis Grann, for their hard work and their belief in my writing.

Finally, eternal thanks go to my longtime friend and champion, John Camp, who is always there when I need him.

Blind
Spot

Transferred Again

● ●

Humidity rolling off of the Mississippi River simmered with the smell of fried garlic and onions and shrimp and sausage, the air thick enough to stab with a knife. A man and a woman walked out of the Eighth District Police Station, slipped on their sunglasses, and shuffled into the gumbo. They were dressed in gray slacks and gray blazers with white shirts. He wore a red tie, and she had a maroon scarf draped around her neck. He was dark-haired, heavy, tall, suntanned. She was pretty, pale, and thin. She stood a foot shorter than he, and her blond hair was cropped close enough to have been done by a barber. Behind the shades, they were sober-faced, bordering on somber.

"That could've gone a helluva lot better," said the woman, unbuttoning her blazer as she walked. "So much for Southern hospitality."

The man loosened his tie and then gave up on it, yanking it off and stuffing it in his pants pocket. "They had their chance. Now it's our case."

"Your case. I'm outta here next week. Remember?"

He laughed. "Where're they shipping you off to? Shreveport? That's a promotion, right?"

"Funny," she said dryly. From across the road, she eyed a pastel building with black iron balcony railing. It looked like every structure on Royal Street, every structure in the French Quarter. "That a bank or a bar or a boutique?"

"Bank."

"Gotta cash a check."

"I want to get back to the office so I can go home," he said.

"Just take a minute."

"They won't cash dick unless you've got an account. I could use some money for the weekend. Let's stop at a station and use the ATM. Need to gas up anyways."

Her eyes narrowed as she stared at the bank, a low building. The closed window shutters dotting the second story resembled dead eyes. Something was bothering her. She tried to push the familiar feeling away and failed. "They'll take my check," she said. "If they don't, we can use their cash machine. They have to have a machine."

"Fine," he grumbled, swiping the sweat off his brow with the palm of his hand. "Let's do it and get out of this sauna."

They crossed the street, weaving around a knot of people standing in the middle of the road. "Good to see all the tourists," said the woman. "The town sure is coming back."

"Yeah, yeah," the man mumbled. He held the bank door open while she stepped inside. He pulled off his shades; she kept hers on. The smells of the street followed them into the building and mixed with the scent of money: fried sausage dipped in ink. The woman peeked over her glasses and surveyed the interior of the bank, a shoe box chilled by an oversized window air conditioner. She saw an "Out of Order" note slapped over the cash machine in the foyer and a "Please Step to Another Window" sign propped in the opening of a teller's window. A girl teller was at the only other window, helping a big guy stuffed into a polo shirt. A big guy stuffed into a tee shirt was waiting his turn. Standing at a counter planted in the middle of the shoe box was a guy in a suit, scribbling with a pen chained to the table. Beyond the tellers' windows were four glass-walled offices; one cube held a man hunched over a desk.

The polo shirt stepped away from the teller's window and left; the tee shirt took his place. The customer at the table dropped the pen, grabbed his slip, and took his spot behind the tee shirt. The woman stepped over to the table and reached into her blazer. While she pulled out her checkbook, she eyed the waiting man. Young. Red hair cut short. Clean-shaven. Well dressed in pinstripes. A nicer suit than her partner's. He turned his head, glanced at her and her companion, and looked away.

Her partner shoved his hands in his pants pockets and stared out one of the windows facing Royal. The sound of a sax penetrated the building. Bourbon Street, running parallel to Royal, was one block over. The clubs were starting to hop as the late afternoon melted into early evening. "Want to grab a beer later tonight? Catch a band?" he asked without turning to face her. "My treat. A goodbye beer."

The woman didn't answer. She dropped her checkbook on the counter and opened it. She reached over, grabbed the bank pen, and pulled it toward her. She started, as if the pen had given her a shock. She stood frozen, head bent down, pen poised over paper but not touching it. A shudder shook her frame, and behind her sunglasses, her closed lids vibrated from rapid eye movement.

Her companion pulled his hands out of his pockets, turned around, and glared at her with impatience. "We should've stopped at a gas station." He turned back to the windows.

She opened her eyes and, with her trembling left hand, slipped off her sunglasses and dropped them on the counter. Her grip on the pen tightened. She pulled it closer—until the chain snapped. She had to let go. She unclenched her right fist and let the pen fall to the floor. She blinked and took a deep breath. Had she really read what she thought she'd read? She had, she told herself. This time she was dead-on. She reached inside her blazer.

The tee shirt finished his business and left. The redhead stepped up to the window.

"Hands up!" the woman hollered. "FBI."

The redhead swung around. His eyes locked on the Glock she had pointed at his chest. He raised his hands in the air. "Ma'am?" The teller saw the gun, gasped, and took a step back from the window. Behind the teller, the man in the glass office looked up from his paperwork. His hand went to the phone on his desk.

The woman's partner swung around. "What the hell?" He pulled out his own pistol and aimed it at the pinstripes while talking to the woman. "What is it?"

Her eyes and gun didn't leave her target. "He's looking to rob the place. His pockets. Be careful. He's armed."

"Don't move!" Keeping his gun on the guy, her partner stepped over to the redhead. With his free hand, he reached into the pin-striped jacket and pulled out a handgun. "Beretta. Nice. Got papers for it?" The redhead didn't respond. "That's not the right answer, my friend." He slipped it into his own pants pocket. He patted the redhead's other pockets. Nothing. He noticed something in the guy's left hand. He reached up and snatched a rectangle of paper. He ran his eyes over the writing. "Amazing. A police station right across the street. It's a . . ."

"I know what it is," said his partner. "I already read it."

         ❀   ❀   ❀

The two agents stood on the sidewalk, watching and talking as the redhead was being shoved into a squad car. "What do we tell them back at the office this time?" the man asked his partner.

"That it was your arrest," she said. "That you recognized him from tapes of the other robberies."

"He wore a ski mask before this."

She sighed. "Make up whatever shit you want, then."

"How'd you figure it out?"

"You know better than to ask."

"I just thought . . ."

"You thought you'd like to join me in Shreveport."

"Hell, no."

"Then don't ask," she said. "Don't ever fucking ask."

One

Spring in Minnesota is a bad blind date: Late in arriving. Disappoint-
ingly cold. Sloppy and frenetic and loud and foul-smelling. Beneath all
of that, glimmers of something dangerous yet desirable.

In the skies above the Mississippi River, bald eagles glide and dip as
they search for dead fish and the animal carcasses that become visible
each spring, when the white cover is pulled back. Dogs bolt from their
yards and head for the woods or the road, lured by the scents released
by the receding snow. Before it finally surrenders, the ice on the lakes
groans and cracks and moves. The winds blow hard and long, rattling
the trees and drying up the puddles. The skunk cabbage pokes through
the mud, emitting an odor that's a cross between garlic and a skunk's
stink. Turkeys rev up their gobbling and put on a show to get the attention of the other birds. The sun rises earlier and loiters like it might stay
all the way through dinner.

The teenager stood at his back stoop. He could smell dinner—pot roast and new potatoes—but he couldn't eat until the dog was kenneled. "Gunner! Here, boy! Gunner!" He clapped his hands together twice. "Come on, boy!"

His father walked out the back door and stood behind him. "You should've put the collar on him."

The boy frowned and shoved his hands in his jacket pockets. "Don't like shocking him."

"Better than watching him run across the highway and get flattened."

"He'll come." The boy went down the steps, put the middle and index fingers of both hands in his mouth, and blew. The whistle did the trick. A German wire-haired pointer came loping out of the pines behind the house. "Good boy, Gunner."

The father squinted into the low sun as the dog galloped toward them. "What's he got in his mouth?"

The boy shrugged. "Something dead. Another squirrel."

The dog stopped at the bottom of the steps, wagged his stubby tail, and dropped his prize at the feet of the younger master. The boy jumped back and almost fell backward on the steps behind him. "Dad!"

His father thumped down and stood next to him. Crouching over, he touched the bloody thing with the tips of his fingers. Without looking up, he said to his son: "Go in the house. Call the sheriff. Call 911."

The boy didn't move. "Dad!"

"Do what I say! Now!" The boy turned and ran up the steps, yanked open the screen door, and went inside. The door slammed behind him. "Sweet Jesus," the father muttered as he stared at the object on the ground.

The mother came out, stood on the stoop, and wiped her hands on her apron. "Food's getting cold." She looked down at her husband's bent back. "What is it?" She took a step down and then another. She saw what he was hunkered over and gasped. Her eyes went past the yard and into the woods, where the sun was starting to slip behind the tallest trees. "Who? What do you think happened? How?"

"God knows."

"Should we take the truck? Go look?"

The man stood up but kept his eyes locked on the object at his feet. The dog darted forward and bent his head down, making a move to retrieve his find. "No!" yelled the man. "Sit!" The dog backed away, sat down, and panted. A spot of blood dotted the wiry hairs of the animal's muzzle.

His wife repeated: "Should we take the truck and go look?" She paused. "What if whoever lost it . . ." Her voice trailed off.

The man shook his head. "Poor bastard who lost this has gotta be dead." He looked up and into the woods. "Sun will be down by the time the sheriff gets here."

The woman turned her head to the side. Her next question was a woman's question: "Is there a wedding ring?"

He looked back down. "It's the right hand."

◊   ◊   ◊

He regained consciousness before dark. Every inch of him ached, waves of agony washing over him and burning him like scalding bathwater. His lips were split and swollen. The taste of his own blood salted the inside of his mouth. He swallowed once. Something small and hard went down his throat, and he almost gagged on his own front tooth. In the midst of the pain and nausea, another sensation pushed to the surface. Confusion. Where was he? The woods. He sat on the ground with his back against a tree, an evergreen. He could smell the pine and feel the needles under him. He shivered. He was cold, and his pants were wet. He'd urinated on himself; he didn't know when. He tried to move and realized he was tied to the tree. Rope coiled around him from his shoulders down to his waist. He looked at his legs in front of him. Rope bound them from his knees down to his ankles. A realization. His vision. One eye was swollen shut, but out of the other he could see. Hardwoods and evergreens were turning into shadows. Lacy patches of twilight spotted the ground. Why could he see? During the beating, his glasses had been knocked off, and he was blind without them. Who'd put them back on his face? He struggled against the ropes, and the intensity of the pain increased. Boiled over. "Oh God!" he moaned to the darkening sky.

The pain was worse one place in particular. He turned his head to the right and looked at his arm, bound to his side. A shaft of fading sun poked through the canopy of pine boughs above him and illuminated the horror perfectly, as if someone held a flashlight there for him. *See that?* His moans contorted into a sob. His right hand was gone. His assailant had taken it off. The fiend had made sure he'd be able to see the stump—by placing his glasses back on his face.

He wanted to scream but didn't have the strength. All he managed was a noise. A hoarse, guttural growl. Dying-animal sound. He shut his mouth and his eyes and took a breath. He worked up some saliva inside his mouth and swallowed, tasting more blood than spit. "God help me," he whispered. His shoulders shook with sobs. "I'm sorry. Help me." As he wept, he remembered his assailant's tears; the bastard had cried even as he beat him. Why? The monster's words throbbed inside his head like a heartbeat. *Life for life. Life for life. Life for life.*

He passed out again, this time for good. His head fell forward, but the glasses stayed on his face. His killer had tied them to his head.

   ◦ ◦ ◦

A month later and a hundred miles south, two brothers stood on the sandy banks of the Mississippi as they fished at Hidden Falls in St. Paul. The park winds along the shoreline at the bend in the Mississippi, near its confluence with the Minnesota River. Though in the middle of an urban area, the boys were surrounded by limestone rock outcroppings and forest land. Across the river from the pair, atop the bluffs, were perched the stone buildings of Fort Snelling, an 1820s military outpost restored as a tourist site.

The pair repeatedly cast their lines out into the middle of the band of water and reeled them back in with disgust. "Anything?" one would yell. "Nothin'," the other would respond. On their hooks was the bait most preferred by Minnesota kids: night crawlers coaxed from the soil with the help of a running hose. Though they talked big talk about catching record sunnies and crappies, they'd take anything that fit in a frying pan—or almost anything.

The ten-year-old started reeling in his line again. There was something on it, but it wasn't fighting like a fish. What was it? The line stopped coming in, jerking to a halt. He cranked the reel hard and it whined. Must have snagged another stick, he figured. The river was high, and there was a lot of junk floating in it. The boy wiggled the tip of the rod up and down a few times, then pulled hard toward his right shoulder. He felt the line loosen, and he resumed his reeling. He stepped closer to the water's edge and stopped cranking. He lifted the tip of his pole into the air. A tangled bundle emerged from the water and swung toward him. His line was wrapped around a branch—and something else. He looked at it and blinked twice. "Lee!" he yelled to his older brother. He dropped the rod on the ground and took a step backward. He tripped over a rock and fell on his butt. "Lee!"

The older boy held on to his own pole and stared out at the river. "I'm not untangling your line again. You've got to learn sometime, you lazy shit."

"Lee!"

The teenager sighed, reeled in his line, and set his rod on the ground. He looked at his younger brother with disgust. "Stupid stick ain't gonna bite you."

"Not a stick!" The boy rolled onto his knees, wrapped one arm around his gut, and vomited. He started coughing and crying.

"What the hell is wrong with you?" The older boy glanced at the pole his brother had dropped along the shore. He jogged over to it. His eyes followed the line. The end of it led to the river's edge. A speedboat had just zoomed past and kicked up a wave. Water curled over the catch so the older boy couldn't see it clearly. He bent over, picked up the rod, and stared at the mess. "Crap!" He dropped the pole and backed away from it. He ran his eyes up and down the shoreline and saw no one. He looked across the river. A wall of trees. With trembling hands, he patted the pockets of his jeans. Empty. Ramming his hands into his jacket pockets, he pulled out his keys. He wrapped his fist around them and went over to his brother, still kneeling on the ground and crying. He pulled the boy up by the collar of his jacket and lifted him to his feet. "Move! To the car." He pushed his brother ahead of him as they crawled up a steep, sandy incline. They both lost their footing and started sliding down. The younger boy grabbed a dried-up vine and pulled himself up to the grassy ledge. His older brother did the same. They ran across an open, mowed area dotted with picnic tables. A tar trail cut across the green expanse. The older boy scanned the black ribbon as they ran but saw no hikers or bikers, no one to help them. He eyed the woods on his left with suspicion and silently cursed himself for picking such a quiet fishing spot.

"Lee!" wailed the younger boy as he ran ahead of his brother.

"Keep moving!" The parking lot was just ahead of them. The teenager's mind was racing. Was his cell phone in the car or sitting on the kitchen table? He tried to visualize the inside of his car and couldn't. All he could see was the thing at the end of his brother's line.

        ◈   ◈   ◈

Just upriver, in the shady wooded bottomlands next to the Mississippi, a man lay facedown. He turned his head to the right and spat out a mouthful of grit and blood. He tried to draw his knees up under him and couldn't. His legs were tied together, from knees to ankles. His left arm was tied behind his back with more coils of rope. He used his free arm to raise himself a few inches. He couldn't stay up; the pain was too great. He groaned and collapsed back in the dirt. He released one last breath and died with his eyes wide open, locked on the bleeding stump at the end of his right wrist.

Two

A line fell between the two of them, dangling in front of their faces. The rope wasn't part of the rigging; it had a noose at the end. Her husband slipped the loop over his head. "Help me this time," he said. She reached over and tightened the noose. The line lifted him while he kicked his legs and tugged at the rope around his neck. He stopped struggling, and she was relieved. Staring at the flat bottoms of his deck shoes, she watched as he continued going up and up until he disappeared.

She ran to the stern to jump off, but saw the water was different this time. The blue was surrounded by tall grasses, like green lashes hedging an eye. In the middle of the eye stood a robed woman, her palms up and her arms stretching down. The woman raised her arms and turned her hands down, as if reaching for the boat. Then the woman turned to stone.

She didn't want to go overboard; she feared sharing the water with the stone figure. Her attention was instead drawn heavenward, the previously *seamless sky now marred by two rounds of light. She shook her fist at the twin moons and screamed three words, a strange phrase she'd never before uttered: "Life for life!"*

Bernadette Saint Clare jerked and sat up; she'd nodded off during her break on the couch. She looked at the utility knife, locked in her hand with the blade pointing out. Sensing something wet running down her cheeks, she feared she'd cut herself in her sleep. She dropped the knife and tentatively touched her face with both hands. She examined her fingers. Damp with tears. "I'm losing it," she muttered, wiping her palms on the thighs of her pants. She retrieved the box cutter, got up, and shuffled across the floor to a sealed box. Kneeling in front of the cube, she slipped the razor under the flap and sliced through the tape. Peering inside, she found mostly framed stuff. She picked up some of the rectangles and set them on the floor next to her. Commendation. Commendation. A couple of awards. A medal. Things given to her over the years by her supervisors and their supervisors. Why had she bothered packing the junk? None of it meant anything. The letters of censure weren't framed, but they were the only part of her file the bosses cared about. She grabbed the edge of a wastebasket and dragged it to her side. She plucked the framed pieces of flattery off the floor and dropped them into the metal can. The *clank* satisfied her. She continued sifting through the box, uncovering a plaque shaped like a badge. *FBI* was engraved in large script. "Famous But Incompetent," she muttered as she chucked the plaque into the wastebasket.

The next layer was family photos. She lifted out an unframed snapshot of her mom and dad standing in front of one of the barns on the farm. All were gone now, her folks dead, the farm sold, and the barn replaced by a townhouse development. The edges of the photo were curling and pocked with pinholes. Over how many different desks in how many different cities had she tacked that photo? She dropped the picture back in the box and dug around until she found the framed high-school portrait of Madonna, the last picture snapped of her, not counting the ones taken by the state troopers and the coroner. Bernadette lifted the photo out of the box. Had it really been twenty years? She touched her fingertips to the blue eyes staring back at her. Would her twin have aged any differently than she? Would Maddy have gray mixed with the blond? Probably not. They would look the same. She and Madonna knew they were identical twins even though everyone else said that wasn't possible because their eyes didn't match. Bernadette had a set of brown eyes, at least up until the moment of the crash.

She set the photo on the floor and rummaged around inside the box. Bernadette spotted her favorite picture, the eight-by-ten of her husband caught in a rare moment of stillness, when he wasn't sailing or rock climbing but was simply sprawled out on the sofa. She got up off the floor, walked over to her desk, and hesitated before propping the photo on top. Maybe it would be better to take the picture home. People in the office would ask about him, and she didn't want to tell the story to a whole new set of co-workers.

She glanced around the office and set the picture down on her desk. Who in the hell was she kidding? What coworkers? There were two other desks in the room, and neither one of them looked occupied. One had an empty letter tray and a computer monitor sitting on top of it; the screen was black and the box under the desk looked dead. The other desk was covered with file folders that reeked of mildew. The cases inside of them probably predated Wounded Knee. The ancient couch she'd napped on could have been requisitioned by Hoover. They'd hidden her away good this time, burying her in a basement office across from the electrical room, on the same level as the parking ramp. At least it was bigger than her last place. What was lower on the bureau food chain? An agent with a basement office in St. Paul, or one with a first-floor closet in Shreveport?

She heard ringing and ran her eyes around the room until she spotted her jacket draped over the chair behind the moldy-files desk. She went over, dug the cell out of her pocket, and flipped it open. "Yeah?"

Her latest boss, Assistant Special Agent in Charge Tony Garcia: "Got a good one for you."

"Let's hear it."

"Couple of kids—the Vang brothers—were doing some fishing and reeled in a nasty trophy this morning. A juicy hand."

She pressed the phone tight to her ear. Sounded intriguing and creepy. Creepy was her specialty. She hadn't expected a case so soon, and found her exhaustion being replaced by excitement. "Location?"

"Hidden Falls. South entrance. Know where that's at?"

"I'm from Minnesota, remember?"

"Figured you didn't know the cities."

He made it sound like she had manure caked on her shoes. "I've got cousins in town." She knew it didn't matter, but had to ask anyway. "Which hand?"

"The right. Why?"

"No reason. Curious." She leaned against the edge of the desk, reached inside the holster tucked into the waist of her jeans, and took out her gun. Checked it. "And why do we care?"

"We care, Agent Saint Clare, because this is the second person separated from his hand. A month ago, we had a dead guy up north. Same deal. Right hand cut off. Body found in the woods. Plus, this second guy has got a history with St. Paul cops. They want it cleared fast, so it doesn't look bad."

"What do you mean?"

"You'll see when you get there."

"This our case or theirs?"

"We can share. There's plenty of treats to pass around." Garcia paused. Cleared his throat. "I'll meet you."

She slipped her gun back in her jeans and gritted her teeth. He was keeping tabs on her like the last one, watching her like she was the latest addition to the zoo. An unpredictable exotic. "I can handle it solo."

"I know," he said. "It's Saturday. Weather's crap. Got nothing better to do."

o   o   o

She hopped in and started up her truck. While the Ford rumbled in front of the Warren Burger Federal Courts Building, Bernadette took inventory of her wardrobe. Dressed in jeans and a hooded St. Louis Rams sweatshirt under a jean jacket, she looked like half the people she arrested. She flipped down the visor and studied her face in the mirror. Her husband had told her she looked like Mia Farrow in *Rosemary's Baby*. She wondered which movie her husband would place her in this morning. Her short, boyish blond hair stuck out in spots, like she'd gone to bed with a wet head. Mia Farrow on a bad-hair day. The red veins in her eyes and the gray smudges under them advertised her lack of sleep. She rarely got enough rest, and last night was worse than usual. She'd stumbled into a new home in the dark and curled up on a bare mattress surrounded by boxes. Her night had been filled with disturbing dreams, and now the nightmares were getting weirder and starting to seep into her daylight hours.

"*Night of the Living Dead*," she said out loud to the mirror.

She fished her shades out of her jacket pocket. Unlike a lot of women, she didn't drag around a shoulder bag. Purses were oversized cosmetic bags, and the only thing she ever smeared on her face was ChapStick. Her husband had always told her she was beautiful without makeup, and she was glad he thought so. She didn't have the skill or patience for applying cosmetics. Now that he was gone, she figured she had even less reason to fuss with her face. She slipped on her shades and checked in the mirror again. Why bother with eye makeup when sunglasses were handy? She flipped the visor up.

Bernadette looked north and south on Robert and hung a U-turn so she was headed south. She stopped for a red light at Kellogg Boulevard. A cold drizzle misted the air and coated her windshield; she clicked on the wipers. The light turned green. She hung a left onto Kellogg and drove a block. She took a right on Jackson Street and went down a short hill and under a railroad bridge before hanging another right, onto Shepard Road. The Mississippi, a meandering band of chocolate studded with barges, was on her left. That damn brown water seemed to be tethered to her, pulling her back like a muddy umbilical cord. All she'd been able to snag were assignments in river states: Missouri. Louisiana. Minnesota. What would be next? Maybe the bureau would ship her off to the state of Mississippi itself.

Bernadette spotted the South Gate to Hidden Falls Park and hung a left. Police tape crisscrossed the entrance, with a uniform stationed on each side of the yellow X. The bigger officer stepped away from his post and went up to the driver's window. "Who're you?"

"FBI."

"Flash me," he said.

She whipped out her ID wallet and held it in front of his nose. "Bernadette Saint Clare."

His eyes went from the ID to her face. "Lose the specs," he said.

She hesitated and then pulled off her sunglasses. His eyes shifted back and forth as he studied her face. Like most people looking at her for the first time, he struggled to figure out which eye to focus on. She hated that; it made her feel like a freak. She slipped her glasses back on. "Okay?"

"Heard you were coming."

She sensed the resentment in his voice. She wondered what else he'd heard about her. Could be it was just the usual pissing match between local cops and the feds. She forced a smile. "What's the skinny?"

"There's a God after all."

She frowned. "What?"

He winked and stood straight. "You're in for a treat, FBI." He stepped away from the truck. He undid his end of the tape, dropped it, and waved her through. She rolled forward a few yards. Before she steered down the steep drive that led to the riverfront park, she glanced through her rearview mirror. The big cop was putting the tape back up. He and the other uniform were laughing, like they were at a picnic.

Three

A crime scene like a thousand other crime scenes, Bernadette thought as she surveyed what was at the bottom of the hill. She'd be the only oddball. Would anyone pick her out? It'd be like an exercise in a child's workbook. *Which object doesn't fit in the picture? Draw a circle around it.*

She pulled in between a squad and a paramedic unit. While she turned off the truck and dropped the keys in her jacket, she took in the view through her windshield. She spotted her boss at a picnic table with two boys, the Vang brothers. A couple of crime-scene photographers. The cops' crime-lab van. Bunch of uniforms and their squads. Two paramedics talking to one of the uniforms. The Ramsey County Medical Examiner's hearse. A gurney sitting behind the hearse, waiting for a body.

She popped open the driver's side and hopped out. While she

walked across the grassy expanse toward the picnic tables, she dug inside her pockets for her notebook and pen. Garcia eyed her from his seat on the picnic bench. He got up and said something to the two boys. They nodded and stayed sitting. The older one rested his elbows on the table and propped up his chin with his hands. The younger one wiped his nose with the back of his jacket sleeve; his eyes were red. Bernadette figured he was the one who'd pulled in the prize. Gross thing for a little kid to see.

As Garcia walked to meet her, Bernadette took in his face and physique. Even under his trench coat, she could see he was built like a weight lifter, with a trim waist and big arms and shoulders. He had olive skin, and short black hair with gray creeping into the sideburns. The buzz cut was getting overgrown, and the ends were starting to brush the tops of his ears. She approved. Bosses who were too meticulous about their grooming and dress were often anal jerks in the office. As Garcia drew closer, his mouth stretched into that tight grin she knew too well, that familiar smile Minnesotans employed to hide their real feelings. She told herself she was reading too much into it. He'd sounded decent over the phone and seemed straightforward when she came into town to talk to him before getting the assignment.

As they met and stopped on the grass, he held out his hand and she took it. He towered over her, but then, so did most people. "How're you doing?" she asked.

"You come from your new place?"

"From the office. I was unpacking."

He eyed her sweatshirt and frowned.

"I was unpacking," she repeated.

"Media's gonna love this one." He scanned the sky above them for news helicopters and saw nothing but gray. The mist was getting heavier, turning into a drizzle that clouded the air like a fog. "Wonder where those dogs are this morning?"

"It's a little early for them. Give them time to have their coffee." She flipped open her notebook. "The dead guy?"

"Sterling Archer."

Bernadette's eyebrows went up. She'd heard about him; he'd made the national news. Archer was a juvenile judge who'd molested a string of children and teens over a dozen years. Most of the victims had been in his courtroom. In one case, he'd elicited sex from both a girl and her mother in exchange for leniency on the bench. Archer's team of attorneys got half of the charges thrown out and, during the trial, tore apart the credibility of the kids. The defense's tactics and the resulting verdict—an acquittal—infuriated the cops and citizens. One of the young women who'd testified committed suicide. Some of the families had publicly vowed revenge.

Bernadette: "A vigilante thing, right? There's gotta be a line of suspects snaking all the way down to the Iowa border."

Garcia: "Maybe. Maybe not. Here's the deal. After he was cut loose, Archer left the state, went to Florida. Miami. No one knew he was back in town except his Realtor lady. He came back for a day—to close the sale of his house."

"Where'd he live?"

"Right up there." Garcia tipped his head toward the top of the hill. "Mississippi River Boulevard."

"Know the neighborhood. Nice little shacks."

"St. Paul Watch Commander said the Realtor lady called the cop shop last night to report her boy missing in action. He didn't show for his closing Friday afternoon, and she was worried."

"So Realtor lady reports Archer missing last night." She nodded toward the brothers sitting at the picnic table. "Then, this morning, the boys reel in a whopper."

"With a ring still on the pinkie finger."

The right side of Bernadette's mouth curled up. For some reason, that detail pleased her. She clicked her pen a couple of times and started writing. "With a ring still on the pinkie." She looked up from the notepad. "What about the rest of him?"

"As the squads are pulling into the South Gate, some hikers parked at the North Gate are giving the cops a jingle. They tripped across the judge halfway between here and there."

"Cops already sweeping the park?"

He nodded. "They found some shoe prints around the body. Could produce some decent casts. They've got some boats doing some checking, too. Maybe they can dredge up the murder weapon."

She looked past him and counted three twenty-foot boats bobbing on the water—one belonging to the Ramsey County Sheriff's Office, one owned by the St. Paul Fire Department, and the third from the St. Paul Police Department. "Damn," she said. "Every copper in this town's got a boat. What about us? Do we have a boat?"

"We could get one if we needed it, but we don't need it."

Bernadette stuffed her notebook in her jacket. "Gonna check out the scene on dry land, then. Get a look at Archer while you finish up with the Vangs."

"Already done interviewing the kids. Cops interviewed them. Nothing much to tell. Didn't see spit or hear spit. Just reeled in some dead guy's hand. The thing rattled the hell out of them. I told them to chill for a while, calm down, and then go home."

"Between you and the cops and their flotilla, what have I got left to do?" She knew what she had left to do, why she'd been called. She wanted to hear him say it. She wished just once *anyone* in authority would officially ask for it. Of course, she knew it would never happen. To ask for it would be an admission, an acknowledgment of an ability they didn't understand and a power that frightened them. She couldn't blame them. At times, it scared her.

The wind picked up and blew the drizzle against their backs. Garcia turned up the collar of his coat. "Let's go have a look-see at the dead guy before this turns into a monsoon."

◦　◦　◦

They didn't speak during the brief hike through the woods. The ground beneath their feet was uneven and covered with fallen branches, dead vines, and low-growing vegetation. Above them, rain pattered the leaves on the trees. Garcia led her to a triangle of police tape wrapped around tree trunks. The yellow stood out like an exotic flower planted in the middle of the brown-and-green forest. At each point of the triangle stood a uniformed officer. All three of the cops were grinning.

"Guys," said Garcia.

Two of them nodded and wiped the smiles off. "Hey," said the third, continuing to grin.

Bernadette eyed the area around the triangle. The corpse wasn't far from the riverfront or the park's paved trail, but it was well hidden by the density of the trees and bushes. She stepped over the tape, hunkered down next to the body, and examined the right arm resting on top of the muddy ground. "He was alive when his hand was taken off."

Garcia hopped over the tape and crouched down next to her. "What makes you so sure?"

She pointed at the stump. "Look at the way the dirt is sort of packed into the end of it. I think he tried to use it for leverage. Push himself up with it."

"Ouch."

Bernadette took her notebook out of her jacket, flipped it open, and wrote while she ran her eyes up and down the body. She'd seen Archer in the newspapers and on television. He'd been a short, obese man with an Alfred Hitchcock belly. Now, facedown in the mud, he looked flat and spread out—a jellyfish washed ashore. He was in khaki slacks and a short-sleeved polo shirt. "I assume there are no other parts missing, but let's check out the B side." She stood up and went around to the body's left side and hunkered down. The left arm and hand were bound behind Archer's back by the rope. She studied the knot resting on top of the body's left shoulder blade. "Well, that's interesting as hell."

"What?" asked Garcia.

She stood up and stepped over to Archer's feet. She crouched down and studied the rope coiled around his lower legs. "Very interesting." She flipped to a clean notebook page and scribbled furiously.

"What?"

She pointed to Archer's bound legs with the pen. "See how nice and neat the rope is coiled. It's a pretty good imitation of a method called 'sheer lashing.' Sailors use it to tie poles together side by side. This loop here—the one by his ankles with the end of the rope threaded through it—see that?"

"Yeah."

"I'm pretty sure that's a clove hitch."

"Clove hitch," Garcia repeated. "I heard of that."

She thumbed toward the knot tied over the shoulder blade. "And that's a double fisherman's knot. Another sailing deal."

"How do you know all that?"

"My husband was into sailing."

"He quit?"

"Died."

"Sorry. Didn't know. New Orleans didn't fill me in on that personal stuff."

Liar, she thought. *You're my boss. They told you everything. You know more about me than I do. That's the bureau's job—knowing.* "That's okay," she said evenly.

Garcia stood up. "So you think the killer's a man of the high seas."

"Or thinks he's one."

"What do you mean by that?"

"These aren't perfect renditions. And, really, there're quicker and more efficient ways to restrain a person. The sheer lashing in particular—talk about overkill. Whoever did this was showing off or really into his cordage."

"But he seems to know *something* about sailing."

"Or fishing. Rock climbing. Michael used to climb, too. They have to know a lot about line. Who else? Magicians. They know about ropes. Or could be it's just a guy who likes to tie knots. Knot guys have their own clubs and magazines and newsletters."

"You're kidding me."

"I met this one guy in New Orleans. A river guy. Worked on a barge. What was the name of his group?" She paused. "The International Guild of Knot Tyers. Something like that. They practice tying knots and investigate new knots and have meetings about knots."

"Whatever floats your boat."

"Was the guy up north tied the same way?"

"Don't know."

"We'll have to find out. His hand turn up?"

"A kid's hunting dog brought it home."

"Lovely," she said.

"At least the pooch didn't eat it." Garcia shoved his own hands in his coat pockets. "We'll have to see if they got shoe prints around that body. Check for a match. See if we're dealing with the same guy."

"It'd be nice if we got matching shoe casts. Nice, too, if the rope job is the same. Regardless . . ."

Garcia finished her sentence: "It's gotta be the same guy."

"My thoughts exactly."

"We keep implying the perp's a *he,* by the way."

"An assumption, but not a wild one. The judge wasn't a small person. Can't see a female overpowering him. This slicing-and-dicing business, can't remember the last time a woman got that creative with a tool. Takes a lot of strength. Stamina." She stood up and wrote in her notebook while she talked. "How often do you see a gal behind the counter of a butcher shop? It's a guy thing. Cutting parts off. Hacking meat and bone."

Garcia hunched his shoulders against the cold. The drizzle had stopped, but it was still windy. "Hacking with what? A knife?"

She went back around to his side of the body and stared at the stump. "Whatever the instrument, had to be sharper than hell. That's a mean, clean chop."

He coughed and paused. Didn't say anything for several seconds. Then: "Need me to clear the scene for you?"

How many times had she heard those words or something close to them? *Need me to clear the scene for you? Want some time alone? Want to hold it? Get a feel for it?* What they really want to say is: *Do that thing you do. The parlor trick. That spooky, ESP, bogeyman mumbo-jumbo. The things-that-go-bump-in-the-night thing that you do. Don't give us the details on how you do it or why you can do it. Just do it, and do it right this time. Solve the case and go away. Don't embarrass us.*

"Need me to clear the scene?" he repeated.

"Not necessary." Bernadette stuffed her notebook in one jacket pocket, and from the other fished out her gloves. She snapped them on. She took out her keys; she kept a pocket knife on the chain.

Garcia eyed the tool. "Doing a field autopsy?"

Bernadette went over to the dead man's ankles and crouched down to study the rope wound around his legs. *The killer had to touch the ends to do the clove hitch,* she thought. She reached over and grabbed the end of rope threaded through the loop and sliced off a few threads. She cupped the threads in her right palm and scrutinized them. They wouldn't be much to hang on to, but she didn't want to take more and compromise evidence. The strands would have to work until she found something more substantial. She closed her knife against her knee and dropped her keys back in her jacket. "Anyone got a bag?"

Garcia patted his pockets. "Not on me." He looked over at the cops. They shook their heads.

"Forget it." With her free hand, she pulled out another glove, shook it open, and dropped the threads inside it. She balled up the glove and shoved it in her right jacket pocket. She stood up, peeled off her gloves, and tucked them in the front pocket of her jeans.

"What else?" he asked.

"The severed hand. I'd like to see it."

"ME's guys have got it."

"Let's check it out," she said.

He looked at the mangled arm and back at her, as if he expected something more. "You're done here?"

"Done," she said flatly.

"Let's take the long way back. Easier going." He stepped outside the triangle.

"You two through, then?" asked one of the uniforms. "ME wants to pack him up and roll him outta here."

Garcia looked at Bernadette, standing inside the triangle. "You good, Agent Saint Clare?"

She ran her eyes around the body one last time. "I'm good." She stepped over the tape. "Thanks," she said to the closest cop.

"Anytime." He thumbed over his shoulder at the corpse. "This made my week."

○   ○   ※

Garcia led Bernadette through the woods and onto the paved path. She had to walk fast to keep up with him: his legs were long, and so was his stride. "How do you like your new office?"

"Lonely," she said, a step behind him. "Quiet in the basement."

"That'll change come the week after next."

A gust of wind made her shiver. She'd forgotten how cold early May could be in Minnesota. "What happens the week after next?"

"The rest of the St. Paul crew gets back from vacation."

"Crew?"

"Okay. Not a crew exactly. One agent. You'll like him. Good, but a little odd."

She pulled a tube of ChapStick out of her pocket, ran a bead along her lips, and dropped the tube back in her jacket. "What's his name, my oddball crewmate?"

"Creed. Ruben Creed."

"Who'd he piss off to end up in the basement in St. Paul?"

Garcia stopped in his tracks. "What?"

Four

She'd already put her foot in it, and it wasn't even her first official day on the job. "Sorry," Bernadette said quickly, stepping next to her boss.

Garcia pivoted around to face her. "Do me a favor. Take those shades off when I'm talking to you, Cat. That's what they call you, right?"

She slipped off her sunglasses. "Cat's good."

He looked at her eyes and blinked. "Why Cat? Like a kitty?"

"Like a dog." She folded the sunglasses and hooked them over the neck of her sweatshirt. "The guys in New Orleans gave me the name. Catahoula. Cattle-and-hunting breed that's popular down south."

He frowned. "I don't get it."

"Catahoula leopard dogs. They're known for having eyes of two different colors."

"Is 'Cat' okay with you?"

"Beats that formal stuff."

"Formal stuff?"

"*Agent This. Agent That.* Hate it."

He folded his arms over his chest. "I know you've been through some personal crap."

"Thought they didn't fill you in on all that."

He ignored her crack and kept going. "And I know you've had some professional issues as well."

"*Issues.* A good word for it."

He sighed, unfolded his arms, and didn't say anything for several seconds. The sound of a speedboat tearing downriver filled the void. He ran both his hands through his hair, folded his arms again, and looked at her. "You've got some special talents. I respect those talents."

She'd already torpedoed herself with her big mouth and figured she might as well go for broke. "Then why am I isolated in a bunker in St. Paul? Why can't I play with the other kids in Minneapolis? Afraid that I'm gonna infect the rest of the class? That I'm gonna scare them? Or maybe I'll give them ideas. Ideas that don't fit into Quantico's textbooks. Is that why Creed is in St. Paul? He scare you, too? What's his *special talent?*"

"Jesus Christ. It isn't about you, okay? We have space problems—as does every other federal agency in every other city in the country. The newest agent in the office always gets St. Paul. As soon as we get a couple of empty desks through transfers or retirements or whatever, you can head across the river. Join the rest of the inmates in the asylum on Washington Avenue. Then I'll send the next newbie to the cellar. But I gotta tell you something. Some of my best folks would rather be tucked away at the Resident Agency in St. Paul. Creed's one of them. He's been in St. Paul forever. Loves it here."

Her eyebrows arched with skepticism. "Loves the basement?"

"He gets to be away from the SAC," he said, referring to the special agent in charge. "Then there's the asshole ASACs like me."

She raised her palms in surrender. "The basement is wonderful. St. Paul is good. It's all good. I'm sorry I opened my mouth."

"This is not some punishment. I asked for you, lady."

Not even attempting to hide her disbelief, she crossed her arms over her chest. "Why?"

"That al-Qaeda cell you ferreted out in St. Louis. Your work on that RICO bust in Baton Rouge. Serial bank robber in New Orleans."

"That last one was my partner's doing."

"Bullshit," he said. "I checked around. It was yours, all the way. You don't like to take the credit, do you?"

"Some of my colleagues would say too much of my work relies on . . ." She searched for the right word. "Hunches."

"Professional jealousy."

"My bosses haven't approved of my methods, either."

"Proof's in the results, and you've had stellar results." He skipped a beat before he added: "Most of the time."

Those last four words made her cringe. *Most of the time.* He'd added that qualifier so she knew how cognizant he was of her previous missteps, the episodes when she'd come up with blanks in trying to use her sight, or sabotaged cases by misinterpreting what she'd observed. "Appreciate the kind words," she said dryly. "Really. The basement in St. Paul is great. Hell. Minneapolis Division *does* cover the Dakotas. Could have ended up in a root cellar in Minot."

"That's the spirit," he said flatly.

Around a bend in the path rattled a gurney flanked by four men. "Can we take it?" asked one of the ME crew.

"All yours," said Garcia. He and Bernadette stepped off the trail and let them by. The pair stepped back on the path and continued walking. "Did you find a decent place to live?"

"Bought a condo. Loft in Lowertown."

"You can roll out of bed and walk to work."

"In five minutes," she said.

"You run? There're some great paths along the river."

"What have they got for dirt trails close to the city? I've got a bike."

"I've seen bicycles along the river downtown. On the trails right here in the park, for that matter. Lots of bikes."

"Not *my* kind of bike." She grinned. "That's okay. I'll figure it out. Reorient myself. Figure out what's where." She paused and then asked: "Still got some churches downtown?"

"Three Catholic churches. Some other denominations, too."

"Catholic works."

The walking path emptied out into the picnic area. The pair cut through it and headed for the parking lot. Half of the uniforms and all of the boats had cleared out. The paramedics were gone. The Vang brothers had left for home. The cops' crime-scene van was still there, but there was no activity around the vehicle. The ME's hearse had a guy leaning against the driver's side. A news helicopter hovered overhead. "There they are," said Garcia, his eyes to the sky.

"We've got a public-information guy?"

"Didn't bother pulling him into this. Let the cops' PIO handle it."

"What about our ERT?" she asked, meaning the Evidence Response Team.

"St. Paul's crime-scene guys are all over it. They want help on that end, they'll ask for it."

She stopped several yards from the hearse. "Did they ask for me?"

Garcia stopped ahead of her and turned around. "They didn't have to. You're what they need."

"What's that supposed to mean? What are they expecting out of me?"

"Don't worry about what they're expecting. Worry about what I'm expecting." He jammed his index finger into his chest. "I'm the only one you've got to please." He turned back around and continued to the hearse, parked in a corner of the lot. She waited a few seconds and went after him.

           ○   ○   ○

Along the front passenger's side of the hearse stood a knot of uniformed cops. As she drew closer, she could feel their eyes on her. She slipped her sunglasses off her sweatshirt, unfolded them, and put them back on. Their voices were low, but she caught fragments of their conversation: ". . . dragging the feds into this . . . little blonde chasing after

Garcia . . . crystal-ball crap . . ." *Great,* she thought. She'd get her usual welcome from the local police. Stares and whispers and shaking heads. The uniforms stopped talking as she came up on the ME's wagon, but they kept staring. She went around to the driver's side of the hearse. As she did, she heard muffled laughter. Then a male voice, one of the cops: "Keep it down, ladies. She's gonna bring out the dead. Send them after us to eat our brains." *Fuck you,* she thought. *The dead would starve if they had to feed on your brains.* She stood next to her boss. He was talking to one of the ME investigators—a big guy with a shaved head.

"My agent, Bernadette Saint Clare," Garcia said to the ME guy.

"How you doing?" asked the guy. "Sam Herman."

Bernadette shook his hand; her small fingers got lost in his grip. "I'm doing good."

"I hear you wanna see my goody bag," Herman said.

"You betcha," she said.

"Let's head to the back of the bus," he said.

She and Garcia followed him and waited while he popped open the back of the hearse. The big guy leaned inside and dug around. The group of cops shuffled to the rear of the vehicle to watch.

Garcia tipped his head down and said into her ear: "You mind an audience, or you want me to chase them away?"

Bernadette figured Garcia was expecting some sort of show, but this wasn't the place for it. She didn't want to tell him that. "I don't care," she whispered. "It's fine."

"Here you go," said Herman, pulling his head out of the vehicle. He turned toward Bernadette and stretched out both arms. A doctor presenting a newborn.

Bernadette peered through the clear plastic while she took out her gloves and snapped them on again. She reached out to retrieve the bundle and then pulled her hands away. She slipped off her sunglasses and leaned closer to the bag. "Holy shit."

"What's wrong?" asked Herman. His eyes darted from her bent head to the package and back to her.

She looked past the investigator and over at the officers. "You'd bet-

Five

· ◦ ○ ◇ ◎ ◈ ◑ ◮ ◐ ◦ ◈ ◑ ◇ ◎ ◎ ◓ ◈ ◈ ◈ ◈ ◎

Herman inspected the hand through the plastic. He glared at Bernadette. "What're you talking about?"

"The index finger, around the cuticle," she said, hanging her sunglasses back on her shirt.

Herman looked down again. After several seconds: "Son-of-a-bitch. How'd we miss it?"

"What is it?" asked Garcia.

She pulled her gloves tighter over her fingers. "Trace of pink polish. On the thumbnail, too. Same spot. Around the cuticle. The deceased wasn't much of a manicurist."

The short cop took his foot off the bumper. His ruddy complexion had turned redder. "Big deal. So maybe Judge Perve wore nail polish."

Bernadette: "Plus, that's a woman's ring."

"She's right," said Herman. "It's a fat lady's hand—not a fat fella's."

Bernadette: "Plus . . ."

"Another plus?" moaned Herman.

"Plus, that hand looks a tad riper than the body. The fat lady was killed before the fat fella." She looked at the short officer. "You're gonna smell her before you see her."

"Crap," spat the short cop. He turned and sprinted to one of the squads. He yanked open the door, got in, grabbed his handset. The rest of the uniforms scattered between the remaining cars.

"Should we hit the woods?" Bernadette asked her boss. "Help them search?"

"That's not why I brought you down here," he said in a low voice.

Bernadette nodded. Time to stop stalling and get to it. She eyed the package. She didn't want the hand; she couldn't haul it around with her. The jewelry would be good, more substantial than the threads. Surely the killer had touched the band during the struggle, or while chopping off and discarding the hand. "I'd like to take the ring," she said to Herman. "Run some . . . tests."

"What kinds of tests?"

"She just saved your ass," snapped Garcia.

The gurney team bumped across the parking lot and stopped at the rear of the hearse. "We're done," said one of the men.

Herman looked up from the bag. "No, you're not."

"The ring," repeated Bernadette. She and Garcia and Herman stepped away from the hearse so the men could slide the body into the wagon.

"You've got to sign for it," said Herman, his attention again locked on the package in his arms. "Paperwork is back at the office."

"You guys could be here all day," she said. "Can we expedite this? Transport the hand to your office ourselves?"

Herman looked up from the bundle and shook his head. "That ain't kosher. I'll send one of the guys on ahead to the office with the fat lady's hand. You go to the office, fill out whatever they want you to fill out. Take the ring from there."

Garcia: "Cat. You know where the ME's digs are?"

"Squat building next to Regions Hospital's parking ramp," said Bernadette. "Looks like a dental lab."

"You got it," said Garcia.

Herman: "How'd we miss it?" He turned around and slipped the bag back into the hearse while his crew gathered around him.

"Miss what?" asked one of the gurney men.

"Shut up," snapped Herman. He slammed the back of the hearse and looked at his group. "Don't move. I gotta make some calls." He went to the front of the wagon.

Bernadette stepped away from the hearse and Garcia followed. "What're you thinking?" he asked.

"I'll bet it turns up in the woods or the river. Thrown away, like the other two."

"The judge's hand? I'll bet you're right."

"And won't it be interesting if they find the woman's body and she's been tied up all nice and neat like the judge?"

"Interesting as hell."

"The guy up north. The judge. The woman." She peeled off her gloves and crammed them back in her jeans. "That would make three—three that we know of. Someone killed each of them. Cut their right hands off. Why? Was there someone somehow victimized by all three of them? Old-fashioned revenge? We were thinking it was a vigilante thing with the judge. Could be the same for the other two. What have you got on the dead guy up north?"

"Hale Olson. The guy's got his own interesting history. Was tangled up in a home invasion and robbery that went sour some years back."

"Another bad man, like Archer."

"Except Hale served his time. Found God in prison and all that. Cleaned up his act, by all accounts. Been behaving since he's been out. Had a steady job up north. Retired up there and stayed."

Bernadette: "Let's say for the sake of argument that, even though Mr. Olson served his time and got religion, someone thinks it wasn't enough. Let's also say the dead lady did something naughty and didn't get punished sufficiently. She's a bad mom who abused her kids. She poisoned her husband. Whatever. We add that up and what does it give us?"

"Easy math. That gives us three dead debits to society. Why cut off the hands, though?"

Bernadette: "Why throw away the hands? That's the bigger question."

Garcia: "What do you mean?"

"Why not take them as sick souvenirs? That's the usual pattern. In this weirdness, the killer treats the hand like waste. Garbage."

"A message," said Garcia. "A symbol of some kind?"

"Maybe the hands themselves aren't the important thing. The action of cutting them off is the key. A statement about what they did. A public judgment against them."

"That narrows it down," said Garcia. "We'll put out an APB for a suspect. *Believes he has the right to judge others.*"

"I know," she said. "Pretty much describes the entire human race. Except we can also add: *Knows how to tie a clove hitch.*"

"Meet you at the ME's." Garcia turned and went to his car.

As Bernadette watched him pull away, she heard sirens. Additional squads were racing back to the park. She slipped her sunglasses back on her face, and looked across the parking lot to the river and surrounding woods. She wondered: *Who are you? Why the right hands?* She knew what she had to do to find the answers, but she wasn't looking forward to it.

◊   ◊   ◊

The ME lab guy was as thin as a broomstick and as tall as one. A white coat hung from his narrow frame, and when he walked the material billowed behind him like a sheet in the wind. The jacket would have been filled out better if it were draped over a coat hanger. "What are you going to do that we can't? The Ramsey County Medical Examiner is one of the best pathologists in the country. What sorts of tests are we talking about here?"

Garcia: "We don't care to disclose that information at this time."

Bernadette gave her boss a sideways glance while she signed on a dotted line. The two agents were sitting at a conference table filling out forms, with the broomstick pacing behind them. They were in the front of the building, in a sunny room—the public face of the medical examiner's office. The lab, where the real work was done, was in back. So was the hand.

The broomstick stopped moving long enough to push his glasses up on his nose. "What are you looking for from this ring? Prints? DNA?" The pacing resumed.

"We don't want to say," said Garcia.

Lab Guy stopped again, planting himself at Garcia's elbow. "Federal arrogance. That's what this is."

"We're all working together on this," said Garcia, continuing to write.

"You come in here and pee on my shoes and tell me it's raining." He turned and headed for the door. Yanked it open and started to step through it. He said over his shoulder: "I'll bring out the ring, but the hand stays in the lab."

Garcia looked at Bernadette. She nodded. "Keep the hand," Garcia said to him.

He walked out, letting the conference-room door slam behind him.

"You think he's pissed?" Bernadette asked dryly. She dropped the pen on the table and pushed the paperwork away from her.

"Let him be pissed," said Garcia. He clicked the pen and looked at it. The side of it carried the address and phone number of the ME's office. "They got their own pens. We should get our own pens." He slipped it inside his blazer.

She retrieved her pen. "This one's from the Ramsey County Public Defender's Office. 'A reasonable doubt at a reasonable price.' Cute." She slipped it inside her jacket.

He drummed his hands on the table. "Everybody's got their own pens. We've definitely got to order up a box. Address. Phone number. The works."

"We don't like people knowing who we are and where we are and what we're doing."

"That's the old FBI," he said. "This is the new and improved FBI. The open FBI. What's the slogan for our pens?"

"Famous But . . ." She quickly stopped herself.

He finished her crack: ". . . Incompetent. I've heard that a million times. Old news. How about Fumbling Bumbling Idiots?"

She smiled. "Haven't heard that one before."

"That's the one I get from the reporters every time we have a high-profile fuckup. Unfortunately, all our fuckups are high-profile."

"That's because we're the fucking FBI," she said.

"How would that look on a pen? 'Because we're the fucking FBI.' No address or phone number or anything. Just that simple statement of fact. Whenever some perp asks us why we can get away with shit, what gives us the authority to bust his butt, we toss him the pen."

She laughed just as the ME lab guy walked back into the room. "Sorry to interrupt your good time," he said. On the table between them, he dropped a plastic bag the size of a sandwich. "Be responsible federal employees and don't lose it."

"Thank you," said Bernadette, reaching for the bag.

"By the way," said the broomstick, "there're a couple of initials inside. You might miss them. Pretty small. Cops are checking to see who's been reported missing. We might have a hit if a name matches up with the initials."

Bernadette: "AH."

"Yeah," said the guy. "How'd you know?"

"Cops won't find anyone with those initials," she said.

"How do you know?" snapped the guy.

Garcia looked at Bernadette as she slipped the bag into her jacket. "I just do," she said.

o   ⌀   ɔ

Bernadette and Garcia both exhaled with relief as they walked out of the building. They didn't say anything to each other until they were standing in the parking lot. The wind had died down and the drizzle had stopped, but it was getting colder. The sky was the color of dirty dishwater. The air hummed with the sound of traffic on the nearby tangle of freeways.

"You would have thought we asked him to please cut off his own hand and give it to us in a Baggie," said Bernadette.

"We're all possessive of our evidence," said Garcia. "I don't blame him. Then we give him this obtuse explanation. *Tests.*"

"Yeah. Guess you're right." Bernadette slipped her left hand inside her jacket pocket and felt the bag with the ring. In her right pocket was the glove containing the threads; she'd decided to hang on to it as a backup in case the jewelry didn't pan out. "I'll keep in touch with the cops and the ME this weekend."

"I can keep tabs on them." He fished his keys out of his coat pocket. "I'll give you the heads-up when all the missing hands and bodies are accounted for."

"You sure?"

"You finish unpacking and then do your deal." He jiggled his keys. "Need any help?"

With which task was he offering assistance? Bernadette answered as if he wanted to help with the first chore, even though she suspected he was more fascinated with the second. "Don't have that much stuff at the office or at home."

"You're a minimalist?"

"A slob. The less I have to take care of, the better."

"I can relate to that," he said. "Worst thing I ever did was buy a house."

"I'll be home. You can catch me on my cell if you need me." She turned away from him, started for her truck.

He snagged the elbow of her jacket. "Cat?"

She faced him. "Yeah?"

"How do you . . ." He stopped in mid-sentence and let go of her sleeve. "Give me a call first thing Monday. Earlier if you . . . uh . . . come up with something."

It took her less than ten minutes to drive through downtown to the loft—not nearly enough time to figure out why Garcia was so fascinated with her abilities. He was unlike any of her previous supervisors, and she couldn't decide if that was a good thing or a bad thing. Her other bosses didn't want to know the details of what she did or how she did it. Garcia was different; he wanted to watch. Was that because he believed in her sight—or because he doubted its veracity? She suspected it was the latter.

Six

While she alternated between unpacking and swearing, Bernadette did her best to ignore the two bundles. The bag containing the ring and the glove balled up with the threads were both perched on a tipped wooden fruit crate—trash left by the condo's previous owner. Every so often she gave the bundles a sideways glance, as if she didn't trust them completely but didn't want to be caught staring.

She bent over a cardboard box, dug around inside, and pulled out a wad of blouses tangled around plastic bags and wire hangers. She stood up and shook out the mess, walked over to the closet, and hung a pair of shirts over the rod. It was a miracle she'd discovered her stereo system right off the bat. Harry Connick, Jr., crooned "The Very Thought of You" while she fished out another top.

Inside the next box was stuff wrapped in newsprint. She picked up one bundle and unraveled the paper. Dishes, filthy from the ink. She pushed the cube over to the kitchen area. The condo was made up of a series of *areas*, as opposed to *rooms*. Except for around the bathroom, there were no walled-in spaces. Her bed area consisted of an oversized ledge jutting out from the wall, with a spiral staircase providing access from the ground level. All the shelf needed was some hay and it could pass for a barn loft.

The condo was her first home purchase. She and Michael had rented because they'd moved so much. He was a freelance writer and could find work anywhere, but her job took them everywhere. Wherever they landed, they'd somehow made her folks' country furniture fit. She wondered if the antiques would ever look right in this funky setting—a loft with twelve-foot ceilings, nine-foot windows, exposed interior brick walls, exposed ductwork, and exposed pipes. Plus, what about her bike? She'd had to sneak it up in the freight elevator. She didn't want to leave it outside, and she sure as hell wasn't going to pay to keep it in the parking ramp. She should've bought a regular house with a real garage. As she set the dirty dishes in the sink, she muttered to herself: "This was a bad call."

◦   ◦   ◦

Bernadette's worst call—made along with her sister—was one she could never face. The two took an ability they were born with and honed it until it was something unnatural.

They'd always been tuned to each other's thoughts; it was expected that twins operated that way. Their mother had bragged about it to her lady friends: "I'm trying to figure out which dolly one is crying for, and the other girl goes and gets it."

Developing the ability to see through each other's eyes seemed the next logical step. They'd concentrate hard on reading each other's mind while staring at a math problem in school. Soon they'd see each other's paper, watch each other's hand writing the answer. The sight was more controllable—turned off and on easier—if the twin doing the viewing held an object belonging to her sister. The possession acted as an antenna.

Once, Maddy was sitting on her bed, scribbling an entry into her journal while her sister was in the barn. Sensing her sister's glance at her diary, Maddy looked around her room and saw the hairbrush from her dresser was missing. Instead of ending Bernadette's spy mission by slamming the journal shut, she practiced an insult the twins had been trying out. She willed her sister's sight out of her eyes.

They coordinated each other's viewing as well. One fall evening in their junior year of high school, Maddy was in the back seat of a Buick with a football player and Bernadette was in a neighbor boy's bed. The girls had exchanged class rings with each other and, at a predetermined hour, slipped the rings out of their pockets for a wild night.

Bernadette and Maddy never told anyone how far they'd taken their ability to share.

That ability changed permanently senior year, on a rainy Saturday in the spring. The girls' father had ordered parts for the John Deere. That afternoon, Maddy took the call from the dealer; the brake pads had arrived.

Maddy banged on the bathroom door. "Where're Mom and Dad?"

Bernadette on the other side of the door: "Left for four o'clock mass."

"Tractor junk's in. Wanna go with to pick it up?"

"Give me a minute to rinse." Bernadette was in the tub, shaving her legs and ripping the hell out of them. Maddy was better at the female stuff.

"They're getting ready to close."

"Wait!" Any excuse to go into town was a good one. Bernadette hopped out of the tub and grabbed a towel, but it was too late. She heard the front door slam and the station wagon skid out of the driveway.

Bernadette stepped back into the tub and turned on the shower. When she reached for the shampoo in one corner, she noticed that Maddy had forgotten her soapy class ring on the ledge. Bernadette picked up the ring, cupped it in her hand, and held it under the stream. The spray in front of her eyes vanished, replaced by a wall of chrome and metal. Bernadette screamed into the water.

The instant before impact, Maddy felt her sister watching the same horror she saw through the windshield. She bucked off her sister's sight. Maddy didn't know her twin was so determined to be with her that Bernadette's vision had to go somewhere—and it landed inside the eyes of the drunken driver. Maddy saved her sister from one gruesome view only to exchange it for another. Bernadette watched from behind the wheel of the truck that killed her sister.

The days after Maddy's death were a fog for the family, and Bernadette's parents either failed to notice the change in their surviving daughter's face, or didn't care. Bernadette herself couldn't have explained how it happened or why, but she knew when. The instant she stepped out of the shower that terrible afternoon, she saw the transformation in the bathroom mirror. She considered the blue left eye her sister's farewell.

It was at Maddy's wake that Bernadette realized her ability to see through the eyes of killers could be permanent.

Helena Smith, a family friend from two farms over, stepped in front of the mourning family and dropped a piece of jewelry into Bernadette's palm. "For good luck," she whispered, and moved on. Bernadette looked down and saw a Mother's Day bracelet. Each charm—shaped like a girl or a boy with a birthstone for a head—represented a child. Bernadette counted eight figures. The newest baby—born only days earlier—hadn't yet been added. Why would Smith give away something so precious?

Bernadette closed her hand around the bracelet, and everything in front of her eyes vanished: the flowers, the crowd, and her own fist wrapped around the jewelry. She saw someone else's hands pressing a pillow into a bassinet. Around the right wrist was a bracelet—the bracelet that had just been dropped into her own hand.

A few days later, another wake was held at the funeral home. The Smiths' infant had been found dead in its bassinet by its father while Helena was at Maddy's wake. Doctors said it was SIDS. Bernadette didn't tell anyone what she had seen, and she was careful not to touch the bracelet with her bare hands when she buried it in the backyard.

o   o   o

Another bad call Bernadette couldn't acknowledge: taking a job with the FBI.

She'd thought she could handle using her sight for the work if she was discreet. During her entire journey on the way to becoming an agent—from the moment she enrolled in criminal-justice classes at Bemidji State in northwestern Minnesota to the day she graduated from the FBI Academy in Quantico, Virginia—she kept her curse of sight a secret. She figured she had no choice. The bureau's Web site, deriding television's portrayal of profilers, said it all:

> FBI Special Agents don't get vibes or experience psychic flashes while walking around fresh crime scenes. It is an exciting world of investigation and research—a world of inductive and deductive reasoning; crime-solving experience; and knowledge of criminal behavior, facts, and statistical probabilities.

Bernadette wouldn't have described her ability as *psychic,* but it sure as hell wasn't something they sanctioned at Quantico. She waited until she passed her two-year probation with the bureau before she used her sight to solve murder cases. Even after that, she didn't tell anyone about it—not even Michael.

Her bosses usually figured out there was something going on and had the good sense to shut up about it. Even when she was solving cases, her superiors didn't want to know how the sight worked. When she went chasing in the wrong direction or led the bureau to pick up the wrong guy, they wanted to know even less.

She'd get transferred, and when she arrived at her new assignment in a new city, she'd get the stares. She'd go to a crime scene and the local cops would have already latched onto a string of rumors and exaggerations, outrageous accounts of crimes she'd supposedly solved or screwed up with supernatural talents. In Louisiana, one fable had her walking the cemeteries at night, consulting with murder victims. She pictured herself sitting on a headstone, taking notes: *Did you get a good look at the man who killed you? Any distinguishing marks or characteristics?*

She'd hoped to work her way into Behavioral Sciences, but it became clear she would never be allowed anywhere near the prestigious unit. They could have tolerated an agent who was odd; Behavioral was filled with them. Bernadette was worse than that. She was strange and inconsistent.

The inconsistencies frustrated even her. Once she'd started seeing through killers' eyes, Bernadette's sight became cloudy and filmy—akin to peering through a soaped-up window. It might work in real time, or show recent history. She could witness the killing itself, or inconsequential scenes from the murderer's life. If she landed in the killer's eyes during his nightmares, she saw fantastic images right out of an abstract painting. Even with concentration and quiet, the sight could fail her. It could also come on suddenly and unexpectedly with a casual touch. Each time she used the thing, it drained her and put her in the emotional shoes of the killer, leaving her angry or depressed or desperate. As murderous as the people she pursued.

Seven

"The naked fat chicks have got to go," muttered Bernadette, standing in the doorway of her new bathroom.

The tub's artsy shower curtain—another castoff from the loft's previous owner—was a vinyl expanse printed with black-and-white images of reclining nude women, all of whom had full hips and handsome breasts. She didn't need to be reminded of her boyish shape every time she took a shower. Besides, the hem was dotted with dark speckles—and those had nothing to do with art. How filthy had the previous owner left the tub? She walked over to the curtain and told herself not to be squeamish about a little mold. She envisioned the shower scene in *Psycho*—one of Michael's all-time favorite movie scenes—and she was the one with the knife. She grabbed the edge of the curtain and ripped it aside. She was relieved. The tub itself—a clawfoot—was spotless, and a gleaming gooseneck extended up from the faucet.

Running a hand through her hair, she decided she'd use the shower immediately, gross curtain or not. She peeled off her clothes and stepped into the tub. With a grimace, she pulled the curtain shut with two fingers. She activated the shower, stood under the spray, and let the hot needles massage her scalp. She closed her eyes and reminded herself of what she had to do later, and wondered how hard it was going to be to find an open church on a Saturday night.

Bernadette dressed in jeans and a sweatshirt, snapped her gun into her holster, and slipped her sunglasses on her face. As soon as she stepped outside, she realized how quickly night was approaching—no one would notice her eyes. She took off her specs and hooked them over the neck of her sweatshirt. Though there was no wind, the temperature had taken a nosedive. She was grateful she'd found her leather bomber jacket packed away under the jeans. She reached inside her jacket as she walked and found her leather gloves, pulled them out, and slipped them on. They were as thin as a second layer of skin, but warm enough to take the bite off the night air—and thick enough to shield her from surprise sights.

An ethnic festival was being held at the same time as a Wild game, filling the sidewalks with an odd mix of humanity: hockey fans stuffed into jerseys, and folk dancers sashaying around in costumes. Her gut rumbled as she walked past a steakhouse. The smell of charred beef was inviting, but the food would have to wait. She was on her way to perform a task best tackled on an empty stomach; God only knew what she'd see this time.

Bernadette wove up and down the tangled streets of downtown, over cobblestone and pavement, under old-fashioned lantern streetlights decorated with hanging flower baskets, and past an office building and a check-cashing joint. She spent more time ogling the people than the scenery, however. She figured there was some sort of theater event or concert at the Ordway Center for the Performing Arts, because suddenly suits and dresses were added to the hockey jerseys and sarongs. As she walked and watched folks, she slipped her right hand into her jacket pocket and felt for the items. They weren't going any-where. She withdrew her hand.

o   o   o

The sun was almost completely down when she found herself standing in front of a Catholic church. She hiked up the steps. "Please don't be locked," she muttered to the massive double doors. She put her hand on one of the knobs, turned, and pushed. The slab of wood creaked open. The interior was a warm, golden glow. She shut the door behind her and stepped deeper inside. Bernadette saw a font against the back wall, went over to it and reached. Remembered her gloves. She pulled them off and stuffed them in her jacket. She dipped her right finger-tips into the holy water and crossed herself. She inhaled the comfort-ing aroma of incense and burning candles. She'd tried other venues and tactics over the years, from hunkering down in her bedroom at night to driving to the countryside and sitting alone in a field. Churches seemed to give her the best results. Their thick walls, high ceilings, shadowy niches, and saint statues invited contemplation and meditation.

Up on the altar, Bernadette saw two middle-aged women, silent and grim-faced as they performed their housekeeping chores. One was re-moving pots of flowers while the other was pushing a carpet sweeper back and forth. The squeak of the sweeper's wheels seemed amplified in the nearly empty church.

Shuffling down the middle aisle of the church was an old woman with a windbreaker pulled over her housedress. The back of the jacket was plastered with the name of a bar. "Tubby's Tavern. Let the good times roll." The tavern lady went to a rack of votives sitting to the right of the altar, lit two candles, and slipped into a front-row pew. Ber-nadette noticed the woman had a round lace doily on top of her head. She remembered her mother forcing her and her sister to wear scarves to church, tying the chiffon tight under their chins. Bernadette brought her hand to her throat. She could still feel that knot of fabric, a tightness that gripped her whenever she first entered a place of worship.

Bernadette unzipped her bomber as she walked down a side aisle. She heard snoring and looked to her right. An old man in a tattered trench coat and baseball cap was slouched in a back pew. He reeked of urine and alcohol. The booze stink brought back another childhood memory—her father's drinking. It didn't get better after Maddy's death. An ugly home movie started up in her mind: Her father at the kitchen table with a full tumbler of whiskey, and another Johnny Cash dirge playing on the radio. Her mother sitting alone in the front room watching television, crying, and knitting. Bernadette told herself she shouldn't be thinking about that now. She had to empty her head of her own clutter to make way for someone else's.

She stepped between some pews and cut across until she was in a bench on the other side of the church. She went down on her knees, rested her arms on the back of the pew in front of her, and folded her hands together. As she shut her eyes, she whispered a five-word prayer she routinely uttered before searching for the truth through the eyes of a murderer.

"Lord, help me see clearly."

Eight

Anna Fontaine once believed silence was golden.

When their daughter ran away from home, her husband called the police and cried out loud, predicting the worst. Anna sat on a front-porch rocker, keeping a wordless vigil until their girl returned.

After their daughter was arrested with a backpack stuffed with pills and pot and a gun, Jerry railed against the school and the cops and the social workers. Anna curled up in bed and prayed the rosary in her head.

During the hour their daughter was alone in Sterling Archer's chambers, Jerry wrung his hands in the hallway and voiced hope for leniency from the juvenile system. His wife sat quietly in a chair, silently worrying and wondering why her child was taking so long with the creepy fat judge.

Months later, Jerry paced and muttered while awaiting the jury in

Archer's sex-abuse trial. Anna stayed glued to a courtroom bench, saying nothing. When the verdict came in, Anna couldn't bring herself to speak to the reporters; she let her husband and the other families lambaste the acquittal.

It wasn't until their daughter died that Anna had an epiphany: silence isn't golden; it's shit.

With the help of one person—a fiery, furious, moral man—Anna found a voice for herself and justice for her daughter. Now she wondered: *Have I damned myself in the process?* She would ask the question—and a slew of others—when he got there. She would talk and question until the breath left her. Silence was no longer her friend.

         *   *   *

She was starting to nod off when he opened the door a crack and popped his head into her room.

"Anna?"

She forced her lids to open. "You came."

"I told you I would." He slipped into the room and closed the door behind him. He stepped next to her bed.

She felt her lids dropping again. Through the slits, she saw him reach out to her and then withdraw his fingers. She thought: *My hero and my coward. You kill, but you're afraid to touch the dying.*

"Anna?"

Her eyes opened wider this time. "All doped up."

"Do you want me to raise the bed more?"

"No," she said.

He tipped his head toward the bed rails. "Shouldn't those be up? Should I put them up?"

She'd already had that fight with the nurses: the rails made her feel trapped. "Leave them down."

"Are you comfortable?"

"They finally got me on the good meds. Why do they save the good shit for the end?" She swallowed and coughed and winced.

He carried a chair to the side of her bed, set it down, and perched on the edge of the seat. "How're you doing?"

She coughed again. "Lousy."

He picked up a cup from her nightstand and shoveled a dot of crushed ice with a spoon. "Thirsty?"

She saw his knuckles were raw, and it repulsed her. She turned her head away. "No thanks. I'm good." She fingered the rosary in her hands. He'd given it to her, and she planned to be buried with it.

"Shall I put away your reading?"

She found him more attentive than her husband and sons combined. "My glasses, too. I'm having trouble with the words. Headache. Dizzy."

"I'll put them where you can find them," he said, picking her glasses out of the book.

As her eyes closed again, she felt the volume being lifted off her thighs. She knew he'd check to see what she'd been reading. She hoped he'd approve, and at the same time hated that she still sought his approval. He had a power and a presence that had drawn her to him and to his cause. He'd convinced her it should be her cause. Jerry hadn't been swayed. Jerry didn't know how far she and this magnetic man had taken things, and she was glad.

She heard him walking across the linoleum floor and remembered the first time she'd watched him cross a room. His size and looks alone would have commanded respect, but his confident gait demanded it. He carried himself like a CEO who was late for his own meeting: he needed to get there, but he also knew it couldn't start without him. She heard the swish of the drapes. She opened her eyes and saw him leaning toward the window. The outside didn't offer much light; night was falling quickly. He turned away from the window and brought the book closer to his face. She'd memorized the words, and spoke them for him in a voice so weak only the two of them could hear:

> "But anyone who strikes another with an iron object, and death ensues, is a murderer; the murderer shall be put to death. Or anyone who strikes another with a stone in hand that could cause

death, and death ensues, is a murderer; the murderer shall be put to death."

Her recitation was interrupted by her coughing. He waited until she stopped hacking and finished it for her, his voice as low as hers but resonating with authority. He paused in the right places and emphasized the right phrases. The cadence moved the message the way a river moves water: smoothly, efficiently, inevitably. She found herself floating along with his words, momentarily forgetting the pain:

"Or anyone who strikes another with a weapon of wood in hand that could cause death, and death ensues, is a murderer; the murderer shall be put to death. The avenger of blood is the one who shall put the murderer to death; when they meet, the avenger of blood shall execute the sentence. Likewise, if someone pushes another from hatred, or hurls something at another, lying in wait, and death ensues, or in enmity strikes another with the hand, and death ensues, then the one who struck the blow shall be put to death; that person is a murderer; the avenger of blood shall put the murderer to death, when they meet."

He lowered the book. "Anna?"

She turned her head away from him and sniffled. "I'm still alive."

"Stop talking like that." He walked back to her bed and set the volume on the nightstand. "Where're Jerry and the boys?"

He was being polite or—more likely—hoping to avoid her husband and kids. "Cafeteria. Sent them to get something to eat. They're not eating right. Making themselves sick."

He walked across the room and glanced outside again. He turned away from the window. "Your family loves you."

"They couldn't do for me what you did for me. What you did for my girl."

"They tried." He put his hands behind his back and returned to her bedside. "They had faith in the system—and it failed them."

"I saw something on television. The cops aren't saying much."

"Don't worry about the authorities."

"I'm not worried about the police. No time left to worry about them." She paused and asked: "Did you cry for him?"

"I cry for all of them. The taking of a life should be done with reverence and sorrow. It shouldn't be a time for celebration. Proverbs tells us how to behave. 'Do not rejoice when your enemies fall, and do not let your heart be glad when they stumble, or else the Lord will see it and be displeased, and turn away his anger from them.' "

Hungry for more details, she continued: "His hand. What did you do with it? The river?"

"The woods."

"Perfect." She appreciated the way he discarded their parts in the wilderness, so an animal or a fish could eat them. She found it satisfying to imagine crows or carp picking at sinners' body parts. A fitting end to their flesh. Biblical and feral at the same time.

As if he'd read her mind, he launched into the Lord's message to Pharaoh as quoted in the book of Ezekiel. " 'I will throw you on the ground, on the open field I will fling you, and will cause all the birds of the air to settle on you, and I will let the wild animals of the whole earth gorge themselves with you. I will strew your flesh on the mountains, and fill the valleys with your carcass. I will drench the land with your flowing blood up to the mountains, and the watercourses will be filled with you.' "

"Lovely," she murmured.

He smiled. "One of my favorites, too."

She posed the one question she had to ask. She'd lain restless all day in her hospital bed, imagining the possible answers. "Did he suffer?"

"Yes." Then he added: "Terribly."

His response sent a rush of warmth through her body. She felt the corners of her mouth turn up. How could she not rejoice when this enemy fell? How could her heart refrain from gladness? She gushed: "Thank you for doing it for me."

"I did it for all of us."

"What about Chris? Will you do it for her?"

"I'm meeting with her later tonight, after her shift."

"She's a decent person," said Anna. "You'll want to help."

"Tell me more about her."

Anna thought about it for a moment and said: "Let her tell you."

"So be it," he said. "Is there anything else you need or want?"

"Yes." She weighed how to make her next request. By asking, she was admitting she had doubts about the righteousness of his mission. She decided to say one word: "Penance."

She found his reaction quick and artificially cheerful: "Go see your parish priest when you get out. Who've they got over there now? Father Timothy, right? He's a good guy."

"Stop it. You know I'm never leaving this place." She blinked back tears. "We're both going to fry."

He scanned the top of the nightstand, spotted a box of tissues, grabbed it, and dipped his hand into the slot at the top. Empty. He tossed it back on the stand. He patted his blazer pockets, pulled out a handkerchief, and held it out to her. "I told you not to worry about the law."

"I'm not afraid of the cops." She reached up and slipped the square of cotton out of his hands. "I'm worried about my soul. Both our souls."

"I've done nothing wrong. You've done nothing wrong."

"I need to be sure. Have to have a clean slate before I . . ." She covered her mouth with the kerchief to stifle a sob. Her hands fell back on the covers with the hankie locked in one fist and the rosary in the other.

They both heard a rolling cart clattering outside. She watched him eyeing the door. As the racket drew closer, the muscles in his neck and jaw tightened. The clatter continued down the hallway, and he relaxed. *My hero and my coward. You're afraid someone will walk in on us. Find us out.*

He turned his attention back to her. "Sometimes it's difficult to figure out why these things happen, but they do. Medicine has its limits. We need to know when to surrender quietly and leave it in God's hands."

Now he was babbling, falling back on his store of comforting clichés. She'd have none of it. "A priest to hear my sins. I have to tell a priest."

"Save your breath. Preserve your strength."

"I can't die with a mortal sin on my soul. I'll never see my daughter again."

The authoritative voice changed. His next words were spoken in something between a pleading whisper and a low growl. "Anna. Please. Be reasonable. Confess to the wrong man and he could turn us in. Ruin everything."

She wasn't going to give in. "If you don't call one for me, Jerry will. I need a priest tonight, before it gets late."

He glanced at the wall clock hanging over her bed. "It's already late." His eyes moved to the erasable board next to the clock. *Today is Saturday.* "And it's the weekend." He folded his hands together and rested them on the edge of the bed. "I'll pray with you, Anna. How about that? Let's both of us pray." He closed his eyes and bent his head down.

She coughed as she made the sign of the cross. The rosary rattled in her fingers as the breath rattled in her lungs. Anna Fontaine thought to herself: *All this for my daughter, and now I'm never going to be with her.*

Nine

Bernadette got up off her knees and sat on the bench. Staring straight ahead at the candles flickering at the front of the church, she inhaled deeply and exhaled slowly. In and out. In and out. In. Out. The breathing exercise reminded Bernadette that she—and not the object she would hold—was in control of her body, in control of her senses. She was the driver; the thing in her hand would be along for the ride. She would take in the sights and decide when she'd had enough, seen enough. She'd stop the ride by letting go of the object. Then came the hard work of processing what she'd observed, dissecting the killer's actions. Though her unearthly curse of sight brought her the visions, she relied on her grounded talents and training to help her analyze what she saw.

She reached into her pocket and pulled out the bag. Through the clear plastic, she studied the white-gold band with eleven tiny diamonds. Pinkie rings used to be reserved for flashy guys, but single women had started wearing a particular kind. They were called "Ah rings." The bands could be worn on either pinkie. She'd seen pictures of the jewelry on television and in women's magazines. Celebrity women—actresses and rock stars—stacked them on their fingers. Most men were clueless about the fashion trend, but she'd recognized the ring immediately when the ME guy at the park showed her the hand. She tipped the bag and held it at different angles until she could see the engraving inside the ring. There it was. "AH." She frowned as she tried to remember what the initials stood for. "Available and happy," she muttered. The rings were meant to celebrate a woman's contentment with the single life. She brought her free hand to her chest and felt for the bands under her sweatshirt. The rings were her widow's jewelry, her dead husband's wedding band and her own worn on a gold chain that never left her neck. "Available and miserable," she said in a low voice.

She opened the bag and took a breath, bracing herself as she tipped the ring into her right palm. She curled her hand around the band and closed her eyes. Imagining she could sense every single one of the diamonds, she started ticking the jewels off in her head. *One, two, three . . .*

The diamond count stopped scrolling through her mind, abruptly replaced by a picture. She inhaled sharply and involuntarily, like a swimmer jumping into a lake. She shuddered. A cold, cold lake.

    o   o   o

The gender and race of the killer are clear. He's looking down at his own hands, folded in front of him. The large white mitts are covered with black hair. She sees blue trousers on his legs, and a blazer over a dark shirt. Not much of a description, but better than nothing. He raises his head and his eyes. He's standing inches from a door. It's oversized, and there's a line slicing down the middle. The two halves part; it's an elevator. He's exiting, hanging a left and heading down a long, dim hallway. The corridor walls are lined with large rectangles—framed paintings or photos—but she can't make out the details of the art. He's moving so quickly the passing pictures are smears of color against the walls.

He stops at a door. Is this an apartment? Maybe not; she can't see a number. He raises his fist to knock. Lowers his hand. He turns his head to one side and sidles up to the door. He's eavesdropping. What is he listening to? He raises his hand again and pushes the door open. Peeks inside. What's this place? She can't tell immediately; it's too dark, and everything's too far away to make out. He enters and runs his eyes around. This is not an apartment; it is a tiny room. In the middle of the cell is a white island. A bed. He walks up to it, slowly. There's a woman under the covers. Long blond hair fans out against the pillow. Her face is a pale oval. Can't see her eyes; they're half shut. He leans closer and reaches for her face—an intimate gesture—and then pulls his hand away. Perhaps he doesn't want to wake her. Her eyes snap open anyway. They're green. Emeralds dotting the white skin. Bernadette finds it impossible to make out any other facial features.

He glances around the room, his eyes landing on an orange chair in a far corner. He walks around the end of the bed and picks up the chair. It's weird, this chair. Ugly and institutional. Behind the pumpkin chair is an expanse of pumpkin drapery, and beneath the drapery is a windowsill littered with squares and rectangles. Books? Photos? Greeting cards? He carries the chair to the bed and sits down.

He reaches toward a piece of furniture parked next to the bed. A small chest of drawers? Doesn't look like normal bedroom stuff. He retrieves something off the top of the chest. A cup and a spoon. He scoops something out of the cup and holds it out to her. No takers. He's dropping the spoon inside the cup and putting them back.

His eyes travel back to the woman. Her body. Something resting on her bed. Beads almost as green as her eyes. A necklace? A gift from him? An open book next to the necklace. He's lifting something out of the crack of the book. A bookmark? He sets the object on the chest. What's wrong with that damn chest? Other shapes behind it. Against the wall. Something glowing. What is all that? Electronics of some kind. His eyes go back to the bed. He's picking up the book and looking at it. Printed words. What are the words? Too small to see. Too dim in the room.

He's standing up with the book and carrying it across the room to the window. He's got the book in one hand while the other is reaching for the drapery cord. The curtains open, and he looks outside. Good boy. What's outside? Where is he? He's looking down. The room is up a few stories. Not too high. Where? When? Dark outside, but there are lights. Streetlights. Traffic lights. Office buildings shining with interior lights. A neon sign. FREE PARKING. There's more to the sign. Part of it is obscured by a low structure in front of the building boasting FREE PARKING. Where is parking a premium? He's in a city. Which city? Minneapolis? Right here in St. Paul? The killer could be anywhere by now. A city outside the state. The area he sees is unfamiliar to her. No distinctive landmarks. His eyes look up and go to the right of FREE PARKING. Two columns. Skyscrapers? No. Too narrow. Monuments?

He's turning away from the window. Bringing the book closer to his eyes. Most of the print is still too small to read. The title or chapter printed at the top of the page is big enough to make out. *Numbers.* What book has that? Is it some sort of reference book?

He closes the book. Walking back to her. Setting the book on the chest. He's walking back to the window. Looking outside. Pivots away from the window. Walking back to the bed. He looks down at his girlfriend. She's speaking. She stops. Probably listening to him yammer. Her mouth is moving again. Something's going on. He's looking at the chest top. Picks up something. A box. Sets it down. He's searching for something. Feeling his clothing. Pulls out something white. Gotta be a kerchief or a scarf. She takes it.

He's looking across the room, against the wall opposite the window. A closed door. Maybe there's someone knocking. He stares back at the white oval draped in blond. Now he's looking above her. The wall behind the bed. Is there a mirror? Please, God, let there be a mirror over the bed. A clock. What time is it, lover boy? The numbers are impossible to read. Must be Roman numerals. The "I"s and "V"s and "X"s all running together. The position of the hands. Eight o'clock? No. Nine o'clock. He's reading something else on the wall. Large words scrawled on a white board. *Today is Saturday.*

Bernadette gasped and reflexively opened her hand. The image washed away. She opened her eyes, lifted her wrist, and checked her watch.

Nine o'clock. Nine o'clock on a Saturday. She used the bag to shield her hand while she retrieved the ring from the bench seat. She crammed the bagged jewelry in her pocket, jumped out of her seat, cut through the pew, and flew out of the church. She jogged down the church steps and ran down the block, pulling on her leather gloves as she went.

Her vision was operating in real time. If she got to her car and drove around town, maybe she'd luck out. See the towers somewhere around the Twin Cities. She stopped at a crosswalk and at that instant realized how wiped out she felt. This had been a tough one. She leaned a hand against a light post. Rising up in her gut were the killer's emotions, a weird combination of satisfaction tempered by something else. Fear? No. Fear was too strong. Concern. He's worried, but only a little. The satisfaction was the predominant sensation, and having that smug feeling coming from a murderer sickened her. She pushed the emotions down and caught her breath while she waited impatiently for the light to change. Cars and trucks zoomed by on the nighttime street in front of her. She smelled charred meat again. She looked across the street at the restaurant emitting the aroma. MICKEY'S DINING CAR, read the neon sign mounted on the roof of the diner. Above that, also in neon: FREE PARKING. A chill crawled up her spine, along with a realization. The killer hadn't been seeing a pair of monuments when he'd glanced outside. She looked back over her shoulder at the building she'd just visited. There they were, rising up on each side of the church. Twin steeples.

Ten

· ◊ ▣ ◊ ▣ ◊ ◙ ◈ ◊ ▣ ◈ ▣ ◈ ◈ ◈ ◊ ◈ ◊ ▣ ◊ ◊

When the light changed, Bernadette ran across the road to Mickey's
Dining Car. She turned and stood on the corner with her back to the
restaurant. Where in the hell was she downtown? She got her bearings.
Mickey's was on Seventh Street at St. Peter Street. From which building
was he looking at the diner's sign? From which window? He was up a
few floors. She looked to her right and saw the Minnesota Children's
Museum on the other side of St. Peter Street. No. That would have
given him a side view of FREE PARKING.

Kitty-corner from the diner was the Ramsey County Juvenile
Service Center. A county building would have a lot of ugly institutional furniture. Orange upholstery would fit right in. She considered
whether the killer could be young. The murderer's hands were large, so
he would have to be a big teenager. She prayed it wasn't a kid. At the
same time, she had to admit it was an interesting possibility. Archer

had pissed off a lot of kids; one could have come after him and then, for some reason or another, ended up at the juvenile center. Not all of what she'd seen through the killer's eyes made sense with that disturbing scenario, however. What would a woman be doing in bed at a kids' detention center? Was the woman a teenage girl? The corrections staff wouldn't let a male be alone with a female in her bedroom—not unless there was some hanky-panky going on. What was that reference book about, then? Was it a kid's math book? She'd check out the view from the juvenile center.

Making a diagonal dash across the intersection, Bernadette narrowly missed getting slammed by a Suburban. The driver laid on the horn. She stood on the corner and looked at the diner, then turned and looked behind her at the windows dotting the detention center. The angle wasn't right; he'd been looking at the sign from up high, but facing straight ahead.

The single-story buildings on West Seventh, directly across the street from the diner, were too low. What was behind them on St. Peter? The traffic was heavy again. She waited until she had a green light and crossed back. Bernadette ran down the sidewalk along St. Peter, passing a check-cashing joint, an empty storefront, a Thai restaurant, and a surface parking lot.

There it was, across from the parking lot. A hospital. The woman in bed had been a patient. That explained the institutional furniture. She remembered the cleanness of the cut to the judge's wrist. Had the amputation been performed by a surgeon or someone else with access to surgical tools? That book or chapter he was reading—*Numbers*—could have been some sort of medical reference, something related to patients' stats. What about the gesture, reaching out to touch her? Maybe he was a medical professional screwing around with a patient.

She crossed against the light. What street was she on now? She figured it should be Eighth. She checked the street sign. Of course it wasn't Eighth. That would make sense, and the streets in St. Paul never made sense. This was Exchange Street. She ran up to the hospital's front entrance in the middle of the block. As she faced the building, she tipped her head back and took in the full height of the building. She counted five floors. Which one was he on? She thought about calling Garcia and asking for help. Too early, she thought. Could turn into a wild-goose chase. She'd go inside, where there were fewer distractions, try to find a quiet corner, and take another peek through the killer's eyes before she went running up and down hospital hallways.

Thunder clapped over her head and she felt a few raindrops. She yanked open one of the glass doors and stepped into the lobby. Behind her, the skies opened up and a curtain of water started falling.

Inside, on the right, she saw a gift shop and coffee stand, both closed. In front of her were a couple of couches. To the left was a larger waiting area. She stepped farther inside and scanned the larger room. More couches. End tables. Coffee tables. A fake fireplace. Floor-to-ceiling bookcases nearly empty of books. One wall of the room was made up of windows that looked out onto the horseshoe drive at the hospital entrance.

A lone dark-haired man was on one of the couches facing the windows. He was sitting down with his feet up on one of the coffee tables. Dressed in blue scrubs, he had an open book on his lap. She studied his hands. They were big enough and hairy enough. Reaching inside her coat, she put her hand on the holstered gun tucked into the waist of her jeans. He looked up from his reading to check his wristwatch and glanced out the windows. She figured he was waiting for a ride to pull up. What was he reading while waiting? He raised the volume closer to his face, and she saw the cover didn't belong to a medical reference. The book, by Anne Tyler, was *The Accidental Tourist.* She exhaled and took her hand off her gun. Did she really think the murderer would be sitting there waiting for her just inside the front doors?

She walked over to a set of café tables parked in front of the dark gift shop, eased herself into one of the chairs, pulled off her gloves, and dropped them on top of the table. Dipping her hand into her pocket, she pulled out the bag with the ring. The idea of fishing out the package containing the strands of rope was tempting, but Bernadette decided to go with the known quantity. This was going to be one of those occasions when she didn't have time to focus. She hoped she could still get a bead on him.

Inhaling deeply and exhaling slowly, she tipped the bag. The ring fell into her right palm. She shut her eyes tight, closed her hand around the band, and said the five words. While she sat in her personal dark-room, the sounds of the hospital and the city surrounding it filled her ears: Gurney bumping down a hallway. Female voice paging X-ray. Distant sirens. Rumbling thunder. Music. Bob Dylan on the radio. Early Dylan. Perfect accompaniment for the downpour outside. "A Hard Rain's A-Gonna Fall." At the same time, the hospital smells invaded her nostrils and crawled down the back of her throat: Antiseptic solution. Cafeteria cooking. Fried something with onions. Coffee, strong and black.

$\diamond$ $\diamond$ $\diamond$

The coffee and guitars began to fade.

$\diamond$ $\diamond$ $\diamond$

Those big hairy hands again. They're holding an open book while he's standing. Not the same book, though. A smaller one. Another reference of some sort? She can't make out the details. He's turning the page. Again, the words are too small for her to read. No big chapter headings this time. Sitting down with the book. Sitting down on what? A chair. There are two more of those chairs in front of him. What color? Cough-syrup orange, like before. He has to be in the same room, the woman's room. He's turning the book pages again. Lifting his arm to his eyes. Hairy wrist with a watch wrapped around it. As with the wall clock, she can't make out the numbers, only the position of the hands. Working in real time. Good. He sets the open book down on his lap. That blue on his legs could be scrubs. Scrubs or jeans. Now he's standing again, the open book in front of his face.

$\diamond$ $\diamond$ $\diamond$

Suddenly it all went black. A light switch flipped off. She waited with her eyes closed. Waited. Nothing. Still black. He'd fallen asleep or passed out or died or—most likely—the connection was broken because she was wiped out. Her hand tightened around the ring. "Return to me," she whispered. Nothing. Might as well be sitting in a closet with a bag over her head. She was wasting time. She opened her eyes but still saw black. She dropped the ring in the bag, took a deep breath, and let it out slowly. Her eyes cleared. Bernadette shoved the bag back in her pocket. She stood up, plucked her gloves off the table, and pulled them on. Time to do it the regular way.

Her eyes darted between the hospital signs and arrows pointing this way and that. Admitting. Cashier. Cafeteria. Chapel. Information Desk. Three different sets of elevators. She headed down the main hallway that sliced through the lobby level and found a bank of elevators on her left, opposite the information desk. She punched the UP button and walked back and forth three times in front of the doors while she waited for one of them to open. A middle one parted and she got in. Two women in scrubs followed her into the elevator. One pressed the fourth-floor button. Bernadette raised her hand and hesitated, mulling over her strategy. She'd start at the top and work her way down. The south side of the hospital had patient rooms facing FREE PARKING. She'd narrow her search down to the correct floor on the south side by studying the angle of its window views. After that it would be a matter of poking her head into each room and looking for one containing a blond female patient with a dark-haired male in attendance.

"Need help finding something?" asked one of the scrubs.

"I'm good." Bernadette pressed the fifth-floor button. While she waited for her floor to come up, she took in the killer's emotional state. He was tranquil. At peace. That pissed her off—and worried her. He'd just murdered two people, and he was as relaxed as someone coming out of a spa.

Eleven

Bernadette quickly eliminated the top level of the hospital: it was up too high. She could see not only FREE PARKING from the windows on the fifth floor, but the rest of the sign—MICKEY'S DINING CAR—as well. She took the stairs down one level, found an empty patient room at the end of the hallway, and slipped inside. She stepped up to the windows and opened the drapes. Through the downpour, Bernadette looked out onto the neon and streetlights and car lights of downtown. The fourth floor was a hit; the sign and the twin church steeples appeared as she'd seen them through his eyes.

She went outside the room and ran her eyes up and down the corridor. She didn't want to get stopped and have to explain herself or be forced to whip out her ID. If she could help it, she didn't even want to ask anyone a question. This lead could still fizzle. At one end of the hallway, she saw a male technician bent over a hospital cart. At the other end were a couple of nurses standing next to each other in front of the nurses' station. The women were immersed in conversation.

The door to the next room was closed, but she heard noise—a male voice. She took a breath and reached inside her coat, putting her right hand on her gun. With her left, she gently pushed the door open a crack. An elderly man was alone, sleeping, while the television set across from his bed blared with a baseball game. She glanced at the score: the Twins were kicking Anaheim's butt at the Metrodome. Quietly closing the door, she backed out of the room and took her hand off her gun. She turned to continue down the hall.

The door to the next room was wide open. She stepped into the doorway. The bed was stripped of linen, and the lights were off. The room had been empty all night. As soon as she stepped back into the corridor to continue her tour, someone behind her touched her shoulder. Bernadette started and turned around. A nurse. Busted.

"Visiting hours are over." She was a little taller than Bernadette and twice as wide. Her upper arms were the size of picnic hams, and her voice was hoarse. She sounded like she'd been yelling at people all day, and she wasn't going to take any grief. The nurse thumbed over her shoulder at a sign on the corridor wall behind her. "You'll have to leave."

Bernadette stole a sideways glance at the next room. The door was propped open, but she couldn't see the patient or the visitors. Probably another dead end. She didn't want to waste any more time doing it the discreet way. Bernadette whipped out her wallet. "I'm with the FBI. Agent Bernadette Saint Clare."

The nurse's eyes widened as she studied the identification. "What's going on?"

Bernadette put away her ID. "I need to check the patients' rooms on this side of the hallway. While I'm doing that, you can get me a list of all the staff working tonight. The professional staff. Doctors, nurses, aides."

The woman's eyes narrowed. "What do you need all that for?"

"I can't disclose that information. This is part of a federal—"

The woman interrupted her: "Federal patient privacy laws. Heard of those? I'm not authorized to hand out anything or let you see anyone. You'll have to go through Administration. They'll be in on Monday."

"This can't wait until Monday!"

The woman planted her fists on her hips. "Turn down the volume. This is a hospital."

"Let me speak to a supervisor."

"You're looking at her."

"I don't have time to fool around!"

"If you don't keep your voice down, I'm going to call Security." She folded the hams in front of her chest. "How do I know that badge is real and that you're really an FBI cop? You think just because you waved that ID in my face I'm gonna hand over a pile of personnel information? Let you bother patients? You come back on Monday with the proper paperwork and go through the right channels." Then, in a voice that was as loud as Bernadette's, she added: "Now, please leave!"

Bernadette hesitated. Arguing in the hallway with Nurse Big Arms wasn't getting anywhere. Maybe she could sway the woman if they sat down together. She lowered her voice to a whisper. "This is really important, and I don't have time. Can we talk somewhere?"

The woman unfolded the hams and pointed toward the nurses' station. "This way."

Bernadette eyed the woman's ID badge. "Thank you, Marcia."

While the two women walked side by side, the nurse started her own questioning.

"What's this about exactly? The dead judge? It's all over the news. Television said the FBI is investigating. You think someone at the hospital is involved?"

◦   ◦   ◦

A frightened man stuck his head out the door of Anna Fontaine's hospital room. He looked down the hall and was relieved to see the backs of the nurse and the FBI agent.

FBI! What has that bastard gotten my wife into?

"Dad?" said a squeaky male voice behind him.

"Shut up and stay here," Jerry Fontaine said to his sons without turning around. He was a soft, chubby man with thinning blond hair combed over the top of his scalp.

He slipped outside the room and chugged for the steps. Giving one last look over his shoulder, he saw the two women going into the nurses' break room. Good. He opened the door and thumped down the stairs. Jerry remembered the bastard had said he was going to attend evening services at the hospital chapel and then head on to another appointment.

        ✿   ✿   ✿

Jerry saw him standing outside the chapel, talking to the hospital's lady minister and smiling. He mistrusted that reptilian grin and despised the man's overall appearance. The snake was too good-looking to be left alone with an impressionable, weak woman like Anna. Other worshippers were spilling out of the room as well. As soon as the hallway crowd dispersed and the chaplain parted ways with the big man, Jerry came up behind him. "Hey!"

He spun around. "Jerry. What's wrong? Is Anna—"

Jerry grabbed him by the shoulder and pulled him back into the chapel. He let the chapel door shut behind them and glanced around the room to make sure no one else was there. "What the hell did you two do? There's an FBI agent on Anna's floor."

"What?"

With the heel of his hand. Jerry swiped a coating of perspiration from his forehead. "I heard her arguing with a nurse."

"What makes you think that has anything to do with me? With your wife?"

Jerry wiped his palms on the thighs of his khakis while he felt sweat collecting under his armpits. He wondered if he was going to drown in his own fluids. "She wanted personnel files or something. I couldn't catch all of it."

"A hospital worker must be in hot water."

"Sounded like it had something to do with the judge." Jerry stepped closer. "So help me God, if you had anything to do with that fat fucker's death, if you've roped my wife into some sort of—"

"Lower your voice."

Jerry whispered his next questions. Even as he asked them, he hoped the bastard would lie to him. He didn't want to know shit: "Did you do it? Did my wife have anything to do with it?"

He posed his own questions in a voice so calm and condescending it made Jerry want to punch him in the mouth: "What does she look like, this FBI person? You said *she*, right? What does this woman look like? Can you describe her to me?"

Jerry stumbled over his response, all the while wondering what the hell the woman's looks had to do with anything. "Didn't . . . I didn't see her face. From behind she looked tiny. Skinny. Short blond hair."

"How was she dressed?"

"What? Leather jacket and jeans. Why?"

"Does that sound like an FBI agent? Come on, Jerry. I'm sure you misunderstood the conversation. I'll bet you overheard them gossiping about what they saw on the news today."

Jerry took a step back, blinked, and considered the possibility. He dragged his shirtsleeve across his sweaty upper lip and said hesitantly: "No. I'm sure . . ."

"You're all wound up because of Anna. Go back upstairs and take care of your wife and kids. Forget about what you *thought* you heard."

Jerry went to the door and put his hand on the handle. "I hope you're right." He yanked open the door and left. He looked over his shoulder as he went and saw the asshole was still inside, peeking into the hallway through a window in the chapel door. "Chickenshit," Jerry muttered, and continued back to his wife's room.

＠　＞　＠

Bernadette's one-on-one with Nurse Big Arms had been a waste of time. The woman's answer was still the same: *Visiting hours are over, so get out.* As Bernadette headed down the hall, she felt the nurse's eyes on her until she stepped into the elevator. The car went down; she held on to the railing with one hand and closed her eyes. The two sessions with the ring had wasted her. Her legs were rubbery, and her empty gut ached. She needed to eat something and go to bed.

She opened her eyes when she felt the car stop and heard the doors open. She half expected a cadre of security guards to be waiting for her, but none materialized. Hanging a right off the elevators, she headed for the exit. She contemplated a third try, and at the same time wondered if she could take it. Would the church be closed by now? When she was this tired, she needed that serene setting. She stopped with her hand on the door and looked outside. The thought of schlepping through the rain in search of a church exhausted her. The hospital had a chapel; maybe that would work. No. She needed the real thing. She opened the door and dashed through the rain, retracing her steps to the church.

Twelve

With eyes closed tight, Bernadette set her elbows on her thighs and rested her face in her hands. She couldn't make herself do it again, couldn't make herself pull off her gloves, dip her hand into her pocket, and take it out. She was too damn drained. A third round with the ring could ruin her for tomorrow, and she wanted Sunday to work on this. She opened her eyes and sat up on the bench, ready to leave. She rubbed her temples, feeling the beginnings of a headache. She'd get something to eat, try to sleep, and get a fresh start in the morning. A call to Garcia could wait twelve hours.

She scanned the front one last time. When she'd first returned to the church, Bernadette was surprised to find it open and the women still cleaning. The altar ladies had quietly disappeared while her eyes were shut. They were probably putting away their supplies; they had to be closing shop soon. She told herself she should leave before they had to kick her out. A clap of thunder shook the church walls and reminded her it was storming outside.

In unison with another clap, she felt a hand on her shoulder. She jumped to her feet and spun around. In the pew behind her stood a tall man in a robe, his face obscured by the garment's hood. She hadn't expected to see a priest at this late hour. "What?" she blurted, and then quickly added, more respectfully, "Yes, Father?"

"I'm sorry if I startled you, daughter."

"No, Father. I'm sorry for staying so late." She turned back around and started shuffling out of the pew. "I'll get out of your hair."

"Wait," he said.

She froze. Bernadette looked over her shoulder and was horrified to see he'd left his pew and was sliding into hers, coming up on her right side. "Father, I really didn't intend to . . ."

He motioned down toward the wooden seat with his left hand. "Sit. Please. You look troubled."

She opened her mouth to respond and then closed it. Slowly lowering back down, Bernadette silently cursed herself for staying so long. For all she knew, this priest had observed her from the sacristy during her first visit. Now she was back and he felt compelled to counsel her. Worse, maybe the altar ladies had summoned him to deal with the crazy woman who kept popping in at night. As he sat down next to her, she avoided looking at him.

"Why are you here this evening?"

"Father . . ." Her voice trailed off. She hadn't been close to a priest in years, and his presence made her nervous. She'd always felt guilty for quitting mass while still using the physical space of the church for her sight. Now here she was, caught in the act by a priest. At the same time, she felt drawn to him. He reeked of incense, a scent that drew her back into her childhood memories of church.

He asked: "What troubles you, daughter?"

His voice was low and deep and carried a solemn resonance that appealed to the remnants of her faith. She folded her hands in her lap and kept her eyes down. Odd that he kept the hood of his robe up over his head, but she didn't want to be rude and stare. "I'm fine, Father," she said to the floor.

"You don't sound fine. You sound exhausted. And you're here at a very late hour. This tells me you're troubled. Would you be more comfortable in the confessional?"

"No," she shot back, more loudly and quickly than she'd intended.

"You're not Catholic?" he asked gently.

She felt bad she'd snapped at him, and fumbled with a response. "No. Yes. I was raised Catholic, but I haven't been to mass in quite a while."

"Why?"

His one-word question filled the cavernous church and ricocheted off its walls. Her excuse was halting and weak, and she hated it the minute it dribbled out of her mouth. "Laziness, I guess. I don't know."

"Do you believe in God?"

This time her answer was swift and sure: "Yes."

"Do you believe He deserves your time and devotion?"

"I give Him my time in private prayer."

"Is that what you're doing here tonight?"

With his personal questions and hooded garb, this priest was rattling the hell out of her. She thought about lying to him, and then reconsidered. She'd never see him again, she figured. Why not tell him the truth? At worst, he'd assume she was mentally ill and leave her alone. She blurted it out: "I see things, Father, and this quiet time in church helps me focus."

He paused and then asked: "What do you mean, daughter? What do you see? What *things*?"

Sensing her palms sweating under the leather, she pulled off her gloves and set them on her lap. She wiped her damp hands on her jeans while she continued. "When I hold certain objects, they enable me to see through someone else's eyes. I see what someone else is seeing."

"I don't understand, daughter."

She shot him a sideways glance and wondered to which order he belonged. His hands were tucked into the robe's baggy sleeves, and the hood remained pulled up over his head. She wished he would take the hood down so she could tell if he was truly trying to understand, or if there was disbelief in his face. "When I hold something that a killer has touched, I can see through that murderer's eyes. I see what he sees."

His left hand came down, to rest in his lap. A large rosary was wrapped around his fist. "Fascinating."

"I know it sounds absurd, Father. I'm sure you find it impossible to believe."

Behind the hood, he chuckled lightly. "*Credo quia absurdum.*"

"What?"

"I believe precisely because it is absurd." He paused and then explained: "I've seen everything and learned to discount nothing."

She appreciated his attitude and forged ahead. "It's an ability I've had for years, and I use it in my job."

"What do you do? What's your job, daughter?"

"I'm an FBI agent."

A long silence. The left hand disappeared back into the robe, as if the sleeves were a muffler warming his mitts. "Has this vision actually worked for you? Have you been able to use it to apprehend criminals?"

"Not every time. There can be . . ." She struggled to find the right word. "Glitches."

"What sorts of *glitches*?"

"I misinterpret what I see, or I can't see clearly enough to get something useful, or it doesn't function at all. It puts me in the emotional shoes of the killer. A horrible place to be. It drains me so badly I can't . . ." She cut herself off. She'd found a sympathetic ear, and now she was rambling. If she wasn't careful, she'd start disclosing company secrets. "You know what, Father? Dumping this on you was a bad idea. Forget the entire conversation." She started to stand.

"Don't go," he said. He unfolded his arms and with his left hand reached toward the sleeve of her jacket.

She was surprised by his gesture, and sat back down. She stared at his hand as it retreated back inside the sleeves of his robe.

"Give me an example of how this operates," he said. "Are you using it on a case right now? What are you seeing?"

He was probing for specifics, and she couldn't give him any. That disappointed her, because she detected authentic interest in his voice. "I can't talk about it. Ongoing investigation."

"When did these visions start visiting you?"

"I had a twin sister. We knew what each other was thinking."

"I've heard twins can do that," he said.

She finished the story in shorthand. "It sort of evolved from there."

"You said you *had* a twin."

Bernadette grimaced. It was her own fault. If she didn't want to talk about it, she shouldn't have mentioned it. "She's dead."

"I'm so sorry."

He fell silent, undoubtedly waiting for details, she thought. She wasn't anxious to provide them.

Finally, he asked tentatively: "An illness?"

"Accident. A guy hit her car. Drunk truck driver."

"So, if you see through the eyes of murderers . . ."

She waited while he thought it through and reached his own conclusion.

"You saw him kill her," he said.

She whispered her answer: "Yes."

"Horrible. To see a loved one die."

"Yes," she said again, in an even smaller voice.

From behind his hood, she heard him take a breath and let it out as he offered his own story. "I'm alone in this world. My family is gone. All I have is God—and this vocation."

She thought about how she struggled to fill her personal void with her career. "Is it enough? Is the priesthood enough?"

"It has to be," he said flatly. "Now, let me ask you something, daughter."

"Go ahead, Father."

"How can you be sure what you're seeing is always the truth?"

Bernadette's brows went up; his question baffled her. "The truth?"

"What if these visions aren't a gift from God, but trickery by Satan?"

His take on her talent dismayed her. She'd found her sight problematic at times, difficult because of its inconsistencies. She'd never thought of it as evil. The possibility she was being used sent an icy chill through her body. "No, no," she sputtered, sounding unconvincing to her own ears. "It's never led me that far astray. Certainly I've made some honest mistakes."

"Were they honest mistakes? The words of Exodus come to mind. 'You shall not spread a false report. You shall not join hands with the wicked to act as a malicious witness. You shall not follow a majority in wrongdoing; when you bear witness in a lawsuit, you shall not side with the majority so as to pervert justice.' "

"I have not *perverted* justice," she shot back.

"Did you condemn innocents while letting the real devils go free? *Respice finem.* Look to the end; consider the end result."

She'd had enough Latin and lecturing for the evening. She pulled her gloves back on and slid away from him, preparing to bolt from the bench. "Thank you for listening, Father. I'll consider what you've said."

"If you want to talk again, I'm here the rest of the week," he offered. "I usually pray at about this time every evening."

She stood in the aisle and looked at his figure. Now he was down on his knees, facing the altar, hood still over his head and arms still tucked into his sleeves. She was curious. "Only through the week?"

"I'm visiting clergy."

She remembered a priest who'd briefly assisted at her parish back home; he'd worn a similar outfit and carried an oversized rosary. She'd found him a wonderful confidant once she got to know him. The name of his order came to her. "Franciscan?"

The hood bobbed in affirmation. "Yes."

She thought about everything else she had to do: Unpacking at home. Unpacking at the office. The case. It'd be a few days before she could free up an evening. "Might come to see you again middle of the week."

"Wednesday?"

"Maybe."

"Excellent, daughter. I look forward to it." He bent his head down.

"I'll leave you to your prayers, Father." She genuflected before the altar and turned to leave.

"Tomorrow is Sunday," he said without looking up. "They have a five o'clock mass at the cathedral for late risers. Short and sweet and to the point."

"Maybe."

"*Maybe* again. You like that word, don't you?"

Bernadette didn't answer. She quickly walked down the aisle and went outside, relieved to be cooled by the rain as she jogged down the steps.

Thirteen

Chris Stannard had taken a booth with window seats—she'd had her choice, since she was the only customer at that hour—and through the glass, she saw him hurrying down the pavement in the rain. Anna's description of the guy had been perfect: he could pass for a pumped-up Clark Gable, tidy mustache and all. She hoped Anna had been equally accurate about the man's willingness to help, eagerness to make things right. She needed a zealot. Anything to get it done.

She followed him with her eyes as he hiked up the steps to the restaurant—a knockoff of an old railroad dining car—and went inside. He didn't notice her at first; his head was bent as he ran his fingers through his wet curls. He wore a tweed blazer over a sweater and jeans. Clark Gable playing the part of a college professor. He looked up, saw her, and headed for her table. As he came up to the booth, she saw fine lines around his eyes betraying his age—well into his thirties—but there was no gray hair mixed with the black. Handsome. Would he find her as attractive as she found him? She reached up and brushed her cheek with the tips of her fingers. The makeup was minimal, but her skin was clear and she'd dabbed on a little perfume. Her brown hair was parted down the middle and styled into a blunt cut that went a few inches past her shoulders. A flattering look for a woman of her years—which was in the same neighborhood as his. The nurse's uniform didn't do any favors for her figure, but she'd had no choice, since she'd gone to the diner right after work.

She stared straight ahead, waiting for him to make the first move. He cleared his throat and extended his hand in front of her face. "Chris? Mrs. Stannard?"

She slid out of the booth, stood up, and gripped his hand. "Sorry," she said. "Zoning out for a minute." He was a head taller than she, and his shoulders seemed to fill the width of the dining car. His size and closeness intimidated her, and she took a step back from him.

"Sorry I'm late." He folded his hands in front of him. "How can I help?"

Her eyes flitted to his large mitts and went back to his face. "This is going to take a while."

"I'm not going anywhere." He waited until she slid back into her side of the booth before he took the bench across the table. "May I buy you a late dinner?"

She shook her head. "Just coffee would be good."

He raised one of his large fingers, and the waitress—an older woman with gray hair in a tight bun behind her head—came to the booth with her pad. She clicked her pen and put it to the paper. "What looks good, kids?"

"Two coffees and . . ." He glanced over at the rack of pies on the lunch counter.

The waitress, in a singsong voice: "We've got banana cream and co-conut cream, blueberry and cherry, pecan and apple, peanut butter and—"

"Peanut butter," he interrupted. "My mother used to make it.

Haven't had it in years." He looked across the table. "Sure you don't want something?"

"Maybe I will try the peanut butter." She smiled.

* * *

She waited until a lull in the conversation. Reaching under the table, she slipped her hand inside the purse on her lap. "This is for you," she said, sliding the envelope across the table.

"I am not a hit man," he whispered, pushing the envelope away from him. Their in-booth jukebox, mounted to the wall just above their table, was winding down on a Roy Orbison pick. "Only the Lonely." It was cranked as loud as it could go.

"You need to support yourself." She pushed the envelope back across the table, and it stuck halfway between them on a patch of something sticky. "Take it."

He scanned the diner. Though the other booths had remained empty, three men in jeans and flannel had just taken stools lining the counter. All three were soaked to the skin. The waitress was busy pouring the trio coffee while they dried their heads and faces with paper napkins.

The big man peeled the white rectangle off the table, set it on his lap, and peeked inside. The envelope was stuffed with large bills. He tucked the top flap closed.

"It's my money." She worried that sounded snotty, and quickly added in her meekest voice: "I've been saving. My husband won't miss it." She took a sip of coffee and glanced through the diner windows. The rain had kept pedestrians off the sidewalks, but the streets were jammed with traffic. A row of cars and trucks were stopped at the lights on West Seventh Street. The lights turned green, and the cars rolled forward, kicking up waves of water. She set down the cup and returned her attention to the man sitting across the table.

Fingering the envelope, he said, "I'm still not sure what you expect me to do with this."

"Use it for the expenses for your . . ." She searched for the right phrase, and remembered what Anna had called them. "Righteous missions."

"What do you know about my expenses? My missions? What did Anna tell you?"

Now I've done it, she thought. He was angry Anna had told her so much. She skipped over his question. "Put the money in the collection plate, then. Do some good with it. Anna said you do good things."

That seemed to appease him, and he tucked the envelope into the inside pocket of his blazer. He picked up his fork and poked at the last corner of his pie. "Why am I here exactly? Not to serve as a charity drop box."

She bit down on her top lip and looked off to the side, at the jukebox. Orbison was over. The Eagles were singing "Hotel California." She undid the top two buttons of her smock and pulled back on the material so he could see the purple on the right side of her chest, below the collarbone. A bruise, like a dead violet pressed into her paper-white skin. "He's smart about it. Beats me where it doesn't show. Avoids the face. Never hits me hard enough to break anything." She pulled her eyes off the jukebox and looked at him. "This isn't the worst of it. I can't show you the worst of it. My back. Breasts."

He dropped his fork and held up his hands. "Stop."

"Afterward, Noah makes me take an ice-water bath. For the swelling. And to punish me for crying. Then he sends me to bed so he can leave the house. He's seeing someone else, I don't even know who. He hasn't slept with me for months, and he's definitely the kind of man who needs it on a regular basis." She buttoned up her blouse. "He hasn't hit our daughter. At least not yet."

"The police?"

"They'd never believe me. Even if they did, he'd get no time. He doesn't have a record. Not even a parking ticket. He said if he ever got nailed he'd take me down with him. Make sure I never see our daughter again. And he could do it. He's got money. The lawyers." She looked up at him. "Anna told you who he is?"

"All she gave me was your name," he said evenly. "You know more about me than I do about you."

"Not true. I don't even know *your* name." She paused, hoping he'd offer it up.

He retrieved his fork, stabbed the chunk of pie. "Your husband . . ." He popped the morsel in his mouth and chewed.

"He's a pharmacist with a serious drug problem. It's become my problem. And it's become other people's problem, even if they don't know it."

His brows furrowed. He set down his fork and pushed his empty plate off to one side. "What do you mean?"

She took a breath and launched into it. "Noah started up by stealing from the inventory. Stealing from the customers. Shorting people their pills. They didn't bother checking. The old people can't see well enough to check. They trusted him. Trusted him with their lives. And he was standing behind the counter, stoned."

"On what?"

"Codeine was his first love. Worked his way up the food pyramid from there. OxyContin was one of his favorites." She picked up her coffee mug, took a sip, and set it down. "He's graduated from the prescription meds, though. Now he's into a more dangerous high. Stuff he has to pay for himself."

He cupped his hands around his coffee. "But if he isn't killing anyone but himself with his addiction . . ."

"That's not all." She looked straight ahead. Past him. She chewed her bottom lip and picked a damp curl off her forehead.

"Mrs. Stannard. This doesn't rise to the level . . ."

"Chris."

"Chris. If this is all there is . . ."

She jumped in. "You don't understand." She reached across the table and clutched his arm. "He's killing people right now. While we're sitting here."

He leaned forward. "Tell me more."

"For years, he's hopped around from one pharmacy to another. Always leaves before anyone gets wise. Never worked at my hospital, thank God. Mostly across town."

"Go on."

"His latest setup gives him access to serious goop. He mixes intravenous bags of medicine that are sold to doctors. Cancer doctors."

"Chemotherapy treatments."

She nodded grimly. "Gemzar. Taxol. Liquid gold."

"Has he been stealing sacks of the stuff? Selling it on the black market?"

"Something worse. More devious." She bit down on her bottom lip again. "He's been diluting it with saline. Billing doctors like he's selling them full-strength medicine."

"How much can he possibly make that way?"

"One doctor can buy a hundred thousand dollars' worth of drugs from him."

"A year?"

"A month."

The big man leaned back in the booth. "Liquid gold is right."

"He came from money, but he always wants more. Needs more. Needs to fund his extracurricular activities." She pushed her own untouched pie to one side and folded her hands together on top of the table. "The money isn't the point, of course. His drug habit isn't the point. His beating me and cheating on me—even that isn't the point. My daughter and I, we could run away. Hide from him. I went back to work for that contingency. Got quite a nest egg going for myself. None of that matters. What matters is—"

"Very sick people are getting watered-down drugs." He sat up straight and asked: "How long has this been going on? How did you figure it out?"

"Noah's had the shop for a couple of years. He spilled his guts to me during one of his drinking jags. That was last winter, right after my mother died of ovarian cancer." She looked out the window again and spoke to the pane of glass. "Her meds were mixed at his place."

"Your mother. I'm sorry."

As she continued staring out the window, she congratulated herself on reading him right. *Definitely a momma's boy.* "Even if he was caught and convicted, he'd never get what he deserves. He needs to get what he deserves. And he needs it soon, before somebody else's mother dies."

She turned away from the glass and looked across the table. "Anna said you can help."

He picked up his coffee cup and cradled it between both hands. "How do you two know each other?"

"From the hospital. Not just from this stay. During her previous visits, too."

"I'm surprised we never ran into each other." He drained his cup and set it down.

"I work third shift mostly. Patients get attached to the night nurse, especially patients in a lot of pain. You're their angel. Coming in with magic shots and pills. Talking to them while the rest of the world is asleep. She noticed a bruise. I opened up." Her voice lowered. "She opened up."

He pulled out his wallet, took out some bills, and tossed them down on the table. "We need to talk in greater detail." As he slipped his wallet back in his pants, he looked toward the diner's glass doors. Two cops were standing inside the restaurant's glass-enclosed foyer. They were snapping the water off their jackets before coming inside. "Elsewhere."

"I've rented an efficiency on Smith Avenue, in the West Side Artists' Block," she offered.

"The contingency."

She nodded. "We can go there."

They slid out of the booth. She picked her purse up off the seat. As he went to the door, he gave a sideways look to the cops taking stools at the counter, next to the flannel guys. He pulled the door open and held it for her. "Where's your car?"

"Hospital ramp." She stepped through the door and into the foyer, hiking her purse strap over her shoulder.

"Mine, too."

They stood in the foyer waiting for the light to change. When it turned green, they ran out into the rain and across the street.

"Is your husband right-handed or left-handed?" he asked as they stepped over the curb.

The question sent a pleasant chill crawling up her back, and she readily answered: "A lefty."

Fourteen

By the time she got home, Bernadette was as wet as a dishrag and looked as appealing as one. Her teeth chattered uncontrollably, and her hands shook as she shoved the key in the lock. That priest had spooked her; all she wanted to do was get inside, get food in her belly, and pull the covers up over her head. The dead bolt wasn't being cooperative, however; it wouldn't turn. She pulled out the key and struggled to steady her hand while she slipped it back in. She tried turning it to the left and to the right. It gave way a little bit in each direction, but not enough to do the trick. Drawing back her right foot, she gave the bottom panel of the door a kick. She pulled the key out a second time and resisted the urge to fling it at the wall.

A male voice bellowed from down the hall. "Hey, kid! What the hell are you doing there?"

The tail end of the shouted question echoed and bounced off the walls.

There . . . there . . . there.

She was so startled she dropped the key. As he walked toward her, she felt her face heating up while the rest of her stayed chilled. He had to be six and a half feet tall. Biceps strained the sleeves of his tee shirt, and a mop of brown curls covered his head. The five o'clock shadow looked genuine as opposed to one of those groomed, catalogue-model beards. He had a strong nose with a prominent aquiline bridge. What did they call it? Roman nose. It fit the rest of him, she thought. He looked like a gladiator. He was pulling something low and long behind him on a leash. A dachshund. The gladiator was walking a wiener dog. As she bent down to retrieve her key, the gladiator stepped up next to her. His jeans were ripped at the knees, and he had sandals on his feet. She straightened up and looked him in the eyes. They were piercing, dark eyes. Surprised eyes. He seemed as startled as she.

"You heard me?" he asked.

"You scared the hell out of me."

"Sorry," he said. "Thought you were messing around with some-body's door. You looked like a kid at first."

"I get that a lot," she said.

He ran his eyes up and down her figure. "I can see I made a terrible mistake, however. You are most definitely a woman—"

She cut off his compliment. "Who're you?"

He folded his arms over his chest, raised his eyes, and nodded toward the ceiling. "I live in the penthouse."

She'd heard about *the penthouse* from her Realtor when she asked about who lived over her. The agent had said it was empty and would probably stay that way for months because the space was too large and expensive to sell quickly. He'd said that the previous resident—a rich attorney—had torn up the entire top floor of the historic building and turned it into his private palace. The Realtor said the rich guy had even laid claim to the building's flat rooftop so he could use it as his own ter-race, leaving the other condo owners without an outdoor place to play and barbecue. After hearing that, she'd taken an instant dislike to this rich guy. She'd immediately resented him and was glad he was no longer living above her. Plus, she'd liked that she wouldn't have anyone clomping overhead.

The Realtor had either lied about the upstairs' being empty or been mistaken about how long it would take to fill it with another resident. A penthouse dweller of some sort was standing in front of her, and she wasn't sure what to think—or say. All she could come up with: "Hi." She turned her back on him to fiddle with the lock.

"Having trouble?"

"Nothing ever comes easy," she said to the door.

"I've got some WD-40 in the penthouse."

She wished he would stop referring to *the penthouse.* "No thanks." She kept wiggling the key back and forth while pushing and pulling and jiggling the doorknob. "I've almost got it."

"Seriously. Let me. I'm used to the temperamental hardware around here."

She let go of the key and knob and backed away from the door. "Go for it."

He extended her the leash and a white plastic bag. "Hold Oscar for a minute, would you?"

She hesitated. The way he was looking at her made her uncomfortable. She felt like this was some sort of test: maybe he wanted to see if she was an animal lover. She accepted the leash but eyeballed the bag. "I'm not good with poop."

"It's empty."

"Fine." She took the bag from him and shoved it in her jacket pocket.

His eyes darted from the leash in her hands to the bag in her pocket. "You're okay with the dog paraphernalia?"

"Fine. Fine. Let's just get to it. Please."

He smiled at her and repeated: "Fine." Stepping up to the door, he took over. "You've got to pull in while turning." He yanked the knob toward him while turning the key to the right. Nothing. "Stubborn bastard."

The gladiator wasn't above swearing. Good. She mistrusted people who didn't swear. She also approved of his top, an Aerosmith tee shirt from their 1997 Nine Lives Tour. She wasn't an Aerosmith fan, but she appreciated that he was one. The gladiator couldn't be the rich attorney guy; he was too normal. He wasn't good at this door detail, however. "I should call a professional," she said to his back.

"Locksmith would charge you big-time on a Saturday night. I've got some acquaintances. They're good at breaking and entering."

"Oh yeah?" The wiener dog pulled on the leash, one of those gadgets that worked like a fishing line. She pushed a button and reeled the dog back in. "Can you call them?"

"Not really. I guess they aren't *that* good. They're in jail."

She let out some line, and Oscar went sniffing down the hall. "I was thinking about the caretaker."

The guy laughed while working the key and knob. "Let me know if you track him down. I've got a few problems of my own in the penthouse."

"I don't want to trouble you any more than I already have," she said. "Maybe I should . . ."

"Got it." He pushed the door open a crack, pulled out the key, and turned around. "Name's August Murrick."

She paused before offering her own name. The building was called Murrick Place. This guy had to be the rich attorney who'd originally torn up the top floor. She was disappointed. "I'm Bernadette Saint Clare."

"FBI agent."

She didn't like that he already knew what she did for a living; she valued her privacy. "You've done your homework."

The right side of his mouth turned up. "You're kind of petite for an agent. What's regulation?"

"They snuck me in under the radar."

"They must like your work."

"Yeah. They just love me." She held out her hand, and he dropped the key in her palm. She handed him the leash and pulled the poop bag out of her pocket.

He took the bag from her. "I'll have to have you over for a drink. We can trade war stories. I'm an attorney. Criminal defense. Dumb-ass drug stuff mostly. I've gone a few rounds with you feds."

You feds. She hated the way he said it, making her sound like a thug with a badge. She shoved her hands in her jacket pockets. "I should get going. Do some more unpacking."

"Need help?"

"No," she said quickly. She took her hands out of her pockets and inched closer to the doorway. "I'm good. You've done enough, and it's late. Probably call it a night myself pretty quick. I want to get up for the Farmers' Market."

"Really nice meeting you. Gets lonely around here sometimes."

"Not exactly a regular neighborhood, is it?"

Oscar yanked on the leash, jerking his owner's arm. "We'll catch you later, then. Gotta finish the inside leg of our nightly tour."

"Inside leg?"

"We meander around inside the building. Then we go outside. Hit the park." The gladiator turned his back on her and went down the hall with his wiener dog leading the way.

"It's pouring outside," she said after them.

"We'll manage," he said over his shoulder.

"Thanks for the help . . ." She hesitated, not knowing what to call him. "Appreciate it."

He raised his free hand in a sort of salute. "Call me Augie," he yelled without turning or stopping. The pair disappeared down a stairwell at the end of the hall.

It occurred to her that he'd taken no notice of her eyes, and she appreciated that. She went inside and closed the door, turning the dead bolt.

Her mind returned to the robed Franciscan. "Two weirdos in one night," she said to herself, sliding the security chain into place. She pushed the priest out of her mind. At least she knew what the second weirdo looked like.

Fifteen

As Chris Stannard took the Smith Avenue High Bridge across the river, she watched the lights of his ancient Volvo sedan in the rearview mirror of her own Lexus SUV. Doing the Lord's work was a low-paying proposition. How could someone living so modestly look down his nose at.an envelope filled with cash? Forget about God. With *money,* all things are possible, and this guy would do well to accept that reality. She was glad she'd insisted he keep the cash.

Her corner unit was one of six apartments that sat above a row of brick storefronts. They both parked on the street in front of the shops and went around to the back, entering the building through an enclosed stairwell. The two of them walked down the hall together, and she stopped in front of the last door. Whereas the other apartments had dark-stained entrances, hers was coated in a glossy layer of white enamel. Even the knob was painted white. As she fiddled with the lock, she inhaled a hated smell. When she unlocked her apartment door and pushed it open, the odor became even stronger.

They stepped inside. "Sorry about the stink," she said, wrinkling her nose.

"What is it? Smells familiar."

She flipped on the lights. "There's a salon right below us."

"My mother ran a hair salon out of our front porch."

"Interesting." She thought: *Momma's Boy heard from again.*

"What else is below?"

She stepped out of her shoes. "Coffee shop. That stinks, too—especially in the morning—but they've got live jazz Wednesday nights. Photo gallery. Pottery studio. That's pretty cool. You can see I've got a few pieces."

She was proud of her place; she'd done a lot with very little. The apartment was no bigger than a large bedroom, and she'd furnished it as such. Instead of the usual fold-out couch or boring daybed, she had a massive sleigh bed with a curving headboard centered against one wall. Matching nightstands topped by matching table lamps were parked on each side of the bed. Most of the opposite wall was taken up by six double-hung windows. The kitchen was masked by a folding screen, and the bathroom was behind a door tucked into a corner of the room. Everything was white. Not antique white or off-white, but the blinding white housepainters use on ceilings. The walls and woodwork were done up in that stark shade, as were the spread on the bed, the Roman blinds folded halfway down the windows, and the screen hiding the kitchen. A fluffy white area rug covered most of the wood floor. Even her adored pottery pieces—chunky covered jars and vases that looked like oversized marshmallows—were ceiling white.

He took a couple of steps inside and kicked off his soggy shoes. "I take it you don't like color."

She tossed her keys and purse on the lone piece of furniture not related to sleeping—a wingback chair. White. "Bet you feel like you're back at the hospital."

He walked into the middle of the room. "Feel like I'm floating."

"On a cloud?"

"*In* a cloud."

"That's what I was after," she said with a satisfied smile. She went behind the kitchen screen and fished a white towel from a drawer under the counter. She went back around the screen and tossed the rag to him. "There you go."

He caught the towel and rubbed his head with it. "Aren't you afraid of getting something dirty?"

She walked over to the windows and lowered the shades the rest of the way. The rainy night disappeared behind the white. "Everything in my life, everything outside these four walls, is sullied and muddled and complicated. I wanted a clean, simple place. White sanctuary."

"I get it," he said.

"For some reason, I knew you would." She let go of the drapery cord and turned around, walking toward him with an outstretched hand. "Give me your blazer."

He slipped out of the wet wool and draped it over his arm. "I'm good."

She took the towel from him and threw it over a row of white radiators that sat under the windows. She wondered what he had in his blazer that he didn't want her to see. A wallet with his identification? She turned away from the radiator and watched him brush and fluff his curls with his fingertips.

"Not very kid-friendly," he said, continuing to run his eyes around her apartment.

"What?" She looked down and unbuttoned her smock. Underneath was a low-cut tank, and she wanted him to see it.

"Aren't you going to take your little girl with you when you leave? Isn't this place for the both of you?"

She pulled off her smock and tossed it next to the wet towel. "Let's not talk about my little girl right now." She paused, then softened her tone. "She's at my sister's for the weekend. Hanging out with her cousins. Having a good time. Being a kid."

She slipped behind the kitchen screen again, rummaged around in a drawer for a corkscrew, and pulled a bottle out of the refrigerator. She closed the fridge with her knee and looked at the label. Not a very good chardonnay, but she suspected Momma's Boy wouldn't know the difference between a good bottle and a box-o'-wine. She popped the cork, grabbed a couple of glasses, and poured. She came out from behind the screen with a glass of wine in each hand. She handed one to him. They clicked their glasses together. "An eye for an eye," she said.

He offered his own words: "Life for life."

"Life for life." She brought the glass to her lips.

While she gulped, he sipped. "Your husband—where is he right now?"

"Out of town. Golf trip with his buds. He won't be back until next week." She gulped again and motioned to the bed with her glass. "Sit."

He picked her purse and keys off the chair and tossed them onto the bed. He lowered himself into the seat. Setting his nearly untouched wineglass on her nightstand, he announced: "Social hour is over. We need to get to work."

She frowned; so much for the grand seduction. Didn't matter, she consoled herself. It seemed he didn't need that extra incentive.

°   •   ο

She sat on her bed with an open day-planner on her thighs while he opened a Hudson's Street Atlas on his lap.

"His flight comes in Wednesday night," she said. "He'll work late Thursday so he can catch up."

"Where's his business?"

"Mendota Heights," she said.

He flipped to the back of the atlas and ran his eyes down the index until he found the page number for Mendota Heights, a St. Paul suburb. He flipped to the middle of the book, turned some pages, and found it. "Here it is."

"His lab is in a business park right off the highway." She slid off the bed and went over to him. Reaching over with her index finger, she pointed to a sliver of land on the right side of the open Hudson's. The strip was on the very bottom of the page, just south of Minnesota 110.

He studied the sliver. "I've been to that part of town, but I'm not intimately familiar. What's around your husband's work?"

"What do you mean? Other businesses? There's a little strip mall down the road. A McDonald's."

"Do you think I plan to go out for burgers?"

"Oh. Okay. Umm. You mean places where you can take and murder him without being—"

"Execute him," he corrected her. "Innocent people are murdered. Your husband is himself a murderer. He is going to be executed. This is an *execution*."

"Execution," she repeated. She disliked the way he was talking to her—as if she were a child reviewing a failed quiz with her teacher.

"I have to use your bathroom." He stood up with the Hudson's and dropped it—still open to Mendota Heights—on her bed. "Start looking for some green space. Woods. Something close to his work."

He walked into the bathroom—his blazer cradled in his arms—and shut the door. She wondered what she had in her bathroom that could cause her problems. What was in the medicine cabinet over the sink? Headache meds and cough meds and a box of tampons. What was in the drawers under the sink? Toilet paper. Tons of cosmetics. Face cream and hand cream. Hairspray and hair gel and a blow dryer. Combs and brushes. On the sink counter—a tube of toothpaste and two toothbrushes.

A ringing phone jarred her out of her mental inventory. She slid off the bed and dashed into the kitchen, scooping the phone off the counter. Staying behind the screen, she kept her voice low as she talked: "I told you not to call tonight . . . Yeah, yeah . . . Absolutely certain . . . Me, too, Cindy." She put the phone down softly, went back to the bed, and retrieved the open map book.

She heard a flush and water running—undoubtedly sound effects for her benefit, as she was sure he'd spent the time snooping. The door popped open, and as he walked out of the bathroom, he asked casually: "On call at the hospital today?"

She was sitting on the bed again, legs crossed. "My kid."

"What's her name, your little girl?"

"Cindy." She was bent over the Hudson's, frowning at the open pages.

"What're you finding?" he asked.

She pulled her eyes off the map. "A nature center has a big chunk of land on the same side of the highway, right next to his place."

"A nature center," he repeated.

"Catholic cemetery down the highway, too. A big one."

"That's right. I'd forgotten it was in Mendota Heights. I've been to funerals there." He walked over to the bed. "There's a risk of being seen by someone visiting a grave."

"What about at night? Like I said, he'll work late Thursday."

"Maybe." He pulled the Hudson's out of her hands and eyed the distances. "The cemetery *would* be closer to his work."

She reached over, opened the drawer in her nightstand, and pulled something out. "Here's what he looks like."

"Good." He took the picture out of her hands and examined it.

Chris had snapped the photo. Dressed in trunks, Noah was stretched out on a lounge chair parked in front of a pool. He had a drink in his hand and a smile on his face. He was looking into the camera and holding the drink up for her. He looked so happy in the picture; she hated it.

"When was this taken?" he asked. "Where?"

"Last winter," she said. "Hawaii. Maui, to be specific. Why?"

"He still looks like this?"

"Right down to the goofy grin. Except in the photo he's got contacts, and he usually doesn't bother with those unless he's got a date. For every day, he wears glasses with black frames. All that's missing is the tape across the bridge."

"Can your husband see without his glasses, or is he pretty much blind without them?"

"He can see okay. I actually think he prefers the nerd look."

"Tell me more about him."

"What else do you want to know? You already heard about how he smacks me around and—"

"His legitimate hobbies. His interests."

She pulled her knees up to her chest. "Golfing. Runs, but only enough to stay in shape for the golf. That's about it."

"Is there a spiritual dimension to this guy? Does he go to church?"

She laughed dryly. "Could be he prays before a tough shot. I don't know."

"May I keep the picture?"

"The *Hudson's*, too, if you like."

So he could keep his place in the atlas, he tucked the photo into the crack. He closed the *Hudson's* over his bookmark.

"Want me along?" she asked.

"I work alone."

She curled her legs tighter up to her chest and wrapped her arms around her knees. She was excited; this was actually going to happen. "Thursday night, then?"

"Thursday night."

She ran her eyes up and down his figure. Whatever his name was, the guy was built. "Sure you don't want another drink?"

"I've got to get home. Tomorrow's Sunday. Church." Pulling on his blazer, he started for the door.

"Wait," she said. "Your name. Anna didn't tell me."

"Good," he said. "At least she kept some things to herself."

"I need to call you something."

He put his hand on the knob. Without turning around, he said: "Reg Neva."

"What kind of name is that?"

"It's Danish." He opened the door, stepped into the hallway, and said over his shoulder: "You should think about going to church." He shut the door.

Chris waited until the sound of his footsteps disappeared down the hallway. "Sanctimonious asshole," she said to the closed door. She snatched her empty wineglass off the nightstand and took it into the kitchen to refill it. Her hands shook as she poured. As handsome as he was, Momma's Boy had still scared the crap out of her.

Sixteen

"Dave Wong's," croaked a male voice.

"Food," Bernadette muttered to herself, and buzzed him up.

The deliveryman—a skinny old guy in need of a shave and a shower—handed her a sack through the doorway. "Here ya go, sis."

"Thanks for making such a late delivery." She handed him a twenty. "Keep the change."

He stuffed the money into the pocket of his purple Minnesota Vikings windbreaker and, with both hands, hiked up his baggy pants. "Thanks, sis." As he turned and headed down the hall, she noticed he had a slight limp and felt sorry for him. She'd give him an even bigger tip next time—and there would be a next time. Bernadette cooked for herself, but didn't particularly enjoy it.

She closed the door and carried the food into the kitchen. She fished two white cartons out of the sack, along with a handful of fortune cookies, a handful of soy-sauce packets, two paper napkins, two plastic forks, and two sets of chopsticks. The take-out joints always sent pairs of utensils, and she never bothered telling them the food was for one: she didn't want to make herself sound pathetic, and she didn't mind having extras. She took both forks and one set of chopsticks and dropped them into a drawer under the kitchen counter. "My new junk-drawer," she said, and closed it.

The chicken fried rice and the beef with broccoli were still steaming hot. "You're my main man, Dave Wong," she said to the cartons. She dug into each container with the chopsticks while flipping through an old copy of *Motocross Action Magazine.* Her eyes lingered over photos from the Southwick National, a race held in Massachusetts. The competitors and their machines were coated in grit. "Looks like fun," she said in between bites of broccoli. Another story profiled a champion rider who was pushing forty. " 'Age hasn't slowed him down one bit,' " read the piece. "Forty isn't old," she groused. An article detailing the latest in goggles reminded her that she had yet to unpack her riding gear.

She reached the bottom of both cartons and dropped the chopsticks into one of the empties. She cracked open the fortune cookies one after another, reading and commenting on the prophecies while discarding the cookies themselves. " 'A well-deserved job promotion is headed your way' . . . That'll be the day . . . 'An unexpected prize will be left on your doorstep' . . . Courtesy of Augie's dog . . . 'Your lucky numbers are 3, 15, 19, 27, 35, and 38' . . . I'll have to buy a Powerball ticket and try those out . . . 'The man of your dreams will arrive soon' . . . I'd have a better chance winning the lottery."

She cleared off the table and got ready for bed. Digging through a box of medicine-cabinet stuff, she found her over-the-counter sleeping meds. The bottle said to take two, but she'd long ago graduated to three. She refused to go to a doctor and get a prescription for something more potent. In her mind, that would be an admission that she had a bigger problem—one requiring a shrink—and she didn't want to acknowledge that she needed that kind of help. She swallowed the pills with a handful of water from the tap.

As she spiraled her way up the steps to her bed, she wondered how the moving men had managed to get her mattress and dresser up the narrow, twisting wrought iron. The architectural feature reminded her of the way old westerns portrayed whorehouses; the brothels always had balconies with wrought-iron railings.

She got to the top of the steps and looked around, seeing boxes and bags everywhere. "What a mess." At one end of the long, narrow space, she spotted a round window, a circle of glass the size of a garbage-can lid. She'd never noticed the portal before. She walked over to the window and stood on her tiptoes to peek out.

Streetlights lined the waterfront and described the gently curving lines of the river. She imagined herself dressed in a frilly nightgown, leaning out the window and calling down to cowboys galloping by on horseback. Then again, since she was on the river, maybe it would be passing towboat crews. "Hey, sailor, want a good time?" she asked the round of glass.

As she shuffled over to her bed, she chuckled dryly. She couldn't remember the last time sex had been about having a good time.

* * *

In the year after Michael's death, Bernadette didn't think about sex, and the idea of ever being paired again evaporated from her head. She'd interviewed murder victims' relatives who were so grief-stricken they'd stopped seeing colors or tasting food. Similarly, she'd become blind to other married people. Couples didn't exist in her dark, single world.

Then, one summer day, she noticed two teenagers strolling in front of her on the sidewalk. The boy reached over and took the girl's hand. The natural, affectionate movement sparked something inside of her.

The desire for sex was rekindled.

At first she'd tried getting what she needed from guys at work, but she quickly learned that was a mistake. It wasn't as much a concern over violating policy—whatever the hell that policy said—as it was a fear of getting a reputation. She didn't want people to fix her up with guys and go out on formal dates, either. She wasn't seeking a relationship; she wanted sex.

She finally fell into a practice she knew was dangerous: sleeping

with strangers. She picked them up in hotel bars, high-class establish-
ments with martini menus and Scotch drinks priced in the double digits. Even more than the venue, she was discriminating about the men.
They had to be well dressed and immaculately groomed. She looked for
professionals attending conferences, or business travelers flying into
town for trade shows. They'd go up to his room. She never gave him
her real name or told him what she did for a living. She always brought
her own condoms—and her Glock. What more did a girl need to stay
safe?

                    ❂   ❈   ❂

She stripped down to her panties and sat on the edge of the mattress
while she fiddled with the clock radio on her nightstand. No matter
which station she turned to, she heard rock music—faint but pounding. She snapped the radio off for a minute and looked toward the ceiling. "Rats in the Cellar" was vibrating over her head. She heard barking,
too. Were Augie and his dog partying right above her? She'd have to
read him the riot act when she saw him again. She turned the radio
back on and continued messing with the knob until she hit on a station
with Sinatra. "When Your Lover Has Gone." Perfect. Sinatra was always
perfect, no matter what the occasion or mood.

Bernadette collapsed back on the bare mattress and pulled the comforter up to her chin. Her eyes popped open; she'd almost forgotten.
She turned the radio down, slid out of bed, and went down on her
knees. She propped her elbows on the mattress edge and folded her
hands together. A smattering of the words she'd exchanged with the
Franciscan invaded her head:

Do you believe in God?

Yes.

Do you believe He deserves your time and devotion?

I give Him my time in private prayer.

She told herself her private prayer was good enough, and then she
launched into her nightly ritual of the Lord's Prayer followed by the
Hail Mary:

"Our Father, Who art in heaven, hallowed be Thy name . . ."

By the end of the Hail Mary, her body was starting to surrender to the pills and exhaustion. She made the sign of the cross, got up off her knees, and crawled back between the covers.

o   o   o

She felt a breeze combing her hair and moisture beading on her skin. She sensed the rolling of the boat under her sneakers and heard the distinctive thump of a wind gust catching the sails. The smell of the lake—a combination of pine and moss and rotting vegetation—invaded her nostrils. This time she was alone on the boat, bobbing and rocking in a space without lines, where the sky and the water dissolved into each other.

The noose dropped and danced in front of her face. She grabbed it and slipped it over her head. "My turn," she said, tightening the loop and waiting for it to lift her and carry her up to him. She saw the end of the line was cut, so she ran to the stern to jump off. From behind, massive arms wrapped around her waist and stopped her from leaping. She scratched and clawed until her captor loosened his hold enough for her to turn around and face him.

"You," she said.

"The man of your dreams," he said.

"What do you want from me?"

"Do you believe in God?" he asked.

"Yes."

"Do you believe He deserves your time and devotion?"

"I give Him my time in private prayer," she said.

"Then stay home. Don't go back to church. He isn't there."

She squirmed. "Who? Who isn't there? God?"

"A good priest." His arms tightened around her.

Instead of pushing him away, she pulled him closer and buried her face in his chest. She whispered his name as if uttering a prayer: "August."

Seventeen

She'd gone to bed with Sinatra and Steven Tyler. Spent the night immersed in a bizarre dream starring her neighbor. Woke up with the weatherman.

"A break in the rain today. We'll have partly cloudy skies over the Twin Cities and a high of sixty degrees. Lows tonight in the mid-forties. Sports are up next. Twins have another home game against . . ."

Bernadette flipped onto her stomach, reached over, and slapped off the radio. She cracked open an eye and checked the time. Almost ten. The radio had been blaring for nearly two hours, and she'd slept through it. "Great," she said, rolling onto her back. She hoped the market was still going. She hopped out of bed and grimaced as her feet hit the cold floor. Her arms wrapped around her torso, she made her way down the spiral. The wrought iron felt like ice on her bare feet. She contemplated turning on the heat in her condo and then immediately chastised herself for the thought. She was a Minnesotan, for God's sake.

Bernadette padded into the bathroom and shut the door. Turned the shower on *hot*, so it steamed up the small room. She stepped into the tub and gingerly pulled over the curtain. Was it her imagination, or had the mold gotten worse overnight? Shades of *The Blob*. While she showered, she made a mental note to put the new curtain at the top of her list.

She pulled on some sweats and a pair of sneakers and her watch. She checked the time. She'd do her grocery shopping before calling Garcia. She grabbed some cash and her keys, slipped her sunglasses over her eyes, locked up, and stepped into the hallway. She walked ten feet and stopped in the middle of the corridor. She checked both ends. No one there. She wanted to try that echo effect.

"Hey, kid!" she yelled to the ceiling. No echo. She felt foolish.

She went outside. The Farmers' Market, at Fifth and Wall Streets in Lowertown, was just a couple of blocks from her place.

⋄   ⋄   ⋄

Hmong embroidery. Hanging flower baskets. Wild rice. Herbs. Home-made soaps. Beeswax candles. Buffalo meat. Lamb. Fresh eggs. Apple cider. Exotic, stinky cheeses. Vendors handing out samples. Aisles packed with people and strollers.

Bernadette spotted a bagel stand on the other side of the market and decided to grab a quick bite before she started loading her arms. She weaved her way through the crowd and got in line. When she got up to the counter, she scanned the selection listed on the sandwich board parked on the ground, to the right of the counter. "Veggie and cream cheese, please. Hold the onions."

"What kind of bagel?" asked the girl behind the counter.

"Sea salt," said Bernadette. "Coffee, too, please. Black."

While she waited for her order, she felt something bumping into the back of her legs. Probably a stroller. She didn't bother turning around. Then the stroller nipped her ankle. She swung around and looked down. "Oscar. Knock it off."

"He likes you."

She looked up. Augie was standing next to her, in the same outfit he'd had on in the hallway. The gladiator lawyer was definitely a slob—a character trait with which she totally empathized. She felt herself softening up. Being rich didn't make him a bad guy. She didn't know what to say to him—she'd never mastered the art of small talk—so she tried to thank him again for his help with the door. "Last night was . . ."

"Last night was amazing," he said with a big grin. "I agree."

A woman pushing a stroller up to the bagel line gave Bernadette a strange look. Bernadette felt her face redden. Smart-ass. She'd get back at him. "Actually, I've had better."

The stroller lady gave an uncomfortable last glance at Bernadette and quickly steered the stroller out of the line.

Augie laughed and put his hand over his heart. "I'm hurt—and surprised."

The bagel clerk handed Bernadette her bagel and coffee. Bernadette smiled at Augie. "I'll bet you're not *that* surprised." She stepped away from the counter.

Augie was on her heels, dragging Oscar behind him. "I'm going to take that as a challenge."

"Don't," said Bernadette without turning or stopping. "I was just giving you some grief." She took a bite out of her bagel while weaving around a knot of shoppers. Realizing she didn't have enough elbow room to wolf down her breakfast comfortably, she searched for a gap in the crowd. The sidewalks across the street from the market were empty.

"Are you seeing anyone?"

"What?" She dashed across the street, eating as she went.

He followed her. "You seeing anyone? Dating anyone? I know you're not living with anyone. Right?"

Stepping between two parked cars, she went onto the sidewalk. Oscar was the one following her now, pulling Augie up onto the pavement. The dog spotted Bernadette's bagel. He stood on his back legs and did a dance in front of her, a sort of pirouette. "I didn't know dachshunds could do that on those tiny little legs," she said in between nibbles.

"Oscar's almost as talented as his owner."

Behind her sunglasses, she rolled her eyes. She took a big bite of her bagel. The dog stopped dancing and rested his front paws on her right shin. She lifted her right leg to push him off and he shifted to her left shin. She sipped her coffee. "Persistent little fella."

"Same has been said about me."

"You're not so little." Looking down at the little dog, she spitefully took a big chomp out of her sandwich. "None for you," she said after swallowing. "Now go away."

"Try 'down,' " said Augie.

"Down!" she said to the dog. Oscar barked once and pulled his paws off her leg.

"You didn't answer my question."

Now the dog was sitting politely. "Good boy." As a reward, she tossed him the remainder of her sandwich. He hopped up and caught it in midair.

"My question," Augie repeated.

She tossed the bagel wrapper and coffee cup into a trash can on the sidewalk.

"What was your question?"

"Seeing anyone?"

She brushed some crumbs off her sweatshirt. "You're damn nosy, mister."

He stepped closer, dragging the dachshund along with him. "Augie."

"You're damn nosy, Augie. You're also loud."

"What?"

"Turn down the Aerosmith, okay?"

"Didn't realize I had it cranked up."

"Well, you did." She inventoried the row of vendors lined up across the street. She'd hit the egg and cheese stalls for lunch fixings. A jug of honey would be good, along with a loaf of bread. She remembered seeing a stall with range-raised poultry. She could throw a chicken in the oven for supper. She stepped off the curb and waited for the traffic to clear so she could cross.

The man and the dog were right behind her. "How about dinner at my place tonight?"

She spun around, ready to give a flat and final no—but she couldn't do it. The gladiator lawyer was too handsome. She felt that craving bubbling up inside her—a hunger that couldn't be satisfied with a bagel—and pressed it down. She didn't need to be sleeping with her neighbor, not her first weekend in town. It was enough that she was already dreaming about him. Mustering a graceful refusal, she said: "That's nice of you, but I'm swamped. Unpacking. Shopping."

"It'll save you time. You won't have to cook. You gotta eat, right?"

He's a pushy bugger, she thought. Probably a good lawyer. Probably good in the sack, too. "I appreciate it, but give me time to settle in first. How about I take a rain check?"

"I'm gonna hold you to it." He bent over and scooped up his dog.

"You betcha. Well, I gotta get some shopping done." She turned to run back across the road to the market.

"You need anything this weekend—hammer, nails, a beer, rock and roll, whatever—hike up to the penthouse and knock," he said after her.

She cringed at the sound of that "p" word again. She'd have to give him a new label for it. *Upstairs* would be good. "Hike upstairs and knock. Got it," she said over her shoulder, and dashed across the street.

It was nearly noon by the time she got home. She was unloading her Farmers' Market groceries onto the kitchen counter when work called. She grabbed her cell phone off the counter. "Yeah?"

Garcia: "Any luck on your end?"

She leaned her back against the counter. She knew what he was asking: *What did you see when you held the junk?* She wasn't sure what to tell him: That the suspect had been in the room of an ailing woman? That she'd been on his heels but was tossed out of the hospital? How much did Garcia *really* want to know? Experience told her the answer was *not much.* She opted to avoid talking about the chase itself and instead give him the end result—that's what the bosses usually wanted. "I have some bare-bones stuff. Vague description of the guy. General idea of what he does for a living. Possibly where he works."

" 'Vague description . . . general idea.' You're sounding like a profiler, Agent Saint Clare. I didn't hire a profiler. I don't buy into that non-sense. The profiles always sound like every other creep on the street. Never helps solve cases. I need something solid. What else you got?"

She opened her mouth to tell him more about the situation and de-fend herself, but she snapped her mouth closed and reconsidered. She'd keep her cards to herself, at least until she got together with him.

"Still there, or did you fall asleep on me?" he asked with irritation.

"Better if we talk in person." She walked across the kitchen and into the living room. "Any news on your end? The cops turn up the woman's body?"

"They're still beating the bushes along the waterfront. Checking for missing-persons reports. Running her prints through the system."

She went over to the couch. She plucked a sheet of bubble wrap off the cushions and sat down, kicked off her sneakers, and put her feet up on the coffee table. "What about that Olson guy up north? The ex-con. Got anything more on the MO on that case? Any shoe casts?"

"No casts, but you're gonna love this."

She heard him shuffling paper. "Don't leave me hanging," she said into the phone.

"Here it is. Had them e-mail me and fax me a pile of papers to the house to supplement what I pulled together from the office. You could be right about that business with the rope. Killer used a bunch of it on Olson. Overkill. Like with the judge. Whether the knots were anything fancy, I don't know—doesn't say in the paperwork here. Just that he was trussed up like a Christmas turkey." He added conciliatorily: "You called that rope thing right."

The rope. She remembered she still had strands in her jacket pocket from the judge's binds, along with the ring. The idea of searching for an empty church on a Sunday and trying to dredge up another vision didn't excite her. She'd give it more time, wait until that night. Maybe she'd take the lazy route first and try the sight from home. She wanted to find out more about the knot-tying, though, and see what the other victim looked like when he was found. She asked Garcia: "They send you photos of the guy up north?"

"They sent me some in a JPEG file, but I'm having trouble with it."

She wondered if her ASAC was computer-illiterate, like half the bosses she'd had. "What're you using to open it up?"

"Huh?"

Computer-illiterate for sure, she decided. Too bad she didn't have her home computer up and running. She didn't want to hunker down in that creepy basement office of hers on a Sunday. Besides, if she really wanted to work the case, she'd have to dig out her Post-its—and they were buried in a box at the loft. "Never mind the photos. Got anything else for me?"

"That's pretty much it. How's the unpacking going?"

She ran her eyes around the space. "Slow."

"My offer to help still stands. Got nothing going on all day."

Garcia needed to get a life, she thought. "Thanks, but I've got to get out of here this afternoon. Buy some things for the house."

"What about tonight? I could come by with a pizza. Bring the pile they sent over on the case up north. Got a smaller stack from the St. Paul cops—they're tighter with their files."

He'd whetted her interest. "What did St. Paul give you?"

"Mostly copies of stuff related to Archer's criminal case. That's where they're starting their search for suspects. Where we should be looking, too, of course."

"Of course." She ran a hand through her hair. She'd love to see if there was a downtown doctor or his family mentioned in those documents. She was tempted to open up to Garcia, but not over the phone. She needed to read his face. He was throwing her off balance with his displays of impatience one minute, and his offers of help the next. "You know what? I might take you up on that pizza offer. Give me a few hours and then swing by."

Garcia: "Good deal."

She hung up and dropped the phone down on the couch cushion. She couldn't remember ever having a boss at the bureau who even sporadically acted like a regular human.

Eighteen

One last box, Bernadette told herself, and then time to run errands. The crate she opened sank her Sunday shopping trip, however. She found her home-office supplies—including her Post-its. "Good deal," she said into the box. Though she was computer-savvy, she'd had great success with her primitive hands-on method of thinking through a case.

She lifted the stack of Post-its out of the box and dropped them on the table. She fished her notebook out of her jacket pocket, went back to the kitchen with it, and sat down to go to work. She huddled over the table, writing and clicking and peeling off Post-its and slapping them on the table. Reading the scribbles in her notebook. Writing on the Post-its again. A dozen times, she cursed and ripped a yellow square into pieces and started over on a fresh sheet.

On a few separate sheets, she listed what the sight told her about the suspect in the local murders. There was the physical description: *Big man. White. Hairy hands. Dark long-sleeved shirt. Blue pants.* Behavior: *Reached out for sick woman? Woman's lover? Read Numbers. Read another book.*

She did another set of Post-its on the ropes: *Sheer lashing. Clove hitch. Double fisherman's knot. Overkill. Show-off.*

Another set for the missing hands: *Right hands hacked off. Thrown away. Victims all alive when cut off? Meaning?*

Post-its for motives in Archer's murder: *Revenge? Robbery ruled out? Lovers' triangle—something sexual?* Taking the possible motives into account, additional squares of paper for possible suspects: *Judge's victims? Family of victims? A cop? A doctor or nurse—took care of victims? Con sentenced by Archer? Bad business deal? Jealous husband?*

She couldn't begin to guess why someone had killed the female. She could only assume it was related to the other two murders. Nevertheless, she gave the woman her own square. All she wrote was: *Woman's murder—motive?*

Since she only knew what Garcia had told her about the case, a one-word list of motives in the northern-Minnesota killing of Hale Olson: *Revenge?* She paused, pen raised over the Post-it she was going to use to list suspects in Olson's slaying. All she knew about the dead ex-con was that he'd been involved in a home invasion, and that it was years back. She wrote: *Victims of home invasion? Doc/nurse who treated victims?* She stopped writing, lifted the pen off the paper, and thought about it some more. Inmates made friends in prison—and enemies. Sometimes the friends were really enemies. Still, he'd been out of prison a long time. Nevertheless, she put the pen back down on the paper and also wrote on the square: *Another ex-con?* She peeled the note off the pad and slapped it on the table.

There were *things to do* notes: *Get threads off rope used on Olson. Tox screens on both men? Tox screen on woman's hand? Keep checking w/ cops—woman's body and Archer's hand turn up? Get hospital personnel files.*

After two hours of thinking and flipping through her notebook and writing and peeling paper off the pad and slapping squares onto the kitchen table, she stopped and looked at the collection of Post-its stuck to the wooden surface in front of her. They were in no particular order; some were positioned sideways, others upside down. A few of them overlapped—not because they were related in some way, but because she hadn't been paying attention when she put them down. She counted them just to count them and came up with eighty-four squares.

She pushed her chair away from the table and stood up, ready for part two of her exercise: organizing the squares. She surveyed the loft, searching for the right canvas. The exposed brick that made up most of the loft's walls wouldn't work. The walls on either side of her front door were Sheetrock, however, and those would do nicely. To the right of the door, she picked out a spread of white in the middle of the wall.

She peeled the notes off the table and carried them over, a few at a time, to the blank wall—a vertical desktop of sorts. She lined them up on the Sheetrock, going from left to right, leaving an inch or so of blank space between the squares. She started at eye level and worked her way down to knee level. After they were all stuck to the wall, she moved them around and grouped them together into categories. The eighty-four squares came together in different groupings to form a handful of larger blocks. Suspect blocks. Victim blocks. Other blocks that came to her. The sum, Bernadette hoped, would become larger than the parts.

She backed away from the wall and stared at it. "Wait. That's not right," she muttered. She went back to the wall and switched two Post-its. She stepped back again. Planting her hands on her hips, she ordered the paper: "Talk to me." She looked for holes in the case and searched for patterns. As with any case, some words jumped off the sheets and begged for attention. She'd learned over the years to take notice of annoying words—they were clues. Sometimes it helped to work it through with another agent, or just a person with whom she felt comfortable and talkative. She had no one like that in Minnesota. Not yet.

Still, someone she'd just met had offered to bend an ear. She folded her arms in front of her and tried to imagine how the conversation would go.

Bless me, Father, for I have a tough homicide case. It's been two months since my last . . .

She laughed dryly, took a step toward the wall, and raised her arms to shuffle some more squares around. That's when she noticed what she'd done. How she'd arranged the yellow slips of paper so there was a vertical white space of wall slicing down the middle of the yellow, and another bar of white cutting horizontally through the top third of the Post-its.

The intersecting lines formed a cross.

Smack in the middle of the cross, where the white lines intersected, was one yellow square of paper. She didn't remember slapping that particular note on the wall, and in fact, couldn't recall writing the three words themselves. She didn't know their meaning relative to her investigation. Still, there they were, penned by her hand: *Life for life.*

Nineteen

A knock diverted Bernadette's attention from the Sheetrock cross. She knew who was at the door. Before she moved away from the wall, she quickly rearranged a few notes to hide the religious symbol. She didn't need her boss shipping her off to the loony bin.

She yanked open the door and found Garcia standing in the hall-way, a glass casserole pan in his hands and a stack of file folders tucked in his armpit. Weaving around her, he went inside. "Hot, hot, hot." He spotted the kitchen and made a beeline for it.

"There's a trivet on the counter," she said after him.

He set down the pan, dropped the files next to it, turned on the faucet, and put his hands under the water. "Didn't think it was still that hot. Left the oven mitts in the car. Halfway down the hall, my fingers started frying."

Bernadette went over to the pan and peered inside, seeing something swimming in a sauce and topped with melted cheese. "Smells fantastic."

He shut off the faucet and wiped his hands on the thighs of his jeans. "Decided to whip up something homemade instead of doing the take-out thing. Enchilada hot dish."

One side of Bernadette's mouth turned up. Hot dish, the Minnesota staple. She was definitely home. Her eyes traveled to the stack of folders. She told herself they'd better eat first, because once she started digging into the files, she wouldn't want to take time for anything else. Bernadette opened a set of cupboards over the counter, took down a pair of dinner plates, and set them on the counter. She pulled open a drawer under the counter and dug out a couple of forks and a serving spoon.

Garcia ran his eyes around her loft. "Looks like a tornado touched down in here."

"Tell me about it." She filled some glasses with water, set them on the counter, and shut off the tap.

He zoned in on a flash of chrome and red that was parked in a corner of the condo. Clothes were draped over the seat and handles. He went over to the bike and pulled off a couple of sweatshirts so he could get a better look. "Honda. Motocross?"

"I use it as more of a trail bike."

"Nice." He tossed the shirts back on the bike. "Looks big for you, though."

"I can handle it." She carried the water glasses over to the table, set them down, and went back to the counter to scoop hot dish onto the plates. She carried the plates and forks over to the table. "This looks great. Was so busy unpacking, I forgot about eating."

He turned away from the bike and shoved his hands in his pockets. "I can help you later."

"You've got better things to do with your Sunday."

"Not really. Sad, isn't it?"

She laughed. "You said it. I didn't."

Garcia stepped over to the table and pulled out a chair. "I like your kitchen set."

She had a round oak table with a fat pedestal base, circled by four ladder-back chairs. "My folks' furniture from the farm." She pulled out the chair across from him and sat down. After he took his seat, she started attacking the food. She stabbed a piece of chicken, blew on it, and popped it into her mouth.

"How is it?" asked Garcia, his fork poised.

"Excellent," she said in between chews. "Thank you so much for bringing it."

"It's a treat being able to cook for someone for a change."

"Know what you mean. A drag just cooking for one."

He eyed her face for a few seconds. "You look tired. Sure this is okay? I can leave the pan here and take off."

"Last night wiped me out, but I'll be okay. Food will help. So will some company." She took another bite.

He shoveled a forkful into his mouth. Without looking up from his plate, he asked: "Your husband—how long has he been gone?"

She picked up her glass and took a sip of water. "Three years this September." She set down the glass and to her own amazement, told him details she usually avoided discussing. "Suicide. He hanged himself with his own rigging," she said, running her index finger around the rim of her water glass. "We were anchored in the middle of nowhere. I had to cut him down. Get us home. I'll never set foot on another sailboat."

"You sold it?"

"Sunk it," she said, satisfaction salting her voice.

He didn't say anything for several seconds. The only sound in the apartment came from a Sinatra CD, the volume turned just high enough to be audible. "Come Fly with Me." Poking his food with his fork, Garcia asked: "How long were you married?"

"Thirteen years." She picked up her fork and did her own poking. "We met at college. Got married right after we graduated."

"Same with me and my wife," he said. "Right out of school."

Bernadette speared a piece of chicken and put it in her mouth. While she chewed, she thought about how to ask her question. Instead of making a query, she decided to put it as a statement. "I figured you were a bachelor."

"A widower. For five years, ten months, and . . ." He looked at his watch. ". . . six days."

"I'm sorry," Bernadette said in a low voice.

For the first time since he'd opened the personal conversation, he looked her in the eyes. "She'd just gotten off work—she was a nurse at an old folks' home—and was driving back to our place. Another car sideswiped her. Ran her off the road and into a ditch and kept going."

In her search for sympathetic words, she offered: "My sister was killed in a car accident."

"But, unlike Maddy's case, they never caught the son-of-a-bitch who killed my wife."

Garcia had not only gone back far enough into her past to find out about her sister and how she'd died, he'd even picked up on her twin's nickname. "You know about Maddy. You've done some digging."

He took a bite of food and washed it down before he answered. "I like to know my people." He set the glass down. "To that end, why did your husband do it?"

"He didn't leave a note, but it was depression." Even as she answered, she wondered why he'd asked such an intensely personal question so early in their working relationship; most people on the job saved the "why" question until they got to know her. The reason for his probing suddenly dropped into her head, and she looked up from her plate with narrowed eyes. "You don't have to worry about me, if that's what you're thinking. It's not like it's contagious."

"If you ever need to talk," he said evenly. "That's all."

"I'm fine."

"Good," he said, returning his attention to his hot dish.

He seemed relieved to have gotten past some personal talk he apparently thought he had to have with her. She wondered if it was some new touchy-feely garbage the bureau was requiring of its bosses. Perhaps Garcia simply required it of himself. She switched to work talk. "Tell me more about my officemate."

"Creed. Good guy. Good agent. Like I said before, a little odd." As if cuing in on the word "odd," Garcia looked up from his plate and stared at the paper-covered wall across the room. Pointing at the notes with his fork, he asked: "What the hell is that all about?"

She cut a tortilla with the side of her fork. "Working the case."

"What about . . ."

His voice trailed off. She knew what was on his mind. *What about that weird-ass sight of yours?* Before he regrouped to ask, she answered: "I use traditional and nontraditional methods."

Garcia dumped a gob of casserole into his mouth and chewed while staring at her notes. He put down his fork, picked up his napkin, dragged it across his mouth, and dropped the wad on the table. He pushed his chair back and stood up. Nodding toward the wall, he asked: "May I?"

"Go for it." As she watched him go over to the notes, she wondered what his reaction would be. Her Post-it charts weren't exactly FBI protocol. Then again, the big shots in D.C. wouldn't know what to make of an ASAC who took Sunday-night hot dish to the home of an underling; it probably violated some federal rule or policy. In his quirky way, Garcia was himself a renegade.

He stopped two yards from the wall and took in the overall design. An art critic studying the lines of a sculpture. He took two steps closer, and two more. He clasped his hands behind his back, bent forward, and started reading the scribbles on individual squares. An appraiser looking for a signature of authenticity. "Fascinating," he said without turning around. "So some of these notes deal with your regular footwork, and some deal with your other method."

Other method. She smiled to herself and said to his back: "Right."

His eyes locked on one square in particular. "Says here, 'Get hospital personnel files.' What's that about?"

"We'll get into that later."

"I see we have something of a physical description," he said, pointing to another block of boxes. "Too bad we can't get more detailed."

"I figure he's a doctor or a nurse or maybe a lab tech," she said. "How about that for more detail?" She stabbed a hunk of chicken and popped it into her mouth.

"What?" Garcia stood straight and spun around to face her.

She chewed and swallowed, set down her fork, and picked up her napkin. Dabbing at the corners of her mouth, she said: "You heard me."

He pivoted back around and ran his eyes over the notes for a couple of minutes. "Help me out here." His voice carried an edge. "I'm not seeing it."

He's defensive because his wife was a nurse, Bernadette thought. She went over to her boss and stood on his right. Extending her arm, she pointed. "There. I grouped them together."

Garcia read the collection of notes. *Reached out for sick woman? Woman's lover? Read Numbers. Read another book.* "I'm confused."

"I *saw* him," she said, emphasizing *saw* so Garcia would understand her meaning. "I saw the killer—last night, at a hospital downtown. He was with a patient. She was in bed. I recorded his movements. His behavior. That little bit of a physical description."

"Okay. So how does that get us to . . . a medical person? You saw him with a scalpel, or wearing scrubs, or what?"

Bernadette found it interesting that Garcia at that moment grudgingly accepted her sight, but apparently had problems with what she deduced from it. Was it because his wife was a nurse, or because of her missteps on past cases? "Forget my goofy notes. Let's finish our hot dish."

He didn't respond; he'd resumed his study of her Post-its. His shoulders were squarer this time; she'd gotten his attention and maybe pissed him off.

"Tony?" she said to his back. She couldn't remember the last ASAC she'd called by first name so readily. She tried it again. Louder. "Tony? How about it? Chow's getting cold."

Unfolding his arms, he turned away from the wall and went back to the table.

⋄   ⋄   ⋄

Garcia insisted she sit while he cleared the table. As he stood over her and reached to pick up her plate, she noticed his ID bracelet—heavy silver chain-link, with *Anthony* written in script on the rectangular nameplate. "Beautiful bracelet."

"Gift from my wife." He unsnapped the bracelet, slipped it off, and turned the nameplate over so Bernadette could see what was written on the back. *I am a Catholic. In case of an accident, please call a priest.* "She always worried about me on the job." He cleared his throat while fumbling to put the bracelet back on his wrist.

Call a priest.

That reminded her. She glanced at Garcia's watch while he fooled with his bracelet. She was missing five o'clock mass at the cathedral. She felt guilty about it, but at the same time told herself she'd made no promises. Then the priest's jab came back to her.

Maybe *again. You like that word, don't you?*

She'd make up for missing mass by meeting with the Franciscan Wednesday night.

⁕ ⊙ ⊙

It was late by the time Garcia left her place. Bernadette was just starting the dishes when she was startled by the sound of someone banging on her door. Her guest was coming back for his pan. She was going to wash it, but if he wanted it that bad, he could have it. She picked it up off the counter and opened the door.

Augie smiled and glanced down at the dirty dish. "What's for dinner?"

"Enchilada hot dish. Past tense." She opened the door wider.

He walked through with Oscar—sans leash—trailing behind. Spotting the glasses and plates on the counter, Augie asked: "Did we have a date this evening?"

"No, we had hot dish with our boss."

Augie crossed her living-room area and headed for her windows. "Hot dish. That's a uniquely Minnesotan way to advance your career."

"He brought it, not that it's any of your business." She closed the door and went back to the kitchen with the pan. She opened her dishwasher and started loading it. "If I were to use food, I would impress him with my Aunt Virg's recipe for molded Jell-O. Three layers, including a lime one containing crushed pineapple and cream cheese."

"Yum." He glanced outside. "Nice view of the parking lot across the street."

She stood straight, a dirty dish in her hand. "I can see the river."

"My view is better."

She felt something on her shin and looked down. Oscar had his front paws up on her leg and was licking the plate in her hand. She tried to shake him off but he wouldn't budge. She gave up and set the plate down on the floor. "Don't you ever feed this poor animal?"

Augie spun around to answer and noticed her Post-it wall. "What's that mess?" He started back across the room for a closer look.

She intercepted him halfway, stepping in front of him to block his path. "Let's pick this up another time, neighbor. I'm getting ready to hit the hay."

He looked over her head at the wall. "Working a case the old-fashioned way, huh? Want to bounce anything off me? I've got a lot of insight into the criminal mind."

She put her hand on his shoulder and started steering him to the door. "I'll bet you do."

He put his hand over hers. She tried to jerk her hand away, but he grabbed it and held it between both of his. "You're hot."

She yanked her hand out of his grasp. "And you feel like a block of ice."

"Hot and cold." Oscar padded between them, and Augie scooped him up, cradling the dog in the crook of his arm. "We've got that 'opposites attract' thing going on."

She pulled open the door. "I never did buy into that theory."

He hesitated before stepping into the hall, his eyes traveling back to the yellow squares. "A cross. Is that significant to your case?"

She'd covered up the intersecting bars of white. How had he spotted it through the jumble of paper? Her eyes met his, and she said evenly: "You're scaring me, counselor. I think you'd better go back upstairs and call it a night before you spread whatever it is you've got."

"I'm the one who should be nervous." He walked through the door. "People who cover their walls with paper scraps end up the subject of those cable-TV crime shows."

"Good night." She closed the door after him.

Twenty

Jerry Fontaine clawed another layer of toilet paper off the roll, blew his nose, and dabbed his eyes. He tossed the soiled tissue onto the coffee table in front of him. The wad joined an ocean of discarded pop cans, crumpled fast-food sacks, dirty paper napkins, and empty Kleenex boxes—the flotsam of a family dashed against the rocks by the loss of its wife and mother. The tabletop was a microcosm of the rest of the house.

Anna had been a quiet and efficient housewife—rather like a high-quality upright vacuum—and the first thing Jerry and the boys noticed after each of her hospitalizations was the immediate increase in clutter. Objects suddenly started appearing on each and every surface, as if dropped by evil gnomes when the humans had their backs turned. Dirty socks and boxers and tee shirts materialized on the bedroom floors. Dirty dishes and empty cereal boxes planted themselves on the kitchen counter. Cans of shaving cream, tubes of toothpaste, and strands of used dental floss littered the top of the bathroom vanity. Newspapers and magazines and junk mail landed pretty much everywhere. Each time Anna returned from the hospital, she was able to restore order by magic. Her very presence seemed to will away the mess.

Now there would be no magic, because there would be no return.

Jerry dropped the roll of toilet paper on the floor and picked up the phone. He glanced down at the legal pad resting on his lap—the only uncluttered horizontal surface in the front room. Anna had drawn up the names and numbers before going into the hospital this last time. Jerry had dutifully phoned family and friends and the mortuary. The florist and their parish priest. He stared at the one number not yet checked off the list. He didn't want to make the call, but Anna would be pissed if the bastard wasn't personally notified. He took a deep breath, sat up straight, and punched in the number. As the phone rang, he prayed to God that a machine would answer.

His prayer wasn't answered.

"Hello."

"Hi. It's Jerry. Jerry Fontaine."

"Is it Anna?"

Jerry put his hand over the mouthpiece and swallowed hard; he didn't want to break down over the phone. "Early this morning."

"I'm sorry."

"She'd want you at the services. At least the wake, if you can manage." Jerry wished he wouldn't make it to anything. He'd had enough of the crusader and his futile cause.

"Any idea when the visitation is going to be? Where?"

"Four to eight on Tuesday. That funeral home on West Seventh Street. The one on the corner that looks like a medieval fortress."

"Tuesday . . . That's tomorrow. So soon."

"Funeral mass is Wednesday morning. It's at a small church south of town. I don't expect anyone but family to make it to that." Jerry paused, wondering if the guy got the hint. Then he put more bluntly: "Burial's gonna be *private*."

"That's all pretty quick."

"She wanted it that way." Jerry had another thought and cleared his throat before he asked. He struggled to make his voice sound casual. "Oh. By the way. Anything come of that FBI woman? She contact you or anything?"

"No, no. Like I said, you must have misunderstood the conversation. I'm sure that woman wasn't even a cop." A moment of silence, then: "You didn't ask anyone at the hospital about it, did you?"

"No. Too much else going on."

"I wouldn't worry about it."

Jerry despised the arrogant tone, but he had to admit the guy was probably correct. If there was an issue, the FBI would have made contact by now. "Yeah. You're right." Jerry sighed. "Gotta go. Gotta make some more calls. The florist and the mortuary and all that."

"I'll say a prayer."

"You do that," Jerry said abruptly, and hung up. He sank back into the couch with relief.

He ran a hand through his thinning hair and wondered where the boys were in the mess that used to be their tidy split-level. Probably playing video games or watching television in their rooms. Jerry figured they were cried out for the moment. Fresh bawling jags awaited them at the wake and the funeral. The burial would be the worst. Then they would have to pick up their house and get on with their lives, because Anna would have wanted it that way. Anna liked things kept tidy.

In a way, his wife's fondness for order had brought the snake into their lives. The man had dragged the Fontaines and other grieving families to one legislative hearing after another in a quest to restore moral order to their world. They'd repeatedly told their stories, bared their souls to rooms filled with strangers, and answered asinine questions from idiot elected officials. At his insistence, they'd vigorously backed a proposal by a Republican senator that would have put a constitutional amendment reauthorizing the death penalty before voters. Jerry had to admit the idea was a long time coming; the state had abolished capital punishment in 1911. Problem was, a majority of lawmakers in both the House and the Senate had to approve putting it on the ballot, and neither body had the balls or the votes to let the people decide. Minnesota would remain one of a dozen states that would never allow the punishment that fit the most heinous crime.

Even after the effort went down in flames—leaving all the families feeling used and abused as much by their *leader* as by the politicians—Anna continued to idolize the snake. Sometimes Jerry wondered if his wife had cheated on him and slept with the slimy creep. He glanced down at the legal pad again, as if one last look would provide the answer to that nagging question. All Jerry saw before him were a series of names and phone numbers penned in Anna's elegant handwriting, followed by sloppy checkmarks made in his own shaky hand. He scratched a check next to the bastard's name and looked at his palm. Stained with ink—the pen was leaking. "Figures," he spat, and tossed the pen and pad on the table. The impact knocked a half-empty Coke can onto the floor. Jerry watched while the brown liquid foamed and settled into the beige carpet. The cat stepped across a copy of *Sports Illustrated*, the telephone bill, and a grocery-store flyer to get to the cola.

"Good kitty," Jerry mumbled as the animal lapped up the puddle.

Twenty-one

Bernadette rose early Monday, intending to go into the office and work the case from the cellar, but she couldn't pull herself away from the files long enough to get dressed. Wrapped in a bathrobe, she sat hunched over the kitchen table with the folders and a legal pad in front of her.

She read the tab. *Olson, Hale D.* The name was followed by a case number. She set it to her right. She counted three more files on Olson. She flipped open the cover of the last one and saw it was a transcript of Olson's trial—at least three inches thick. She couldn't believe the cops up north had gone all the way back and dug up those old court documents. She appreciated their thoroughness, but nevertheless closed the file. She didn't want to immerse herself in Hale's ancient adventures just yet. She stacked all of Olson's files into a separate pile and pushed them off to the side.

She dug into the Archer files. Now and then she interrupted her silent scratching and scribbling to hiss words of contempt:

"Disgusting."

By the time she was halfway through the folders, she felt filthy inside and out. She took a break to wash her face, drag a comb through her hair, and pull on a pair of sweats and a tee shirt. She went to the kitchen, opened the fridge, chugged some apple cider straight out of the jug, and put it back.

Sitting back down at the table, she started flipping through the files again. She lifted a girl's high-school portrait out of the papers. Bernadette had seen that shade of blond hair paired with those striking emerald eyes once before—on that woman in the hospital bed. This had to be the woman's daughter. Dead daughter.

Behind the color portrait was another photo—a gray morgue-shot taken after the girl's death—and tucked behind that was a medical examiner's report. Bernadette grabbed a pad and pen and started writing. When she got to the cause of death, she paused in her note-taking. The girl had committed suicide—a drug overdose, according to the report. Her parents found her body, in her own bed. A pang of sympathy stabbed Bernadette's gut; she brushed it aside.

She picked her cell off the table and called Directory Assistance to get the hospital number. When she was connected to Patient Information, she asked for the dead girl's mother, named in the report. Bernadette became suspicious when, without explanation, she was switched to a nurse instead of the room.

"Nurses' station."

The woman didn't sound like Nurse Big Arms; Bernadette was relieved. "Anna Fontaine's room."

The voice on the other end asked gingerly: "Uh, are you a member of the family?"

"Yeah."

A few seconds of silence, and then: "I'm sorry. Anna passed away earlier this morning."

Bernadette panicked, then scanned the report for the father of the dead girl. "Is Gerald . . . um, Jerry there?"

"Already left. Asked me to tell callers the services are being handled by . . ." The sound of paper shuffling. "I can't find it right now. Wait. Here it is. That mortuary on West Seventh Street. The big one on the corner. I've got a number."

Bernadette jotted the name and phone on a scrap of paper. "Thanks."

She punched in the funeral home, got a recording, hung up. She considered trying Jerry Fontaine at home, but thought about it some more. Perhaps she'd seen Anna Fontaine through the eyes of her spouse. She'd have to get a good look at the new widower, study his hands and his mannerisms. Something told her he wasn't the killer, but she had to be sure. Besides, hanging around the bereaved husband could get her to the right guy.

She hit redial, and this time a live person answered at the mortuary. Bernadette asked the man: "Anna Fontaine—has her wake been set yet?"

 ⚘   ⚘   ⚘

She was standing in front of the open refrigerator contemplating what she could grab for a late lunch when her cell rang. She slammed the fridge door and scooped the phone off the counter. "Yeah?"

Garcia, and he was incensed: "Where in the hell are you?"

"Thought I'd work from home today."

"This ain't the Big Easy, Agent Saint Clare. You want to work from home, you call in and make a request."

She gritted her teeth. "Yes, sir."

"You finished with those files?"

Her eyes went to the folders on the kitchen table. "Not yet."

"What have you been doing all morning?"

"The woman in the hospital bed. I tracked her down. Anna Fontaine."

"And . . ."

"And she's dead. Died this morning." Before Garcia could pipe in with more questions, she quickly added: "Wake's tomorrow. I'm going to the funeral home to scope it out."

"Who is . . . who was this Fontaine woman? What's her connection to anything?"

"She was the mother of one of Archer's victims. The daughter raided the medicine cabinet after that awful verdict came in."

"I remember that mess. So now the mother is dead. A regular Greek tragedy." He sighed. "Last thing we need is a grieving family calling a press conference."

"I'll be respectful."

"Be incognito," he said. "Put on your black suit and lean against a wall."

His instructions surprised her. She had been about to suggest the same tactic, expecting him to shoot it down. "Sounds good."

"Anybody asks, you're—I don't know—someone she met while she was hospitalized. You brought her pudding."

"Hopefully, nobody asks."

"Looking at the family at all? The husband?"

She didn't want to tell Garcia too much. "Maybe the husband. Yeah."

He said smugly, "Sounds like that doctor theory of yours is circling the drain."

"We'll see who shows up," she said.

Twenty-two

She was running late. Standing in her slacks and a bra, Bernadette was ironing an oxford shirt atop the kitchen table late afternoon Tuesday, minutes before the wake was to start. When she heard a knock, she tried to ignore it. Three more knocks were followed by an impatient bang. "Coming!" she yelled. She set down the iron, pulled on the warm cotton, and headed for the door. "This better be good," she mumbled, buttoning as she went. She threw open the door and found Augie standing in the hallway. "August. I don't have time to . . ."

He walked around her and went inside. "How about drinks tonight at my place? I've got a bottle of champagne chilling in the fridge. I'll blow the dust out of a couple of flutes, put on some tunes. We can—"

"Can't," she said, the door still open and her hand on the knob. "Gotta go to a wake."

He buried his hands in his pants pockets and frowned. "Do my feet stink or something?"

She stifled a grin as she took in his outfit—the same one he'd worn since the first night she met him, except that he'd exchanged the torn jeans for ratty sweatpants. She wondered if his Aerosmith Nine Lives Tour tee shirt would stand up by itself. "How could your feet smell when they get so much fresh air? I've never seen you in socks, neighbor. Don't those tootsies ever get chilly in sandals?"

"I'm hot-blooded." Flashing her a wicked grin, he folded his arms in front of him. "Unfortunately, at the rate we're going, you'll never get close enough to feel the burn."

She blinked twice and closed the door. "August—"

"Augie," he corrected her.

"Augie, I have to take off."

"Excuses, excuses. *I'm busy unpacking. I'm tired. I'm visiting dead folks. I've got to chase after some terrorists.* You're giving me a complex." Navigating around some boxes, he made his way to a window and glanced outside. "My view is still better."

She checked her watch. "I've got to get moving."

"Always in a hurry," he grumbled. "Life's too short. Bet you haven't even gone for a walk by the river."

"I just got to town. Give me a chance." As she fastened her shirt at the cuffs, one of the buttons came off in her hand. Mouthing a curse, she went back to her closet to find another top.

"Looks deceptively tranquil and harmless, especially from up here," he said to the glass.

"What does?" She peeled off the offending oxford, dropped it at her feet, and reached for a silk blouse preserved in a dry cleaner's bag. "What're you babbling about?"

"The river. It's sort of like life in general. People underestimate it. Think it's stable and predictable and safe to play on. They get careless and sloppy. Die." He turned away from the glass and spotted her bare shoulders as she slipped into her blouse.

She kept her back turned to him as she buttoned up the silk.

"Promise I won't do any belly flops off the bridges or play on the freeway. That should keep me from dying for a while."

"Speaking of death . . . anyone I know?" he asked.

She scanned the floor of her closet for shoes and bent over to retrieve a pair of dark pumps. "What?"

"Who died? I know everybody in town."

She stepped into her shoes. "Anna Fontaine."

"Don't know her. Is the wake business or pleasure?"

"Can't talk about it," she said, tucking her blouse into her slacks. "In fact, forget I mentioned her name."

"It's business, then."

She fished a belt through the loops of her slacks and buckled it. "August—"

"Augie," he said. "Drinks after the visitation, then. You'll need cheering up. Despite what the Irish claim, wakes are a sad affair."

"Sure." She walked to the front door and pulled it open, motioning him through with her open hand. "You gotta go or you're gonna make me later than I already am."

He walked across the loft and stepped out the door. He pivoted around and lifted his arms over his head, hooking his hands over the top of the door frame. "One more thing."

Bernadette shot a quick look at his biceps, massive and rippling and filling the entire opening. She visualized those arms wrapped around her body, and quickly banished the image. "What?" she said impatiently. "I gotta go."

He leaned inside and said in a low, conspiratorial voice: "You've got a nice back, neighbor lady."

She felt her face reddening and lowered her eyes. "Sorry about that."

He smiled. "Don't get me wrong. I'm not complaining."

She raised her eyes and offered an embarrassed grin. "I'm in a rush."

He pulled his hands off the door frame and pointed a finger at her. "Don't get rushed tonight. Don't get sloppy." He headed down the hall.

"Where do you get off?" she muttered to his back, and closed the door after him.

Twenty-three

Where does he get off? simmered Jerry Fontaine.

Jerry was just inside the front door, fishing a pack of cigs out of his pants pocket, when the snake slithered into the mortuary and glided right past him. No hello and handshake. No signing the guest book and tucking a check in the memorial-gift box. He elbowed past a crowd of others in the hallway and dove right into the throng inside the chapel. To top it off, the reptile was dressed better than the grieving husband— and smelled better than half the women in the place. Jerry got a whiff of his cologne as he whipped past. Probably expensive. Not like Jerry's drugstore aftershave.

Jerry went outside, lit up, and defensively assessed his funeral attire. The slate suit with its narrow lapels was dated, but his sons had reassured him that the silver tie was a contemporary width. The outfit was further redeemed by the crispness of his pressed white shirt. He reached up and laid his palm over his heart. Anna had ironed the shirt—and starched the hell out of it. There'd be no more crisp shirts at their house; neither he nor the boys had the ability or the desire to iron. That was all right. He sold preowned vehicles for a living, and people expected his ilk to look wrinkled. He tapped a tube of cigarette ash to the ground and at the same time inspected the shine on his black wingtips. He'd polished the shoes just before leaving home, having miraculously discovered the long-missing electric buffer in the front-hall closet. Anna would have credited the angels for the find, or chalked it up to one of those saints good at locating lost items. Which saint was that? He couldn't remember. In his mind, they all melded together—except for St. Francis of Assisi. Jerry could remember him as the patron saint of animals because the fellow was always standing around with a bird on his shoulder.

Jerry nodded to a trio of women clicking down the sidewalk on their way to the mortuary. One of the gals reached out and squeezed his upper arm as she passed him on the walk. "We're praying for ya, Jer." He grimaced a thank-you. They were in Anna's prayer group. They'd sent enough Bundt cakes to the house to open a bakery, but he knew that generosity would end the minute his wife's coffin hit the dirt. He wasn't cut from the same churchy cloth—the fact that he was out-side puffing away was testimony to that. In fact, they would probably comment on his sinful loitering the minute they got inside.

He took a deep pull off his cigarette, released a cloud, and checked his watch. Where were the boys? They'd run off with their friends to grab some burgers and should've been back half an hour ago. It didn't look good if the deceased's immediate family was AWOL just as the wake was really getting rolling. He took one last pull and held it, enjoy-ing the coolness of the menthol. He blew out the smoke and reluctantly threw down the butt. He turned and faced the mortuary with trepida-tion. It was like looking into the mouth of a beast, an old enemy to whom he'd lost his daughter and now his wife. He felt tears welling up in his eyes.

No crying, you big baby, he told himself. Jerry stood straight, ad-justed his tie, and hiked up his pants. As he headed for the door, he ventured one last look over his shoulder. No sons in sight. Worthless turds. Not like their sister. They'd better remember his cheeseburgers. Anna would have made sandwiches. So would their daughter. His heart lifted for a moment as he envisioned the two women making sandwiches together up in heaven.

His stomach rumbling, Jerry went back inside.

Bernadette pulled her gloves tighter over her fingers as she hurried up the walk. She put her hand on the knob, pushed open the heavy wooden door, and stepped into the lobby. As the door closed behind her, she inhaled the odors. Funeral flowers and women's perfume and men's cologne. Faint cigarette fumes. Beneath all of that, she detected something musty. Funeral homes always carried that musty undercurrent. If the souls of the dead had a scent, it would be that musty odor.

She saw a hallway to the right and another to the left, with a chapel at the end of each corridor. Both rooms were jammed with mourners; the funeral home was hosting two wakes that evening. "Excuse me," said an elderly male voice behind her. Bernadette turned around and saw she was blocking a group of older men. She stepped to one side, stumbling over an apology as they went by. She hated wakes and funerals to begin with, and attending a stranger's services by herself was torture.

She went deeper inside and, ahead of her, saw a magnetic sign perched on a tripod. "Gladys Johnson" had an arrow pointing to the left, whereas "Anna Fontaine" mourners were directed to the right. She hung a right, went down the hallway, and stopped at a podium sitting just outside the chapel. Atop the stand, a guest book sat open and ready for visitors to sign. She reflexively reached for a pen and stopped herself. Time to take away names rather than leave one. She checked and, seeing no one behind her, flipped through the signed pages, scouting for someone who'd used a doctor's title. No luck.

She picked up a memorial prayer card from a stack sitting next to the book. The front had a picture of Our Lady of Guadalupe. She turned the card over and read, "In loving memory of Anna Fontaine," followed by a prayer:

> *Our Lady of Guadalupe,*
> *mystical rose. Since you are*
> *the ever-Virgin Mary and*
> *Mother of the true God,*
> *obtain for us from your holy*
> *Son the grace of a firm and*
> *a sure hope. In the midst of*
> *our anguish, struggle, and*
> *distress, defend us from the*
> *power of the enemy, and at*
> *the hour of our death receive*
> *our soul in Heaven. Amen.*

She slipped the card into the pocket of her slacks. Next to the cards were envelopes for memorials. She picked one up, opened the flap, and slipped a twenty-dollar bill inside. She tucked it closed and—without signing the front—dropped the envelope into the slot on top of the podium.

Bernadette walked into the chapel and found it so packed with people and flowers she couldn't immediately spot the casket. Running her eyes around the room, she counted lots of gray heads. A few young couples dressed in jeans were hauling kids around the room with them. The majority of mourners were well-dressed middle-aged couples—Anna's contemporaries, she guessed. A wall of people on the left parted, and she saw a glint of dark, glossy wood. She negotiated her way through the crowd, aiming for the kneeler planted alongside the coffin. She'd say a quick prayer and then snoop around the crowd for her guy.

Before she knelt, she studied the figure in the coffin. Anna Fontaine was as Bernadette had spied her through the killer's eyes, except better defined—like starting out with an artist's sketch and filling it in with greater detail and color. Blond hair fanned out over the casket's satin pillow, the same way it had fanned out over the bed linen. Anna's complexion actually carried more color in death than it had in life—courtesy of the mortician's makeup palette. Resting in the corpse's lap was that chain of green beads held by the hospital patient—and now Bernadette could see it was a rosary and not a necklace. A small detail, she told herself, but perhaps she wouldn't have made the mistake had she been truer to her Catholic faith.

She went down on her knees and folded her hands in front of her.

      ◊   ◊   ◊

Jerry sneaked into the hallway as members of Anna's prayer group started distributing rosaries to the chapel crowd. He needed a fortifying smoke before wedging himself back inside the sardine can. His sons had finally shown up—without his burgers—and they could suffer without him for a while. As he yanked open the front door, he heard the cadence of group prayer begin behind him. He slipped outside, and was immediately immersed in a sense of guilty relief.

He didn't want to be seen by anyone glancing out the mortuary's front windows, so he headed for the public sidewalk that ran along the mortuary's front yard. Keeping his back turned to the building, he lit up another cig and took a heavy drag. Exhaling, he watched the nighttime traffic going back and forth on the street in front of him. He spotted an empty bus-stop bench on the corner and went for it. He lowered himself down with a sigh and stretched his legs out in front of him.

Behind him, he heard footsteps heading down the mortuary's walk. They sounded like a woman's high heels. Fearing a tongue-lashing if he was caught by one of the church ladies, he slunk down on the bench. As the *click-clack* faded, he turned and peeked over the back of the bench. He saw a blond woman heading down the sidewalk that ran along the side of the mortuary. Someone else had bailed from the rosary recitation and was fleeing to her car. *Good for her,* thought Jerry. He wondered who it was; he couldn't recognize her from the back, but she looked vaguely familiar. He shrugged and resumed his smoke.

A couple of minutes later, Jerry heard a man's heavy footfall and turned around in his seat again. The reptile himself was clomping down the mortuary walk. Instead of following the woman down the sidewalk to the back parking lot, he hooked in the other direction, cutting across the front lawn, and disappearing between the mortuary and the building next door. *Weird bastard.* Jerry turned back around to face the street. He hoped the snake would follow the Bundt cakes and vanish as soon as Anna was buried. He took a long pull, held it, and exhaled. Flicking the butt in the gutter, he eyed the corner liquor store across the road. He made a mental note to pick up a bottle on his way home. *Tonight would be a good night to get lit.*

He dropped his face into his hands and wept.

⋄   ⋄   ⋄

Bernadette reached inside her blazer and touched the butt of her Glock.

Don't get rushed tonight. Don't get sloppy.

Why had she let Augie spook her? She withdrew her hand and kept going down the walk that ran along the side of the funeral home. She'd cut her watch short by exiting as the rosary was beginning, but she'd been uncomfortable lurking around Anna Fontaine's gathering. Praying with the dead woman's people would have been excruciating.

The evening had been a waste. As she'd suspected, the husband was not the killer. His demeanor was too meek, and his plump hands were not the murderer's hands. She'd observed the other mourners but noticed no one behaving oddly. She'd been especially watchful of the area around the casket, studying large adult males in particular. Granted, the place was so full it was difficult to scrutinize every person. She'd periodically checked the podium in the hall for fresh signatures—again searching for doctors. She'd even asked a few folks if anyone from the hospital was in attendance, but nothing came of her search for a medical person. Fortunately, no one had asked her much of anything. As Garcia had requested, she'd kept her vigil low-key. Covert. She'd even been tempted to leave her gun at home, but then that damn Augie had dropped in with his ominous words.

They get careless and sloppy. Die.

As the sidewalk emptied into the parking lot, she pulled her blazer tight around her body. The night air was cool and damp and reeked of wet leaves, a smell that belonged to the late fall instead of the spring. Her truck was in the far corner of the tar rectangle, and she sliced a diagonal path to get to it. The blackness of the tar seemed to melt into the blackness of the night. The lot had none of its own lighting. Weak ambient illumination was provided by a streetlamp planted on the street that ran alongside the mortuary.

She was in the middle of the lot, standing between two rows of cars, when she heard the snap of a twig. She froze. Where had the sound come from? Another crack. Her eyes darted to the bushes lining the back of the parking lot. She sensed someone peering out from the darkness, watching her. The man she was hunting?

Bernadette reached inside her blazer and unsnapped her holster. She withdrew her hand and continued walking, but more slowly. She went another fifty feet before she slipped her hand back inside her jacket and pulled out her gun. She kept going, a slow but steady pace. The sound of the street traffic buzzing past the front of the mortuary seemed muffled and distant compared with the deafening thump of her shoes on the tar.

She deviated from the diagonal and cut between two minivans, heading straight for the back of the lot. Beyond the bushes was an alley—the ideal escape route for someone hiding in the hedge.

Bernadette allowed a distance of ten feet between herself and the bushes as she walked from one end of the hedge to the other, aiming the gun straight at the greenery. Was it her imagination, or could she smell him, smell his aftershave? Something cheap and musky. She struggled to maintain a steady, stern voice and to keep her volume below a panicky shout: "FBI . . . Step out with your hands in the air . . . I know you're in there . . . I heard you."

When she got to one corner of the back lot, she went around the bushes and crunched along the gravel alley behind it. "FBI . . . Come out now . . . Hands in the air." She saw nothing, but the strip of shrubbery was dense enough to hide someone inside it. When she reached the end of the row of bushes, she stopped walking and scanned the alley, shared on both sides by residential garages and fenced backyards. Every other garage had a yard light mounted to its side. No one in sight.

Bernadette navigated around the bushes so she was back inside the lot and walked until she was in the middle of the line of greenery. She crouched down, arms extended. From the lower vantage point, she ran her eyes up and down the hedge. She stood straight and listened. Silence. Even the traffic from the front of the building seemed to have vanished. She lowered her arms, took two steps back, and waited.

"Long gone," she sighed. She holstered her gun, turned on her heel, and went to her truck, glancing over her shoulder while she walked.

Twenty-four

Talk about careless and sloppy, she thought. She lifted her fist to knock and realized his door was already open a crack. Typical bachelor. She didn't want to barge in and catch him walking out of the shower. She smiled to herself. Would that be such a bad thing? Besides, he'd already seen her half dressed. She issued a two-word warning—"It's Bernadette!"—and slipped into his place.

"My God," she whispered. She closed the door and leaned her back against it, afraid to walk farther inside.

Votives glowed on every sill—and there were better than a dozen windows lining the walls. More votives were scattered in groupings on the marble floor, like nighttime campfires dotting an open field. To her right, chunky pillar candles covered the kitchen island and littered the counters. On the left, a forest of tapered candles flickered atop a baby grand—the only visible piece of furniture. The windows were uncovered, no light fixtures hung from the ceiling, not a single potted plant decorated the floor. Yet, with the hundreds of candles, Augie's place was warm and inviting and romantic.

She took three steps inside. "This isn't fair, damn you."

"Not very neighborly," said a voice behind her.

She spun around. "August."

He was dressed in black slacks and a black turtleneck finished off by black socks. In each hand, he carried a flute of champagne. He passed one over to her and clinked his glass with hers. "To improved neighbor relations."

"Neighbor relations." As she sipped, she ran her eyes up and down his figure. "You clean up real good."

He motioned toward her black slip dress with his flute. "Slinky. You changed for me."

"No, I didn't," she said defensively. Then, with a smile: "Yes, I did."

"We both picked black. Instead of that opposites-attract thing, we're onto that matchy-matchy thing." He looked down at her feet. "And we're both shoeless."

She looked down at her own naked legs and feet. "I thought I'd one-up you in the barefoot department. Plus, my feet are killing me." She sipped and glanced around the room. "Your mood lighting is amazing, Augie. But where's the furniture?"

"I keep scaring away decorators," he said.

"I wonder why." She took a drink and moved toward the piano. "You were right about tonight."

He followed her, snatching a magnum of champagne off the kitchen island as he went. "Right about what?"

Running an index finger across the keys, she said: "Needs tuning."

He tipped back his glass and drained it. "Don't play much anymore."

She looked at her fingertip. "Don't clean much, either."

"Maid's on vacation." He stepped next to her, refilled his glass, and topped off hers. "Right about what?"

Bernadette took a long drink and shuddered at the coldness of it. "Being careful."

"The wake," he said. "What happened?"

"You don't want to know." She swallowed and shuddered again.

"Tell me," he insisted.

She raised her glass toward him. "Maybe after a few more of these."

○   ○   ○

She was on her back in his bed, a massive four-poster—the only furniture in the cavernous master suite. Her small figure was drowning in the sea of down blankets and down pillows and satiny sheets. Savoring the sinking sensation, she snuggled deeper under the covers.

Standing by the side of the bed, he looked down at her and asked: "Are you sure about this? You don't know me."

His words seemed to be out of sync with the movement of his lips, as if he were an actor in a foreign movie mouthing dubbed dialogue. She'd had way too much champagne. She didn't care. "I'm sure."

He peeled off his turtleneck, stepped out of his slacks and boxers. She drank in his body while candles danced on the floor behind him. He was dark and muscled, with a broad chest that was surprisingly smooth, almost hairless.

"I want to see you." With one hand, he yanked off the top covers. His eyes went to the two gold bands resting against her skin. "What's that on your necklace?"

"Don't worry about it."

He reached down and clamped one large hand over the waist of her panties. "You won't need these." In one swift, brutal motion, he pulled them down and off and dropped them to the floor. He fell on top of her and forced her thighs apart with his knees. She reached down to guide him inside her, but he pushed her hand aside. "Not yet," he breathed in her ear. He wrapped his left hand over her right wrist and brought her arm up over her head, pinning her against the mattress. With his right hand, he kneaded her breasts.

She arched her back, pressing her pelvis into his. "Please."

"I want you to wait."

"You're mean," she whispered sleepily, drunkenly.

He laughed and moved his mouth to her nipples. "You taste like sugar," he murmured, his words echoing as if he'd uttered them in a cave or a canyon or their building's hallway.

Sugar . . . sugar . . . sugar.

His breath and his skin were cold, but moisture beaded his fore-head. A drop of perspiration rolled down the side of his face and fell between her breasts. With her free hand, she reached down to grab the comforter and pull it over their bodies, but she couldn't find the cover. "I'm freezing."

"I'll warm you."

"Hurry."

When he finally entered her, she was wet and ready for him. Still, she gasped. He slowed his thrusts and said: "I'm hurting you."

"Yes," she said, wrapping her legs around his hips. "It's good."

In the candlelight, she heard his rock music pounding a beat. At the same time, she swore she heard her own favorite singer crooning some-where distant. Aerosmith and Sinatra, a strange combination. Jack Daniel's with a martini chaser.

◦   ◦   ◦

It was the middle of the night when she rolled out of his bed. The can-dles on the bedroom floor had gone out. In the dark, she tried to feel around the massive bed for him so she could give him a good-night kiss, but her hands became lost in the piles of pillows and humps of down. She gave up and turned around to feel around the floor for her dress and panties. She gathered them in her arms and started to tiptoe out of his bedroom. The door was open to the main living area, and she could see a faint glow. A few candles remained lit out there. She'd douse them before leaving, so the place wouldn't go up in flames.

In the blackness of the bedroom, a muscular arm snaked around her midriff. "Come back to my bed."

"I have to get up early," she whispered, hugging her clothing to her naked front.

"I don't care." He kissed the side of her neck and pressed his front against her back as his hands moved under her bundle and cupped her breasts. "Stay."

She could feel his erection. "You don't play fair, and I really have to go."

"Just a little longer. Lie with me a little longer. Please."

The tone of his voice stabbed her heart. He sounded as lonely and hungry as she could be on her worst nights. She unfolded her arms and let her clothes drop to the floor. He scooped her up. She twined her arms around his neck as he carried her back to bed. "Don't let me fall asleep again. I have to wake up in my own bed."

"I'll carry you there myself," he said, setting her down amid the blankets and pillows and tangled sheets.

Twenty-five

A hangover. She hadn't had one of those in a while. At least Augie had made good on his promise and deposited her in her own bed. She crawled out of it Wednesday morning with throbbing temples and a queasy stomach. With her eyes half shut, she hobbled downstairs and into the bathroom.

A hot shower took the edge off her headache, but did nothing to dilute the memory of his hands and mouth all over her. She prayed she hadn't made a horrible mistake by sleeping with him. In the same instant, she hoped it wouldn't be the last time. He'd been an amazing lover.

She reluctantly pulled on some work clothes—navy-blue slacks and a white blouse topped by a navy blazer—and headed out the door. She checked her watch as she hustled down the sidewalk and saw it was not quite seven-thirty. She had time to grab a coffee and a pastry on her way to the cellar.

While she stood in line at the café, she thought about her game plan for work. No way in hell was she going to tell her boss she'd been followed out to her car during the wake. Nothing good would come of it, Bernadette concluded. He'd be furious with her over something, be it failing to identify the suspect at the visitation, trying to apprehend the guy solo, or letting the killer get away from her.

o   a   o

Garcia was leaning against the edge of her desk waiting for her, one of her FBI commendations in his hand. He offered her a dry greeting as she walked through the office door. "Good afternoon, Agent Saint Clare."

She had her coffee cup in one hand and a morsel of Danish in the other. She didn't know what to do with the pastry except pop it her mouth and swallow. After taking a sip of coffee to wash it down, she coughed and sputtered a greeting: "Hey."

His face wearing the disgusted expression of someone who'd just discovered a hair in his soup, Garcia held up the plaque with two fingers. "Found this in the garbage."

"My mistake." She took another sip of coffee and thought: *Jesus. He digs through my trash. Plus, he said "Agent Saint Clare." Gonna be a bad day in the basement.*

"Found some other *mistakes* in the trash." He set the award down on her desk. "How'd it go last night? *See* anyone you liked?"

The way he'd said *see*—she'd pretend she didn't catch the dig. Dropping her coffee cup into a wastebasket, she said evenly: "Didn't observe anyone suspicious."

"The husband?"

"Not our man."

He suddenly noticed her empty hands. "Where're those files I dropped off at your place?"

"On my kitchen table. Was gonna go through them at home after I straightened up in here."

"Let me see if I got this right. You were gonna fix up the office and then go home to do your office work?"

She realized how ridiculous that sounded, but didn't know what else to say except "Yes."

He picked the plaque up and examined it while talking to her. "You don't want to be here, do you?"

She buried her hands in her blazer pockets. "I told you. Basement's fine. St. Paul is—"

He cut her off. "I mean the bureau."

Her eyes widened. "What? I want to be with the bureau. I love this job."

"Sure you do," he said tiredly. He carried the plaque over to the wastebasket, dropped the award inside, and stepped around her to get to the door.

She said to his back, "I do."

He put his hand on the knob and said, without turning around, "Finish up with those files by tomorrow, Agent Saint Clare. I don't care *where* you read them. Take them into the damn john if you want." He yanked open the door and walked out.

"I *do* like my job," she said to the closed door.

°   °   °

Bernadette ate lunch at a downtown deli, hardly tasting the sandwich. She went home and sat at the kitchen table, sifting through the remainder of the Archer folders and scratching notes. She told herself she'd tackle the Olson pile the next day. She had trouble concentrating, and found herself rereading entire pages because she couldn't remember what she'd just seen. Garcia's words combined with her fumble at the wake left her feeling insecure about her work and her sight. Her decision to get drunk and sleep with Augie didn't leave her feeling any better about her personal life.

She really needed to see the Franciscan that night—if for no other reason than to hear someone validate her existence on the planet. Any good priest could do that.

Twenty-six

She was surprised to find the front doors open but not a soul in the pews. The church was dimly lit, making Bernadette wonder if the Franciscan had forgotten about their midweek rendezvous. She decided to give him a chance and wait around a while.

She took a back bench, off to one side. Bernadette shuffled into the pew and went down on her knees, unzipping her bomber but leaving on her gloves. She folded her hands together and propped them on the back of the bench in front of her. The church was so quiet she was sure she could hear her own heart beating. She rested her forehead on top of her hands and closed her eyes. Reflecting on what had brought her to this place, she replayed bits of conversation in her head.

Come back to my bed.

You don't play fair, and I really have to go.

Just a little longer. Lie with me a little longer. Please.

You don't want to be here, do you?

I want to be with the bureau, I love this job.

Sure you do.

I do . . . I do . . . I do.

"I do," she said out loud—more loudly than she'd intended.

She opened her eyes and lifted her head off her hands. She half expected someone to shush her for being disorderly in church, but she remained the lone congregant. She glanced at a saint standing against the wall, just across the aisle from where she knelt. He was frozen in a niche and cloaked in shadows, but she saw enough detail to know he was St. Patrick. She recognized the staff in his hand, and could see the snakes writhing at his feet. *Help me slay my serpents, St. Patrick,* she silently petitioned.

She was startled by the sound of footsteps and looked toward the noise. With the grace and flutter of a wind-tossed leaf, his robed figure suddenly glided onto the altar. In one practiced, fluid motion, he simultaneously genuflected and made the sign of the cross. He was still wearing the hood pulled over his head; that couldn't be regulation for his order. She speculated that this particular man had embraced this manner of dress and calling to hide from the world. She smiled bitterly to herself. An insecure priest counseling an insecure woman. Which cliché applied? "The blind leading the blind"? "It takes one to know one"?

Bernadette bent her head as if she were immersed in prayer. She watched him out of the corner of her eye as he floated down an aisle on the opposite side of the church. He went to the front doors. She stole a look over her shoulder and saw him turn the dead bolt on the door. *Why is he locking the two of us inside?*

She quickly snapped her head back around and faced the front, looking down but keeping her eyes wide open. He hurried back up the aisle, again genuflected and crossed himself on the altar, and went into the sacristy without acknowledging her presence. Perhaps she'd hidden herself too well. Besides, she'd sought him out, and it was rude to make him traverse the church to come to her. She slid out of the pew and headed closer to the altar, stopping at a pew in the second row. Like all

Catholics—practicing or not—she shied away from sitting in the very front. She slid between the benches and again went down on her knees, this time making the sign of the cross before tipping her head.

He walked out onto the altar again. With his back to the pews, he genuflected and crossed himself. Stepping off the altar, he headed down her aisle. She was baffled when, instead of coming up next to her, he took the pew behind hers.

"Good to see you again, daughter."

"Good to . . ." Still kneeling, she glanced over her right shoulder. With the rosary wrapped around his left fingers, he had folded his hands together and was resting them on the back of her pew. "Why are you sitting there, Father?"

"Thought you'd be more comfortable this way, should there be anything . . . sensitive you wish to confide. Confess."

She faced the front again. "Why the shortage of lights? Trying to save on the electricity bill?"

"This church is usually closed and dark at this hour, daughter. As a courtesy, the parish priest let me keep the front door open for you."

"Is that why you locked up after I got here?"

She detected a slight halting in his voice as he answered. "Yes . . . We can't have other visitors coming in this late. Who knows who could walk through the door?"

She realized she'd been interrogating him as if he were one of her suspects, and she felt bad about it. She tried to make amends. "You went through a lot of trouble, and I appreciate it. You didn't even know I would show."

"But you did. Why have you come, daughter? Need to talk? Something personal troubling you? Something spiritual?" He paused and then added: "Something about work?"

"They're all three usually intertwined," she said.

"How can I help?"

She pulled her hands off the back of the front pew, got up off her knees, and sat down on the bench. "First let me get something off my chest about what you said before. If that's okay."

"Go ahead," he said, in a voice just above a whisper.

He stayed kneeling, his hands still perched on the back of her bench, just to the right of her shoulders. The intimacy of his voice and the closeness of his figure made her uncomfortable. Perhaps a confessional would have been better. She was tempted to go back on her knees to put distance between her and him, but she thought he'd find that odd. She stayed where she sat and continued. "When you suggested my sight might be Satan's work . . ."

"Yes."

"It's got to be the opposite."

"God's work?"

"Yes," she said defensively.

"What makes you so sure, daughter?"

"I was at home, working through an investigation. I was sticking some stuff up on the wall. Post-its." She paused, knowing he'd find that in itself an unorthodox way to work, let alone how she generated the observations in the first place. "The notes contained clues I'd . . . um . . . picked up in the case."

"Clues you'd obtained through these visions?"

"Through regular footwork, too," she added quickly.

"Please. Go on."

"So I'm slapping these yellow squares up on the Sheetrock. Arranging them in a way that makes sense. Categorizing them. Rearranging. I step back when I'm finished and take a look."

"And?"

"And, without realizing it, I'd positioned the notes up on the wall so they formed a cross."

The long silence that followed told her she'd disturbed him with this story. She shouldn't have told him, shouldn't have come back at all. This guy was going to freak out on her. The whole thing was yet another bad call on her part.

Confirming her fears, he hissed his next words into her right ear: "A paper cross? Trickery, daughter. Demons twisting your hands and your heart."

"There are . . . no such things as demons," she said weakly.

"Demons come in many forms, daughter. Read Timothy in the New

Testament. 'Now the Spirit expressly says that in later times some will renounce the faith by paying attention to deceitful spirits and teachings of demons, through the hypocrisy of liars whose consciences are seared with a hot iron.' "

"Are you calling me a liar, or are you saying I'm stupid enough to listen to one? I'm not sure which is worse, Father."

His tone softened. "If you could tell me about your visions, what you've seen . . ."

She swallowed hard. Now *he* had agitated *her*, and she needed to regain control. "I can't. Ongoing investigation."

"How convenient—for the devil."

She started to stand. "I apologize for taking your time. This was a bad idea, my coming here and dumping on you, especially since I can't give you the full picture."

Suddenly changing his tone, he said gently: "Surely there are things you can tell me without jeopardizing your investigation. I need to know more before I can judge whether you're being led down the wrong road. Can you tell me generally whom you suspect in this case? The sort of soul who may be arrested as a result of these visions?"

She reluctantly lowered herself again. "He works at a hospital. Spends time with patients."

"What makes you believe that? What's led you to that conclusion?"

"He was in a room with a sick woman. I think he was studying a book about patients' stats or vitals."

"What, daughter? I don't understand. A book about patients' vital signs?"

"I was using my sight. Seeing through the murderer's eyes. This guy, the killer, was reading a reference book with a chapter or page titled 'Numbers.' I assume it was . . ."

"A book in the Bible," he breathed.

"What are you saying? What was I looking at?" She turned around in her seat and stared at him. "You know what I was seeing?"

"Numbers," said the voice behind the hood. "You were looking at Numbers. The fourth book of the Pentateuch."

"What's that?" she asked.

"You should know this, daughter. The Pentateuch is the first five books of the Bible."

"And one of those books, the fourth one, is called . . ."

"Numbers," he repeated.

"I thought he was looking at patient stats or something."

He got up off his knees and sat down, fingering the rosary as he answered. She saw his hands were trembling. Now he was starting to believe in her ability, and it frightened him. "It does have *something* to do with statistics," he said. "The book deals with events during the Israelites' travels in the wilderness. The name—Numbers—refers to the censuses that God instructs Moses to take at the beginning and end of the wilderness period."

"You aren't shortening the translation for me? Simplifying it?"

"No," he said.

"You're sure, Father? Numbers? It's just called Numbers?"

He said mechanically: " 'The Lord spoke to Moses in the wilderness of Sinai, in the tent of meeting, on the first day of the second month, in the second year after they had come out of the land of Egypt, saying: Take a census of the whole congregation of Israelites, in their clans, by ancestral houses, according to the number of names, every male individually; from twenty years old and upward, everyone in Israel able to go to war. You and Aaron shall enroll them, company by company.' "

"I'll take that as a yes," she said. She sat forward, burying her face in her hands.

"What's wrong? This isn't the answer you wanted or expected?"

"Changes everything," she said through her fingers. "My assumptions were wrong. I've got to start over. Go in a different direction."

"Tell me more about what you saw. Perhaps I can help you . . ."

She sat up straight. "You've already helped more than you can imagine."

She felt a hand on her shoulder and started. He was kneeling directly behind her, and she didn't like it. "You came here to tell me more. There are other things bothering you, matters beyond work."

She stood up. "That's not important now."

Behind her, he stood up as well. "Daughter . . ."

"Thank you, Father." She slid out of the pew and ran down the aisle without looking back. She unbolted the door, pulled it open, and disappeared into the night without another word to her confessor.

◊   ◊   ◊

Bernadette shivered as she hurried down the sidewalk toward her condo, but she didn't pin the sensation on the evening chill. The Franciscan's behavior—locking the door and sitting behind her—had been bizarre. Though she trusted the information he'd given her, she didn't trust him. Her instincts had told her to stay away from the robed man. There'd be no more late-night counseling sessions. To hell with validation.

Twenty-seven

· ·

She revisited the wall Thursday morning.

Bernadette concentrated on the squares containing information she'd collected through her sight. With the revelation that the man had read a Bible and not a medical reference book, the way she'd interpreted what she'd seen through the murderer's eyes was now in question.

The physical description of the killer remained valid. *Big man. White. Hairy hands. Dark long-sleeved shirt. Blue pants.* What about the killer's behavior toward the patient? She moved to peel off *Reached out for sick woman? Woman's lover?* She lowered her hands. Those would still work, even if the guy was religious. In fact, Holy Rollers could be the most convincing actors, leading double lives and keeping lovers.

Read Numbers. Read another book. She had no idea what the second book was, but the Franciscan had educated her on the first. She snatched the square off the wall and crumpled it. On a fresh sheet, she hastily scrawled, *Read Bible passage from Numbers* and pressed it back onto the Sheetrock.

She took a step back and planted her hands on her hips. The new addition to the wall was vital. The killer was more than simply religious. He'd read the book at length, lingering over it. Who would do that? Her hands grew cold as the answer came to her. That couldn't be who had followed her to the funeral-home parking lot—or could it?

Why would a member of the religious community kill people and hack off their hands? A youthful memory drifted into her head, something from Sunday school. A verse every Christian would recognize. Was the name of a pastor buried in her unread Olson files? Had she missed the mention of a minister during her read of the Archer case? She turned and stared at the folders piled across the room, on her kitchen table. With the help of the Franciscan, she could now think clearly enough to find the answer—one clergyman helping her nail another one. "Thanks, Father," she muttered.

The phone rang, jarring her out of her trance. She went over to the kitchen counter, picked it up, and answered distractedly. "Yeah?"

"What have you been doing all morning?" Garcia paused and then answered his own question: "The Post-its. Stop wasting time on—"

She interrupted him. "Our guy isn't a medical professional after all."

"Who is it, then?"

She hadn't fixed on a specific faith, and surprised herself with the two words that popped out of her mouth. "Catholic priest."

Dead air on Garcia's end, and then: "I'm coming over."

* * *

As soon as she threw open her front door, she regretted not changing into work clothes while waiting for his arrival. He was dressed in a dark suit and red tie. His shirt—so white it blinded her—looked professionally pressed. He stepped into her apartment, a black trench coat thrown over one arm. She extended her hands. "Can I take your jacket?"

"No thanks," he said, running his eyes down the length of her figure and frowning at her jeans.

"I was so busy going over my notes . . ."

"Right," he said dryly.

She closed the door and nodded toward the kitchen. "Let's sit down."

He walked into the kitchen, threw his coat over the back of a chair, and waited while she sat down across from him. He dropped down onto his seat. "Man of the cloth? This better be rock solid."

Man of the cloth. He'd said it reverently—not flippantly. Was she going to have trouble convincing her boss of a priest's guilt because Garcia was a pious man? Maybe that's why he didn't completely discount her sight: he believed in ethereal things. She didn't want to criticize Garcia's spirituality when it could turn him into her ally. She offered him a concession: "Maybe I'm jumping the gun on this priest idea."

"Serious charge to go throwing around, especially in this town. In case you haven't noticed, the St. Paul Cathedral sits higher in the city skyline than the State Capitol Building. Catholicism's a pretty big deal here."

The only words that came to her mind next were the ones from Sunday school, a Bible verse Garcia had to recognize if he was indeed a person of faith: "If your hand causes you to sin . . ."

"What're you saying? A priest is killing people and hacking off their hands as some sort of—what?—divine retribution?"

"I'm open to other possibilities." She pushed the Olson stack across the table. "Let's flip through these files. Why don't you take our pal Hale? See if anything jumps out at you after hearing my theory."

"My pleasure." He pulled the pile closer and opened the top folder. She started sifting through Archer's folder again, in case she'd missed something.

For twenty-five minutes, they read without speaking. Each took a few notes and scribbled a few doodles. Then, without raising his eyes from his papers, Garcia said: "This might be a leap. The Olson case— not his murder, but the one where he's on trial for murder—has got a priest. Future priest."

Her head jerked up. "What?"

"That family. The one Olson and his buddies slaughtered." He looked up from the file. "The only survivor was the son. He was away at college. Ended up in seminary school."

"What are you looking at?"

"Victim-impact statement. Son's name is . . ." Garcia flipped to the second page, third page, fourth page. He continued turning until he found the signature at the bottom of the last page of the lengthy hand-written letter. "Damian Quaid."

Bernadette dropped her pen, stood up, and leaned across the table. She grabbed the victim's statement, pulled it toward her, and spun it around so it was right-side-up for her eyes. Her heart started racing. She could taste the adrenaline flooding her mouth, metallic and excit-ing. Forcing herself to sit down again, she ran her eyes over the page and found neat, almost elegant script—more feminine than masculine. Her sight locked on the signature. *Damian Quaid*. She reached out to touch the name and froze. The papers were photocopies of the letter, she told herself, not the original. She'd get nothing from the writing. She went back to the first page of the statement and saw the date. "I vaguely remember reading about the case. Where would I have been back then? College? Just out of college?"

"Quaid was the first of the three kids to go off to college. He was in school in the Twin Cities when it happened. You're probably about the same age."

"Give me the CliffsNotes version," she said, nodding toward the pile in front of Garcia. "Where'd it happen? What happened? Who were the Quaids anyway?"

Garcia turned some pages, read some more, and announced: "No-body important. Mother ran an electrolysis business and beauty parlor out of the house. Dad repaired small engines and removed stumps."

Bernadette: "Sounds like the family of every kid I grew up with. If you didn't farm and you couldn't land a job in town, you did a mish-mash of things to make ends meet. Sometimes you farmed *and* worked in town *and* repaired small engines on the side. Where'd they live?"

Garcia rifled through the file until he found a narrative of sorts buried in a criminal complaint. "Quaid's childhood home was some sixty miles west of Minneapolis, between Dassel and Darwin." He looked up and added: "Those are dinky rural communities sharing a couple of thousand souls between them, if that."

"I'm familiar with dinky rural communities."

Garcia: "Family's two-story house was tucked into the woods on the north side of U.S. 12. Across the street were railroad tracks that ran parallel to the highway."

Bernadette: "Something tells me those railroad tracks are players in all this."

"Fall night. Three drifters hopped off the boxcar they'd been riding, darted across the road, and headed for the first house they saw. The Quaids' place. The front door was unlocked." Garcia paused in his recitation to offer an editorial comment. "Stupid. Why do people leave their doors unlocked?"

She smiled sadly. "In the country, even careful people leave their doors unlocked. We're naïve fools, I guess. Trust people not to walk in and butcher us."

He continued: "Using rope they'd found in the shed, they strapped husband and wife into chairs facing each other. When the robbers couldn't find the money they wanted, they dragged the daughters upstairs, raped them on their parents' bed, and sliced their throats with a kitchen knife while the girls lay next to each other. They went downstairs and finished Mom and Dad with the same knife they'd used on the daughters."

She shuddered. "Horrible."

"Then the trio went on to the next home down the road." Garcia ran his eyes down the text and turned to the next page. Grinning grimly, he said: "This is where our three friends messed up big-time. Behind door number two was a family of hunters, with their own arsenal. Two of the robbers were shot dead."

"Lovely," she said.

"The third went on trial for the rapes and murders."

"Olson. What'd he do then? Claim insanity?"

Garcia: "The more reliable and frequently used SODDI defense."

Bernadette: "Some other dude did it."

Garcia lifted a copy of a newspaper clipping and read a reporter's account: " 'Olson blamed his dead colleagues for the murders and testified that he'd unwittingly stood outside while his buddies ran amok inside. His testimony on the stand was punctuated by his own tears; he repeatedly took off his bifocals and wiped his eyes. His defense attorney also pointed to the defendant's age—at nearly fifty, he was twice the age of his late partners.' "

Bernadette: "Let me guess how this story ends. Since there were no witnesses to the slaughter, and because the defendant had no prior violence on his record, the jury gave the guy the benefit of the doubt. He was found guilty of lesser charges."

"Juries," he said flatly.

"If the defendant's a good actor and he's got a slick attorney . . ."

Garcia pointed to the file. "In this case, Olson really lucked out. I recognize the name. Didn't realize it'd been her case."

"She's that good?"

"Cut her teeth on a bunch of tough cases in the boondocks. Ditched the public pretender's office for a real job. Became a prosecutor for Hennepin County. That's how I know her."

"She's in town, then?" Bernadette returned her attention to the victim-impact statement.

"Got recruited by a law firm in Milwaukee. See her around once in a while. She's got ties here."

A dark thought crossing her mind, Bernadette took her eyes off her reading. "She a big gal by any chance? Has a thing for jewelry and nail polish?"

"How'd you know? What difference does it make if she . . ." Garcia stopped in mid-sentence as it came to him.

"Why don't I call her law firm with some excuse this afternoon? Something related to a case. That way we don't raise any alarms prematurely. All we need to do is confirm she showed up for work this week, with her right hand intact."

"St. Paul PD and our folks are already checking missing persons," he said.

"Could be no one knows she's missing yet. The hand turned up over the weekend. If she's supposed to be on vacation . . ."

"We should run it through the Milwaukee FO," he said.

"Nah. Let me deal with it. What's her name? Name of her firm?"

"We don't need to scare the crap out of anyone. The case is ancient history. It's hard to believe that after all these years, the son would—"

Bernadette cut him off. "His entire family was wasted."

Garcia tore a clean sheet off a legal pad and started writing. "Be discreet."

"My middle name."

He slid the paper across the table. She retrieved it and read it. "Marta Younges. Jansen, Milinkovich and Younges. Her name's on the door, huh?"

He snatched the paper back. "I'll make the call. I know her. I think I've got her firm's number in my cell's database."

Bernadette's mouth hardened. His mistrust of her was getting tough to swallow. "Whatever you want, sir."

"I'll take care of it right now." He pushed his chair back and stood up. "Excuse me."

He pulled his cell out of his pants pocket and walked to the living room, punching in a number as he went. He turned his back to her as he spoke into the phone. She fumed for thirty seconds before returning to her reading.

After a polite opening, the tone of the victim-impact statement took a dramatic turn. The words were beyond angry. They were furious. Vindictive. Righteous. Peppered throughout were Bible verses. Her eyes darted back and forth as she raced to take in each line. No turn-the-other-cheek stuff for this guy.

Garcia turned around and walked back into the kitchen, the cell glued to his ear. "I'm on hold," he told her.

"Listen to what he told the judge. 'I can't taste the food I eat—and I eat only to stay alive. I can't focus enough to drive a car or watch television or listen to music, let alone do my classwork. I can't sleep for more than a few hours each night. I am constantly awakened by a recurring noise. I imagine the screams of my mother and my father and my sisters as they beg for their lives.' "

She skipped a few paragraphs and went to the bottom of the page.

"Look here. He sees two reasons to live—and he ties them together in the same sentence. Plus, here's the mention of our lady lawyer. 'One night of wanton rape and bloodletting by Mr. Olson—and believe me, he was one of the killers, despite what his lying attorney says—has left me less than an orphan. I am a man alone in the world. I have no reason to live except for this religious vocation. It calls to me and pulls me out of the depths of misery. The priesthood—along with my quest for justice—gives me purpose and a mission.' "

She flipped to the last page of the statement. " 'This man—this devil—may be able to walk out of prison one day, but he will never be able to walk away from his guilt and his sin. The Lord will see that justice is served, be it in this life or the next. I only hope it is in this one so I am around to see it and revel in it. I would like to watch him suffer the way he made my family suffer. I pray he shall be compelled to give eye for eye, tooth for tooth, hand for hand, foot for foot, burn for burn, wound for wound, stripe for stripe. Most important, life for life.' "

Garcia held up his hand to quiet her. While he spoke into the phone, she glanced across the room at the square of paper she'd slapped into the middle of the white cross. *Life for life.* How had she known to write those three words? What did the phrase mean? Did it mean anything? She quickly looked away from the wall and back at her boss. He was closing his phone.

"What did her office say?"

"She was in the Twin Cities all last week. Shuttled around between friends' houses. She was supposed to drive back to Milwaukee middle of this week, in time for a deposition today." He dropped the cell back in his pocket. "She didn't show up at the office this morning. They're figuring she's still on the road, on her way in. Problem is, they can't ring her up on her cell."

Bernadette fixed her eyes on him: "Problem is, she's dead."

Twenty-eight

"Gotta take a look at this Father Quaid," said Garcia.

"Know another priest who can give us some inside info on the guy?" asked Bernadette. "Someone who's been in the business a while? Knows everybody?"

"As a matter of fact, I do." He fished his cell out of his pocket and flipped it open.

"How about you introduce me and then let me take it from there?" she asked.

"This is my parish priest I'm thinking of tapping. How about *I* ask him the questions and *you* keep slogging through the files?"

Garcia was afraid she was going to insult his pastor, step on some sacred toes. He was probably right. She'd let him make the call. Besides, the pastor was his resource, not hers. She went over to the table and sat down. "Sure."

"You keep an ear tuned," he said. "I'll try the rectory."

Bernadette watched as he sat down across from her and started punching in a number. She noticed he didn't have to look it up in his database; he knew it by heart.

He put the phone to his ear. "Scribble any additional questions and shove them under my snout."

She picked up her pen and clicked nervously while Garcia waited for someone to answer.

"Father Pete? Anthony Garcia."

Bernadette grinned. When it came to the priest, her boss was *Anthony*, not *Tony*. She dropped the pen and drummed her fingers on the table while listening to Garcia's precursory pleasantries:

"How're you doing? . . . I'm good, thanks . . . How's the planning for the fall festival? . . . Really? . . . What do you need? Maybe I can scare up some toy badges or balloons . . . Yeah. Yeah. They say FBI on 'em . . . No. No pens. Sorry."

⁕ ⁑ ⁂

Garcia lost patience with the notes Bernadette repeatedly passed under his nose. He said into the phone: "Father Pete. I've got an agent working the case. Bernadette Saint Clare. She's sitting right here. Got some questions of her own she'd like to run by you. Mind if I put her on?" Bernadette reached across the table for the phone, and Garcia held up his free hand to stop her. "Sure. We can do that. Where you want us to meet you?" Garcia listened to the priest's answer and laughed. "Maybe we can squeeze in a few frames."

⁕ ⁑ ⁂

Bernadette followed Garcia in her truck. He'd wanted her to ride with him in the fleet car he'd driven over from Minneapolis, but she despised the Crown Vic. With its no-frills government interior and dark "pretend we're not really here" exterior, the Vicky looked like a G-man with tires. Might as well slap lights on the hood and get it over with, she thought.

She had no trouble keeping up as Garcia inched through downtown

St. Paul's stop-and-go traffic. They turned onto Rice Street and took it north for less than two miles, ending up in a working-class neighborhood called the North End.

She was a little surprised when they pulled up in front of a Catholic-school gymnasium, but she didn't say anything while she followed Garcia into the blocky building. As they jogged down the stairs to the basement, she heard the distinctive clatter of balls knocking down pins. Garcia pushed the stairwell door open, and the two of them stepped into a tiny bowling alley.

She unzipped her jacket and ran her eyes around the place, a dimly lit rectangle with a low ceiling and wood-paneled walls. She counted eight lanes, half of them being used by gray-haired league bowlers. A snack bar with an abbreviated menu—pizza, hot dogs, nachos, candy bars, beer, and pop—was tucked into one back corner. Parked on stools in front of the bar were two old men, each nursing a cup of coffee. In the other back corner—the one closest to the door—was an unmanned counter with an old-fashioned cash register on top of it and shelves filled with bowling shoes behind it. The wood floors and countertops were spotless, but the place nevertheless smelled like burned cheese and the insides of old shoes.

Bernadette felt a hand on her shoulder and pivoted around to face a man dressed in black slacks, a black short-sleeved shirt with a white Roman collar, and bowling shoes. Garcia's contact.

"Agent Saint Clare?" The priest was a skinny sixty-something guy who stood even shorter than Bernadette. A halo of white hair hovered around his pink, damp face. Behind his wire-rimmed bifocals were milky eyes that looked overdue for cataract surgery.

He extended his bony hand, and she took it in her gloved one. "Thank you for taking the time, Father."

The priest released her hand and went over to her boss. The smaller man threw his arms around Garcia's shoulders. Father Pete looked like a kid hugging his dad and sounded like a grandfather chastising his neglectful grandson. "How are you, Anthony? Why haven't you come by to see me? I haven't seen you in church for a month."

"Sorry," said Garcia, his face flushing. "Busy."

Father Pete released Garcia and pointed to a lone dining table planted between the snack bar and the lanes. "I ordered a pizza and some pops for us."

Bernadette and Garcia stepped next to the table, a square of Formica surrounded by four metal folding chairs. They waited until Father Pete sat down. Garcia took a seat to the priest's right, and Bernadette sat to the clergyman's left. A few yards away, the sounds of the alley continued: Balls hitting the lanes and rolling. Pins tumbling. Bowlers hollering. The racket of pins being reset.

"How's your game?" asked Bernadette, peeling off her gloves and stuffing them in her jacket pockets.

"Not bad," said Father Pete, a grin turning up his thin lips. "I've been consistently scoring two hundred plus."

"I could use some lessons," said Garcia, unbuttoning his trench coat.

"How did you happen to end up with a bowling alley under your school gym?" asked Bernadette.

"Fifty years ago, we had a priest who liked to bowl," said the priest. "The schoolchildren love it. We've got a phys-ed unit on bowling for the junior high."

A busty, freckled waitress materialized next to the table with a greasy circle of cheese in her hands. She set the pizza down in the middle of the square. "Sprite okay, Fadder?"

"Wonderful, Elizabeth," said the priest. The young woman turned and went back to the bar. "And napkins and plates, please," he said after her.

Elizabeth returned with three cans of pop and a stack of napkins, but forgot the plates.

Bernadette and Garcia reached for pizza, but sheepishly pulled their hands away when the priest said: "Let us offer thanks."

All three made the sign of the cross and bowed their heads, but the two agents let the priest say the prayer. "Bless us, O Lord, and these Thy gifts, which we are about to receive from Thy bounty, through Christ our Lord. Amen."

"Amen," echoed both agents, again crossing themselves.

"Let's eat," said Father Pete. He picked up a wedge of pizza, folded it in half, and tucked it into his mouth.

Bernadette eyed the snack-bar clock—an oversized one that probably came from the school gym. She had to move this along. She took a sip of Sprite, set down the can, and charged ahead. "From listening to Tony's end—Anthony's end—of the phone conversation, sounds like you only know this Father Quaid from reputation. You never sat down and had a conversation with him."

Father Pete chewed and swallowed. "We never talked, but I did catch his show twice. First time, as a visitor to his church. I remember it vividly. I happened to be in street clothes, so I doubt he knew another priest was in attendance. Had he known, he might have toned it down."

Garcia: "Toned it down?"

The priest nodded and reached for another slice of pizza. "The homily. I have to give him credit for brevity. Short and to the point. No gray in his message. The Ten Commandments are not a suggestion. Break the rules and the punishment should fit the crime. The Bible is the last word. 'If any harm follows, then you shall give life for life, eye for eye, tooth for tooth, hand for hand, foot for foot, burn for burn, wound for wound, stripe for stripe . . . I will punish you according to the fruit of your doings.' And so forth."

Garcia and Bernadette looked across the table at each other. "Sounds familiar," said Bernadette.

Father Pete chomped off the point of his pizza slice, took a sip of pop, and continued. "Then he repeated the official catechism of the church: the death penalty is justified under certain narrow circumstances—if it is the only possible way of effectively defending human lives against an unjust aggressor—but those circumstances are rare or nonexistent, since the state has ways to deal with criminals."

Garcia: "I take it he didn't stop there."

The priest shook his head. "Then he laid out *the facts* to his congregation: modern society has created animals who can be stopped one way and one way only, and that is through the use of the death penalty."

Bernadette: "I assume church leadership didn't like that part of his homily."

"Not at all. He even earned himself a nasty little nickname." Father Pete took another bite of pizza, chewed, and swallowed. "Death Penalty Padre."

"Nice," said Bernadette.

"To their credit, the bishops tried working with him," said the priest, dabbing at the corners of his mouth with a napkin. "They made him e-mail his homilies to them before he delivered them, so they could edit if necessary. After a few weeks of that, they were under the assumption Quaid was back on track. They discovered he'd been sending them bogus sermons. He was still delivering his brimstone blather from the pulpit."

"Stubborn," said Garcia.

"Angry," said Father Pete. "But what really got his fanny in hot water was his lobbying."

Bernadette: "Lobbying?"

"Up on the Hill. That's where I suffered through his routine again, during a legislative hearing."

Garcia picked up a wedge of pizza and set it down on a napkin. "What was the hearing about?"

Father Pete took a drink of pop. "Every few years, one legislator or another tries to get the death penalty reinstated in Minnesota. An exercise in futility, of course. It will never happen here."

Bernadette: "Father Quaid was up there speaking?"

"In favor of the measure," said the priest.

Garcia: "And you were sitting on the opposite side of the room."

"With the archbishop himself."

Bernadette's brows went up. "What was the gist of Father Quaid's testimony?"

"If I had to characterize it . . ." The priest took another drink, set down the can, and covered his mouth for a moment while he stifled a burp. "I would describe his presentation as heavy on the Old Testament, just like his homilies."

Bernadette: "Back up for a minute. I don't get it. The Bible is the Bible is the Bible. Right? Old Testament, New Testament—isn't the message the same regarding the death penalty?"

Garcia jumped in. "Correct me if I'm wrong, Father Pete . . ."

"I always do, son."

"One school of thought says capital punishment is allowed in the Old Testament but not in the New Testament. There's another camp that says it's allowed in both books."

"Not *allowed*," said the priest. "*Mandated*. Mandated in both books. That's the position Damian Quaid took, running counter to the position of his own church. He was, in a word, a heretic."

Bernadette: "Did Father Quaid nominate any candidates for death row? Did he name any names? Get personal in any way?"

"I know he had some sort of tragedy in his life that inspired this quest of his, but I was late for the hearing and only caught the second half of his act—the part where he waves the Good Book around and rants about biblical justice." Father Pete tipped back his Sprite and emptied it. He set it down, but kept the can between his hands as he continued. "And, by the way, it isn't *Father* Quaid. Not any longer."

Bernadette: "Terminated?"

"Left the priesthood before he could be given the boot." Father Pete bent the tab of the pop can up and down.

"Hard to be both a parish priest *and* a legislative lobbyist for the death penalty," said Bernadette.

"And a prison chaplain," said the priest, ripping off the tab and dropping it in his can.

Garcia leaned back in his seat. "Why would he want to do *that* while he's up at the Capitol making a case for the electric chair?"

"Keep your friends close and your sociopaths closer," said Bernadette.

The priest eyed the pizza with only a few pieces missing. "Aren't you two going to help me out on this?"

Bernadette picked up a slice, nibbled off the point, and asked: "Know anybody who knows Quaid? Knows where he hangs out? How he makes a living these days? A friend? Relative? A guy who roomed with him in seminary school?"

Father Pete shook his head. "Sorry."

Garcia: "Where can we get our hands on some decent photos of the guy?"

"Archdiocese may have something from his seminary days or his ordination, but those would be years old." The priest took off his glasses, wiped them with a napkin, and put the specs back on his face. "For heaven's sake, Anthony. You're the FBI! Don't you people have fingerprints and DNA samples and mug shots of everybody and his uncle?"

"No recent mugs," Garcia said with a small smile. "Federal budget cuts and all that."

"One more thing," said Bernadette, setting her wedge of pizza on a rectangle of napkin. "You know if Quaid sails or rock-climbs or camps or does anything outdoorsy like that?"

"He's a large, muscular person, but I have no idea . . ."

"I was looking for some sort of knot-tying hobby," she said.

"Does macramé qualify?" asked the priest.

Garcia: "Come again?"

"He was known for his wall hangings and plant hangers and other such objets d'art. Woven crosses and whatnot. Some of the stuff even decorates the walls of the chancery." The priest paused and added, "I myself thought they were hideous monstrosities."

Bernadette: "Hideous monstrosities fit the bill."

"My understanding is, his father had been in the Navy and devoted a lot of time to fiddling with rope." The priest folded his arms in front of him. "Don't suppose you can tell me . . ."

Garcia shook his head. "Can't talk about it."

"Really must have stepped in it if he's got two federal agents on his tail," said the priest.

The waitress came up to the table with a cardboard box. "Wanna take the leftovers back to the rectory, Fadder?"

"I suppose we shouldn't waste food. Thank you, Elizabeth." The priest looked at the two agents while the young woman reached between them and started loading the carton with congealed wedges. "How about some raffle tickets? Five dollars a chance. You could win a large-screen television."

Twenty-nine

The two agents stood on the sidewalk in front of the gymnasium/bowling alley, shoving raffle tickets into their pants pockets.

"Tell me again where you *saw* Quaid," said Garcia, pulling his car keys out of his coat pocket.

"Downtown hospital," said Bernadette. "The one down the street from the old dining car."

"And he was visiting this woman who later died?"

"Yup."

"I'd like some . . ." He searched for the right phrase. "Independent confirmation that he was there."

She gritted her teeth and worked to steady her voice. "Hospital personnel," she offered.

"If we can check informally. Quietly." He jiggled his keys. "Of all the folks who work at a hospital, who would notice a controversial, disgraced priest?"

"Ex-priest," she corrected him.

"Ex-priest. Who would recognize him bumping around the hallways? Who would know Quaid right off the bat?"

"How about another priest? The hospital chaplain—I'll call on the chaplain."

"You do that." Garcia buttoned up his trench coat. "I'm heading back to Minneapolis. Gonna see if Marta Younges has shown up for work by some miracle. If not, gonna put in a call to the Milwaukee FO and tell them what's going on. What *might* be going on."

"Super Lawyer's dead," said Bernadette.

"Too early to sound an alarm." He started for the Vicky, saying over his shoulder, "Check in periodically."

"Thanks for the vote of confidence," Bernadette mumbled as she went to her truck.

      ◊   ◊   ◊

Bernadette parked on the street a block down from the hospital. She went through the front doors, cut across the lobby, and found the information desk situated in the center of the main floor. She didn't bother flashing her ID or her name, and the blue-haired hospital volunteer in the blue smock didn't ask for either. The blue lady pointed Bernadette back outside with the news that the hospital's clergyman was a clergywoman named Tabitha O'Rourke who spent some afternoons volunteering a block away, at a downtown charity clothes closet.

"Whatever *that* is," said the blue lady, using the eraser end of her pencil to push her eyeglasses up against the bridge of her nose. "Probably some kind of hippie thing."

      ◊   ◊   ◊

The blue lady was more or less correct. The charity clothes closet was located in a storefront that had once housed a head shop. A dozen psychedelic stickers advertising various brands of rolling papers, bongs, and pipes were plastered along the top and bottom of the plate-glass window. The storefront's current tenant had obviously attempted to remove the paraphernalia ads—most of the stickers had their corners peeled off—but in each case, the meat of the message had stubbornly stayed in place. *Juicy Jays Flavored Papers. Hempire: Winner of High Times Cannabis Cup 2000 for "Best Hemp Product." The Original Sixshooter Pipe.* Bernadette stepped up to the shop's glass door and paused to take in the neon-green sticker plastered at exactly her eye level. *Badassbuds—Seeds for the Connoisseur.* She pulled open the door, and a set of brass bells hanging from the top of the door announced her entrance. She walked inside, the badass door closing behind her with another jingle.

The square space reeked of unwashed bodies and mothballs, and resembled a large walk-in closet. To her right and left were clothing racks on wheels lined up parallel to the walls. Each rack had a theme. One was filled with jeans, another with jackets and coats. One was loaded with tops—shirts and blouses and sweatshirts and sweaters. Another had a meager collection of office attire—outdated dresses and a few men's suits—hanging from wire clothes hangers. Last stop was the ladies' lingerie department, a rack crammed with robes and nightgowns and slips and bras. Plastic laundry baskets, sitting on the linoleum floor in front of the racks, continued the themes: Sock basket. Baby-clothes basket. Shoe basket. Handbag basket. Sitting against the center of the back wall was a card table piled with recycled paper grocery bags. Also against the back wall, on either side of the table, were swinging half-doors like those found in department-store changing areas. The one on the left had a handmade cardboard placard taped to the top of it. *Men/Hombres.* The right one was *Women/Mujeres.* Each fitting room was occupied. Behind the *Hombres* door, two hairy, pale legs were stepping into a pair of trousers. *Mujeres* had a forest of limbs pulling on jeans; the sound of a child's giggles emanated from behind the half-door.

"Anyone home?" Bernadette yelled.

"Yes," said a female voice, sounding muffled. The lingerie rack shivered, and a tall, curvaceous woman stepped out from between two chenille bathrobes. "Can I help you?"

Bernadette hesitated, not knowing what to call a female chaplain with the unlikely name of Tabitha. "Reverend Tabby"? The woman's appearance threw her off, too. She'd expected someone who looked like a middle-aged nun, but Tabitha O'Rourke could have passed for an old Farrah Fawcett. She sported long yellow feathery hair parted slightly off center and salted with streaks of gray. Her face was too tan, especially for a Minnesotan coming off a long winter, and her teeth were the sort of bleached white that came from a box. She wore a white peasant blouse tucked into tight jeans, Birkenstock sandals, and ragg-wool socks.

Deciding to drop her own name and title before tackling the lady minister's, Bernadette pulled out her ID wallet and walked up to the woman. "I'm Agent Bernadette Saint Clare, with the FBI. You are . . ."

The woman studied the badge while she answered. "Pastor Tabitha O'Rourke."

Bernadette snapped her wallet shut and stuffed it back in her pocket. "I've got a few questions related to a case I'm working on."

The pastor crossed her arms in front of her. "What's the problem? If this is about all those pothead signs out front, that operation was shut down a long time ago, and I in no way endorse—"

"This has to do with the hospital."

"Is someone at the hospital in trouble? I should be sending you to Administration."

Bernadette whipped out her pal Nurse Big Arms as a reference. "I've already spoken with Marcia, the supervisor up on four."

"This going to take long?" She walked across the closet floor and glanced outside through the storefront glass. "I've got a truck coming in soon, and I'm here by myself."

"Are you the only minister working at the hospital?"

O'Rourke turned around. "The only one on staff, but patients have their own clergy visit."

"Would they check in with you before making their rounds?" asked Bernadette.

"Not necessarily. Some pop their heads into my office to say hello. I know many of the other religious around town . . . What's this about?"

Bernadette unzipped her jacket. The closet was an oven. "Were you at the hospital Saturday night?"

Pastor Tabitha buried her hands in the pockets of her jeans. "Yeah."

"See any other clergy hanging around?"

"Damian Quaid," she said quickly. "During one of my evening services in the hospital chapel."

"Did he say anything?"

"Not much. *Hi.* That's about it."

"You don't know why he was there? Where he'd been and where he was headed after the service?"

"No."

"Was he alone, or with someone?"

"Alone."

"Can you describe his demeanor? Did he seem upset or angry?"

"Not either one of those." She pulled her hands out of her pockets. "But, hey, I don't know him all that well. Before Saturday night, the last time I laid eyes on him was at an interfaith workshop thing across the river. Five years ago maybe. Even then, we didn't talk. We just sort of screamed across the table at each other."

Bernadette frowned. "What do you mean?"

"We were both speaking on capital punishment." She tucked a band of blond-gray behind her right ear and said smugly: "I was against it, of course."

"And he was for it."

"You got it."

The door to the women's changing stall swung open, and a plump, barefoot young woman with bobbed brown hair stepped out. Behind her trailed two toddler girls. The woman's gut was pouring out over the waistband of the jeans, and the girls were drowning in their second-hand pants. Tired pastel tee shirts topped the three. The woman looked at the reverend. "Whadya think? They're Tommies and everything."

Pastor Tabitha: "They look great, Jenna."

Bernadette eyed the pastor but didn't say anything. The trio disappeared back inside the fitting room.

The roar of a truck engine shook the building. A semi pulled up in front of the shop, the wide sides of the trailer filling the storefront windows. Pastor Tabitha pivoted around and looked through the glass. "Damnit. I told them to park in back."

"May I call you at the hospital if I have other questions?" Bernadette said to the back of the blond-gray head.

"I guess." She went to the coat rack, yanked a lime ski jacket off its wire hanger, and pulled it on. She put her hand on the door and looked back at Bernadette. "Gotta go."

"Please don't mention our conversation to anyone," said Bernadette. "This is part of an ongoing investigation."

"Let me ask one question."

"I'll answer it if I can," said Bernadette.

"You feds can seek the death penalty, right?"

"For certain serious crimes."

"I have no idea why you're going after this Quaid," said the pastor. "But wouldn't it be poetic justice if, after all his years of lobbying for capital punishment, he ends up getting executed himself?"

Before Bernadette could respond, Pastor Tabitha was out the door, a blur of green and blond.

Bernadette went over to the women's fitting room. She reached into her pants pocket, pulled out some folded bills, and peeled off three twenties. She said to the stall door: "Found these on the floor. Think you dropped them." Bernadette reached over the top of the door with the cash. The money was quickly snatched.

"Yeah, I did," said Jenna. "I did drop them. Thanks."

"Those jeans . . ." Bernadette hesitated. "They do look good on you."

"Thanks."

Bernadette turned and, with a jingle, followed Pastor Tabitha out the door.

o   e   a

Bernadette drove back to Lowertown and called her boss from her place. Garcia: "What'd you get?"

"The ex-priest was there Saturday night. Pastor Tabby didn't know why. He attended one of her masses. Services."

"Quaid was at the hospital? Saturday night?"

She was furious that he was so surprised. She swallowed hard and said: "Yeah. Just like I said."

"We need . . ."

"We need a lot before we can go after him." She didn't want to tell Garcia that she planned to go another round with the ring. With the help of Father Pete and Pastor Tabby, she'd accumulated some background on this guy. She wanted to take another trip through Quaid's eyes, using her newly acquired knowledge. It wouldn't change what she saw, but it would help her interpret it more clearly—akin to having a travel guide in a foreign city. She wouldn't hop on that creepy tour until nightfall. "I've got some ideas. Let me keep working it."

"I'm punching out," he said. "Reach me at home on my cell if anything pops."

She remembered something: "Did you get a hold of Super Lawyer?"

"No," he said. "She never showed at work."

"You called the Milwaukee FO, then? They know we're on it?"

"They're gonna work it from their end, with the local coppers." He paused and added: "They might come up with something different."

"Something different." *He still doesn't believe completely*, she thought. "Fine," she said, and snapped her cell closed.

Thirty

Sighing heavily, Noah Stannard reached under his glasses to rub his eyes with his thumb and forefinger. He was sitting at a desk, trying to reconcile the numbers in his monthly corporate bank statement with the chicken scratches in his business checkbook. His wife had been doing his accounting for years with no problem, but suddenly it wasn't working out. Checks were bouncing all over town. He had no idea what he really had in the bank, and he had to figure it out fast.

Noah Stannard was a nice guy who, for a limited period of time, and only in certain areas of his life, had had it all figured out. He correctly figured he needed A's in high school to get into a good college and had to study his ass off as an undergrad to get into pharmacy school. He figured he'd marry a woman who was pretty and a virgin when they walked down the aisle—and he did just that. He was also right when he figured that if he worked hard he'd build up his business and be able to live in a nice house and drive nice cars and take nice golf trips. Buy nice things. He even had a good read of the bedroom routine: if he ran four mornings a week and watched his diet and kept his body in shape, he'd be able to perform well enough to keep his wife happy in the sack the other three mornings a week.

Eighteen years into his marriage, Noah Stannard realized he'd made a miscalculation. His figuring had been off, especially when it came to his wife. The sex had dried up, and every time he made a move on her in bed to restart it—rubbed his foot against her leg or stroked her shoulder with his fingers—she rolled away from him like he was a leper. She was dressing strangely. She'd wear long-sleeved shirts during the day and show up for bed in flannel pajamas. In all their years of marriage, she'd only worn oversized tee shirts—or nothing at all. She used to make fun of women who slept in flannel. Now it was as if she was trying to keep her skin from being exposed to his. He'd tried to talk about it, and she'd mumbled something about "change of life" and "hot flashes." He'd asked her, if she was having hot flashes, then why in the hell was she dressing like she was freezing? She didn't answer. Clammed up.

She'd been plenty talkative during the early years of their marriage. Unfortunately, he hadn't been listening then. He was too busy getting his lab going, paying off those student loans, sweating the mortgage. He had to admit he still wasn't much of a listener. Something in the female voice—maybe its high pitch or its tone—made his mind wander. Chris would yap about the hospital and he'd struggle to concentrate, put a smile on his face, and nod. The second honeymoon in Hawaii over the winter hadn't helped the marriage. If anything, it had caused her to grow more distant, more inscrutable, less talkative. He found himself tuning out the little bit that she was saying. After they got back, she started working more hours at the hospital. He figured she wanted to get away from the house. That was fine by him.

The phone call bothered him, though. Some woman had called the house earlier in the spring and asked for Chris and then hung up. He'd pulled the number up on caller ID. He'd punched it in and got a phone in a nightclub.

"Marquis de Sadie's."

"Where are you?" he'd asked the girl who'd answered the phone.

"Minneapolis. Warehouse District. Need directions?"

He and Chris never went to the Warehouse District. That was for the young and the hip, and they were neither. Then he'd thought about the name of the bar and asked: "What kind of club is this?"

The girl had laughed and hung up.

They should've had kids, Noah Stannard figured. Kids would've made her happy. Kids would have kept her busy and tied to the house and away from his books.

He stewed about these things while he struggled to make sense of the numbers in front of him. The business should be doing better, he thought. His relationship with oncologists all over town was fabulous. They appreciated his good work. He had a greater understanding of the disease than most pharmacists, a greater sympathy for the patients. His mother had died of breast cancer when he was a teenager. His mother-in-law had died of ovarian cancer. He'd liked his mother-in-law.

He punched another set of numbers into the calculator and cursed. That couldn't be right. Was he even deeper in the red than he thought? What were these cash withdrawals? They were on his bank statement, but not in his check register. He'd call the bank in the morning. He tossed the calculator down on the desk and ran his fingers through his hair. He pushed his chair back, put his feet up on top of his desk, and folded his hands on his lap.

As he always did when he was tired, he started questioning whether running his own show was worth it. He could have signed on with a big lab, worked saner hours, and taken home a decent paycheck. He glanced at the stuff hanging on his office walls, stuff that told him a decent paycheck wouldn't have been good enough. That oak-framed Johns Hopkins degree hadn't come cheaply, nor had those nifty matted shots of him golfing St. Andrews, golfing Ballybunion. Half Moon Bay. The Greenbrier. No. A decent paycheck wouldn't have been good enough.

Stannard pulled his feet off his desk and stood up, took his jacket off the back of his chair, and pulled it on. He gathered the statements, stacking them into a pile to take the work home. She'd been going to bed earlier and earlier. He'd have plenty of time alone to figure it out. He snapped off his desk lamp and locked up his office, checking his watch as he went. Noah Stannard was a creature of habit. When he worked nights, he always made it home just in time for the start of a particular program on the Golf Channel.

He inhaled the sharp night air as he walked to his silver Mercedes sedan, one of his favorite niceties purchased with the help of the lab. His was the only car in the parking lot, a dimly lit tar expanse that sat in front of the business complex and ran along Minnesota 110. Behind the complex was a cemetery—three hundred acres of rolling land that became dark and deserted every day at dusk. A line of fencing separated the cemetery from the road, but the chain-link stopped before it reached the back of the complex. The only thing separating the businesses from the graveyard was a band of trees and shrubs. A patch of woods.

Stannard gave no thought to the woods or the cemetery or his own isolation as he shuffled to his sedan with an armload of paperwork and a head filled with numbers. He was preoccupied with trying to figure things out.

Thirty-one

Eyes closed and dressed only in her panties, she was flat on her back on her mattress. Her left arm rested alongside her body. Her right hand was curled into a ball and sat on her chest, between her breasts. So pale and cool, she could have been a corpse awaiting autopsy on a coroner's slab.

A jumpy corpse.

Each time Bernadette saw Quaid strike a blow, her fist jerked away from her body, as if it were reflexively pulling away from a hot frying pan. Her breathing was shallow and quick, a frightened animal's pant. Her lids were closed tight, but a trickle of water managed to escape from the outside corner of the left eye. Maddy's blue eye.

She sees Quaid holding the guy up with one hand and cranking back the other, winding up for another punch. Before Quaid can take his swing, the guy folds and goes down on the ground. Quaid stands over the man, nudging him in the side with the tip of his shoe. She wonders if the guy is dead. Hard to tell—he's facedown in the grass. Where is this place? It's the woods at night. Is she seeing in real time? There's a light coming from somewhere, shining down from up high and casting strange shadows. The moon? No. Too bright. The guy lifts up his head. Quaid cranks back his right foot and rams it forward. He kicks the guy in the side. Another kick. Another. The man curls into a tight ball and covers his head with his arms. Quaid's still kicking. Kicking. Quaid picks the guy up and drags him to his feet again. Even in the dim of night and with her cloudy vision, she can see the man's face is a mess. He's got a triangle of raw meat where his nose used to be, a bloody hole instead of a mouth, red running down his windbreaker. There's embroidery or printing on the jacket. Is it the guy's name? The name of his workplace? Anything that could be a guide? Quaid yanks him by the front of the jacket, pulling him closer. She can make out the letters. *Stannard Pharmaceuticals. Remember that name,* she tells herself. Quaid lands another punch in the face. The guy's head flips and flops on his neck like a newborn's. There's no fight left in him, no resistance. A second slug from Quaid. A third. She notices for the first time—the bastard is wearing gloves. Quaid lets go of the guy, and the man goes down on his back. Quaid turns away from the guy. Is he finished? No. He bends over and picks up two objects: a bundle of rope and an ax.

◦   ◦   ◦

Bernadette did something she rarely had energy for while using her curse of sight. She screamed: "No! God! An ax!"

An instant later came pounding on her door and an alarmed male voice, calling for her by her nickname: "Cat! Cat!"

"No!"

Three thumps were followed by the sound of splintering wood as Garcia kicked in the door. He took two steps inside and froze. The loft was pitch-black except for a band of white spilling in from the hallway behind him. "Cat!" He turned around and fumbled along the wall next to the door, seeking a switch but feeling only Post-its. He gathered a fistful of papers in his hand and ripped them down in frustration. His eyes followed the hallway light. He could see the twisting staircase and went for it. He put one foot on the first rung, looked up, and yelled, "Cat?"

"An ax! God, no!"

"Jesus!" Garcia took the steps two at a time. When he got to the top, he reached into his jacket and pulled out his gun. He put his left hand ahead of him to feel around as he shuffled forward in the dark. His legs bumped the side of the mattress. He leaned over and, with his free hand, felt around.

The surprise sensation—his warm, rough hand clamping over her bare shoulder—startled her and interrupted the private screening of the horror movie. Her right fist unfolded and released the ring. The jewelry tumbled off her body and landed on the mattress. As her eyes cleared, she spoke his name—not in surprise or relief but as a flat statement of fact, a recognition that he was there with her in her bedroom. "Tony."

"You're alone?"

"Yes," she answered.

"Thought someone was chopping you up," he said into the blackness. He holstered his Glock and sat down on the edge of the mattress.

"Sorry I scared you." She forgot her own nakedness and sat up. "Quaid's taking another one. I just saw it. I have no idea who. Where. Some poor guy. In the woods. But I got the name of a company off the guy's jacket. Maybe his employer. If we can call and find out where he's supposed to be tonight . . ."

He stood up. "Sure it wasn't a bad dream?"

"Dammit!" she spat. "You think I don't know the difference between . . ." She realized she was about to take her boss's head off for no good reason. The murderer's emotions were boiling around inside of her, and she had to regain control. She took a deep breath, let it out, and said in a low voice: "No. It wasn't a bad dream."

"The name of the company."

"Stannard Pharmaceuticals."

"Get dressed. I'll make some calls from downstairs. If I get something, we'll hit the road with it."

"Good. That's good."

He pivoted around and stumbled over something in the dark. "Where in the hell are the light switches in this attic?"

"Don't move. You'll fall overboard and end up with a broken neck."

"Pleasant image."

"I'll flip on a couple of the overheads." Her face grew hot as she realized she wasn't wearing a bra. She felt around the mattress, found her sweatshirt, and yanked it over her head. When trying the sight at home, she sometimes undressed to help her relax quicker and get to it easier. It had worked this time, and she decided it was worth a little embarrassment. She reached down, felt her abdomen, and was grateful she'd kept her Jockeys on. She slid off the mattress, her feet landing on a pile of clothes. She stepped into her jeans and frantically pulled them up over her hips. She had no idea what Garcia could and couldn't see.

"I'm waiting," he said.

She shuffled to the far end of the narrow space and felt the set of switches to the right of the porthole. She flipped both of them up. Her sleeping loft and the area at the bottom of the steps were illuminated by the ceiling's recessed can lights. She turned around and saw him going down the stairs. "Be careful," she said to his back. "Keep a hand on the railing."

"I'm not an old lady," he snapped without turning around.

She remembered the ring. She went back to the bed and found it and the plastic bag on top of the mattress. Using the plastic to shield her hand, she picked up the ring and turned the bag inside out. She crammed the package in her pants pocket.

"The name again," Garcia yelled from downstairs.

"Stannard Pharmaceuticals," she yelled back. She closed her eyes and spelled it out loud from memory.

"Got it," he hollered. "Hurry your ass. Grab your piece. In case this pans out."

"In case this pans out," she snarled under her breath while she pulled on her socks.

She reached for her sneakers and stopped, went back to the bed, and sat down on the edge of it. Bernadette twined her arms around her gut and bent in half. The killer's emotions were still raging through her body like a high fever. The rush of someone else's feelings made her weak and wobbly and confused. She was angry—not unusual when she was recovering from seeing through a murderer's eyes—but at the same time, she wanted to bawl her eyes out. Fury and sadness. What was that about?

⊙   ⊙   ⊙

When she came down the steps, she saw Garcia sitting at her kitchen table with his cell to his ear and a pen in his hand. He finished writing, closed the phone, and stuffed it in his jacket. Without making eye contact with her, he said, "We'll take my POS. It's parked out front."

The right side of her mouth curled up into a satisfied smirk. "So it panned out?"

"Found a company by that name. Called it. Got a recording. The guy leaving the message identified himself as Noah Stannard. Called the after-hours number and Stannard's residence. Both times, got a machine. The house message says, 'Chris and I aren't home.' I assume Chris is the wife. Then tried the pharmacy again. Still got a recording. I say we go to the Stannard house, bang on the door. See if we can scare up the guy or the wife and get some info about lab employees."

"No," she said. "Let's try the pharmacy first."

He opened his mouth to argue with her and then closed it. He ripped the sheet of paper off the pad, crammed it inside his jacket, and got up from the table. "Ready to roll?"

She grabbed her bomber off a chair and pulled it on. She took her gloves out of the jacket and slipped them over her fingers. "Ready."

Thirty-two

Mendota Heights was a twelve-minute drive from downtown. He piloted his piece of shit—a white Pontiac Grand Am with a dented driver's door and a primed front-left-quarter panel waiting for a paint job—onto Shepard Road. She squinted through the windshield, which had a foot-long crack snaking horizontally across the passenger's side. With every bump in the road, the crack seemed to grow an inch toward the driver's side. "Where'd you get this heap of yours?"

"Police auction." He steered around a slow-moving minivan. "It's loaded. Faster than it should be."

"I can see that."

He was taking a left, turning onto Interstate 35E heading south, before Bernadette realized she had no idea what had brought him to her place that night.

"Why'd you come over?"

"To see if you wanted to grab a beer. I know it's late, but I couldn't sit still at home. Too much rattling around in my head. This case . . ."

"I know what you mean." Another question occurred to her: "How'd you get into the building? When you came up with the hot dish, too—I didn't buzz you in that time, either. Has some guy been letting you in? My neighbor Augie is the only sign of life I've seen in my building."

Garcia frowned at her. "Augie?"

She eyed her boss, the odd look he flashed her. Maybe Garcia and Augie had a history. Better not tell her boss too much. "August Murrick. He's a lawyer. Bumped into him in the hallway and again at the Farmers' Market. He said he's had some federal drug cases. I take it you know the guy, that he's the one who let you in."

"I don't know who let me up. A couple of your neighbors. You should talk to them about letting strangers into the building, especially so late at night." Garcia paused and then continued. "Murricks are a big family around town. They're all lawyers and developers and financiers. Which Murrick are you talking about?"

"Augie."

Garcia gave her that look again. "That's not right. You've got the name wrong."

"It's really August. He told me to call him Augie."

Garcia blinked. "Must have been another Murrick who moved in. August Murrick is—"

"Maybe I got it wrong," Bernadette interrupted. She just wanted to drop it. She didn't want to hear about any bad blood between her boss and Augie. She was already in turmoil over sleeping with the guy.

She kept her mouth shut and didn't say anything else until they were steering onto Highway 110 in Mendota Heights. "Should we try calling the lab again?"

"Go for it. My cell's on the seat between us. Pharmacy's the last number I punched in."

She picked up his phone, flipped it open, and hit redial. She put the phone to her ear and listened to a male voice giving the pharmacy's address and asking callers to leave a name, phone number, and account number. Then the voice gave an after-hours phone number: "If this is an emergency, call me—Noah Stannard—on my cell at . . ." She snapped the cell shut. Her hand—the hand that held the phone—grew cold. The chill spread up her arm, crawled down her throat, and landed in her gut like a deep drink of ice water. She knew the man in the recording was the one she'd witnessed getting beaten. Dropping Garcia's phone on the seat, she asked: "Can't you go any faster?"

"I'm already flying."

She believed what she'd seen was in real time, but she couldn't be sure. There'd been no clock or watch. She wondered if she should pull off her gloves, whip out the ring, and give it another go right there in the car. An instant later, she told herself she'd never get a decent result; she didn't know why she'd bothered bringing the jewelry with her. She was exhausted and wired at the same time. She wished she was driving; she wanted something to do. "Should we call for backup? Clue in the cops?"

Garcia steered around a station wagon. "Let's wait and see what we come up with here. At this hour, could be there's nobody at this lab place."

"You think this is a wild-goose chase."

He passed a Volkswagen Beetle that seemed to be standing still. "I didn't say that."

"You're thinking it."

"So you're a mind reader, too," he said dryly.

She snapped her head back and forth, looking to the right and left along the highway. "Did we miss our turn? I think we're headed in the wrong direction."

"Taking a back way in." He hung a squealing right at the next intersection, sped down the street, and hung another right.

The collection of commercial buildings running along Minnesota 110 was deceptive. Behind the businesses were nice homes surrounded by old hardwoods, massive pine trees, and empty fields. The suburb resembled a patch of countryside. As if to reinforce that impression, a deer suddenly stepped into the middle of the road in front of the car. She pointed through the windshield. "Tony!"

"I see it." He braked, and the car skidded to a stop ten feet from the animal. The deer stared into the headlights and then finished its trip across the road, disappearing into a stand of trees between two houses. Garcia took his foot off the brake, and the car rolled forward a yard.

"Wait," said Bernadette, searching the darkness around them. "There's gotta be more."

He stopped the car again and eyed both sides of the street. Sure enough, two more deer galloped across the road, following the first. He waited a few more seconds and then applied the gas, continuing on a little slower.

As they approached the next intersection, the car lights shone ahead to an expanse of mowed land. "Golf course?" she asked.

"Graveyard," said Garcia.

"Now I see the headstones," she said. The largest monuments— towering crosses and statues—seemed to glow with their own light.

He braked at the corner and looked up and down the road. No cars. No surprise. It was late on a work night in a quiet suburb. He hung a right. "Pharmacy should be coming up on the left, after the cemetery. At the top of the hill."

As they shot up the incline, Bernadette glanced back over her shoulder. The higher vantage point gave her a view of a cemetery pond, a spot of water circled by tall grasses. Where had she seen that pond before?

She turned her head back around. Her eyes followed the fencing on the left as it went up the hill. On the other side of the chain-link, she saw row after row of chunky headstones, boxy soldiers standing guard over the dead. At the far end of the cemetery, near where the fencing stopped, she saw a stone figure standing alone at the top of the incline. A statue perched on a pedestal.

The robed woman who'd visited her dreams days earlier, while she was unpacking at the office.

"Tony."

"What?"

"Pull over."

They were nearly at the crest of the hill. He slowed but didn't stop. "Where?"

"Here. Now."

Garcia jerked the Pontiac over to the right, parked on the shoulder, and punched off the headlights. He yanked the keys out of the ignition and shoved them in his pocket. "Where're we going?"

She pointed at the statue, straight across the road from the car. A nearby streetlight illuminated that end of the cemetery, as well as the edge of a swatch of woods that ran between the graveyard and the business park. "That's where we want to be."

"You sure? Did you see something?"

"Yeah."

Garcia reached under his seat and fished out a flashlight. He held it up and clicked it on and off. "Want it?"

"You take it. I've got great night vision. Plus, there's plenty of light from the street."

"Okay." He shoved the flashlight in his coat pocket. He threw open his door and hopped out. He closed the door and stood next to the Pontiac, waiting for her to come around to his side. Together, they jogged across the street and went down into a ditch that ran between the road and the cemetery. They crouched in the tall grasses. Garcia peeked over the tops of the weeds and took stock of the area immediately around the statue. The ground was mowed and clear of shrubs and trees. The monument was flanked by its own lighting—Roman columns topped by white globes as big as beach balls and as bright as floodlights. No place to duck unless someone was huddled against the statue's pedestal. He tipped his head toward her and asked in a low voice: "What're you thinking? Our guy's hiding behind the statue of the Virgin Mary?"

She squinted into the night. "Not behind the monument. In the woods next to it."

"What're we going to find?"

Was he expecting some sort of instant psychic reading? No. He still doubted her. More likely, he was just thinking out loud. She gave him her best guesses. "Fairy-tale ending: Quaid is standing over the dead guy, admiring his handiwork while he wipes his ax off in the grass. We've got him cold. Real-life ending: Quaid's long gone, and all we've got is the dead guy. No fingerprints. No weapons. A shoe print. Maybe. If we're lucky."

"There's no possibility there's a live guy?"

She thought about the beating. Quaid picking up the rope and ax. Even if what she'd seen had been in real time, they were too late. "No possibility."

He pulled out his piece. "I'll go into the woods from the street side."

She took out her gun. "I'll go in from the back of the commercial buildings."

Garcia crawled out of the ditch and headed for the woods. Bernadette stayed in the weeds and ran through the ditch, following the road up to the business complex. Climbing out of the ditch, she jogged onto a narrow strip of mowed grass that ran between the business center and the woods. She stopped and took a breath. She was grateful for the yard lights mounted against the one-story building behind her. They and the streetlight helped her search for a gap in the greenery, a likely entrance for a man dragging another man. Spotting what she was looking for, she dashed between some trees.

She followed a dirt path that sliced a straight line toward the graveyard. She guessed business-park workers had worn the trail when they'd trekked to the cemetery for lunchtime walks. As she ran, she scanned the wall of trees on either side of her. To her right, she saw a narrower trail forking off from the main one, and took it. The secondary path spilled into a clearing that would have been big enough to accommodate a picnic table. In the middle of the circle of dirt and flattened weeds was a hump of clothing.

Noah Stannard.

Thirty-three

She holstered her gun and went over to him.

Like the judge, the pharmacist was bound with rope and missing a hand. Packaged as tight as he was, and on his back with his legs straight out, he resembled a mummy laid to rest in the woods. As she went down on her knees by Stannard's left side, it struck her that her run through the woods had been too well illuminated. The yard lights and streetlights alone couldn't have shone her way so brightly. She looked up. Her view traveled above the tree line and stopped at the cemetery's edge. She saw the tops of the lamps planted next to the Virgin Mary. Twin globes. The twin moons from her dream. The chill started creeping back into her body like a virus trying to wear her down. She shook it off and returned her attention to Stannard.

She yanked off her right glove, reached over, and felt his neck for a pulse. Nothing. His face—or what was left of it—was turned toward her. She could see he wore glasses; they'd fallen off and were in two pieces on the ground, next to his head. She didn't know why, but the sight of the busted frames appalled her more than the spectacle of all the blood. "What did you do to deserve this?" she whispered.

She withdrew her hand from his neck and sat back on her heels. Scanning the ground around the body, she didn't see a weapon or a footprint or any other piece of evidence. The crime-scene guys—be they from the bureau or a local agency—would have to go through their routine. Did she have the time and the energy and the power of concentration to do her thing before Garcia stumbled across her and the body? What could she hold? The ring again, or something from this murder? Then she remembered: Quaid had wised up and worn gloves. Too bad. Something from Stannard's slaying would have felt right, would have brought her closer to this victim. No matter. She reached inside her pocket and pulled out the bag.

In the woods behind her, she heard a crunching noise. Bernadette quickly shoved the bag back in her jacket, stood up, and pulled out her gun. Garcia ran into the clearing with his flashlight in one hand and his Glock in the other. "Cat!"

"Real-life ending." She holstered her weapon and stepped to the side so he could get a full view of the body on the ground behind her.

"That's what I figured. Almost stepped on his hand in the woods." He shone the beam at the name embroidered on the front of the jacket. *Stannard Pharmaceuticals.* "You really did see something," he said, a hint of awe in his voice. He shoved his flashlight in his jacket but held on to his gun. Looking past her and the corpse, Garcia peered warily into the trees.

She knew what he was thinking. "Forget it. He's long gone."

"Let's make sure." He nodded toward the business park. "Let's check out the dead guy's office."

She took out her gun and followed him out of the woods. While they ran, Garcia called for assistance.

◊   ◊   ◊

They circled the business center and found nothing. All the entrances were locked; the guy had closed up shop before Quaid took him.

The two agents hunkered against the side of the building. "Now what?" asked Bernadette.

Garcia pointed toward the parking area. As the two of them jogged toward the lot, sirens could be heard in the distance. "Here comes the gang," said Garcia. As he and Bernadette stepped onto the tar, he ran his eyes up and down the highway, searching for flashing lights.

"Which gang? Whose case is this, boss man?"

"You shouldn't have to ask. With all the weirdness in this case? The way it crosses jurisdictions all over the place. Dead judges and dead businesspeople. It's yours, lady."

She pointed to a car sitting alone in front of the building, under a lot light. "Victim's vehicle."

"Mercedes. Nice."

They went up to the sedan, locked as tight as the building. On the ground next to the driver's side were a set of car keys and a scattering of paperwork. Garcia and Bernadette crouched next to the papers for a closer look. "Bank statements," she said. "Stannard's name is all over them."

"Think the killing's connected to money?"

"Only marginally—if at all. This rampage ain't about getting rich. It's about getting even the Old Testament way."

Garcia stood up and put away his gun. "An eye for an eye."

She stood up and holstered her Glock. The sirens were closing in. She glanced in the direction of the woods. "Let's get back to our pharmacist before the Marines land. I want to show you something strange in the eye-for-an-eye department."

⁕ ⁕ ⁕

She knelt by Stannard again. "Check out the hiccup in Father Quaid's MO."

Garcia went down next to her, took out his flashlight, and trained the beam on the stump. "Wrong hand."

"Yup."

Garcia shrugged. "Maybe it's because he's left-handed."

"Could be."

He clicked off his flashlight and shoved it in his jacket pocket. "Another unpleasant question for the guy's wife. *Was* he left-handed?"

"Stannard's definitely married?"

Garcia nodded. "He had a band on his finger."

"Wonder if they've got kids," she said.

"If they've got kids, they're minus one parent."

Her jaw tightened. If Quaid were in front of her at that moment, she would have cut his head off. "I'd like to pick up the scumbag now, but on what grounds do we hold him? The evidence I've collected is . . . um . . . usually inadmissable in court. Otherwise, all we've got is a shoe print. I suppose we could interview the husband of that Fontaine woman and—"

Garcia interrupted her. "Let's drive over to Quaid's place right now and see if he's got anything we can use."

She got up off her knees. "We know where he lives?"

"After I left your place this afternoon, I went back to the office and dug into the driver's-license database. Tapped some of our massive federal resources." Garcia pulled a scrap of paper out of his pocket.

Bernadette watched him tipping the square this way and that so he could read it by the shine of the cemetery- and streetlights. While she'd been searching for Quaid her way, Garcia had been doing some digging using his own tools. They'd make a good team, if only he could learn to take her seriously *before* the bodies started turning up.

"It's a St. Paul address," he announced. "Cathedral Hill neighborhood, I think. Could be a bogus address. Old address. Father Pete said he'd heard the guy had moved back to the sticks after he left the priesthood. But who knows? We could get lucky. There are those rare occasions when you ring the doorbell and the one you're looking for is the person who answers."

"Happens every day on television," she said.

They heard what sounded like a bull barreling through the woods. Overhead, a helicopter hovered. "Our crew's here," Garcia said. He stuffed the address back in his jacket and took out his car keys. "Let's brief the gang and then hit the road."

"What if he doesn't come to the door when we ring? We don't have a—"

He raised his hand and interrupted her. "Don't worry about it."

Bernadette: "Because we're the fucking FBI."

Thirty-four

○ ○

Startled by the tap on her apartment door, Chris Stannard almost dropped her drink. Had Cindy forgotten her key again? She checked the clock on the microwave oven. The numbers were out of focus. She squinted and concentrated on the glowing digits until she could read them. Too early for Cindy to be showing up.

The voice on the other side of the door: "Reg Neva. Open up before I wake the neighbors."

"Okay, okay." She took a fortifying gulp of liquor, set her glass down on the kitchen counter, and tightened the belt around her robe. Opening the door, she peered through the gap. "What do you want?"

"We agreed to meet here tonight."

"Gimme a minute." She closed the door, went over to her nightstand, and reached inside her purse. Taking out her perfume, she dabbed a dot on her throat and rubbed a line of scent between her breasts. She went back to the door, moving her hand to unlatch the security chain. She hesitated. Had she agreed to get together with him tonight? Could be. She couldn't remember. She took down the chain and let him inside. She closed the door after him, quickly combed her hair with her fingers, and turned around to face him. Resting her back against the door, Chris took in his figure. Through her dizzy, whiskey eyes, he looked even better than before. He smelled good, too. Sweat and the outdoors. Too bad he didn't want her. She wished she still had that whiskey in her hand.

He folded his arms in front of him. "I just came from your castle in Sunfish Lake."

She didn't like hearing that. "What the hell were you doing there?"

"Looking for you."

Two questions swam through the alcohol and floated to the top of her head. *If we'd agreed on meeting here tonight, why had he tried the house first? How did he find the house?* She blurted the second question out loud: "How'd you find my house?"

"The address was all over your husband's business papers. Sunfish Lake's down the highway from Mendota Heights." He smiled. "Easy to find."

"Excuse me a second," she said numbly. She really wanted that drink. She went back into the kitchen and retrieved her tumbler. The ice was melted. She opened the freezer, pulled a handful of cubes out of the plastic bag, and dropped them into her glass.

"We need to talk," he said.

"So talk." She eyed her glass. Too much ice; now she needed more whiskey. Chris snatched the bottle off the counter and poured.

"Come out here and look at me."

"Did you do it?" Resting one hand against the edge of the counter, she waited motionless in the kitchen for the answer.

A long silence before he said, from the other side of the screen: "He's dead."

His two words sent a rush of excitement through her body. She opened the cupboard and took down a second tumbler. She fished another fistful of ice out of the freezer and plopped the cubes into the fresh glass. She picked up the whiskey bottle and held it in front of her face. Getting a bit low. She filled his glass halfway. She weaved around the screen with a drink in each hand. Passing one to him, she said: "Bet you could use this."

He went over to her bed and set his glass on her nightstand. "We need to talk."

"You already said that." While she took a long drink, she inspected his clothes. Dark spots on his jacket and jeans. Red dots on his sneakers. Scuffs on his gloved hands. Signs he'd been in a battle. Another emotion started invading her body. Guilt. She fought the feeling. Rattling the ice in her glass, she said evenly: "He put up a fight."

He clasped his hands behind his back. "It's late. Where's your daughter?"

Setting down her own glass and reaching to pick up his, she kept talking as if she hadn't heard his question. "If you don't like the hard stuff, I've got some wine. Red or white?"

"Your daughter."

She took a sip of whiskey and attempted to feign confusion. "What daughter? What're you . . . ?"

"*What daughter?* That's exactly the question your husband asked— as I was executing him." He leaned against her mattress. "Tell me," he said. "The truth this time."

Screw it, she thought. He'd find out eventually, and there was nothing he could do about it. The deed was done. "Threw the daughter in as an extra. For a little sympathy."

"Clever."

She worked to make her voice sound light. Carefree. "A toast. To sympathy for the devil." She raised her glass and spilled on the carpet. A stain on the white; she'd clean it up in the morning. She put the glass to her lips and drained it.

"What part of your story was true, then?"

Chris felt her belt start to loosen, but she didn't move to tighten it. Maybe he'd get a peek at something under her robe and get distracted. Stop asking so many questions. She threw her shoulders back. "What do you mean?"

"What part of your story was true?"

"The part where Noah's a self-centered pig."

"Your husband watering down the meds was . . ."

"Fiction."

"It sounded so real. Detailed."

He sounded and looked calm, so she kept going. "Oh, it happened all right. In another state. With another medicine man. Not with my guy. My honest, boring golf guy. He'd never have the imagination."

"The bruises?"

"My girlfriend. We like it rough."

"The Cindy on the phone."

"You got it." She reached to set the glass on the nightstand and missed. The tumbler hit the floor with a thud.

"You lied." He added as an afterthought: "And you're . . . a *lesbian*."

"Bisexual. Get it right, Padre." She turned her back on him and headed to the kitchen, swaying as she went. Her shoulder bumped the edge of the screen before she disappeared behind it. She opened the cupboard and took down a third glass. She'd skip the ice this time. She emptied the remains of the bottle into the glass.

"Was Anna in on this? Was Anna one of your . . . conquests?"

The glass in her hand, she walked around the divider. "I liked Anna. I really did. I told you. She opened up to me. She was sick, and she opened up to me."

"So you befriended a dying patient and she told you about me, about my mission. You concocted this story and fed it to her—all so you could get to me."

She was spilling out of her robe, but her visitor was showing no interest. She was starting to get pissed off about it. She told herself he was obviously put off by her sexual orientation. *You're . . . a lesbian.* He'd hardly been able to say the word. *Was Anna one of your . . . conquests?* Sanctimonious asshole. She'd rub it in a little. "My *lover* cooked up the big lie, actually. She used to rep for a drug company. Very smart woman, my *lover*."

"Two smart women taking advantage of a naïve dying woman."

Chris put the glass to her lips and tipped it back, swallowed hard, and shuddered. When she came up for air: "We had our reasons. They were good reasons, Padre."

"Stop calling me that." He got up off the edge of her bed and stood straight and stiff.

"Fine." She went over to the windows and looked outside while sipping. *My late husband,* she thought. *I have to start using that phrase now. He deserved it. Noah deserved it. We had our reasons. They were good reasons.*

"God doesn't like liars," hissed the man behind her.

She wanted to tell him to get the hell out, but she resisted. "Yeah, well . . ."

"No man who practices deceit shall dwell in my house; no man who utters lies shall continue in my presence."

"Give it a rest. Beating the drum for the death penalty, the holy-mission crap—that's just an excuse. You like killing assholes. Blowing off steam. What a hypocrite you are, Padre." She emptied her drink in one last gulp and turned to face him. She suddenly noticed how hardened his face had become. Attempting to soften her words, she threw herself in his camp. "But, then, we're all hypocrites, aren't we?"

"The words of their mouths are mischief and deceit; they have ceased to act wisely and do good. They plot mischief while on their beds; they are set on a way that is not good; they do not reject evil."

She didn't know what he was saying, and it frightened her. He took a step in her direction. Her eyes darted from his face to his leather-clad hands and back to his face. "You'd better leave now."

He took another step in her direction. "Why?"

She backed away from him. "Cindy's going to be showing up any minute."

Another step. "Good. She's in for a big surprise. Big surprise for the big liar. The big *lover.*"

Her back bumped the wall. "I'll scream."

He kept coming. "And alert the police? Is that what you want? Maybe they'll let you and your lesbian share a cell."

She hurled the glass at him. He dodged, and the tumbler hit the floor, shattering. He stepped up to her, stood inches from her. She could see the tears streaming down his face, and that terrified her more than anything else he'd done or said. "Why are you crying? Stop crying." She raised both her palms to try to keep him away. Fend him off.

He brushed her hands away with a sweep of his arm. "Stop talking." His right hand shot up, and the vise clamped around her throat. "I don't want to hear you talk."

Weeping, he dragged her to the center of the room, away from the windows.

Thirty-five

When Garcia and Bernadette couldn't rouse Quaid by ringing his apartment from the lobby, they used the phone to call the caretaker.

"What?" rasped a male voice.

Bernadette noted the name over the buzzer: "Mr. Lyle. We're with the FBI. We need to get into a tenant's place."

Lyle: "Lemme see some identification."

She took out her ID wallet and held it up to the surveillance camera. Garcia followed suit. "Okay?" she asked into the phone.

"I can't see nothin' with this damn equipment," Lyle said. "Come back when it's light out."

Bernadette: "We need to get in now."

"It's the middle of the night."

Bernadette: "Sir. You could be charged with—"

Before hearing what he could be charged with, Lyle interrupted: "Meet me topside." He hung up and buzzed them in.

Bernadette's nose wrinkled as she and Garcia hiked up the stairs to the third floor. The place smelled musty and perfumed at the same time. The inside of an old lady's purse. The stink fit the building's frumpy look. The stucco exterior of the cube was painted a dated aquamarine, as were the hallway walls and ceilings and radiators.

Lyle was waiting for them, standing barefoot in the middle of the corridor outside his apartment. His bathrobe barely fit around his barrel middle. His gray hair hung in two braids, a red bandana was wrapped around his forehead, and a gold stud dotted his left earlobe. He looked like a fat Willie Nelson. At his side, his fist was wrapped around a baseball bat. The tip was down, but the guy looked prepared to bring it up quick. The two agents stopped short of swinging distance and held up their wallets again. Lyle studied their badges and photos while scratching his stubbly face with his free hand. "Good enough," he declared. He relaxed his grip and rested the business end of the bat on top of his foot. "So whose tits are caught in Uncle Sam's wringer?"

Garcia: "We need to check out Damian Quaid."

"Why?" Lyle asked.

Garcia: "Can't say."

The caretaker's eyes widened. "Is it bad enough that I should be throwing him out on the street come morning?"

Garcia: "Can't comment on that."

The guy said to no one in particular: "I knew that geek was up to no good."

Bernadette: "Sir, we'd like to get in."

Lyle tucked a stray strand of hair behind his ear. "I suppose I should be asking you for a search warrant or some such thing. Being the feds, I'm sure you've got all your ducks in a row on that rigmarole."

The agents didn't say anything.

"Not that I'm pals with that individual downstairs. Wouldn't mind getting rid of him and putting something normal in there."

Garcia lifted his wrist and checked his watch.

Lyle: "You guys can't tell me what he did, huh?"

Bernadette shook her head.

"Don't move," said the caretaker. He padded into his apartment, closing the door behind him. A minute later, he opened the door and handed Bernadette a key. "Basement efficiency, across the hall from the laundry room."

"Anyone else living down there?" she asked.

Lyle shook his head. "Just the hermit and the Maytags. His door's the one with the cross on it. I caught him slapping one of them things on the laundry-room door and I told him to take it down. My washing machines are nondenominational."

Garcia: "Don't suppose you know if he's home."

The guy shrugged. "Saw him take off earlier. Didn't notice him come back in, but who knows? Like I said, me and the geek ain't exactly tight."

Bernadette: "Could be a while. What should we do with the key when we're through?"

The caretaker covered his mouth and yawned. "Lock up. Slide the thing under my door."

"By the way—keep this visit of ours under wraps," said Garcia. "It's a matter of . . . national security."

"Sure it is," Lyle said dryly. With his thumb and index finger, he made the zipper sign across his lips. "Mum's the word."

Lyle shut the door. The agents heard him dead-bolt it and slide the security chain into place.

Bernadette looked at her boss as the two agents went down the stairs. "I think people are getting jaded. Bored with that particular excuse."

"National security?"

"Yeah," she said. "Overused."

"Come up with another one if you want."

Their feet touched down in the basement hallway. Bernadette drew her weapon and said in a low voice: "I'm starting to favor that pen slogan of yours."

"Because we're the fucking FBI." Garcia unsnapped his holster and took out his Glock. They headed down the corridor, sticking close to the wall. Their way was dimly lit by a lone lightbulb dangling from a broken ceiling fixture in the middle of the hallway. The air was warm and moist and reeked of fabric softener. The old lady's purse had morphed into an old lady's clothes basket. They got to the laundry room. Light peeked out from the bottom of the closed door. Bernadette squatted with her back against the wall on one side of the door, and Garcia did the same on the other side. They listened, heard nothing. Garcia nodded. She pivoted around, put her gloved hand on the knob, and turned. Pushed the door open. The brightly lit room was filled with machines, but empty of people. She gently pulled the door shut.

They moved across the hall and took their places, one on each side of the crucifix door. They saw only a dark band along the threshold. Hunkered down, Bernadette put her ear to the wood but heard no movement on the other side of the door. She knocked twice and held her breath. Silence. She slipped the key in the hole and turned. The click of the dead bolt seemed loud enough to alert the entire building. The agents froze, waiting for a reaction from someone inside the apartment. When no one came to the door, she wrapped her hand around the knob, gently turned, and pushed the door open.

The apartment was a black, lifeless cave—with the exception of one light, one bit of movement coming from a computer monitor tucked into a corner. Three words repeatedly crawled across. Damian Quaid's screen saver: *Life for life.*

While Garcia navigated across the floor by the glow of the hallway light, Bernadette felt the wall alongside the door. She touched a light switch and flipped it up.

Behind her, Garcia gasped. "Take a look at his wallpaper."

Thirty-six

⸙ ⸙

Bernadette went to Garcia's side and stood at his shoulder, taking in the newspaper and magazine clippings. She put away her weapon. "Why did I expect to see something like this?"

Garcia holstered his gun. "Let's do some speed-reading."

She stepped to one end of the wall, and he went to the other. The two stretched and bent and shuffled their feet, moving toward the middle while they read. "People who paper their walls like this tend to end up on those cable-TV crime shows," she said.

"What?"

"Never mind. Just repeating something a neighbor said the other day."

After several minutes, Garcia stood straight and stepped back. "As far as I can tell, these charming felonies have nothing to do with our man—or with each other, for that matter. They're all unrelated."

She got on her hands and knees to read a clip that brushed the floor. "They're all horrible crimes."

"Beyond that, I don't see any common denominators. They aren't even local. They're from all over the place."

Bernadette got to her feet and dusted off her knees. She stepped back to take in the whole thing again. A couple of recent high-profile murders were excluded from Quaid's wallpaper job. Absent were the kidnapping and butchering of a pregnant woman in Texas by her ex-husband, the rape-murder of a teenage girl in Florida by a neighbor, and the California killing of twin toddlers at the hands of their mother. Stories from other states were missing as well. Why collect news from some locales and not from others? What trait did the states on the wall share? It suddenly occurred to her. She pointed to individual clippings in the collage. "Minnesota and Wisconsin. That one tacked way up there, near the ceiling, is from Iowa. The two below it are from Michigan. Alaska. One out of Hawaii. Michigan again. More out of Wisconsin. The states in his collection have one big thing in common."

"What?"

Bernadette: "They don't have the death penalty. Nearly every state *without* capital punishment is represented."

"I don't see Vermont. And what about—"

She interrupted him: "The missing ones probably haven't had a juicy murder recently."

Garcia lifted up the corner of a Detroit triple murder to read what was behind it. "You're right. Here's an abduction and murder out of Rhode Island." He let go of the scrap. "Think he's got plans to branch out to these other states?"

"Not if we have something to say about it."

"Right about that." Garcia peeked under another clip and another. Some were four layers thick. Four murders deep. He kept talking while he read. "On the other hand, you have to wonder if Quaid's right. These scum should get drawn and quartered. Personally, I'm a big fan of the death penalty."

"So we should let him go about his business. Play judge and jury and executioner and God and whatever else he wants to play."

"I didn't say that. I can see why Quaid thinks they should get what they deserve. That's all. Why should some piece of garbage walk around—live and breathe and eat and take a dump at taxpayer expense—while his victims are six feet under? Hell. Some of them don't even get time. Look at the judge. Don't you tire of the bad guys getting off so light?"

"I see what you're saying." She was tired of looking at the newspaper wall. Too depressing. She turned around and stared at the other walls, decorated with a motley collection of crosses and icons. The crucifixes were plastic, and the tapestries were the sort of rags sold by street vendors. The velvet painting of the Last Supper would have been right at home next to a velvet Elvis portrait. Quaid's basement efficiency reminded her of the bargain basement of a religious bookstore. She blurted something she'd normally contain in her head: "All this Catholic paraphernalia. My mother would have loved it, God rest her soul."

Garcia pulled his eyes off the collage and snapped his head around to stare at her. She stared right back and asked him: "What?"

He returned his attention to the clippings. "A spiritual utterance out of your mouth. You don't seem particularly religious."

She was offended. "I was raised Catholic, you know."

He turned away from the wall and pointed to the computer. "Think you can do anything with that? You know how those boxes work better than I do."

She ran her eyes over the monitor. It looked tempting—a treasure chest waiting to be cracked open. Memories of her past rash decisions at crime scenes—and the discipline that resulted—reeled her back in. "I'd hate to accidentally mess up some evidence."

"Your call," he said.

She thought Garcia sounded disappointed. "I don't know spit about computer forensics," she added.

"Don't worry about it. Let's snoop around the Vatican the old-fashioned way." He pulled some gloves out of his jacket and snapped then on. He started with the furniture, getting down on his knees and checking under the couch. "Pretty clean for a bachelor pad."

She went over to a weight bench, parked against one wall with dumbbells and barbells on the floor around it. "He keeps in shape."

"Girlie weights," spat Garcia without turning around. "I saw that equipment when we walked in."

She eyed the bar positioned over the bench and added up the numbers stamped on the side of the round plates. "Counting the bar itself, I'll bet he's pressing close to two hundred pounds."

"I do that in my sleep."

She went over to the apartment's only closet and pulled open the door. A row of footwear covered the floor. Each sneaker or dress shoe was with its mate, and all the pairs were lined up with toes pointing to the back of the closet. Over the shoes, a solid wall of clothes hung from a bar. The short-sleeved shirts were together, facing the same way. Then all the long-sleeved shirts. Then the slacks. Last came the blazers. "I wonder if he'd come over and do my closets."

Garcia crawled to his feet and stared at the rope art hanging on the wall behind the couch. "Did you catch this? The knot-tying that you were talking about. That Father Pete confirmed."

"I noticed," she said, still eyeing the jammed but neat closet. Most of the stuff was black or gray. Even if Quaid was no longer a priest, he was dressing like one. A flowery panel of material hiding amid the dark ones caught her attention. Wrestling it out of the wedge of clothes, she held the oddball up by the hanger. She blinked three times before her eyes registered that it was one of those aprons beauty salons draped over customers to protect their clothing.

"Find something?" asked Garcia. He went over to the kitchen and started opening and closing drawers and cabinets.

"Apron from a beauty parlor." She crammed the drape back into the closet, making sure she returned it to its spot between the blazers and the slacks.

Garcia opened the refrigerator and held his nose while he looked inside. "Apron? Wonder what the hell that's about." He closed the refrigerator and opened the top freezer compartment.

She glanced over at him. "Any body parts on ice? A hand or two?"

"Frozen peas and fish sticks. Blue Bunny Rocky Road."

She took down a jacket hanging from a door hook and checked the pockets. Found only lint. "What's the worst thing you ever found in a freezer?"

He lifted up the bag of peas and pushed aside the box of fish sticks. "Does a walk-in freezer count?"

"No. That's really a room." She hung the jacket back on the hook.

"Chest okay?" He started to close Quaid's freezer door and then reconsidered. He reached inside and retrieved the ice-cream bucket.

"Works for me." She crouched down and lifted the lid off a shoe box. Empty.

"Found a guy and his parrot in a commercial chest freezer. Frozen solid. It was a Mafia thing." He wrestled with the ice-cream bucket's slippery top. "Your turn. Worst thing ever. Same rule. Chest freezer or fridge freezer. No walk-ins."

"Fridge freezer. A guy's privates."

Garcia grimaced. "Ouch."

"At first I thought it was fake. You know."

He stopped struggling with the lid for a moment and looked at her with raised brows. "Fake?"

"One of those hollow dildos people fill with water and stash in the freezer." She quickly added: "I only know about those because I went to a bachelorette party. Instead of regular cubes in the punch, they had ice shaped like penises."

"Hilarious."

She frowned. "Where did I leave off with this? Oh yeah. The guy's ex-girlfriend separated the guy from his privates after she killed him. Then the psycho took the penis home with her." Bernadette pushed aside the shoes and felt around the back of the closet, behind the wall of clothes. She sat back on her heels and looked over at Garcia, who was working the lid again. "Found it in an ice-cream bucket, as a matter of fact. An empty pint of Ben and Jerry's."

"I'll be really impressed if you can remember the flavor."

"Chunky Monkey."

The top popped off, and Garcia looked inside. "No hands. No parrots. No penises. Not even a frozen dildo." He snapped the lid back on the bucket and returned the container to the freezer.

She got up off her knees and stood on her tiptoes to check the shelf over the clothes bar. Sweaters and sweatshirts, folded into neat rectangles and stacked like sandwiches. "I'm coming up with a whole lotta nothing so far."

Garcia headed for Quaid's bathroom. "I'll see if the john's got any goodies."

"Grab some hair while you're in there," she said after him. "Got a bag for it?"

"Yes, Mom." He walked through.

She closed the closet. "Anything jump out at you?"

"A woman's dressing table," he said from the other side of the bathroom door. The sound of dresser drawers being opened and closed.

"Weird." She crossed the room to investigate a collection of electronic equipment he had parked in a corner. A cheap television set sat on a wobbly stand. Next to that was a cheap stereo system. On the floor next to the stereo was a CD wallet. She picked it up and paged through it. Classical religious music. Bach. Handel. Mozart. Beethoven. A smattering of country gospel by Tennessee Ernie Ford. Some religious sets by Elvis. The score from *The Passion of the Christ*. None of it was to her taste. She closed the wallet and set it down.

Bernadette turned around and looked at the computer monitor again, gritting her teeth, as Quaid's self-righteous screen saver scrolled across repeatedly. "Maybe I *could* check out the history of his Web searches. That shouldn't mess up anything too badly. I hope."

"What'd you say?" Garcia called from the bathroom.

"Nothing." She walked over to the desk and sat down on the edge of the office chair. She reached for the mouse and stopped, contemplating the gloves on her hands. No. She didn't want to take them off; she wasn't ready to use her curse of sight. Not now, not here. She needed her energy to concentrate on regular investigative work. She pulled the leather tighter over her fingers.

"We gotta move this operation along," Garcia said, poking his head through the bathroom doorway. "Our guy could show up any minute."

"Something tells me we have some time," she said over her shoulder.

He watched her cup her hand over the mouse. "Change of heart?"

"Yeah."

Garcia popped his head back inside the bathroom. "It's your show, Cat."

"Maybe this time it really is," she said in a low voice. She rolled the mouse and noticed what was under it. The pad showed a man dressed in a dark suit and tie topped by a dark hat and sunglasses—like one of the Blues Brothers guys. The words printed across the pad read: *On a Mission from God.*

"Delusional maniac."

She jiggled the mouse again, and Quaid's desktop appeared, as spare as his apartment. Only a handful of icons on the screen, and all neatly stacked to one side, on the left. At the bottom of the totem pole was his e-mail. She wondered if she could check it without messing up anything. She braced herself, set the cursor over the icon, and opened his mail.

"Zip," she said. Nothing in his out basket. Nothing in his in basket. Even his wastebasket of deleted mail was empty. Either he never corresponded with anyone, or he'd been meticulous about cleaning out his files. The bureau's computer geeks would have to dig deeper. She hit the "X" on the top right of the screen and returned to the desktop.

She clicked on the Internet Explorer icon and it opened to Google. She moved the cursor to the top of the screen and clicked on the arrow curled in a counterclockwise direction. The history icon.

The screen split, with Google still open on her right and Quaid's Internet history on the left. She stared at the hunk of screen on her left. "Son-of-a-gun," she said, louder than she intended.

Garcia came out of the bathroom, stuffing a plastic bag in his pocket. "What?"

"His history—what he's looked at while on the Net—is cleared except for today."

Garcia stood behind her, with a hand on the back of her chair. "Do most folks know how to do that? Why would they do that? Who would do it?"

"A guy surfing for some porn would do it, so his wife or his girl-friend or his officemates wouldn't see what he's been into."

Garcia: "Why would a guy living alone erase his history?"

"Maybe he's just naturally neat and meticulous and anal and secre-tive," she offered.

"Or maybe he's worried about getting caught one day," he said.

"Today could be that day." As she moved the cursor to Quaid's In-ternet file folders, she sensed her boss leaning over her shoulder, breathing down her back. "Tony."

"What?"

"Why don't you keep sniffing around this joint while I poke around here? When I'm done, I'll give you the executive summary. It won't take long, since I've only got today's history." She checked her watch. "Soon to become yesterday's history."

He took his hand off the chair. "I'm making you nervous."

"Hell, yes."

He resumed his sweep of the apartment.

⊘　⊘　⊘

Fifteen minutes later, she summoned him back. "Tony."

"Be right there." He dropped a cushion back on the couch and went over to her. He took his former position, with one hand clamped over the back of her chair. He glanced at the monitor. The screen saver was back on; she'd already finished. He took his hand off the chair and took a step back, shoving his hands in his jacket. "What'd you come up with?"

She spun around in the office chair and faced him. "Quaid did some checking on Stannard. Most of it seemed superficial. He just plugged in the guy's name. Looked up some professional stuff. An article Stannard wrote for a medical journal. A piece on cancer treatments."

"What else?"

"He also looked up OxyContin."

"Powerful medicine."

"If we assume Quaid is continuing his pattern of punishing bad guys, then maybe this means the pharmacist was dealing the drug."

Garcia folded his arms in front of him. "Doesn't seem serious enough for Quaid's biblical-justice bit."

"Maybe a kid died after taking the drug. Could be Stannard wasn't even dealing. He filled a prescription wrong, and then someone croaked."

Garcia shook his head. "Doesn't feel right."

"Quaid was checking out the wife, too. 'Chris' was the name you heard on the machine, correct?"

"Yeah."

"Quaid plugged in Chris Stannard's name and then a Smith Avenue address and then the name of this building in St. Paul, which is located at aforementioned address. West Side Artists' Block."

"I think our next stop should be the West Side Artists' Block," said Garcia.

"I agree." She pushed the chair back from the desk and stood up. That's when she noticed the fat envelope sitting on the desktop, tucked next to the base of the monitor. "What have we got here?" She picked it up and pulled out the flap.

"What is it?" asked Garcia.

She reached inside and carefully extracted the green stack, holding it up for Garcia to see. "Think he's been dipping into the collection plate?"

"What size bills?"

She set the envelope on the desk so she could flip through the layers. "Hundreds. Lots of hundreds. Few thousand bucks total, at least."

"Could be our holy man's got some folks funding his overall scheme. Bunch of pissed-off rich guys who wanted that death penalty passed."

She picked up the envelope and examined the front and back, but found no writing or markings. She sniffed the white paper and wrinkled her nose. "What should I do with it?"

Garcia: "Leave it. We've got to come back to the Vatican with the proper paperwork."

She slipped the stack back into the envelope, tucked in the flap, and returned the envelope to its spot on the desk. "A perfumed envelope with money. I don't know why, but I don't think we're talking group financing here."

Thirty-seven

Passing the Smith Avenue building, they scanned the storefronts on their right. "Doesn't look promising," grumbled Garcia, taking in the row of dark windows as he drove.

Bernadette snapped her head around and looked over her shoulder while they continued south on Smith. "There's a light coming from the second story, on the end."

He looked in the rearview mirror. "Could be there's apartments above the artsy-fartsy shops. Let's check it out." He slowed the Grand Am and hung a right and another right, parking the Pontiac on the street in the residential neighborhood one block over.

The pair approached the shops from the back, jogging onto a tar strip behind the stores. The lot ran the length of the complex, but was only wide enough for two rows of cars. The back row had a set of cars and pickups lined up one after another. The two agents slipped between a sedan and a truck parked on the end.

Bernadette counted the vehicles. "If you figure one parking spot for each unit, there must be six apartments upstairs," she said in a low voice.

They heard a crack and ducked down. More cracks. The noise stopped for several seconds and then resumed. "What is that?" Garcia rose from his squatting position and squinted into the darkness. A floodlight was mounted against the building near the roofline, but it was dim and dirty.

Bernadette straightened up and ran her eyes around the parking lot. The racket stopped and then picked up again—with a gust of wind. She pointed to the rear of the building. "Now I see it. Back door. Wind's banging it. Someone left it open."

Garcia drew his weapon while he eyed the door, situated less than fifty feet from where they were standing. Whenever the door blew open, a faint light became visible from the other side. "Someone was in a hurry."

"A hurry to get inside, or a hurry to leave?" She unsnapped her holster and drew her Glock.

He darted out from their hiding spot, and she followed. They ran up the short stoop and went inside, leaving the door flapping behind them. Garcia flattened himself against one side of the stairwell, and she hunkered against the opposite wall. Their eyes went to the top of the steps. They saw only a naked bulb hanging from the ceiling by a frayed cord. The bulb danced and blinked as the door banged and a breeze rolled up the stairs. Beyond the bulb was an open door. Garcia whispered: "The hallway for the apartments."

He took the stairs slowly, hugging the wall as he ascended. She did the same on her side. When they were halfway up the long, steep stairwell, the slamming stopped. In unison, the agents turned their heads and looked to the bottom of the steps. Bernadette trained her Glock at the closed door and waited. The door stayed closed.

They resumed their climb, the bare wood creaking with each step they took. They got to the top of the landing and went through the doorway. They were in the middle of a dingy corridor painted the same aquamarine as the hallway of Quaid's apartment building. Instead of a musty perfume odor, however, they detected another stink. An old ladies' beauty shop. Garcia looked to the left, and Bernadette to the right. Each counted three doors. Garcia leaned into her ear. "Your pick."

Her eyes were pulled to the right, to the apartment at the end of the hall. It had a white door, whereas all the others were stained brown. "The white one. That's the unit that we saw lit up from the street."

He followed her down the corridor. When they got to the end, they stood with their backs against the wall, one on each side of the white door. That's when Bernadette saw the smudge on her side of the doorknob. A dot of red spotting the white. Pivoting around, she cranked her foot up and brought it down on the bottom quarter of the door.

Garcia jumped next to her. "Again. On three. One, two, three." They kicked in unison, and the door slammed open.

Thirty-eight

Her eyes were wide open, and so was her mouth. Red stained her lips and chin and throat and the front of her bathrobe. The blood had dripped down her neck and formed an oval puddle on the rug beneath her.

Garcia maneuvered around the body and checked behind the kitchen screen while Bernadette took the bathroom. They met back at the body, one standing on each side. Garcia took out his cell and called for an ambulance and assistance. He snapped the phone closed and dropped it back in his jacket pocket. Keeping his gun in his hand, he glanced through the open doorway into the hall. "I'm going to do a sweep of the rest of the—"

She cut him off. "Do what you want, but he's gone. We were too slow." She paused. "I was too slow."

His jaw stiffened. "We got here as soon as we could."

Bernadette holstered her gun and nodded toward the woman on the floor. "Not soon enough to help Mrs. Stannard."

"We don't even know if that's who we've got here."

"Let's solve the mystery," she said, tipping her head toward the purse on the nightstand. She reached into the bag, fished out a wallet, and flipped it open to the driver's license. Holding the open wallet in front of his face, she said: "Chris Stannard." She snapped it closed and dropped it back into the purse. "Mystery solved."

"Watch the attitude, Cat." He disappeared into the hallway.

She inspected the apartment from where she was standing. The coppery smell of blood was mixed with another stink that frequently permeated murder scenes: booze. On the nightstand, next to the purse, she spotted a drinking glass with a quarter inch of amber liquid and ice in it. The dregs of a cocktail. On the area rug, between the nightstand and the body, was a tumbler on its side. Halfway across the room was a broken glass on the wood floor. Something had happened in the middle of the room. A drunken fight between Stannard and Quaid? Another smell was sandwiched between the booze and the blood: stale perfume. The vanilla scent from the envelope in Quaid's apartment. Chris Stannard had given him the money. Why? Was Quaid blackmailing her, or was she bribing him? Was Quaid little more than a paid assassin? She hoped not; it would make the case much less intriguing.

She went down beside the corpse, her knees at the top of Stannard's head. She ran her eyes over the length of the body. The woman wore white anklets, dotted with red that was undoubtedly her own blood. Her legs were bare. The bathrobe was wrapped around her upper body and tied with a belt, but the robe had fallen open below the knot. She was wearing baggy cotton briefs, not the kind of thing women usually wore under their jeans. Too bulky. The panties sure as hell weren't worn for a romantic encounter, either. They were the kind of comfortable clothing women slept in, especially when combined with ankle socks. Stannard might have willingly let Quaid into her place, but she hadn't been expecting him. She was getting ready to hit the sack.

Bernadette looked over at the bed and its linen, so frilly and feminine. It had to be the woman's bed alone, her apartment alone. Had she and her husband split up? Was it over the drugs? How had Quaid gotten involved? Why was the wife targeted in addition to the husband? Were both tangled up in narcotics? Or did Quaid go after them for something unrelated to the OxyContin?

Peering down into the woman's face, Bernadette noticed there were no cuts or bruises around Stannard's eyes or on her forehead. All the blood came from the mouth. A lot of blood for a cut lip, or even a knocked-out tooth. She leaned forward and looked down into the woman's gaping mouth.

Garcia materialized in the doorway. "Neighbors didn't hear squat. No yelling or screaming."

"I'm not surprised," she muttered while her eyes stayed focused on the woman's mouth.

As he holstered his gun, the sound of sirens again peppered the night air. "You know, we don't even know if it was him. MO is all wrong. No rope. No missing hands."

Bernadette sat back on her heels. "No tongue."

He stepped into the apartment. "No shit?"

Bernadette scanned the floor around the body. "I wonder what he did with it?"

"Why would he start in on tongues?"

She glanced back at the dead woman's face. "Maybe she said something he didn't like. Something sacrilegious. Sinful."

"Doesn't sound serious enough for our holy man. There's gotta be more to it. Quaid's set his revenge bar higher than that—he's been going after killers and sex fiends. And how does her killing tie in with the husband's murder?"

Bernadette folded her arms in front of her. Sirens sounded right outside the apartment's windows. "The money in Quaid's apartment—how about the obvious? She paid Quaid to kill her husband?"

Garcia held up his hand. "Stop. How do we know the wad was from her?"

"The stink on the envelope in Quaid's apartment. I smell the same perfume here."

"Why does she have Quaid kill her husband?"

"Who knows what marital turmoil they had going on." Bernadette threw her hand toward the bed and the apartment beyond it. "Obviously, if the woman had her own place, they were having problems. Maybe he had a girlfriend. She had a boyfriend."

"Then the murder-for-hire arrangement turns sour. Holy Man comes over here for more money and doesn't get it."

Bernadette: "I still don't think this was about money."

"Okay. Comes over for something else and doesn't get it. Whatever. Fights with Mrs. Stannard. Kills her. Cuts out her tongue."

The thump of feet down the corridor. Bernadette and Garcia looked toward the open door while whipping out their identification. A big blond uniformed cop with a square haircut stuck his head through the door without stepping into the apartment. He eyed their badges and photos. "Hey, FBI."

Bernadette and Garcia together: "Hey." They closed their wallets and stuffed them back in their pockets.

The blond cop struggled to focus on one of Bernadette's eyes, gave up, and looked at Garcia instead. "Got a woman in the squad. She was getting out of her ride while we were pulling up. She's all worked up. Might have had a little something to drink, too. Says she owns one of the shops downstairs."

Garcia: "Tell her the stores are okay. She can come back in the morning and check for herself."

"That ain't why she's worked up." The blond cop's eyes went to the floor, but he didn't say anything about the body.

A second officer—a young guy with red hair—poked his head into the apartment. He spotted the woman on the floor. "Damn. She ain't significant no more."

Bernadette: "What?"

The blond cop: "The shop lady says her 'significant other' lives up here."

The agents looked at each other. The right side of Bernadette's mouth curled into a crooked grin. "There's our boyfriend. Except she's a girlfriend."

Garcia to the blond cop: "What's the shop lady's name?"

The officer reached into his jacket pocket and pulled out a notepad. Looked at it. "Cynthia. Spelled with a 'y.' Holmes, like in the detective books."

"Do me a favor," said Garcia. "Take Sherlock's sister to the station and park her in a room for us. Give her a cup of coffee. Would you do that, please?"

The redhead, his eyes still on the corpse: "What should we tell her?"

Garcia: "Don't tell her a thing. We'll deal with it. Okay?"

The blond shoved his pad back in his pocket and gave them the thumbs-up. He and the redhead turned around to leave.

"Hold on, guys," said Bernadette.

The two officers pivoted back around. The blond: "Yeah?"

"What's the problem?" Garcia asked her.

Bernadette to the cops: "Bring her up here. Don't tell her anything. Just bring her up. And don't let anybody else come up. Not our people or yours. I want you two and the shop lady and that's it."

The redhead's brows went up. He glance down at the body again, and up at Bernadette. "You sure?"

"I'm sure," she said.

"Whatever you want," said the blond. He patted his partner on the shoulder, and the two of them turned around and thumped back down the hall.

Garcia: "You think Sherlock's sister is involved?"

"Up to her significant eyeballs."

Thirty-nine

Cynthia Holmes backed out of her lover's apartment, fell to her knees in the hallway, wrapped one arm around her gut, and vomited. She was a tall reed with olive skin and short black hair that hugged her head like a bathing cap. She was younger than Chris Stannard by a dozen years and was decked out in a younger woman's accoutrements: Biker jacket and tight jeans. Doc Martens on her feet and a layer of makeup on her face. With her head down—hiccupping and crying and puking— Holmes looked like a teenage boy sick after his first drunk. She smelled like a drunken teenager, too. The pink vomit reeked of fruity alcohol.

The redheaded cop stood on one side of the kneeling woman, and his blond partner stood on the other. The officers were stone-faced while Bernadette and Garcia questioned Holmes.

Bernadette: "What happened here, Ms. Holmes? Who killed your girlfriend?"

"She's not my girlfriend," Holmes said to the floor. "I don't know her."

Garcia: "What happened, Cynthia? We're here to help."

"I don't know," the woman hiccupped. She raised her torso and looked into the apartment. She folded back down, vomited a second time, and resumed her crying.

Bernadette stepped through the doorway into the hall. She stood at the sobbing woman's head. "Sit up, Ms. Holmes."

"Nooo," sobbed Holmes.

"Sit up and look at me," Bernadette said to the top of the woman's head. Holmes stayed bent, her shoulders shaking.

Garcia walked out of the apartment and stepped next to Bernadette. The sympathetic dad's voice: "Look, Cynthia. You screwed up. Tell us about it and we'll go easy on you. Let the county charge it out."

Bernadette: "Make us work for it and we'll nail your ass to the wall, Ms. Holmes. Federal charges. Federal time. Federal prison. Big law."

Garcia: "Your choice, Cynthia. Tell us what happened. Maybe it wasn't your fault. This was all Mrs. Stannard's idea. You went along for the ride. Hell, you even tried to talk her out of the scheme."

"That's not what Mr. Stannard told us, of course." Bernadette eyed Garcia, waiting for him to jump in with a contribution.

"He said this was all your doing," said Garcia.

Holmes's shoulders stopped shaking. She wiped her nose with her hand and then wiped the hand on the thigh of her jeans. "He's alive?"

Bernadette: "Your hired hand didn't finish the job."

Garcia, getting into the yarn: "Mr. Stannard knew about you, Cynthia. He knew about this apartment. He'd followed Chris here once."

"You're full of shit," Holmes snarled. "He didn't know jack."

"Then how'd we know to come here?" asked Bernadette.

Holmes hiccupped once and slowly righted herself, until she was sitting on her heels. She twined both arms around her middle. She kept her eyes closed and her head turned to one side while she spoke. Her mascara had run, and a black line sliced from the bottom of each eye down to her cheeks. "Chris hated his guts. She wanted to get rid of him but still keep his money and his house. It was *her* plan. I told her we didn't need to take him out, that we didn't need his money. But my girl likes to buy stuff."

Garcia: "How'd your girl recruit help?"

Holmes opened her eyes but kept her head turned. "She met this woman in the hospital. A patient."

Bernadette interrupted: "The patient's name."

"Anna something," Holmes said, sniffing. "Last name started with an 'F.' "

Bernadette: "Go on. We're listening."

"This Anna person told Chris about a priest who went after bad people. Punished them the way they're supposed to be punished." Holmes turned her head and looked up at the two detectives. "If you know what I mean."

"The priest's name," said Bernadette.

"Reg," said Holmes. "Reg Neva."

Garcia frowned. "What?"

"It's Danish," said Holmes. "At least, that's what he told Chris."

"How did Chris convince this Reg that her husband was bad?" asked Garcia.

Holmes offered a small, satisfied smile. "When I was working as a drug rep a few years back, I heard about a pharmacist. In Florida or California or someplace. He got rich watering down cancer drugs and reselling them. Real asshole. Beat his wife and daughter. On top of all that, he was an addict. Stole prescription meds."

Bernadette looked at Garcia. "There's the OxyContin."

"Keep going," Garcia told Holmes.

"Not much else to tell," said Holmes. "Chris lifted the story and made it her pussy husband's story. She turned around and told it to this Reg Neva."

"Only problem is, looks like your hired hand found out about it. Figured out you used him. A couple of geniuses, you and Chris."

"This Reg," said Garcia. "Think if we pulled together some photos you could pick him out of the lot?"

"Never laid eyes on him." Holmes looked from the face of one agent to the other, and then at the cops flanking her. "This was all Chris's doing. She met up with him. Set it all up."

Bernadette stepped off to the side so the dead woman on the floor was again in Holmes's direct line of sight. "How fortunate for you that Mrs. Stannard is dead now. Can't defend herself."

"Fuck you! I loved her!" Holmes yelled. She crawled to her feet and stumbled backward, hitting the wall.

"You loved her so much you went out and started celebrating her husband's death without her," said Bernadette. "Isn't that right, Ms. Holmes?"

"He *is* dead? You fuckin' liars. You pieces of shit. You played me. You fucking . . ." Holmes halted her diatribe and glared at Bernadette. "You got a weird look, lady. Somebody punch you in the eyeball?"

Bernadette threw out her own jab. "Were you and Reggy in on this together? Are you supposed to meet him somewhere later? Or maybe he was your drinking buddy tonight. Your bed buddy. You a switch hitter, Ms. Holmes? Were you screwing him on the side?"

Holmes reached into her jacket and pulled something out, drew back her right arm, and lunged for Bernadette. "FBI cunt!"

Bernadette grabbed Holmes's raised wrist with her left hand. The two cops moved in to help. "Back off," barked Bernadette. "This one's mine." The agent plowed her right fist into the woman's stomach. Holmes gasped and dropped what was in her right hand—a hunting knife. Bernadette kicked the blade off to the side, twisted the woman's wrist, spun her around, and slammed her face into the wall. Bernadette forced Holmes's wrist up toward her shoulder blade.

The woman hollered into the wall: "Get off me! FBI cunt! I want a lawyer. You hear me? I want a lawyer! I'm not saying shit until I talk to a lawyer!"

"Take the lady to the station and hold her for us," Garcia told the officers. "Tell the rest of the crew they can come up and do their deal. And tell the crime-scene guys we're missing a tongue."

"A tongue," repeated the redheaded cop.

"A tongue?!" Holmes howled.

Bernadette said into the woman's ear: "That's how your hired killer repaid his lying clients."

"I didn't hire him!" Holmes started squirming.

Pushing the woman's wrist tighter against her back, Bernadette said: "Don't move."

Holmes froze. "Okay, okay."

Bernadette let go of the woman's wrist and stepped away.

"Behave yourself," the blond officer said to Holmes's back. He snapped the cuffs on the woman's wrists and spun her back around. He and his partner each took an arm and walked her down the hall.

"I want a lawyer," Holmes bellowed.

The agents turned around and together looked through the open doorway at the corpse on the floor.

"We sure this Reg Neva is really Quaid?" asked Garcia.

"Spell it backward," said Bernadette. "It's too easy. He must have thought the gals were really stupid."

Garcia ran the letters through his head. "Arrogant scumbag."

Bernadette: "Let's put out a bulletin for Quaid and post some people to watch his apartment."

"You think he's headed back to the Vatican?"

"Doubt it," she said. "The earlier killings were planned. This thing with the woman is clearly a cluster: broken glass on the floor, booze everywhere, tons of blood. This one could have him worried. If he's got a brain in his head, he won't go home."

"Where is he, then?"

She took a bracing breath and slipped her hand inside her jacket pocket. "I'll have to go see."

Garcia folded his arms in front of his chest. "I want to watch how this works, Cat."

She opened her mouth to respond, to fight him on it. His expectant expression made her change her mind. "Fine," she said brusquely.

"What do you need? What can I do?"

She eyed him. He was serious; he really wanted to help. "You think that priest pal of yours would open up shop for us?"

Forty

Reg Neva is on the run. Bernadette sees his fists locked around his steering wheel. Those big hands of his are bare; he's removed the killing gloves. Quaid's attention keeps shifting from the view through the windshield to his rearview mirror. He's worried about being followed or stopped. He slows and brakes as the rig in front of him stops. Blinking signal lights on the semi tell her the truck is hanging a left, but the driver must wait for opposing traffic to go by. With yellow lines running down the middle, and vehicles braking to turn, this isn't a freeway. The semi trucks and steady traffic indicate it's not a side street, either. Must be a highway. Quaid drums his fingers on the steering wheel while waiting for the truck to turn. He looks in his rearview mirror and to the right, steers around the semi, and resumes his drive. His eyes dart to the dashboard. He's monitoring his speed, because too slow or too fast would draw attention. Quaid's in a hurry, but he's being careful.

What borders the road he's driving? Woods, maybe. Too dark to tell. Doesn't help that he's focused on driving instead of sightseeing. Ahead is an illuminated area. A city? A sign is coming up by the side of the road, just outside this place. The name of a town or a village? Quaid pays little mind to the sign, so she can't make out the words as he rolls past. Not a very large place, whatever it is. Could be nothing more than a collection of businesses at an intersection. She finds nothing familiar or telling about the buildings. Quaid cruises through, and now the place is in his rearview mirror.

Traffic has thinned. Bernadette sees no headlights from opposing cars. She spots no taillights from vehicles in front of Quaid. This has to be a rural area, she thinks. He's relaxing. He's stopped checking his rearview mirror and has increased his speed. His right hand leaves the steering wheel to fiddle with the radio buttons. Maybe he's listening for news reports on the killings. No. He pushes a CD into the car's player and cranks up the volume. Clearly he's more relaxed—and cocky.

Slowing to make a right turn. Quaid's headlights shine down a driveway. Before she can get a decent look at the surroundings, he brakes, puts the car in park, and snaps off the lights. He stays sitting in the car, blackness all around him. She knows this blackness, remembers it from her childhood. It's a blackness impossible to find in the city. Quaid's frozen behind the wheel for such a long time, Bernadette thinks he intends to sleep there.

He throws open the driver's door and swings his legs outside. Standing up, he raises his eyes heavenward. He's looking for stars, but there are none visible. This is a cloudy night. Windy, too. She can distinguish the tops of the trees, skeletal arms swaying and reaching for the sky. Turns around and digs under the driver's seat, searching for something. He pulls it out and examines it by the car's dome light. What is it? A handgun. Quaid puts it in his pocket. More rummaging under the seat. A flashlight. *Good,* she thinks. Better to see. He shuts the car door and walks with the flashlight, punching it on and aiming it yards ahead of him. Where in the hell is he? Heading for a house. Bernadette wonders: Whose house? Where? No address on the front. He's looking around him as he heads for the steps. It's an older two-story home surrounded by trees. He's hiking up the front stoop, shining the beam ahead of him with one hand and fingering something else with the other. What is he fingering? Keys. Quaid shoves them in the lock, pushes the door open, and steps through.

He runs the beam around the inside. It's a walled front porch. Weird front porch. A handful of foggy mirrors are spaced along the back of the rectangular space. Quaid turns around and secures the door behind him. Jiggles and pulls on the handle to make sure. Yes. Definitely locked. He's very careful—or fearful.

He pivots around, leans his back against the door, and closes his eyes tight. Resting? Thinking? He opens his eyes and, in a couple of strides, steps up to the next door. Quaid shoves the key in the lock and turns. He pauses, hand wrapped around the knob. He isn't moving. Is he afraid of going inside? Why? What's inside? He pushes the door open and steps over the threshold.

Quaid's swaying side to side, as if he's going to faint. If he passes out, she could lose the connection. Is he stoned or drunk? No. He was fine while he was driving. Perhaps the exhaustion has caught up with him now that he's stopped running. Maybe he's crazy. Hallucinating. Is it his emotions? Something about this place? He's better now. Steadies himself. Shining the light around the room. Furniture covered with drop cloths and bedsheets. Could double for the inside of a morgue or a haunted house. Whose house? Where is it? How can she find it? The lights go on. She can see much better. The place still looks right out of a horror flick. The set of a B movie.

He turns around and cranks the dead bolt, locking the door behind him. Navigating around all the drop cloths and heading into the dining room. A tarp covers a large piece of furniture—probably the dining-room table. He's flipping on more lights as he goes. He's afraid of the dark. Afraid of ghosts. *Be afraid,* she thinks. The more lights the better.

He's in the kitchen, switching on lights. He goes to some cupboards over the counter, to the left of the sink. Opens the door and takes down four tins. She can't read the labels. He goes into a drawer under the counter and takes out a can opener. From another drawer, he pulls out a fork. He knows his way around this kitchen. Opens the cans and shovels the chow into his mouth. Rinses the empties before tossing them into the trash can under the sink. Quaid opens the tap and lets the water run while he takes down a glass. Fills the glass, guzzles down the water. Refills it and guzzles some more. Homicide makes a man hungry and thirsty.

He sets the glass on the counter and turns around to head out of the room. Stops in the middle of the kitchen and goes back to the sink. He's forgotten something. He reaches into his jacket and takes something out. Sets it in the sink. What is it? A white container of some sort. A small jar. Hard to see. If only he'd lean closer to it or pick it up. What's in the jar? He starts to lift the lid, but he turns his head away. She suspects he's dumping the jar's contents into the sink, but she can't tell for sure. He's looking away. Why?

He reaches for a switch to the right of the sink, against the backsplash. The garbage disposal. He's going to destroy what's in the sink. Is it evidence? Changing his mind, he withdraws his hand. Good. Excellent. He swivels the faucet so it's over the side of the sink without the disposal. Turns on the hot water, grabs a bar of soap, and scrubs his hands under the stream. Scrubbing and scrubbing and scrubbing. Getting under his nails. Shuts off the water and wipes his hands on his pants.

Back into the dining room. Through the front room. Up the stairs. He's at home in this house. No hesitation. No stumbling around. No turning off lights once they're on, either. Even in familiar surroundings, he's afraid of the dark. Very afraid. She can feel his fear. At the top of the stairs, he turns on the hallway light. He's going into a room at the end of the hall and turning on the light. Two twin beds, all made up with feminine quilts. Big flowers and butterflies. Stuffed animals piled against the pillows. Two girls share this room. Mounted over each headboard, a cross fashioned out of rope. Quaid's creepy craft. He goes deeper inside. His eyes linger over one of the beds. He picks up a stuffed rabbit and hugs it to his chest. Her vision starts to blur; he's tearing up. He sets the toy down.

Moving on to a room next door. The lights go on. One larger bed with a plain brown spread on top, and no stuffed animals. A guy's room. Another macramé cross on the wall. No loitering here. Back down the hall and into a third room. He flicks on the lights. Vatican: The Sequel. Virgin Mary statue on the dresser. Candles in jars. Crucifix over the headboard. Quaid's stepping over to the bed. Unlike the others, this one is bare. No pillows or comforter. What's that stain on top of the mattress? Two rusty spots. Bernadette recognizes the color all too well: dried blood. People died on this mattress, and he kept it. He didn't clean it or cover it up or even flip it over to hide the blood. Why did he keep it? Who died here? He had two sisters. They died on this bed. This is his family home. She sees him extend his hand, reaching for the stains. He pulls his fingers back. He's turning away from the bloody souvenir. Leaving his dead sisters. He goes across the room to another door. A closet? He puts his hand on the knob, but doesn't open the door. Stands there motionless, staring at the panel of wood. What's this about?

He finally lets go of the knob and leaves the room. Goes down the hall to another room. This must be the last room on this level. The lights go on. He's walking inside. It's the bathroom. He's closing the door. Why? He's alone in the house. There's a mirror on the door. He's looking at himself. She can see him in the mirror. For the first time, she can observe this villain head to toe. Quaid's tall and muscular. Doesn't fit her idea of the way a priest should look. Ex-priest. He should be small and wiry, or round like Santa Claus. He's too built, this guy. Dangerous. She wishes he'd step closer to the door mirror so she could make out his face more clearly. Instead, he steps away and goes to the vanity. Starts taking stuff out of his pockets and dumping the junk on the counter. Flashlight. Keys. Billfold. There it is again—the gun. He's still got it. What kind of gun is it? What are we up against? Looks like a revolver. That humpbacked shape is familiar. The frame is extended, covering all but the very tip of the hammer. Easy to hide; not so easy to shoot—unless he's had practice. She prays he hasn't had practice.

Quaid's taking off his clothes. There's gotta be blood. Is he going to throw the clothes away? No. He's opening a little square door in the wall. The laundry chute. Dropping the duds down to the laundry

Forty-one

° °

Unfolding her fist, Bernadette dropped the ring on the church bench. At the sound of the *clink,* she opened her eyes and was surprised to see an altar in front of her. Drained and confused, she struggled to remember where she was and how she'd gotten there.

A male voice punched through her fog: "You okay?"

She blinked and turned her head toward the sound. Her vision was still cloudy. She blinked two more times and the film melted away, revealing Garcia sitting next to her on a church bench.

"Did you see anything?" he asked.

She didn't know how to answer him. She needed a few minutes to collect herself, orient herself, process what she'd seen, and put it into words. Quaid's emotions were still coursing through her. She felt exhaustion and something beneath that, something that made her anxious. Fear? Was it her own fear, or that of the killer?

Using the ring retrieval as an excuse to buy time, she slid away from Garcia. She pulled a work glove out of her pocket, slipped it on, and picked up the band.

"Agent Saint Clare? You all right? What'd you see?"

"Gimme a minute." She peeled off the glove so it was inside out, with the ring safely tucked in the ball of latex. She jammed the package in her jacket pocket. She took a couple of calming breaths and turned in the pew to respond to Garcia, answering his questions in order. "I'm okay. I saw Quaid at home."

"Back at the apartment?"

"No. His family home."

"Are you sure about that?"

"I saw his mom's beauty shop, and the bed where his sisters . . ." She stood up and felt dizzy. She lowered herself back onto the bench. Glancing toward the altar, she noticed Father Pete igniting candles with a long brass pole. "How long have we been here? Is it already time for morning services?"

They were sitting close to the front, and she'd spoken louder than she'd intended. The priest turned around. "Don't mind me. Mass isn't for hours yet. Thought I'd putter around up here. Try out our new lighter, see if the altar boys will be able to work it without setting fire to the place." He lowered the flame at the end of the rod. "I hope God answers your prayers, Bernadette. Let me know if you need me later, at the hospital." The priest turned around and headed to another set of candles with the lighter.

She was perplexed by the priest's words.

Leaning into her ear, Garcia enlightened her: "I told him you had an aunt on her deathbed. You needed to spend some time in church."

Bernadette had no idea Garcia had cooked up such a lame lie to get the priest out of bed. She whispered out of the side of her mouth: "He opened shop for that? In the middle of the night?"

Garcia whispered back: "I couldn't tell him why we really needed the church." His eyes narrowed. "Could I, Agent Saint Clare?"

She stared at Garcia for a few seconds, wondering why he'd suddenly pulled out the formal stuff. *Agent Saint Clare.* She returned her attention to the altar. She approved of Father Pete. He fit one of the two physical profiles she judged proper for a priest; plus, he'd given them some good dirt on Quaid. She raised her voice loud enough for the priest to hear: "Thanks for letting us in, Father Pete."

"We're sorry about the odd hour," said Garcia. He glanced at Bernadette when he added: "We won't waste your time again."

"You know me, Anthony," the priest said over his shoulder. "I never sleep anymore."

Garcia turned in his seat and studied her face. "Looks like you could use some sleep. Eyes are all bloodshot. Face white as a sheet."

She smiled weakly. "I'll live. Let's get back in that fine ride of yours and head for the woods. We can talk during the drive. Think you can find Quaid's place?"

"It was all over the old trial documents. His family lived between Dassel and Darwin, off of U.S. 12. A straight shot west of the cities. They had pictures of the outside of the joint."

She wanted to compare what she'd seen inside the home with photos of the place. "Did you see interior crime-scene shots?"

"A ton of them."

"Let's trade notes while we're on the road."

He fished his car keys out of his pocket and held them in his hand, but didn't make a move to get up. "How sure are you about what you saw, Agent Saint Clare? About where Quaid is hiding?"

"What're you saying?" She scrutinized his face. His mouth was set hard. Plus that *Agent Saint Clare* garbage. What happened to *Cat*? What in the hell was going on with him?

"Let's talk outside." Garcia slid out of the pew and started down the aisle.

She got up and went after him. He was waiting for her at the double doors. As he held one side open for her, she walked through and blurted: "He has a gun."

"We have guns." He let go of the door and followed her outside. They started down the steps together, each zipping up against the cold morning air. A faded photocopy of the moon was peeking out from behind the clouds.

She stood next to the front passenger's door of the Pontiac and looked over the roof at Garcia. "We should call for backup."

"Not yet." He opened the driver's door, got in, and started the car.

She hopped inside and slammed the door shut. "Why not? We know he did it. We've got enough to take him."

"Have we?" Garcia put the car in drive and made a squealing U-turn in front of the church. "Let's see if he's home before we call in the cavalry and embarrass ourselves. Okay?"

"Okay," she said in a low voice.

Deflated and exhausted, she stared through the windshield into the early-morning darkness. More than any of her previous supervisors, Garcia had shown an interest in her sight. He'd wanted to watch. Now he was snapping at her and putting distance between the two of them, behaving like a guy trying to kick a weekend fling out of his bed before heading off to work. What had changed?

Garcia braked at a light. "If this doesn't pan out, Agent Saint Clare, let's head back into the office and reassess what we have. Maybe we need to take a more conventional approach."

Turning her head away from him, she slipped into her own formal language. "Yes, sir."

As she stared outside the passenger window, she caught a glimpse of her own reflection in the mirrored surface of a neighborhood hardware-store window. She looked like a worn little woman—nothing special at all. With that observation, the reason for Garcia's transformation landed in her gut with a sickening thud. He'd watched her using the sight, and it had somehow disappointed him, let him down. Maybe it wasn't mystical enough or spiritual enough for the nice Catholic boy. He'd hoped to see a halo materialize over her head, or hear a celestial choir. Hear her talking in tongues. After the buildup in his head, he was disillusioned. All he'd witnessed was a small, tired woman sitting on a church bench, her hand wrapped around a bit of jewelry. She told herself it was all her own fault: she'd let down her guard and trusted another human being. Big mistake. Worse, she'd given that person a glimpse of how she used her sight. "I shouldn't have let you watch," she muttered, more to herself than to him.

"Watch what?" he asked dryly.

"It wasn't what you expected," she said to the glass. "Now you're pissed off."

"I'm not pissed off."

"Skeptical, then."

She held her breath, waiting for him to deny that he doubted her. He stayed silent.

The light changed, and he accelerated. They didn't speak as he steered the Grand Am onto Interstate 94 heading west. Traffic was spotty, and with few obstacles to maneuver around, Garcia was able to keep the pedal to the floor. Ten miles after hopping onto I-94, they took the exit for Interstate 394. The Pontiac sped west through a couple of Minneapolis suburbs before the highway turned into U.S. 12. From there, they'd be at Quaid's place in under an hour.

As they entered the town of Long Lake and passed the narrow body of water bearing the same name, Garcia reached over and snapped on the radio. An oldies rock station was in the middle of an Aerosmith tribute. "Sweet Emotion" filled the inside of the car.

Bernadette stared through the passenger window and felt a headache coming on. She'd already spent too much time listening to Steven Tyler through the ceiling. She didn't say anything, though. The music was preferable to the grinding silence.

They cruised past three more lakes and went through four more towns before Garcia lowered the volume on the radio and spoke. "You wanted to discuss the details of what you saw inside Quaid's home?"

"I saw a bed with twin stains in a bedroom with religious paraphernalia. I saw two other bedrooms. I saw a kitchen and a weird-ass porch salon and—"

He cut her off: "All stuff you could have seen in the file. Sure you didn't look at that file even briefly?"

"No, I didn't." She paused, struggling to keep her temper and voice under control. "Doesn't matter, sir. All the bureau would care about is that he's there and that we get him."

"Let's hope he *is* there, Agent Saint Clare." Garcia reached over and turned the volume back up on "Rats in the Cellar."

She couldn't take another guitar riff. "Can you switch stations, sir? Augie has been keeping me up at night with that stuff."

Garcia jerked the car to the side of the road and slammed on the brakes. He shoved it into park and snapped off the radio. "What did you say?"

She froze. She'd done something or said something that infuriated him. Was it residual anger over their church visit? She didn't know what to apologize for, so she went with the most obvious. "I'm sorry. The station's fine. The music. Whatever. It's your car, sir."

"Stop with the *sir* crap."

"Then you stop with the *Agent Saint Clare* crap."

"What did you say about August Murrick?"

She frowned, confused by his line of questioning. Had he snapped because she'd mentioned Augie again? Garcia obviously had some weird grudge against the guy. She wanted to get off the subject. "Nothing. Let's keep going."

"Answer my question."

She turned away from the window and looked at him. Even by the dim glow of the dashboard, she could read his expression. Garcia was genuinely worried. "Augie and his stupid mutt. They've been cranking the Aerosmith late at night."

"Someone in your building didn't tell you some inside dirt about August Murrick, did they? Stuff only the cops should know?"

"What stuff? What are you talking about? I told you I bumped into the guy. That he lives upstairs."

Garcia's eyes widened. "He *used to* live upstairs."

"He still does. With that wiener dog of his. Oscar. They've been partying upstairs from me. I had to tell him to turn it down."

"You didn't mention the dog or the music before. That would have clued me in that it wasn't another Murrick you saw. That you really . . ." His words trailed off.

She didn't like the horrified look on his face or the shakiness of his voice. An icicle shot up Bernadette's spine and wrapped around her middle. "That I really what? What's going on? You're scaring me, Tony."

Turning his head away from her, he said to the driver's window: "August Murrick is dead. So is his dog."

Forty-two

Her heart pounded as her mind frantically backtracked. During their first meeting, she'd been alone with Augie and Oscar in the hallway; there'd been no one else to hear them or see them. What about at the crowded Farmers' Market the next morning? Had someone besides her interacted with the man and his dog? Taken notice of them? She remembered the woman in line at the bagel stand, staring at Bernadette and nervously wheeling away her stroller. The mother didn't want to be near a woman carrying on a conversation with thin air. Augie's warning about the wake had been prophetic, as if he had some supernatural insight. His place had been sparsely furnished and dusty for good reason: no one was living there!

I slept with a . . .

She couldn't even finish the thought, let alone say it out loud.

All of it was coming true. The stories they'd told about her in Louisiana. The tales they'd spun around New Orleans about her talking to the dead. The warning from the Franciscan.

Demons twisting your hands and your heart.

She instinctively reached up and put her hand over her chest—the spot where, beneath her clothing, her husband's wedding band hung from a chain next to her own ring. "That can't be. How can that be?"

Snapping his head back around to look at her, Garcia barked: "You tell me!"

She bunched her hand over her talisman. While outwardly denying the dead, Bernadette silently prayed to them. She petitioned her husband and her sister and her parents to make it all go away. "You're wrong or I'm wrong or someone's jerking me around. It was a different Murrick."

"His body was found in the basement of his own building. Your building. Murrick Place."

"Stop."

"Police figured it was because of a meth case Augie had lost. Not even a federal one—a pissant one. His clients blamed him, and hired someone to execute him and his dog. One bullet each to the head. Cops never caught the guys."

She put her hands over her face. "No."

Garcia kept going. "It was all over the local news, but that was months ago. You were down south. I doubt the papers there ran anything."

"Stop."

"And the details were never published."

She was shaking her head. "That's enough."

"Murrick was a big rock-and-roll fan. He was wearing an Aerosmith shirt when he died. I only know that because I've got a cousin in St. Paul Homicide. Ironic, actually. The tee said something about . . ."

"Nine lives," she said through her fingers.

"Exactly," he breathed.

"Dear God," she prayed into her palms.

"You've been seeing spirits? Talking to a dead guy and his dead dog? Is that what you're fucking telling me?"

"No," she said into her hands. "That's not right." She couldn't tell him she'd done more than talk to a spirit; she'd made love with him.

He put a hand on her shoulder. "You need to . . ."

"I don't need to do anything." She pushed his hand away. She didn't want to hear about how she needed to get some sleep or take some time off or see a shrink. She turned around and threw open the car door and jumped out. She didn't know where they'd stopped. Somewhere with woods. She didn't care. She started to run for the trees, her way illuminated by the Pontiac's headlights. Behind her, she heard his car door slam and his footsteps crunching. His voice.

"Cat! Stop!"

Bernadette set her sights on a black gap between two pines. She told herself if she could make it to the evergreens and run into the forest, she could emerge from the other side of the woods a different person, a normal human being with two brown eyes and no extraordinary skills. A regular woman with a quiet job and a living husband. Living lover. Kids and a house in the country. The woman she'd always wanted to be.

"Agent Saint Clare!" he yelled after her.

She ignored the voice behind her and kept going. Almost there. A normal life just beyond those trees.

He tackled her from behind, and they both went down on the ground.

"No!" she screamed into the grass.

"What're you running from? Where're you going?"

"Let me go! I'm a freak!"

"You're not a freak!" He sat up and gathered her into his arms.

She buried her face in his jacket while pounding on his chest with her fists. "I don't talk to the dead! I don't see the dead! I don't! That's not what I do!"

Forty-three

Damian Quaid slipped naked between the covers of his childhood bed. Staring up at the ceiling, he counted out loud.

"One . . . two . . . three . . . four . . . five . . . six . . ."

When he was in grade school and studying the planets, his mother arranged a constellation of plastic and paper glow-in-the-dark stars over his bed. There were 299. There used to be three hundred, but one of the paper ones had fallen off long ago.

"Thirty-three . . . thirty-four . . . thirty-five . . . thirty-six . . ."

The counting relaxed him, frequently helped him nod off.

"Fifty-seven . . . fifty-eight . . . fifty-nine . . . sixty . . ."

The exercise wouldn't work tonight. He stopped at ninety-nine and rolled onto his side. He kicked off the covers, threw his legs over the side of the bed, and sat up. He reached over and snatched a compact paperback Bible off the nightstand, cracked the book open to a random page, and started to read. He'd landed on Paul's Letter to the Ephesians 2:17–19.

> So he came and proclaimed peace to you who were far off and peace to those who were near; for through him both of us have access in one Spirit to the Father. So then you are no longer strangers and aliens, but you are citizens with the saints, and also members of the household of God . . .

Quaid tried to concentrate and continue, but they were conciliatory words and he wasn't in a forgiving, generous mood. He snapped the book closed and dropped it back on the table. Wondered if he should go downstairs and turn on the television to catch the local news. Maybe there was something about his last two executions. Checking the night-stand clock, he saw it was too early. There wouldn't be any local news on until six or seven, and that was hours away.

Opening a drawer in the nightstand, he rummaged around for some clean socks and boxers and a tee shirt. Quaid stood up and went to the closet and yanked a flannel shirt and a pair of jeans off the hangers. An old barn coat. As he buttoned up his shirt, he thought about the shed and its contents. The ropes. The blades. The small engines. The aroma of motor oil and gasoline and sawdust and metal. He'd spend some time organizing the ropes and sharpening the tools, getting select ones ready for the next mission. Quaid was already formulating a way to choose his next fiend. He'd abandon his original list and pick a different state, another one without the death penalty. Perhaps Iowa or Wisconsin or someplace out east. He'd start reading up on the worst crimes ever committed in those places. A check of the Internet and the newspapers would reveal who was due for release, or who'd never gotten prison time in the first place. His candidates would have no connection to Minnesota or him or anyone he knew. His execution of them would be a purely selfless action. God would be proud of him, and there'd be no chance of getting caught by the authorities.

Quaid started down the hall and remembered he'd dropped some essentials on the bathroom counter. He stepped into the bathroom and scooped the keys and the flashlight off the counter, and dropped them in his coat pockets. He crammed his wallet in the back pocket of his jeans. Finally, the gun. He picked it up and held it in his hand for a few seconds, enjoying the shape of the thing, and the color. Like his weight-lifting gloves, the revolver made him feel strong and manly and in control. He slipped the weapon into the front pocket of his jeans.

He went down the stairs and into the kitchen, stepped into some barn boots he kept by the back door and went outside. He locked the door behind him and then paused at the top of the stoop to listen. The wind had died down, allowing him to hear the frogs in the pond. The clouds had thinned, and he could see a splash of stars. He was home. Clicking on the flashlight, he thumped down the stairs and headed for the metal shed planted half a football field away from the house.

Quaid was stepping onto the driveway, between the house and the shop, when he heard movement in the woods. It wasn't the wind; the noise was too concentrated. He froze and ran the beam across the wall of trees that bordered the property. More rustling. He switched the flashlight to his left hand and put his right palm over the bulging front pocket of his jeans. "I've got a gun," he yelled into the darkness.

A fat raccoon waddled out of the greenery, stopped, and stared directly into the light with its bandit eyes. Behind it trailed five kits; they stopped behind their mother.

Quaid slipped his hand into his jeans and slid his gun out of his pocket. Shooting with one hand looked easy on television westerns. His revolver had a fierce recoil that made such fancy firing difficult. He'd been practicing with cans behind the house, and this would be an opportunity to see if his work was paying off.

He raised his right hand and reconsidered. What if, instead, he rested his gun hand on top of his flashlight hand? He'd seen that technique—or something like it—on a cop show. He brought his left wrist under his right hand.

The mother raccoon wasn't budging. She was staring at the light as she stood less than twenty feet away. Behind her, the kits were moving around, playfully jostling for position.

"Steady," he said out loud. He put his finger on the trigger and aimed for the mother's face, so much like a robber's masked face. He inhaled and started counting in his head. *One, two . . .*

On *three,* he exhaled and squeezed the trigger.

The animal exploded. Her kits turned and ran into the woods. Grinning with satisfaction, he followed their retreat with the beam of his flashlight. She'd been an easy target. A man or a woman wouldn't be so motionless, so accommodating. Still, he'd proved to himself that he'd gotten better at firing the thing. As with the rope-tying, all it took was practice.

He lowered the gun and slipped it into his coat pocket. Shining the light on the ground ahead of him, he continued making his way to the shop.

The shed looked like a small airplane hangar. A half-cylinder of metal made up the roof and long sides. The metal end wall facing the highway had a double garage door and a heavy wooden storm door. His father had installed the garage doors—and constructed the building close to the driveway—so on occasion he could veer off the gravel and steer his truck directly into the shed to unload it. On the opposite end of the cylinder—facing the pond and the woods beyond it—was another metal end wall with another wooden storm door. One large, wood-framed window was mounted on each side of the door. The structure sat on a concrete slab, was wired for electricity, and was easily warmed with a couple of space heaters.

Quaid went around to the far end of the shed. He'd installed a security lamp against the back of the building; the light went on every night at dusk unless he shut it off manually from inside the shed. He punched off the flashlight and stashed it in his coat pocket. He shoved a key in the dead-bolt lock—something he'd added to the door after his family was killed—and turned. He pushed the door open, and left it open while he felt the wall just inside the doorway. He flipped the switch up, and the fluorescent tubes mounted to the ceiling flickered and filled with white light. He yanked his keys out of the lock and closed the door behind him. Quaid turned the lock on the dead bolt while nervously eyeing the naked glass on either side of the door. This night in particular—a night that saw him tricked into performing a mistaken execution and then forced into conducting an impromptu one—he felt ill at ease with the uncovered windows. They made him feel vulnerable. They faced the pond and the woods, and he knew bad things could come out of the woods in the country—especially after dark.

Quaid ran his eyes around, zoning in on the rag bucket he kept in the far corner of the shed. He crossed the room and picked through the heap of material—socks with holes, ripped tee shirts, a worn flannel shirt, and other scraps he used to wipe his hands. He pulled out two bath towels and threw them over his arm. Snatching a hammer and a fistful of nails off one of the benches, he went to work dressing the windows with makeshift curtains. The towels had a couple of holes in them—that's why they were in the rag bucket—but they'd be enough to keep someone from seeing directly inside.

After nailing the cloth to the window frames, he surveyed the rest of the shop. The space was the width of a triple car garage and was at least as long as the house. He felt comfortable and protected under the metal. The ribs that curved up the walls and ceiling made him feel as if he were inside the mouth of a whale. It was a safe, fortified shelter, a place untouched by violence. Though the murderers had stolen rope from the shed, none of the slaughtering had taken place in the shop. No blood stained the slab. No ghosts hid in the corners.

Each of the long walls was lined with a workbench that stretched from end to end. Stationed here and there along the benches were tall, backless chairs that allowed him to sit down and work. As a kid, he and his father would sit side by side on the stools and work silently on rope projects. When he grew older, he was allowed to help with the machines people brought for repair. His father started him on the push lawn-mowers, letting him work on sharpening the blades with a large hand file. It was a simple, mind-numbing chore that Quaid still enjoyed. He found something satisfying about dragging the file over the edge of the blades until they looked and felt dangerous enough to do the job. The screeching, grating noise made by metal against metal sounded like exotic, ethereal music. Angels rubbing their wings together.

He had an old gas mower parked in a corner of the shop. Perfect, he thought. He'd work on those blades a while, until his body and his mind started to unwind. Quaid went over to the mower, picked it up, and set it on its side on top of the bench. Before going any further with his repair job, he took one safety precaution his careful father had taught him: he pulled the spark-plug wire from the top side to ensure that the mower wouldn't start up accidentally.

He needed a wrench to remove the blade from the underside. Taking an inventory of the tools hanging from the pegboard over the bench, he saw the wrench and took it down, leaving a black outline of the wrench behind. His father had used a laundry marker to draw around the tools as they hung from the board. That way, when something was taken down it was obvious where it needed to be put back.

A single nut held the blade up against the lawn mower's deck. After applying a little muscle, he was able to loosen and remove the nut. He slipped off the blade and clamped it in a vise mounted at the far end of the bench.

Quaid scanned the pegboard again and saw an empty rectangle. He'd taken down the ten-inch mill file during an earlier visit and failed to put it back. His father would have disapproved. Scanning the bench running along the opposite wall, he spotted the file, retrieved it, and dropped it next to the vise. He took down a set of safety goggles and slipped them over his eyes, tightened the vise's grip on the blade, and went to work.

Using long, broad strokes away from him, he followed the forty-five-degree factory angle of the cutting edge. As his father had instructed him, he kept the pressure firm and pushed the file and his arms from his shoulders, not his wrists. The scraping sound was as soothing and relaxing as any piece by Beethoven or Bach. Each stroke had its own rhythm and music and yet remained connected to the action before it and after it. Movements of a sonata written for metal.

When he was finished with the mower, he moved on to other garden tools. All the shovels needed work, and they would take a while, since there were five of them. He used a bar clamp to hold each to the bench. He started on the left side of each blade and filed to the center. Then he switched to the right side of the blade and worked toward the middle. His arm movements were long and smooth and consistent. Each shovel took about fifty strokes. Most folks didn't think of sharpening shovels, but his father had taught him that sharp shovels made digging much easier. They went through the soil like it was butter and cut roots with no problems. While he worked, Quaid wondered if they could slice through other things easily, too, and made a mental note to bring the sharpest of the lot on a mission.

He propped the last shovel up against the shed wall and took a break. Leaning one hand against the edge of the workbench, he dragged his coat sleeve across his forehead and then across his upper lip and mustache. He'd worked up a sweat; he liked that. He unbuttoned the coat, yanked it off, and dropped it over one of the stools. Searching the ribbed walls for more tools in need of sharpening, his eyes landed on the collection of axes hanging from the pegboard.

Forty-four

· ⸱

Am I losing my mind?

For the remainder of the drive, the two of them didn't talk. While Garcia kept the radio off and concentrated on driving, Bernadette kept her head turned away from him and stared through the passenger window. She was embarrassed she'd had a breakdown in front of her boss, and feared her outburst had endangered her career more than any of her previous gaffes on the job. Even before the big scene, Garcia's attitude toward her and her sight had been all over the board: Curious. Supportive. Skeptical. Resentful. Now there was evidence his underling could see dead people and dead dogs. She didn't know how he was taking this latest bit of news. Not well, she suspected.

Dead people. Dead dogs.

Had she really conversed with a ghost? Touched him? Had sex with him? Would he come to her bed again—invited or not? Those questions made her head spin, but the others were no less dizzying: Was Augie a benign spirit or something malignant? Why did he know so much about her? How had he been able to warn her about the wake? Would other phantoms start materializing in front of her? How was she supposed to use this ability? Was it God who gave her this, or Satan? She knew the answer the Franciscan would give her. She could almost hear him now, in that judgmental voice:

You're sleeping with the devil, daughter.

The biggest, most troubling question she kept asking herself:

Am I losing my mind?

As they entered the town of Dassel, she quieted the screaming in her mind and broke the silence inside the car. "Is it coming up?"

"Yeah." Garcia's eyes were glued to the north side of the road. "Two-story house with woods on either side of it. Enclosed front porch. I'll know it when I see it."

"It's after Dassel?"

"But before Darwin, home of the largest twine ball rolled by one man."

Relieved at his small talk, Bernadette grinned. "What?"

"It was the biggest twine ball *period* until some asshole town in Kansas hopped on the bandwagon. Still, Darwin's twine ball is the only whopper rolled by *one* guy."

"He still working on it?"

Garcia: "He died."

"Maybe he'll pay me a visit next," she said dryly.

Garcia steered around a semi that had stopped in front of him to make a left. "Do you need to talk?"

"No. No. Don't worry," she said, stumbling over her words and regretting her feeble joke. "My head's back in the game."

Garcia pointed through her window. "Good, 'cause that looks like the place. Joint's lit up like a Christmas tree."

Her head swiveled to the right. She looked over her shoulder as they passed a farmhouse with lights on in nearly every window. "He's afraid of the dark," she said.

"How do you know?"

"I just do," she said.

Garcia slowed and steered the Grand Am to the right, pulling it off the highway and out of sight of the house. The car bumped onto a narrow strip of weeds that bordered the woods. He put it in park, punched off the headlights, and shut off the car. "I say we leave the car here and hike through the woods. Enter the place from the back."

"Sounds like a plan."

Garcia took out his gun and slipped it into his jacket pocket. "As soon as we see what we're dealing with here, we'll call for backup."

She took out her Glock and checked it. Slipped it back in her holster. "Still not convinced we've got the right psycho?"

"Not sure *I've* got the right house." Garcia opened his door, jumped out, and started digging under the driver's seat.

She opened the passenger door and hopped out. "That's the only problem? There isn't something else you want to say to me?"

He pulled out his flashlight, stood up with it, and clicked it on. "I've come around. You've obviously got something going on. An expertise or a power or whatever the hell you want to call it. We've got the right man. Was all your work."

"All *our* work," she said, closing the passenger door.

o   o   o

They entered from where Garcia had parked the Pontiac, heading north into the woods. Garcia took point, keeping the flashlight ahead of them, and aimed down. The ground was spongy and smelled of rain and moss. Struggling to keep their path straight, they stepped over logs and weaved between evergreens and hardwoods. After twenty minutes of trudging in near blackness, they figured they were deep enough and turned east, toward the house. When they broke through the trees, they found themselves next to a small body of water, its shoreline encircled by reeds and weeds and tall grasses. The two agents hunkered down next to each other. Garcia punched off his flashlight. They were on the far side of a pond behind Quaid's house. The windows in back of the house, glowing as brightly as those in the front, were reflected in the surface of the water. From across the pool and to their left, they spotted a metal shack that took up nearly as much real estate as the house. A light attached to the back of the shed also shone on the pond surface and illuminated that end of the shack.

Bernadette squinted into the night. "There're a door and two windows on this side of the outbuilding," she whispered.

Garcia: "The what?"

"That metal shed."

"*Outbuilding.* Is that a farmer word or what?"

"Funny." She squinted some more. "I can't tell if there's someone inside the shed. Yard light is too bright."

"I think that's Quaid's ride," said Garcia, pointing to the Volvo parked in the driveway that ran between the house and the metal building.

Bernadette: "Now what?"

"You tell me," he said. "You've been in that house once already. I've only seen photos."

"Yeah." She paused and tried to think above the din of the croaking. "Let's get closer. Follow the edge of the water to the back of the house."

With Bernadette leading the way, the pair bent down and crept to the right, following the pond's shoreline. The grasses hid all but the tops of their heads.

Garcia grunted behind her. She stopped and spun around, pushing a reed away from her face. "You okay?"

"Almost went down. Slipped on a slimy rock."

"Probably a frog." She turned around and continued heading toward the back of the house. She kept her eyes trained on the windows, in case Quaid or someone else peeked through the curtains.

The two of them reached the side of the pool nearest to the house and stopped. They crouched next to each other amid the reeds and weeds. The horseshoe of woods that started at the far side of the pond curled up along both sides of the property, so that there were trees wrapping around the west side of the house and the east side of the metal building. But the inside of the horseshoe—the yard between the pond and the back of the buildings, and the area between the shed and the house—was mowed short and was clear of trees.

Garcia slipped his flashlight in his jacket pocket. "We could beeline it to the back door from here. Hope no one sees us."

"Bad idea," she said.

"Dive back into the bushes and follow the tree line?"

"Better idea."

"It'll take twice as long, and I'm sick of nature." He stood up and bolted out of the reeds.

"Maniac," she said, and went after him.

They both stopped at the bottom of the steps and squatted down as they looked up at the back of the house. The windows along the first and second floors were covered with drapes sheer enough to reveal that the interior of the home was lit, but dense enough to keep them from seeing inside. The only help was a horizontal gap between the curtains covering one window—a square of glass that looked out over the porch. From what Bernadette could remember during her earlier tour of the house—and knowing how farmhouses were laid out and decorated—Bernadette figured it was the window over the kitchen sink. The gap was created by the café curtains. She leaned into Garcia's ear: "I'll take the stairs. Try to see in."

He nodded and told her the obvious: "Be careful."

Staying crouched, she took out her gun and slowly mounted the handful of steps. The wood creaked as she went up. *Damn frogs,* she thought. Now that she needed their masking croaks, they seemed to have gone silent. She expelled a breath of relief when she reached the porch landing, a rectangle of uneven boards covered by an overhang and railed by weathered spindles.

Two round aluminum trash barrels sat under the kitchen window. One, containing cans and bottles, was uncovered. She peered inside and sniffed. Didn't see or smell anything suspicious. Anything dead. With her free hand, she lifted the lid of the other barrel. She looked down. By the light coming from the square window, she could see the barrel was empty. Not even a garbage bag inside. She replaced the lid. Standing on her tiptoes, she looked up at the window. She was too short to see through the gap, especially with the barrels blocking her way and keeping her from getting closer. Moving the barrels wouldn't help—and would make too much racket.

Bernadette holstered her gun and crawled on top of the garbage-barrel lid, staying on her knees. She steadied herself by resting her palms on the trim at the bottom of the window. As she sat up on her knees, she felt the lid beneath her start to pucker and give way. She leaned on the window ledge to relieve the weight on the lid. Peeking through the break in the curtains, she saw the kitchen with all the lights on, but no people inside. Holding her breath, she put her ear to the glass. Heard no voices or music or television.

She spotted a doorway leading to another room, but had trouble seeing beyond it. She knew, from her earlier look inside the house, that it led to the dining room. Anything on the counters? Nothing but canisters on the counter opposite the sink. Now she could get a peek at what he'd dumped inside the sink, what he'd almost destroyed. She raised herself a little higher and flattened her face against the glass to get a view of the sink. What she saw resting against the porcelain made her stomach churn. One word came to mind: *Monster.*

Forty-five

She let go of the window ledge and slid off the lid. As her feet hit the porch, the empty barrel tipped toward her. She reached for the can, steadied it, and righted it as gently as she could. Her attention darted to the kitchen window. No one looking out. She let go of the can and waved Garcia up. He took the steps slowly, grimacing with each groan of the boards. Once he reached the top, she told him in a hoarse growl: "Tongue's in the sink."

Garcia grimly shook his head from side to side and then asked in a low voice. "No Quaid?"

"No Quaid," she repeated.

He pointed to the back door. Bernadette nodded, drew her gun, and planted herself on one side of the entry. He took out his pistol, went up to the door, and put his hand on the knob. He turned to the right and pushed. It didn't budge. He turned to the left and pushed again.

Harder. "Bolted," he whispered. He let go and took a step back. He ran his eyes from the top of the door to the bottom.

Bernadette knew what he was considering, and she didn't like it. Old farmhouses were as solid as bricks, and it would take more than one or two kicks to bring down the door. The murderer inside would have plenty of time to grab his gun. Since Quaid was paranoid—no wonder, since intruders had taken out his entire family—the windows were undoubtedly sealed as well. They needed to find a weak spot in the barricade—an unlatched bathroom window or a rotten basement door. Bemadette grabbed Garcia by the elbow and nodded to the steps. They both padded down. At the bottom, she whispered: "Let's see if there's a cellar."

"What about the front?"

She shook her head. "Saw him lock it up after he went inside."

"Lead the way," he said.

They went around to the wooded side of the house. Bernadette kept her gun out, but Garcia holstered his and took out his flashlight. While Garcia trained the beam on the side of the building, the pair walked the length of the foundation from the back of the house to the front. A band of mowed grass a yard wide gave them enough room to walk without wrestling against branches and bushes. No doors on that side. No windows, either. They retraced their steps and returned to the back-yard. They squatted next to each other at the back corner of the house, abutting the woods. "There's gotta be windows or something along the other side," she said.

Garcia looked across the barren yard to the back of the shed, with its bright yard light. "If there's someone in there, they could see us. There's no cover between the shed and that side of the house. Nothing. Plus, that floodlight won't do us any favors."

"We'll stay low and work fast." Her turn to dart out. She crouched down as she ran, stopping when she got to the other back corner.

Garcia came up behind her. "Let's go."

They started up along the side of the house, again checking the foundation. Even with the illumination from the shed, they needed the flashlight in the inky blackness of the country night. A third of the way to the front, they came across a door. "Bingo," she said. "Basement."

They took the same position as before: Bernadette on one side with her gun, and Garcia working the knob. "Tight as a drum," Garcia whispered. He let go of the knob, and they continued walking.

"Stop," she whispered when they were near the middle of the house. She motioned with the barrel of her gun.

Garcia aimed the light and saw where she was pointing. A boarded basement window. "Perfect."

He set the flashlight on the ground so the beam illuminated the board. Bernadette holstered her gun. They went down on their knees and worked at prying off the slab of plywood. Bernadette was able to slip her fingers under one of the top corners of the board, but she couldn't lift it off the window frame. "Stuck," she sputtered.

"Let me," said Garcia. She took her hands off the board and shuffled over to give him room. He gripped the corner and pulled. They heard the squeak of nails pulling away from the wood. "Almost there."

She wrapped both of her hands over the top edge of the plywood and pulled with him. The board cracked in half and came off in their fists. Garcia placed the board on the ground behind them and started pulling at the remaining slat of wood, nailed firmly to the bottom of the window. "Wait," said Bernadette. She retrieved the flashlight, trained the beam over the window, and ducked her head down to get a look. There was nothing on the other side of the plywood. No glass or screen or window curtain. Just the blackness of the old home's basement. A mildew odor wafted up from inside the cellar.

"Let me finish." Elbowing her aside, Garcia clamped his hands over the top of the board and pulled. The bottom half came off in one piece.

"You won't fit," she whispered.

He studied the dark rectangle and concluded she was right. "All that enchilada hot dish."

"I'll slide through and open the cellar door for you," she said.

He picked up the flashlight and handed it to her. "Check it out before you dive in."

Bernadette stuck her head inside the hole and swept the basement with the beam. She held her breath while she took her survey; the musty smell was overpowering. Right below her was the laundry slop tub. She'd aim to land in that. Next to the tub was an old wringer washer. She looked to one side and saw the stairs leading to the basement door they'd passed outside. Across the room were floor-to-ceiling shelves lining the wall opposite the window; they were filled with dusty jars. She scrutinized the contents, half expecting to see body parts floating in the brine, but noticed only peaches and beans and tomatoes and pickles. Against another wall was a workbench, and a pegboard covered with tools. Hammers and hand saws and pliers and screwdrivers. She held the light over the hardware and squinted, but didn't see anything spattered with blood or bone. She pulled her head out of the hole.

"Anything?" Garcia asked.

"The usual basement junk." She sat back on her heels and handed him the flashlight so her hands would be free. She decided to go feet-first, sliding in on her belly. She turned around and started shimmying backward into the hole while holding on to the bottom of the window frame. She was through up to her waist when she felt the rim of the tub flush against the wall. She let go of the window and slid down into the tub with a soft thud.

Garcia stuck his head through the rectangle and looked down at her. "You okay?"

"Ducky," she said in a low voice. Bernadette reached up and took the flashlight from him.

"Unlock the basement door and let me in."

"In a second." She stepped out of the tub. Something skittered across the floor in front of her feet, and she stumbled back against the side of the tub. She followed the rodent with her flashlight as it ducked into a hole in the basement wall.

Garcia, whispering through the window: "What's wrong? What happened?"

"Nothing. Stupid mouse."

"Unlock the door."

"In a second," she repeated. She wanted to take her time and look around without him.

Bernadette went over to the washing machine and shone the light inside. Empty. She ran the beam around the floor and stopped when it landed on a pile of clothes mounded in a corner of the room. Aiming the light up at the ceiling, she found the mouth of the chute. Something was stuck and hanging down, and she went over to it. A tee shirt dangled just over her head. She shone the light up and didn't see anything red against the white. She hunkered over the pile on the floor, but couldn't spot any blood. More work for the lab guys, she figured.

She walked the perimeter of the dank room, breathing through her mouth as she went. Bernadette felt something in her hair—cobwebs or spiders or both—and waved her free hand over her head. Since the fat lady's hand needed to be matched to a body, she looked for a fresh mortar job in the walls or the floor. She knew it was a long shot; Quaid's practice had been to discard the bodies as well as the parts. Still, he'd kept Chris Stannard's tongue, so maybe he'd brought other souvenirs back to the old homestead. She shone the light between the canned goods, but detected nothing amiss behind them. Examined the dates on the peaches and judged them ready for a museum. Quaid was hanging on to the jars for sentimental reasons. The labels, penned by a feminine hand, had to be in his mother's writing or his sisters' script. A picture flashed in her head, a snapshot from her curse of sight: Quaid hugging a stuffed toy. She felt a twinge of pity and waved it aside with the same revulsion she'd demonstrated for the cobwebs.

Forty-six

∙ ∙

Quaid hung up the file and dusted off his hands. He picked his coat up off the stool and slipped it on. Before switching off the light, he inspected the pegboard one last time. His eyes traveled to the far end, landing on one space. The outline had been empty for some time. He'd taken the tool with him; it had been a dependable companion on all of his missions. Now it was in the trunk of his car, covered with blood. Since he was home, he could reward the ax with a proper cleaning and sharpening.

He opened the door and set one foot outside. He froze with the door ajar and his hand on the knob. He backed up into the shed, gently closing the door. He snapped off the interior light and leaned his shoulder against the door.

Quaid stayed motionless while he struggled to calm himself. He couldn't believe he'd seen a man crouched next to the house. It was happening again. Of all the houses scattered across all the rural roads, his home had been targeted. Another stranger on another dark night. He'd been even more cautious than his parents; he'd locked all the doors. So the thief was breaking in through a window instead—the one busted window he'd put off repairing.

His horror over another home invasion spun him into a personal time warp. Suddenly everything that had happened since his family was slaughtered—the knock on his dormitory door when the police presented the horrible news, the murder trial, his entrance into religious life, his flight from the priesthood, the executions—was erased from his memory. He was back where it all began, his family being butchered anew.

He couldn't utter a formal prayer; all he could muster was a three-word entreaty: "God help me." He chanted it again and again, his voice getting weaker and more plaintive as his body crumpled against the door. "God help me . . . God help me . . . God help me." Finally, all that escaped from his lips was a hoarse puff of air, a one-word plea to anyone: "Help."

As Quaid curled up on the floor of the shed, he tried to strike a deal: make the bad guy go away and he would work hard to be a better person. He would go to mass every day. He'd pray more. He'd do anything if God spared him, if the Lord let him survive. In the midst of his negotiations, he hugged his knees tight to his chest and felt something hard in the pocket of his barn coat. The terrified, powerless victim evaporated in a flash of confidence and anger.

He wiped the tears off his cheeks and rose to his feet. He was furious at his own gutlessness and growled an order to himself: "Don't be a coward this time." He thrust his hand in his coat and felt the hard edges of the gun. The thief had picked the wrong countryside, the wrong house, the wrong robbery victim. The words of Job:

> Their strong steps are shortened, and their own schemes throw them down. For they are thrust into a net by their own feet, and they walk into a pitfall. A trap seizes them by the heel; a snare lays hold of them.

A rope is hid for them in the ground, a trap for them in the path. Terrors frighten them on every side, and chase them at their heels.

Quaid vowed that this stranger arriving in the middle of the night would know terror akin to that suffered by his family. When he threw open the door, light from the outside security lamp poured into the shed. A white swath fell across one of the pegboards, illuminating a set of axes. Quaid took it as a sign to use the tools with which he was most comfortable. He snatched one of the axes off the board, ran through the open door, and sprinted across the lawn to the dark hump hunkered against the side of the house.

The man was still crouched facing the window; the idiot hadn't yet figured out that he'd never fit through. Quaid saw no other activity around the outside of the house and noticed no shadows moving around inside, on the other side of the curtains. The robber was alone. Quaid resisted the urge to yell a warning or a curse as he ran. He wanted to take the thief by surprise, knock him cold, and drag him to the shed. Finish him there, amid the tools and the rope. The wind had started to pick up, and Quaid was glad. The rustling trees masked the sound of his footsteps. He was almost on top of the stranger before the man looked over his shoulder. The man started to stand, but it was too late. Quaid swung the side of the ax against the robber's forehead, and the man flew flat onto his back.

      ⊕   ⊙   ⊛

Bernadette figured Garcia had waited long enough. She headed for the stairs leading up to the basement door, put one foot on the first step and heard a noise. She clicked off the flashlight and looked up at the ceiling. Another noise, this one a muffled cry—and it hadn't come from inside the house. Her eyes went to the broken window. She pocketed the flashlight and drew her gun. Holding her breath, she stood motionless in the pitch black.

Forty-seven

Fists fastened around the ax handle, Quaid crouched down next to the stranger and peered through the compact rectangle into the blackness of the basement. He thought he saw a spark of light in the cellar. He waited, but saw nothing more. Heard nothing. Reassured, he dropped the ax on the ground and stood up. He dismissed the flash, blaming it on the excitement of the moment. No one else could have gotten in; even a child would have trouble fitting through that tiny window.

He looked down at his catch and nudged him in the side with the toe of his boot. No response. Quaid leaned over, hooked his arms under the robber's armpits, and dragged him to the workshop. As he drew closer to the light cast by the security lamp, Quaid could see the man was shorter than he but broader in the chest and shoulders. The guy pumped iron; extra rope would be in order. As soon as the stranger's feet cleared the threshold, Quaid unhooked his arms from the thief's pits and dropped him on his back. He stepped around the body, closed the shed, and locked the door. He flipped on the interior light and reached for the switch next to it.

○   ○   ○

Bernadette heard a door slam and immediately recognized the tinny sound as coming from the outbuilding. Taking the steps two at a time, she ran for the basement door. She locked her free fist over the doorknob and turned. Pushed and pulled and jiggled. The thing was bolted. She felt around for the lock, found the dead-bolt knob, and turned. Yanked on the door handle. Still locked tight. She turned and ran down the steps, holstering her gun as she went. She climbed back into the laundry tub and crawled out the basement window. Jumped to her feet and cut across the yard.

Bernadette was halfway to the shack when the light mounted over the building's door went black. Without the glare of the exterior light, she could see the interior was lit, a glow escaping through the ratty curtains. She ducked under one of the windows and drew her gun. Raising her head, she peeked through a hole near the bottom of the drapes. She peered straight ahead and couldn't see anything but the garage door on the other end of the shed. She angled her head to one side and spotted a workbench with tools mounted over it against one of the long walls. She switched eyes and shifted her head around until she could see the other long wall.

Garcia was on the floor, his figure parallel to the workbench that ran along that wall. She couldn't tell if her boss was conscious; he was facedown on the concrete with his arms behind him. He wasn't moving, but she had to believe he was alive. Quaid was on his knees next to him, twining rope around his victim's wrists. If he'd already killed Garcia, he wouldn't bother binding him. Or would he? Could be the ex-priest had gone off the deep end. Quaid tied off the rope and sat back on his heels. Bernadette could see the maniac had wrapped Garcia good and tight. She recognized the tie job: Quaid had used the same sort of thing on the judge.

Quaid reached up to the bench and pulled down another bundle of line. He moved to Garcia's feet and started coiling around the ankles. Bernadette wished she could see Quaid's face; with his back to the window, she couldn't judge his disposition. Maybe he was talking to Garcia, threatening a conscious man. Threatening him with what? She didn't see a gun or a knife, but there were plenty of other possible weapons hanging from the walls. What did Quaid have planned for Garcia? Had he gone through Garcia's pockets? Taken his service weapon? Checked Garcia's identification? Did Quaid know he'd assaulted a federal agent? Would he give a damn? Would it enrage Quaid even more than dealing with a civilian?

These structures were never well insulated; she'd be able to pick up something through the walls. She lowered her head and put her ear to the cold ribbed metal. What she heard confused her at first. When she figured out what she was listening to, her body stiffened with anxiety. In a voice hoarse with self-righteous fury, Quaid was quoting Scripture. She had no idea what part of the Bible Quaid was twisting to his own use. It sounded like the Old Testament:

> "Your doom has come to you, O inhabitant of the land. The time has come, the day is near—of tumult, not of reveling on the mountains. Soon now I will pour out my wrath upon you; I will spend my anger against you. I will judge you according to your ways, and punish you for all your abominations. My eye will not spare; I will have no pity. I will punish you according to your ways, while your abominations are among you. Then you shall know that it is I the Lord who strike."

She couldn't tell if Garcia was awake. Alive. She'd hoped to hear something out of him. A word. A grunt. All she could make out was Quaid's diatribe—and she had a feeling the former priest didn't care if he had a conscious audience or not, a living audience or not. She lifted her ear off the wall and took a bracing breath. With her free hand, she pulled her cell out of her pocket. She contemplated calling for help, but it would take too long for the bureau's people to get there, and she didn't know if she could trust the locals with a hostage situation. She dropped the phone back in her pocket and adjusted her grip on her gun. She could only trust herself. Bernadette weighed the sturdiness of the door between the two windows. Too heavy for her to take down with one or two kicks, and she was sure Quaid had locked it as tight as his Fort Knox house. The garage door on the other side of the shed was out of the question: she couldn't see well enough through the curtains to take aim through a window. She needed to lure him outside.

Bernadette raised her head and peered through the tattered drapes again. He was no longer kneeling by his captive. She angled her head around and spotted Quaid standing along the other long wall. The view she'd gotten of him by way of his bathroom mirror hadn't prepared her for the real deal. He was even taller than she'd expected, and more squarely built. His shoulders seemed to crowd the long, narrow space. His hands were as big as her face, and appeared fully capable of murder—with or without the assistance of hardware. *His hands.* There was something familiar about them.

Quaid's head started jerking back and forth and up and down. He was taking stock of the equipment hanging over the bench. His eyes seemed to rest on one object in particular. "Bastard," she whispered. She started to stand, preparing to go through the window. With her leather gloves, she could punch the glass. From another hole in the drapes, she saw Quaid extend his arm and then pull his hand back. He turned around and faced her; he was going for the door. She ducked and dashed around to the wooded side of the building.

＊　＊　＊

He decided to go out to the car and fetch the tool he'd already bloodied. Didn't matter if it was dull. In fact, dull would be good; let the thief suffer. He didn't want to use one of his freshly honed blades only to have to clean and sharpen it again. He stepped up to the door, turned the dead bolt, and put his hand on the knob. As he pulled the door open, he heard a noise behind him, a groan. He turned around and said to the figure on the floor: "You picked the wrong house, mister." Another moan. Quaid didn't want to listen to that any longer.

He spun around and went over to the rag bucket, fished out a torn tee shirt black with motor oil, and took it over to his captive. He bent over, grabbed a fistful of the fiend's scalp and hair, and yanked his face up off the floor. Quaid plugged the guy's mouth with the rag and studied his forehead for a moment. "You should have a doctor check that goose egg, buddy." Despite the gag, the man managed another moan. Quaid reached into his own pocket and pulled out his gun. Held it in front of the stranger. "Shut the hell up, or you'll eat this for dessert." Quaid let go of the hair; the thief's head slapped the concrete.

He stood over his captive for a minute and ran his eyes over the length of the stranger's body, wondering if there was a wallet on him, a knife, or a gun. Quaid was in no big hurry to find out. He'd wait until it was finished and then go through the guy's pockets. He knew the names of all the others he'd executed, and he wanted to know this one's name.

Quaid went outside, leaving the door open behind him. Fear had been replaced by bravado. He pulled his flashlight out of his pocket, clicked it on, and shone it ahead of him as he walked. With his other hand, he kept his grip on his gun.

      a   o   o

When Bernadette heard his groans through the open door, she felt a weight lift from her chest. Garcia was alive, and conscious enough to make noise.

From her hiding place, Bernadette watched Quaid's back as he headed across the yard. Out in the open night air, he looked smaller and more manageable. More mortal. At the same time, she could also see he had the gun. He seemed to swagger as he walked with it. She fantasized about firing into his back, but that wasn't her style. Besides, it was nighttime, and even the best shooters missed moving targets in the dark. If she missed, she could be screwed and Garcia could be dead.

Quaid was aiming his flashlight in the direction of the driveway; he was going to his car for something. She didn't have much time. She wanted to get Quaid into the light, but away from Garcia. A shootout in that narrow shack could turn sour real fast. Her eyes moved across the yard to the house. She'd lure Quaid inside and take him there.

Darting out from the side of the building, Bernadette ran for the rear of the house.

∘   ∘   ∘

As he hovered over the open car trunk, Quaid considered the proper punishment for the violation. The stranger had tried to break into another man's home to rob and kill him and perhaps sodomize him. Had Quaid not stopped him, the man would have kicked down the door to get inside and commit his crimes.

Kicked down the door. Kicked and walked inside. It came to Quaid. A foot had to go, or an entire leg. Both legs. Quaid set the flashlight down on the bed and picked up the gloves, grimacing as he pulled them on. They were stiff with dried blood and felt tight on his fingers. He flexed his hands to loosen the leather. The fit was as snug as that of his weight-lifting gloves, and he liked that.

∘   ∘   ∘

Bernadette jogged up the back steps and onto the porch. With the light from the kitchen window, she could see well enough to aim. She raised her arms and pulled the trigger, dispatching the lock in a shower of splinters. She kicked open the door and went inside. As she ran across the kitchen floor, she shot a glance over to the counter and thought about what she'd seen through the window: the woman's tongue against the porcelain. A slice of Garcia could have joined Stannard's flesh in the sink.

No trial for this killer, she vowed. She'd make no phone calls until it was all over.

Forty-eight

○ ○

At the sound of the gunshot, Quaid's head whipped around. He'd been mistaken. The thief had an accomplice, and the animal had just shot his way into the house. Quaid pulled out his gun and, with his other hand, reached down and retrieved the ax from the bed of the trunk. He ran to the back of the house, stood at the bottom of the stairs, and uttered words that sounded closer to a command than a prayer: "Be with me now, God." As he ran up the steps, his grip on both weapons tightened while his hold on reality started to slip away. From inside the house, he heard their screams. He imagined terrible, gurgling shrieks and one-word pleas for mercy.

Please! Don't! Please!

No! Stop!

God! Help!

"I'm coming!" he yelled as he ran through the back door and

charged into the kitchen. "Hang on, Mother! Father! I'm coming! Girls! I'm coming!"

He skidded to a stop when he got to the living room. The cloth-covered furniture became animated. Souls were circling him, surrounding him, taunting. They were demons and devils, the ghosts of the evil sinners he'd executed. They'd come back to claim him and drag him down to hell with them, prevent him from saving his family. He closed his eyes and took a breath. Opened his eyes. The ghosts had vanished. He shook his head and blinked his eyes twice. They were still gone, but he didn't believe it. They were hiding, that's all. He'd have to flush them out.

◦ ◦ ◦

Bernadette froze in the middle of the upstairs hallway. She listened to Quaid thumping around and hollering. She didn't know what he was doing and couldn't understand what he was saying. A loud bang made her jump. It sounded like furniture being tipped. More yelling. She moved closer to the steps and still couldn't decipher the words. Before she could figure out what to do next, she had to see what was going on downstairs.

She ducked into a bedroom and closed the door all but a crack. She turned around and was shocked by the spectacle of the stained mattress, baking under the ceiling light. Only a head case would keep such a horrid souvenir, with its two rusty stains set together like enormous, sorrowful eyes.

Her attention was drawn across the room, to a closed door she'd seen during her earlier tour. Unlike the rest of the house, the closet would be dark. Could she focus with the maniac right below her? Could she use her sight again so soon? This case had already pushed her way beyond her usual limits. She told herself there'd be no harm in trying. She'd know right away if it was going to fail. There'd be plenty of time to abandon the effort, switch gears, and go downstairs.

Bernadette shut her eyes and took a calming breath. The air was different in this room, thick with residual pain. Another feeling: intense fear. Not just from the bed; from elsewhere.

She started at the sound of another downstairs thump. "Get moving," she muttered to herself.

She crossed the room to the closet, opened the door, and inhaled sharply. "Unreal," she whispered. It appeared Quaid had kept every article of clothing ever owned by his parents, including his mother's wedding dress. Hanging at one end of the rod, the gown was a creepy keepsake, a ghostly puff of satin and chiffon preserved in plastic like a body in the morgue. Another thump, this one directly below her. She stepped inside the closet, closed the door behind her, and slipped between two scratchy wool blazers—Sunday clothes once worn by Quaid's father? She swore she could smell aftershave, something cheap and spicy. After all these years, could she still detect the dead man's cologne? Or was it his son's scent? She felt light-headed and nauseous about either possibility.

Bernadette crammed herself against the back wall, behind the wedding dress. She batted the plastic away from her face; she felt as if the dress were trying to suffocate her. With her back against the wall, she slid down to the floor and curled her knees to her chest. A shudder shook her frame. This position in this closet was familiar. A feeling that was not her own—intense terror—started to wash over her. The sensation was muddying her head. "Shake it off," she muttered to herself.

She pulled off her gloves and buried them in one jacket pocket, and out of the other she retrieved the wad of latex. She hesitated, ready to unfold the package. A sharp crack sounded beneath her. *Great.* Now he was shooting up the place. She had to find out what he was up to, so she could take him out effectively and completely. Bernadette spilled the ring into her right hand. Curling her fist around the band, she closed her eyes.

Nothing was visible, save the blackness of her own lids locked tight. She took a long, deep breath through her nose and let it out through her mouth. A bit of plastic brushed her cheek; she didn't fight it this time. Softly, she said the words: "Lord, help me see clearly."

Forty-nine

He's on a rampage, searching for the intruders who'd blasted a hole in the back door. That's the only reasonable explanation, Bernadette thinks. Otherwise, why would he be doing this? Quaid's ricocheting from one piece of furniture to the next, pulling off sheets and knocking over end tables. The downstairs is a disaster, a sea of cloth and wood and cushions. He's bending over an armchair, pulling off the seat, and hurling the cushion across the room like a fat Frisbee. The cushion takes a lamp down with it. He's not through with the chair; he's kicking it and knocking it over.

He's stopping and taking a break from his tantrum, dabbing the perspiration off his forehead with the sleeve of his jacket. As he wipes, she can see there's something in his gloved right hand. What is it? In the long mirror mounted over the dining-room buffet, she sees his reflection. He's taking a step back, allowing her to see more of him. He's got an ax in his right hand. His coat is open, and she can see there's something tucked into the waist of his pants. She can't make out the details of the object; she deduces it's the gun.

He's turning away from the mirror and resuming his rioting. He's on his knees, looking under the couch, lifting up the skirt that runs along the bottom, and waving the ax under the sofa. Doesn't make any sense, she thinks. The sagging piece is too low to hide anyone or anything. He gets up off his knees, squats facing the couch, and locks his free hand under the front. With one thrust, he flips the thing onto its back.

He stands and whirls around, hunting for his next target. His eyes land on a door at the foot of the stairs, and he runs over to it and yanks it open. Winter gear hanging from a rod. He's diving into the closet and tearing the stuff off the hangers. Throwing coats down on the floor behind him, one after another. Barn coats and down jackets fly over his shoulder. Some of the jackets are pink—his sisters' winter wear.

The closet is empty, with only the bare dowel and a couple of empty wire hangers. He reaches up and grabs the rod with his fist and pulls the pole down. Tosses it behind him. He's stepping deeper into the closet and, with both hands, raising the ax over his head. Quaid's bringing the blade down, chopping a hole in the plaster. White dust flies into his face. He keeps chopping and hacking. Bernadette is mystified. Why is he doing this? Is there something stored behind the plaster wall? Cash? Other treasures? A body? The wooden slats behind the plaster are visible now. There's nothing hidden there. Nothing. He's still hacking away. His eyes are watering. He props the ax in a corner of the closet, shrugs off his coat, and tosses it down. Pulls off his gloves and drops them on top of the coat. Wipes his face with the hem of his shirt. Good—she can see much better.

He pivots around and steps out of the closet, wading through the pile of winter gear. He's kicking at the coats, getting them out of his way. The toe of his boot snags a pink puff of material. He falls to his knees amid the mound of clothing and gathers the cotton candy into his arms. Cradles it and rocks it like a baby. Lifts the jacket closer to his face. Dots of water drop onto the shiny material; he's weeping. He burrows his face into the fabric. Bernadette is buried in the jacket along with him, forced to join Quaid in his dark, downy misery.

It seems to last an hour, this black pause. He finally lifts his head and sets down the jacket. Quaid crawls to his feet, but his eyes linger over the pink. He doesn't want to give up on his baby. Dead cotton-candy baby. He pulls his eyes off the floor, shuffles back into the closet, and retrieves the ax. Picks his way through the mess he's made—plaster and coats and jackets and upended furniture—and heads for the stairs.

He puts one foot on the first step and looks up. He freezes, his sight locked at the top of the stairs. Bernadette wonders: What is he waiting for? What is he looking at? She sees nothing at the top of the steps but the second-floor hallway. Is this more of his madness? Maybe he's simply bracing himself for the fight with the intruder. Perhaps his fury has cooled off and has been replaced by fear. Fear and healthy common sense.

He's starting up the stairs. Slowly and deliberately, he's taking one step at a time while his attention is staying fixed on the lighted corridor at the top. With his free hand, he holds on to the rails as he goes. Halfway there, he stops his ascent, takes his hand off the rail, and turns his head. He's eyeing the bottom of the stairs. Is he having second thoughts? She can't let him go back outside. Quaid might flee or—worse—finish off Garcia. She has to keep the maniac focused on the second floor.

She concentrates. Struggles to keep her sight functioning while also executing a physical maneuver. The effort is draining. She feels sweat collecting under her armpits and beading above her upper lip. She does it. Kicks out one of her bent legs. Did it work? Did her foot even make contact with something—the closet wall or door? She can't tell. Yes. He hears a bump. He snaps his head back around and looks toward the second floor with wide eyes. She wrestles with her other leg. It shoots out and makes contact with a solid surface. He raises his eyes to the ceiling and shifts the ax from his left hand to his right. So why isn't he heading upstairs? The noises didn't attract him; they frightened him. Damn. She needs to do something different.

She remembers the way her shouts brought Garcia rushing to her bedside. Quaid's immersion in the pink jacket tells her he's thinking about his sisters. What would the sound of a female voice do to him? Could it send him running upstairs or fleeing back down? Could she even manage to speak again—this time consciously instead of reflexively? She opens her mouth and wills a sound to come out. Anything. A word. A scream. What comes out shocks her. His name. She manages to yell his first name. *Damian!* Or did she imagine it? No. He's running up the stairs now, taking the steps two at a time. She hadn't anticipated such speed from a big man.

He's thumping down the hall and running into the girls' room. His vision sweeps across both beds. He goes to the closet and yanks open the door. A wall of pink clothes. He spins around and goes back into the hall. Running into his own room. The brown bed. No one there. He falls to his knees and checks underneath the mattress. He jumps to his feet, pivots around, and in one stride goes to his closet. Throws open the door. A raincoat and a windbreaker and a collection of polo shirts, all dangling from wire hangers. He rips them down. Nothing behind the clothes. He closes the door and runs out of the room. Now the bathroom. She can see him in the mirror as he runs into the small space. His reflection reminds her he still has the gun tucked into the waist of his pants. As if he reads her mind, he sets the ax down on the bathroom counter and draws the gun out of his pants. He's rushing out into the hall and heading for the last room on the second floor, his parents' room.

He's standing in the doorway and taking in the bed. The mattress. He blinks. Something's wrong, Bernadette thinks. She figures it out: Quaid sees the twin stains and realizes that both girls are dead, and that the voice he'd heard couldn't possibly belong to one of his sisters. Ice water floods Bernadette's body as Quaid takes his attention off the mattress and stares at the closet door. He's walking across the room. Bernadette knows she should drop the ring and draw her weapon, but she can't stop watching through his eyes. Being physically close to a killer while watching through his eyes is hypnotic. Mesmerizing. Intoxicating.

He puts his hand on the knob and rips the door open. It slams against the wall. The contents of the closet flash before his eyes. Before her eyes. She thinks: He can't see me; the gown is hiding me. The billowy heap of chiffon and plastic has become her protector. But for how long? She orders herself to uncurl her fingers, drop the ring, and draw her weapon. Nothing happens. Her fist is frozen around the band, and the rest of her is paralyzed as well. She sees his left hand reaching out for the wedding dress, the tips of his fingers touching the plastic. With his right hand, he's bringing up the gun. This is it, she thinks. He's going to pull back the gown and see her and shoot her. She will watch her own face take a bullet. She will die on the floor of a closet in a house planted in the middle of nowhere. She isn't frightened; the idea calms and relaxes her. At the same time, she wonders if what she is doing is tantamount to suicide.

Without warning and for no apparent reason, he yanks his hand away. The gun still raised, he swivels around and peers through the bedroom door into the hallway. Quaid's eyes dart down to the pistol; he shifts his finger to the trigger. He glances up again and heads for the door. She figures someone is moving around downstairs. Who? Quaid pops his head outside the bedroom and sweeps the corridor with his eyes. He's slipping out the door and stepping into the hallway. He's bringing up his left hand and extending his arms.

Garcia.

Garcia must be in the house. Does he still have his gun, or did Quaid take it? Does he realize Quaid is armed? Garcia can't possibly know what waits for him at the top of the stairs.

She swallows hard and tries to force open her mouth to emit another noise, but her lips feel as if they've been sewn together. Bernadette switches her focus to the hand cupping the band. She again wills her fist to open, and again it refuses to unfold. She switches tactics and squeezes harder. It's working; she senses her fingers curling into a smaller ball. As the metal bites into her palm, she makes herself feel every diamond dotting the band. The ring seems to throb against her skin—as if it has its own heartbeat. She tells herself the ring is a red-hot circle burning a hole into her flesh. She tightens her hand. Her pain—both real and imagined—flares. Her reflexes take over; her hand snaps open and the jewelry drops to the floor. She blinks, and the scene in the second-floor hallway melts away.

⚬   ⚬   ⚬

Her sight is her own, but her emotions are Quaid's.

Fifty

Bracing his outstretched arms in preparation for firing, Quaid moved in the direction of the stairway. He stopped, startled by the sound of footsteps coming from another direction. He swung around with his gun.

Unbelievable! Standing in the doorway of his parents' bedroom was the blond woman. The FBI agent.

She was more astute than he'd anticipated; she'd tracked him down to his home. It was his own fault. He'd had three chances to kill her and passed them up. There'd be no letting her go this time. For the first time he got a good look at her eyes. Strange eyes. Devil eyes. A devil girl partnered with the devil man in the shed. The guy had to be another agent, but Quaid didn't care. They were home invaders with badges. Both were evil—and both would be dead soon. He aimed for her chest.

"FBI! Drop it!"

"Why should I listen to a nut case?" he growled. "Fantastic nonsense about visions and a paper cross."

Her mouth dropped open, and her gun lowered a fraction. She blinked and barked back: "Drop the gun now!"

He could see he'd knocked her off balance. Up until that moment, she'd had no idea that her confessor was the man she'd pursued and cornered. He sneered. "Dense, psychotic little woman."

"Drop your gun or I'll blow your fucking head off!"

She sounded as furious as he felt. Lethal. He worked to moderate his own voice, again becoming the priest on the bench, her hooded confidant. "You're out of control, daughter. Deeply disturbed. You need help."

"How did you find me? Tell me!" she demanded.

"Someone from the hospital overheard you. Pointed you out to me. The rest was easy. I followed you to church. Slipped into my costume."

"You helped me," she said. "I was on the wrong track and you re-directed me. Why?"

He couldn't answer her question without doubting his own sanity, so he turned it around and asked her: "How did *you* find *me*? I was careful."

"Very careful." Her voice had calmed, but her aim stayed at his chest. "I told you in church how I know things. Some things."

Her answer angered him, and he abandoned his cloak of reason. "Satanic. Unhallowed. A load of crap. You're a delusional fake cop."

"Not fake," she said. "That's another federal agent you've got tied up in your shed."

"I don't give a damn who or what you are." He kept his gun pointed at her, but his eyes shifted to the stairs. He was sure he'd heard something earlier, someone coming up the steps. Were there three intruders? Three devils? The girl, the one in the shed, and a third running around downstairs. He'd been dropped into his family's nightmare. "You broke into my house. You're on my property."

"We've been following your trail of bodies. We know you killed Chris Stannard. Noah Stannard. The judge. That other woman. We found her hand. Who was she? What did you do with the body?"

The right side of his mouth curled up. Quaid wanted to make sure the tally was complete. "Don't forget the deviant who slaughtered my family. I *executed* him, too. The woman was his lawyer. Marta Younges. The one who'd gotten him off so lightly. The rest of her is rotting somewhere along the river. Feeding the crows. 'The corpses of this people will be food for the birds of the air, and for the animals of the earth; and no one will frighten them away.' Read your Jeremiah."

"You're a murderer."

"Didn't murder any of them. All of them were executed according to God's laws. God's justice. Life for life. I'm sorry to say it, FBI lady: you're next."

Her gun still trained on him, she took a step out of the doorway and into the hall. "What gives you the authority? Who died and left you in charge of dishing up revenge?"

As the words tumbled out of her mouth, he felt a tear snaking out of the far corner of his eye, down to the edge of his upturned mouth. There would be two put to death that night. The man in the shed, and this crazy woman standing with him in the hallway. What would he take from her? The blue one? The brown one? Both? He'd have to educate her. Make her understand before he sent her to hell without her eyes. He cleared his throat and began. "The Lord's message to Moses. 'Anyone who strikes another with an iron object, and death ensues, is a murderer; the murderer shall be put to death. Or anyone who strikes another with a stone in hand that could cause death, and death ensues, is a murderer; the murderer shall be put to death. Or anyone who strikes another with a weapon of wood in hand that could cause death, and death ensues, is a murderer; the murderer shall be put to death.' " Quaid paused and studied her face to see if any of this was sinking in, but he couldn't read past her blue-brown. Strange. Demonic. Seductive in a way. Yes. Both eyes would have to go. He asked: "Are you listening, little lady? Do you comprehend what this is about?"

"You couldn't even cut it as a priest. What makes you think you've got the moral standing to judge and execute?"

He ignored her insult and her question. "Let me finish up with your Bible lesson. The Book of Numbers continues: 'The avenger of blood is the one who shall put the murderer to death; when they meet, the avenger of blood shall execute the sentence.' " He adjusted his grip on his gun. "So, you see, I'm the avenger of blood."

"A failed priest."

His smile flattened and his eyes hardened; he'd had enough of this give-and-take. "I left the priesthood of my own free will."

"You bailed before they could boot you out. Your self-serving reading of the Bible is a bunch of garbage."

"Shut up." He took a step away from her, toward the stairs. At that moment he wanted to distance himself from Devil Girl and her accusations. Her strange eyes, he'd hold them in the palms of his hands soon enough.

She raised her gun a little higher. "What does the Bible say about hypocrites?"

That word again; he hated it. "I am not a hypocrite!"

"Coward."

Another word he despised, and one he'd used on himself. "You don't know anything about it. What I've been through. What others have been through. People who have lost mothers and fathers and daughters and sons. You're after me? You've got your gun pointed at me? Why aren't you after the real criminals?" Quaid raised his eyes to the ceiling. "Let them be put to shame and dishonor who seek after my life. Let them be turned back and confounded who devise evil against me. Let them be like chaff before the wind, with the angel of the Lord driving them on."

"Why should God answer the prayers of a murderer—and a coward?" She took another step closer.

"Stop there!"

°　°　°

Bernadette froze, her gun and her eyes riveted to this dark, handsome man with his dark, ugly soul. He'd stunned her with the revelation that he was the priest from her church visits. He'd set her up to find him— whether he could admit it to himself or not. Why did he want to be caught? Was he trying to exit in a blaze of glory? "Do you see yourself as a hero? A martyr? You're two paragraphs in the back of the newspaper. Just another sick killer. Another coward."

"I am not a coward! If I'd been here, don't you think I would have defended them? Don't you think I would have given my life? Don't you think I wanted to die with them? My sister's cries still ring in my ears. I hear them pleading for their lives. Their honor."

Bernadette blinked. Why had he suddenly taken off on a rant about defending his family? How could he hear . . . ?

She gasped. The terror she'd felt in the closet. The familiarity of that position in that tight space. Now she understood. He'd been hiding while his family was being butchered. He'd curled his legs up to his chest and done nothing. "You were here all along. You were home when they were killed. Your mother and your father and your sisters—"

"Shut up! I was at school! I was gone! I wasn't here! I wasn't!"

"They didn't even call out your name, did they? They didn't want the killers to know you were there. They died protecting you. My God. What a thing to carry around!"

He took another step toward the stairs. "I wasn't home! I didn't hear anything! I wasn't in the closet! I wasn't!"

"Liar." She took a step in his direction.

His finger moved to the trigger. "Stop where you are! Stop moving or I'll finish it now!"

She needed to draw him in for the kill. Anything short of a square hit to the chest wasn't going to stop this guy. Her shot would have to be perfect, and she wasn't feeling confident. Her head was cloudy and her arms were heavy. She'd finally shrugged off his emotional state, only to find her own psyche crippled and weak. She softened her tone and tried to find their common ground. "Think you're the only one who's suffered a loss in this life? Take a number."

"What do you know about suffering?"

"My sister. That wasn't a fabrication." The story tumbled out easier than she expected, a completion of the confession she'd started on the church bench. "The drunk driver. He's walking around. Living and breathing. Getting up in the morning and going to work and coming home and having dinner with his family. Going to church on Sundays.

The same church Maddy was buried from. The same church! You think I like that? I stopped going because of him. I'm the coward, and he's the brave saint going to mass. Do you know how many times I've fantasized about hitting him with my truck? Seeing him roll up over the hood?"

She took a breath and continued, speaking more slowly and with less conviction. "But he did his time. Served his sentence. He's out and it's over and that's how it works."

Quaid lowered his gun an inch and moved his finger away from the trigger, but stayed where he stood, one stride from the edge of the stairs. "Shouldn't be how it works. That isn't God's justice; it's man's way. Flawed and unfair. Easy on the criminals and tough on the victims."

A part of her agreed with him. She knew her retort was flimsy, but it was the truth: "It's the best we can do."

"I can do better. I *am* doing better. You and your friend in the shed, you should have left me alone. Let me do my work. Accomplish my missions. We're on the same side."

Her eyes darted to his chest. A wide target, but was she close enough? "People can't take the law into their own hands. Run around executing other people. We've got to work within the system, as imperfect as it is."

"I gave the system a chance. The state of Minnesota turned its back on the death penalty. Turned its back on all of us."

The thump of a heavy footstep made both snap their heads toward the stairs. Quaid pivoted around to face the steps. A male voice booming up from the first floor. "FBI! Don't move!"

"Tony," Bernadette hollered. "He's armed."

Quaid stepped to the edge of the stairs and addressed the man at the bottom. "Get out of my house!"

The voice from downstairs: "Drop it, Father Quaid!"

Father. The sound of a stranger's voice addressing Quaid by his former title made him hesitate. He adjusted his grip on his gun.

Bernadette steadied her arms and squeezed the trigger. At the same time, two shots rang from downstairs. All three bullets found their mark: Quaid was hit twice from the front and once from the side. He jerked like a man who'd been shocked by an electrical jolt. He dropped his gun and brought both his hands to his chest. Brought his palms up and looked at the red. Turning his head toward Bernadette, he opened his mouth as if to say something to her. He bent forward and tumbled down the stairs.

She lowered her Glock and ran to the top of the steps, relieved to see Garcia standing alive at the bottom. At his feet was Quaid, sprawled on his back with his arms extended straight out and his feet still resting on the bottom step, crossed at the ankles. A sloppy crucifixion. "Sweet Jesus," Bernadette breathed. A prayer, not a curse.

Garcia holstered his gun, pulled out his cell, and called for help. He dropped his cell back in his pocket and went down on his knees next to the wounded man. Glancing up at Bernadette, Garcia said: "You can put it away."

She pocketed her Glock and started down the stairs. "Dead?"

Garcia nodded grimly. "Close to it."

She reached the bottom of the steps and hunkered down on the other side of Quaid, across from her boss. She noticed red lines on Garcia's wrists. "How did you get loose?"

Garcia held up his right wrist and jiggled his Catholic ID bracelet. "Makes a good saw. I just needed something to distract him so I could use it." He lowered his wrist. "You played it right—drawing him into the house with the gunshot. A firefight in that tin can would have been a bad deal."

Quaid's eyes were closed but his lips were moving. "He's saying something." Bernadette leaned down and turned her ear to his mouth.

Garcia asked in a low voice: "A confession?"

Bernadette held up her hand to quiet Garcia and drew closer to the bloody figure on the floor. She whispered into Quaid's ear: "Don't understand." As the dying man's lips moved again, Bernadette nodded and put her hand on his shoulder.

Garcia: "What does he want? Is he making a confession?"

A final puff of air escaped from Quaid's lips. Air leaking from a balloon. His eyes popped open and his head rolled to one side, toward Bernadette.

She sat back on her heels. "He's gone."

Garcia reached over and searched for a pulse against the side of Quaid's neck. He cupped his hand and held it over the man's nose and mouth to feel for breath. He pulled his hand away. "What did he say?"

"Three words," she said. *"A good priest."*

Garcia stared at the body and frowned. "He wanted last rites? He wanted us to call a priest? He didn't deserve it."

The sound of distant sirens made Bernadette look toward the front door. She turned back to her boss and answered his question: "No. I don't think that was it. He didn't want a priest."

"What, then?"

"He wanted me to know. Wanted us to know. *A good priest.* That's what he was, or what he could have been, if all the crap hadn't rained down on his life."

"He dumped his vocation and turned into an ax murderer. Literally. *Good priest*, my ass." Garcia stood up and swayed, grabbing the stairway banister for support.

"What's wrong?"

He let go of the railing and touched his forehead with his fingertips, felt the bump, and grimaced. "I've got one mother of a headache."

"Got to get you to a hospital."

"It can wait. We got plenty to do here. Our folks need to be briefed. Locals are gonna have a few questions about what went down in their backyard and why those asshole feds didn't clue them in."

Outside, a half dozen sirens wound down as squad and ambulance lights flashed against the curtains. "Speak of the devil," said Bernadette.

"Speak of the devil," Garcia repeated. As he headed for the front door, he said over his shoulder: "Sheriff's here. Get up and get your game face on. I'll do the talking for both of us."

"Sounds like a plan," she said after him. Bernadette watched his back to make sure he wasn't going to turn around again. She made the sign of the cross and struggled to come up with a quick formal prayer. All she could manage: "May God have mercy on your soul."

She stood up and gave one last look at the dead man. She wondered if she should keep Quaid's sad secret—that he'd been in the house hiding when his family was murdered. What about her own secret? Could she ever tell her boss how the killer had deceived her and helped her at the same time? As she followed Garcia to the front door, she remembered the words she'd exchanged with her ghost lover in her dream.

Then stay home. Don't go back to church. He isn't there.

Who? Who isn't there? God?

A good priest.

Fifty-one

He walked through her condo door—without opening the door—
while Bernadette was on her knees unpacking a crate of wineglasses.
Frightened, she dropped a goblet on the floor and jumped to her feet.
"Hey!"

"Not finished unpacking *yet*? Pathetic. And alone on a Saturday
night? More pathetic still."

"It's Sunday." She stumbled backward. "Go away."

He pointed to the broken glass. "Should I get a broom?"

She held up her hands to fend him off. "Use it to fly away."

"Wanted to congratulate you on the case. See if you wanted to—"

She cut him off. "I don't want to do anything with you."

He folded his arms over his chest. "Not very neighborly."

She backed up until she felt the sofa behind her legs. She put her hand
over the front pocket of her jeans and was disappointed she felt no bulge;

she'd left her gun on the kitchen counter. Then she told herself she was being ridiculous—she couldn't kill a ghost. "You're not my neighbor. You're a dead guy. Get the hell away from me."

The right side of his mouth curled up into a smirk. "You weren't so eager to part ways last time we were together."

She wondered if her heart was pounding so loud it would drown out her words. "I didn't know you were . . ."

"So good in the sack?"

"This has never happened to me before," she said defensively. "It's not like I go around getting drunk with dead guys and hopping into their beds."

The crooked smile vanished from his face. "It was a first for me, too. All of this is new."

Was she the only living person able to make contact with him? Her fear was immediately overshadowed by intense curiosity. Maybe she could unravel how all of this worked. Could be it was connected to her sight. She lowered herself onto the couch, but sat on the edge in case she needed to escape quickly. "Let me get this straight. No one else has seen you? This haunting thing isn't your regular gig?"

He shoved his hands in his pants pockets, stepped over the glass, and went around the box. "I made enough racket once to keep a couple from buying my place. The Realtor blamed it on pigeons or rats or some such nonsense. A little boy downstairs can see Oscar, but not me. Go figure. His parents told the kid not to pet strange dogs. If only they knew *how* strange."

"Why can I see you? Is it something about me? Something about you? Something with this building? How were we able to . . ."

"Do it like bunnies?"

She frowned. "That's not how I'd put it, but yes. How?"

"I have no idea why or how. I do know that it was wonderful. I hope you don't push me away. Please don't push me away. I've been so lonely, and now there's someone who can see me and talk to me. Touch me."

She crossed her arms in front of her. "We can't . . . I can't let that happen again."

He opened his mouth to respond and then closed it. He thumbed to an armchair parked to the right of the couch. "May I?"

"Go ahead."

"Appreciate it." He plopped onto the cushion.

"What's with the popping in or materializing or whatever? There was a time when you bothered to knock."

He rapped twice on her coffee table. "How's that?"

"Hilarious."

He crossed his ankle over his knee. Oscar appeared on his lap. Augie stroked the dog's back. "Bad dog. You should have knocked first."

Bernadette started at the dachshund. "How did you make the dog do that? Appear like that?"

Augie ignored her question and ran his eyes around her condo. "Looks like you're getting settled in. Nice. The motorcycle is a unique decorating touch. Didn't notice it before."

"It's a dirt bike."

"I should get one for my place. More interesting than a piano."

"Your place. What happens when they sell it? Where're you and Oscar gonna go then?"

He stopped petting his dog and flashed a wicked grin. "No one will *ever* want to buy my joint. I guarantee it."

She had to smile along with him. "You're evil."

"Maybe that's why I'm stuck here."

Suddenly a dozen topics popped into her head. Life and death and the angels and the devil. A single question rose above the clutter. She had to pose it, even though she feared the answer. "Have you seen him?"

His brows furrowed. "Who?"

She immediately regretted asking; it would be better not to know. "Forget it."

"Your Michael?"

Her stomach fluttered; Augie knew her husband's name. She leaned forward, hungry for details. "He's at peace? Happy? What's it like for him? Is he in a better place?"

"How should I know? I'm stuck here. Unless a lot has changed since I was in Sunday school, a warehouse overlooking the Mississippi River is not the definition of heaven. I'm waiting for that *better place* myself."

"You know too much about me and about the case. You knew my husband's name. How did you know his name?"

"Look," he sputtered, losing patience with her questions. "There's a lot I don't know, and a lot I do."

"How? You must have some insight into the afterlife."

"Why must I?"

She jumped out of her seat. "Because you're a spirit or ghost or a poltergeist or whatever you want to call yourself! What *do* you call yourself?"

"*Dead guy.* Your terminology. Works fine for me."

"Asshole dead guy." She walked around the couch and headed into the kitchen. Bernadette yanked open the refrigerator and leaned one hand against the door. She prayed he'd be gone by the time she turned around. She pulled out a bottle of beer.

"I could go for three of those," he yelled after her.

"Thirsty dead guy," she muttered, pulling out two additional bottles and plucking a magnetic bottle opener off the refrigerator. She dropped it all on the coffee table in front of the sofa.

"St. Pauli," he said, picking up one of the bottles and popping off the top. "Excellent. This would have been my pick for a last drink—had those bloodthirsty animals allowed a last drink."

She sat down and watched while he chugged. Through the green glass, she saw the beer disappear as he swallowed. "How does it work?"

He set his half-empty bottle down on the table and stifled a burp. "What?"

Before she answered, she picked up a bottle, pried off the cap, and took a long drink. She held the bottle on her lap, between her thighs. "How can you drink if you're dead, and what about food? Your dog must poop. You were carrying a poop bag when we met."

Oscar looked at the bottles on the table and whined. Augie retrieved his beer, cupped his hand in front of the dog, and poured a puddle into his palm. The dog lapped it up. "Boozehound."

"August," said Bernadette. "Augie. How does it work? How do you do things?"

He wiped his hand on his pants. "Elaborate. What *things?*"

"How did you light up your condo for me?"

"Let's just say no one else in this building can hold a candle to our lovemaking—because they can't find their candles."

"You stole all that stuff from the other lofts."

"I prefer the term *spirited away.*"

"Semantics. What about the champagne? How can you pour it? How can you drink? Can you get drunk?"

Augie tipped back the bottle and polished off his beer. He set the bottle down and reached for another. "I intend to. Hope you've got more in the fridge."

"Dammit. Answer my questions."

He yanked off the top of his second beer and tossed the cap and opener on the table. "Jesus H. Christ. *Can you get drunk? Does your pooch poop? Have you seen my suicidal hubby?* Is that the best you can do? No wonder the bureau is so fucked up. What about the big stuff? Holy crap. How about *Is there a heaven and a hell? Does God exist and is He pissed at us?*"

"Is He?"

"How should I know?" He lifted the beer to his mouth, tipped it back, and gulped.

"That's why I didn't ask those big questions." She pulled the bottle from between her legs, took a long drink, and set her St. Pauli on the table. "You obviously don't know. You can't even tell me why you can drink beer. For a dead dude, you're very ignorant about the hereafter. Maybe you need to take a night class. Read one of those dummy books—*Life After Death for Dummies.*"

He laughed in the middle of a chug, coughed, and wiped his nose with the back of his hand. "Man, that feels good."

"What?"

"Beer up my nose. Haven't had beer up my nose since . . ." His voice trailed off.

"Do you think you're still here—haunting the place, or whatever you call it—because there're some loose ends related to your murder? I could help. Garcia says they never caught the guys."

His face seemed to darken for a moment. "They never caught the guys because they've got it all wrong. And, for that matter, Garcia's got it all wrong about his wife."

Her eyes widened. "Tell me."

"That's another conversation, on another dark and windy night." He took a swig of beer. "My turn. I'd like to fire off some questions about the crazy-priest case."

"Why? You knew about shit happening in the case before I did. That warning about the wake. Thanks for that, by the way."

"No problem. Like I told you: some things I know and some I don't."

"That dream. You were trying to warn me then, too. *A good priest.*"

"Dream? Now you lost me."

She scrutinized his face and couldn't tell if he was lying. Probably better not to know. "Never mind," she said.

He polished off his beer. "Now, what about my questions?"

"It's only been a week since we got our guy, and the file is still open." She picked up her beer and took a sip. Wiped her mouth with the back of her hand. "But what the hell. Who're you gonna tell, right? Fire away."

"Did you ever find Marta's body?"

"Along the river, not far from where we found Archer. She was trussed up like the others."

"How did the son-of-a-bitch lure her back to Minnesota so he could nail her?"

"He didn't need a ploy to get Marta back to town. She had family and friends here. She bopped back and forth all the time. Unfortunately, that's why no one reported her missing immediately. Work thought she'd extended her visit back home, and the folks here thought she was headed back to Milwaukee."

"How'd he get her into the park, though? How'd he get all of them into the woods?"

"We think he forced them into his car trunk, drove them to the edge of the woods, and then marched them deeper inside at gunpoint. That's our theory, at least. We found kick marks inside his car trunk." Augie seemed genuinely curious and had good questions. The remnants of the lawyer in him? She found herself interested in what he had to say. "Does that sound plausible, counselor?"

He smiled. "All circumstantial evidence, but I won't raise any objections."

"What else you wanna know?"

"Archer's hand ever turn up?"

"Still missing. Raccoon food."

"Serves him right. Too bad Quaid didn't chop off the perve's rod and feed it to the squirrels."

Her brows went up. "The noble defense attorney shows his true colors."

"You know what most of us *really* think of our clients. Speaking of felons . . . Who was next on Quaid's list? Was there a list?"

"There was." She took a long drink. "Our computer guys found it in Quaid's electronic files. He'd used his position in the prison ministry to snoop around and assemble a list of guys he wanted to execute after they got out."

"What's wrong with that? I like that. It's better than the catch-and-release we have going on now."

"Some of the folks on his list weren't cons; they were judges and defense attorneys."

"Kill all the lawyers and let God sort 'em out."

She grinned. "You morphed two different bumper stickers with that one."

"What set this all in motion was the home invasion and murders?"

"And his own inaction."

His brows furrowed. "Come again?"

She hesitated. She didn't know why, but she was about to tell Augie something she hadn't even told Garcia. "Quaid hid in a closet in his parents' bedroom while just outside the door his sisters were being raped and knifed. Imagine hearing those noises and being frozen with fear."

"That's understandable, actually."

"But then he did the unthinkable," she said. "He didn't call the police or paramedics from the house. Didn't go to the neighbors for help. He went all the way back to school and hid under the covers until the cops tracked him down to tell him his entire family had been wasted."

"Was that a calculated move? Did he do all that to avoid being labeled a chickenshit, or was it some form of shock? Did he even remember witnessing what he'd witnessed back home?"

"I don't know. Really don't."

"Then again, what does it matter?" asked Augie. "He's dead. Saved the courts the trouble of a trial; plus, he managed to take some other scum down before he bit the dust."

She finished off her beer and set the bottle on the table. "You're in a vindictive mood this evening."

Rolling his empty between his palms, he said somberly: "Try getting murdered. Changes your outlook completely. I'd like to come back as an electric chair."

"Is there such a thing as reincarnation?"

"How should I know?"

"What good are you? You can't tell me anything."

He set the bottle on the table. "That isn't true. Isn't true at all. My very presence here tells you it ain't over when we think it's over."

She got up from the couch and went to one of the windows to glance at the river. The lights illuminating the water had never seemed sharper. Brighter. "I didn't think death was the end. I have to know what comes next."

"I can't tell you what comes next for you," he said to her back. "I can only show you what came next for me. What difference does it make? All you need to know is, we continue to exist in some form after our bodies quit on us."

"That isn't good enough." Turning away from the window, she faced him and rubbed her arms over her sweatshirt. She felt a draft. Maybe her houseguest had brought it inside with him. "I need more information."

"Why? Do you want to see if you backed the right horse?"

"What?"

"The right faith. The correct god."

She laughed dryly and headed for the kitchen. "I'm not much on organized religion."

"You're Catholic."

"I *was* Catholic. Now I'm not anything." She pulled open the refrigerator and rested her hand against the top of the door.

"Once a Catholic, always a Catholic." He paused, and then added: "I know you still pray."

She didn't want to think about *how* he knew. "So what? That doesn't make me Catholic. Since when do you need a church membership card to pray?" She thought: *This is insane; I'm discussing my faith with a dead guy. And he's drinking my beer.*

"So why do you need details about the hereafter? For argument's sake, tell me this: If you knew a certain religion had the correct god dialed in, what would you do? Would you run out and join that church?"

"I doubt the Almighty gives a damn where I bend my knee."

"You didn't answer my question."

She scoured the shelves inside the fridge. A stick of butter. A carton of eggs with one egg inside. A bowl of mushy strawberries. She pulled her head out of the refrigerator and glared at him. "Know what? I don't want to talk about religion anymore. Boring and depressing."

"Whatever you want." He put his feet up on the coffee table. "So what's the verdict? Got anything to eat?"

"Looks grim, counselor."

Oscar barked twice and jumped off his owner's lap. The dog clicked across the floor and joined Bernadette in the kitchen. He stood next to her and stared up into the fridge.

"Oscar," yelled Augie. "Get out of there."

Bernadette leaned into the fridge and pulled out three green bottles of St. Pauli and one brown bottle. She examined the oddball; it had a buffalo head on the front. "How about a Headstrong pale ale?"

"Never heard of it."

She slammed the fridge door and carried the bottles to the living room, with the dog at her heels. "Liquor store was clearing out some singles. Wanted to try something different." She deposited the bottles on the coffee table and sat down on the couch.

He got up off the chair and sat down next to her. He picked up the brown bottle and read the label. "Big Hole Brewing Company. Belgrade, Montana. I'll take a chance." He popped off the top. "Can't kill me, right?"

She watched him take a drink. "If you don't like it, you can give it to Oscar."

He hiccupped. "No. It's good."

She opened another St. Pauli for herself. "There's plenty of other beers in the fridge. Not much else."

He took a second guzzle and burped. "We could order a pizza."

She checked her watch. "Kind of late to be filling our bellies. I'd never get to sleep, and I've got to get up and go to work in the morning."

Oscar hopped up on the vacated chair, circled the cushion twice, and plopped down into a ball. "Oscar," said Augie. He pointed to the floor. "Down."

"It's okay." She took a sip of St. Pauli. "He doesn't shed, does he?"

"Not even when he was alive."

She took another bump off her beer and set the bottle on the table. Checked her watch again. Who was she fooling? She wasn't going to get any sleep. Not after tipping a few with a dead guy. Handsome dead guy.

"You know what? I *could* go for a pizza. Know who delivers to downtown this late on a Sunday?"

"There's a joint on West Seventh Street. They make great deep-dish."

"Deep-dish? That'll take forever."

"All I've got is time."

Fifty-two

Her visitors left as suddenly as they'd appeared. She got up off the couch to put the pizza leftovers in the refrigerator, and when she turned around, they were both gone. Dead guy and his dead dog. Relieved and exhausted, she wound her way up the steps to her sleeping loft and collapsed on top of the covers.

She woke up Monday morning with a headache and a gut ache, but both started to dissipate as she showered. While she stood in the bathroom toweling off, she wondered if he was watching. She put it out of her head; there was nothing she could do about it if he was spying on her.

She pulled on one of her usual suits—dark slacks and dark blazer over a white blouse—slipped her Glock into her holster, and headed outside.

The sidewalks were crowded with men and women dressed in everything from suits to jeans, and the downtown streets were jammed with cars and trucks and buses and delivery vans. The sharp spring air was a splash of cold water on her face, and smelled of exhaust and rain-dampened concrete. On her way to the federal building, she stopped to pick up a cup of coffee and a scone. She debated getting two of each, in case Garcia dropped by on his way to Minneapolis, but decided her boss could get his own.

＊　＊　＊

While she jogged down the steps to the basement, she slipped off her sunglasses. She walked into her office and started. One of the two empty desks across from hers was now occupied. Agent Ruben Creed, her cellmate in the dungeon, was back from vacation this week. He had his back to the door. He was a skinny African-American guy with close-cropped salt-and-pepper hair. She could see he was tall; he was hunched over his computer like a giant comma. She remembered Garcia had said Creed loved the cellar in St. Paul and had been there for years. She told herself to avoid making any wisecracks about their digs; Creed could take offense. She frowned at the bag in her hand; she should've gotten a pastry for her coworker. She walked up to him and said to his back, "How were the Cayman Islands?"

He swiveled around in his chair and looked up at her, his mouth agape. "Huh?"

"Isn't that where you went? How was the weather?"

He nodded, his eyes locked on hers. "Hot."

She forced a smile and wished she'd kept her shades over her eyes. She tried to think of something more to ask about his trip. "Heard you're big into scuba diving. What's that like? I've always wanted to—"

He interrupted her. "Don't try it; it's too dangerous."

She thought she detected the remnants of a Southern accent and used it as an opening to tell him a little bit about herself. "Where're you from originally? The job shuffled me around Louisiana for quite a while." He didn't answer her question, and she didn't know what else to say, so she extended her paper bag. "How about a welcome-back scone?"

He looked at the sack and back at her. "Who're you?"

Quite a greeting, she thought. She pulled back the bag and thrust out her hand. "Agent Bernadette Saint Clare."

He stared at her hand for a moment and slowly extended his own. "Hey."

Bernadette thought he seemed uncomfortable touching her. She wondered if he'd heard stories from New Orleans. He probably thought she was going to read his mind or mess with his brain or infect him in some way. She let go of his bony hand and held up the sack. "Sure I can't interest you in breakfast?"

"No thank you," he stammered, his eyes again focused on her face.

Bernadette headed for her own desk, sat down, and dropped her bag on top of a pile of folders. She reached inside the sack and fished out the drink and the scone. She lifted off the cup cover, sipped, and shuddered. The coffee was cold and bitter. She snapped the lid back on. She took a bite of the scone. As dry and flavorless as sawdust.

Garcia walked in as she was stuffing the cup and scone back in the bag. "That looks good."

"Looks can be deceiving." She set the sack in the wastebasket next to her desk.

Garcia sat on the edge of her desk. "Let's get out of here and get some good grub. There's a place in the skyway. I've got something to tell you, and I'd rather do it with a hot meal in my stomach."

She thumbed over her shoulder to the desk behind her and said in a low voice, "What about . . . ?"

Garcia glanced over at where she was pointing. "What?"

She turned in her chair and was surprised to see Creed was no longer at his computer. She ran her eyes around the room. "He was here a minute ago. Did you pass him in the hall?"

He frowned. "Who?"

"Agent Creed."

Garcia swallowed once and asked, "What did he look like?"

She said in a whisper, so Creed wouldn't hear if he suddenly walked back in: "String bean with graying hair. Southern string bean, by the sound of his voice. Dark-skinned . . ."

"Cat." Garcia got up off her desk and stood straight.

Her eyes widened as she looked up at her boss. "Don't tell me that wasn't him. That someone snuck past security and . . ."

"Nobody snuck past anybody." Garcia rested one hand on the back of her chair. "You described Creed perfectly, right down to the drawl. Southern string bean with hair."

She scanned the room again. "Where is he, then?"

Garcia rubbed his forehead with his hand. "On his way home—in a body bag."

Bernadette felt an icy draft and twined her arms around her body. She looked straight ahead. She didn't want to face Garcia, didn't want to see the fear in his eyes.

"He died over the weekend. Some sort of accident. We're collecting details. By the looks of it, he was killed . . ."

"Scuba diving," she said numbly.

Garcia took his hand off her chair. "How did you know?"

She bent her head down and covered her face with both hands. Through her fingers, she answered: "He more or less told me."

"Shit," spat Garcia.

She took her hands down. "Sorry if I've upset you. I know you worked with him a long time. Sorry."

"Stop apologizing." He walked over to Creed's desk and eyed the monitor on top. "Next time you see him, ask him what happened to the files on—"

She blurted: "I can't believe how well you're taking this."

"I'm getting used to it. How scary is that?" He headed for the door. "Breakfast offer is still good. I want to hear what else Creed told you."

She stood up and went after her boss. "He didn't say a helluva lot."

"Always was a reticent bastard," Garcia grumbled. He stopped in the doorway and turned. Glancing around the office nervously, he asked: "You think he heard that?"

She shrugged. "How do I know?"

"*How do I know* isn't a good answer. We've got to work on polishing this particular talent of yours, Cat."

Slipping on her shades, she followed him out of the cellar and up the stairs. "We've got time. I'm not going anywhere."